I0708441

"The means of transport to the alternate world, the beings Kaitlynn encounters there, and the emotion and poignancy of her and her compatriots' plight all lift this story beyond the everyday fantasy."
-Helen Whistleberry, Author of *Black Pine Cove*

"This book starts as a somber, touching, human slice of life and turns into an epic fantastical adventure. It has pretty much everything you could ask."
– Jacob Faust, Author of *Cracked*

"I don't want to give too much away but I laughed, cried, and felt the character's frustrations on their journey."
– Dawn Hosmer, Author of Bits & Pieces

"The Stairs in the Woods is author Matt Cesca's debut effort. It's a well-written piece and should satisfy most any fan of the genre."
-Michael A. McLellan, Author of *In the Shadow of the Hanging Tree*

"Combining a love story with mythical creatures in an unknown world has just the right amount of magic for this compulsive reader."
- Elizabeth M. Carola, Author of *The Oathing Stone*

Books By the Author

The Stairs in the Woods

The Forbidden Scrolls Trilogy
The Forbidden Scrolls
Redemption & Ruin
The Last Sorcerers

The Miranda Project Trilogy
The Miranda Project

Anthologies
Autumn Nights: 13 Spooky Fall Reads (contributor)

THE STAIRS IN THE WOODS

MATTHEW CESCA

N386 PUBLISHING

Copyright © Matthew Cesca, 2018

All rights reserved.

No part of this book may be reproduced in any form on by an electronic or mechanical means, including information storage and retrieval systems, without permission in writing from the publisher, except by a reviewer who may quote brief passages in a review.

This is a work of fiction. Names, characters, places, and incidents either are the product of the author's imagination or are used fictitiously. Any resemblance to actual persons, living or dead, events, or locales is entirely coincidental.

This story includes adult language, sexual themes and nudity, as well as fantasy violence and gore. There are also Heavy themes surrounding both cancer and divorce. Reader discretion is advised.

Learn more about the author and his works at https://www.mattcesca.com/

Edited by Vanessa Redmon https://nessacessity.com

Cover Art by Fay Lane https://faylane.com/

For Jessica,

She always believed in me, even when I did not.

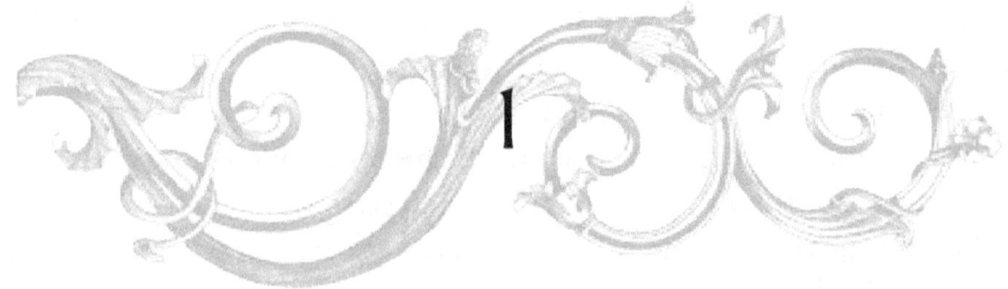

1

Kaitlynn had absolutely nothing to wear. But when it's sixty-three degrees outside on a January day in Connecticut and most of your clothes are still back home in Arizona, picking out the perfect outfit isn't necessarily the easiest thing in the world to do.

But that's New England weather for you. Three days ago, four feet of snow had dropped from the sky in the latest named superstorm. Naming storms that weren't hurricanes was a new trend that Kaitlynn wasn't sure she could get behind. In fact, she'd already forgotten the name of the one that had just roared through town like a jilted lover looking for revenge. "They used to just call them nor'easters," she thought to herself with a sigh that was barely audible despite the silence in her bedroom.

As she looked out the window at the deep snowdrifts and the bright sunshine that reflected off them like the light off a collection of mirrors, she felt at a loss for what to wear today. "What kind of outfit really says springtime with snow boots?" she wondered. The question in her mind made her think back to the posters she remembered seeing in the Scottsdale Fashion Mall, with the girls wearing the short shorts with the pockets hanging below the cutoffs and pairs of expensive Ugg Boots with the white fur sticking out from within them. "Eski-ho's," her friend Jess had called them as they had walked past the advertisements one Saturday afternoon with an armload of shopping bags. She chuckled at the memory and decided on a pair of jeans and one of the few short sleeve t-shirts she had hastily stuffed into her suitcase two months ago. She tossed her clothes on and then gave a wry smile. She missed her friends and her old life; the life that she hoped to go back to when this was all over.

After fixing her shoulder length chocolate brown hair into a ponytail and taking a cursory glance in the mirror to check her appearance, Kaitlynn stepped out into the hall. She crept to the next room and paused outside the door. Outside, she took a few deep breaths and let them exhale in a slow, quiet rhythm. This was her new sad morning ritual as she steeled herself for what was on the other side of the door. She faked her best smile and knocked three times in rapid succession.

"Come in," she heard him say from the other side of the door. She turned the doorknob with trepidation and stepped inside.

"Good morning!" she said in her best cheery voice as she passed through the door.

On the best of days, the emaciated man lying in the bed still looked like her father. But the best of days were fewer and farther between. His skin had yellowed with jaundice and sagged as the muscles had atrophied over the past few months. The chemotherapy had taken almost all of his dark brown hair from him as well. He looked up at her with his dark eyes, which now looked like they had sunken into the cracks and grooves of his face. A pang of guilt hit her then as she recalled missing her old life when her father needed her here so much right now.

"It's a great day outside today," she continued, doing her best to keep a cheer in her voice despite the lump in her throat. "Springtime in January if you can believe it. You want me to set you up on the porch today?"

"Oh," he replied, his voice far more strained than it used to be. "Springtime you say? It's not even Groundhog Day yet."

"It's already in the sixties and expected to get warmer," she said, maintaining her best Barbie-doll smile as well as she could. "Just warm enough for you to yell at the squirrels trying to get into the birdfeeder if you'd like." They both chuckled at that. Yelling at the squirrels was one of her dad's favorite past times in the spring and summer months. He'd even gone so far as to wrap an old slinky around the top of the pole that the bird feeder hung from to stop the critters from stealing food from its intended recipients.

"Well, I didn't put the bird feed out for them," he said with a wry grin, and then let out a light cough. Kaitlynn came over, a look of concern spreading on her face where her plastered-on smile had been. He reached over and pushed the button on the hospital bed, raising himself up to her as she leaned in to kiss him on the forehead. "I'm fine, just a cough," he said, waving his hand dismissively at her. "Cancer's down in my gut, not in my lungs. I'll live to see tomorrow." He grinned at her and though she didn't feel much better, she flashed him a smile again.

"Okay, I'll get the deck chairs out for us," she said, and then patted her father lovingly on the cheek. "I'll help you get out there and then join you after I make breakfast."

He smiled at her as she glanced back before exiting the room and heading out to the garage to get the deck chairs. She chuckled to herself at the idea of hanging out outside all day in January, in Connecticut, but hanging out on the deck with her father was a tradition in the summertime. She wasn't so sure Dad was going to make it that long, so she'd take the chance to get one more cherished memory in while she still could.

The diagnosis had come as a shock to her when her father had called just before Thanksgiving. It wasn't just any cancer either, but stage four pancreatic cancer; most often one of the hardest to detect until it was too late. That had been the case with her dad, Danny Jenson. The doctors had told him that he had only six months to live at most, and that was two months ago now. Kaitlynn had packed up what she could as quickly as possible and then flown back home to be with him until the end. She was an only child; her parents had long since divorced. They'd not been on speaking terms for even longer than that. She never asked why and had always told herself that she didn't want to know the details.

Her mother had gotten full custody, as women back then often did and moved her all the way across the country to Arizona when she was fourteen. Since then, she'd had to mediate between them to plan any visits to see her father until she was eighteen; her parents couldn't work anything out between each other peaceably. And then she'd had to work out all the financial details for her to go to college as well. Her parents couldn't even talk to each other politely enough to do that either. She'd learned to grow up far sooner than most of her friends and take care of herself early on in her life, but she did her best not to resent her parents for that fact. Well, not anymore at least. She'd had enough therapy in her mid-twenties for that.

She pulled on a pair of fashionable boots that went to just below her knees before stepping out onto the deck with the first of the chairs, and then she went and got the other one. Thankfully, the teenage boy next door had shoveled off the deck for them the day after the storm for fifteen dollars. Kaitlynn was also pretty sure that he'd had a bit of a crush on her too, otherwise, she doubted he would have done the job for so little. While Kaitlynn hadn't expected to be using the deck so soon, she wanted to make sure that it didn't get damaged by the weight of the snow. She knew she'd likely have to sell the house before summer and didn't want to be doing major repairs before trying to move back home and attempting to restart her life.

After setting up the chairs in their usual spots, she caressed the sliding glass door open, slipped back inside and headed down the hallway to her father's room. She was grateful that the house was a raised ranch style, and she could keep her father upstairs for the most part so as not to have to worry about him falling down the stairs while trying to get to the living room below in his current condition. She rapped lightly on the door again in the same pattern as before. "Ready?" she asked, and then she slipped into the room.

Her father had adjusted the top half of the hospital bed into a fully upright position and started to slide his legs out by the time she had come into the room. She glided around to the side of the bed, stuck out her arm for him, and helped him up off the bed and down into the wheelchair that had been folded up in the corner of the room by the bed.

"I hate this thing," he said, his tone brisk and defiant. "If it's my time to go, I can live with that. But a man should be able to walk to his grave if he wants."

Kaitlynn tried to stifle her emotions as best as she could, but a single tear slipped down her face. She wiped it away before her father could see, and then said, "Personally, I think this was all part of your master plan to get me to move back home. Congrats, it worked." She smiled and gave him a peck on the cheek. She then rolled him down the hallway and out to the open sliding glass door before offering him her arm to walk him to the deck chair. She lifted him up with an abundance of caution. He was much lighter than he had ever been before, and she found it disconcerting how easily she could bear his weight considering he was a good four inches taller than she was.

After setting him down in the deck chair, she smiled and said, "Breakfast will be ready in about ten minutes or so." She slid back inside, pulling the screen door closed behind her, and started pulling out pans, cracking eggs, and toasting bread. When everything was done, she grabbed two tray tables, set them up outside and then scooped up the two plates. After setting them down, she went back inside, grabbed two glasses of orange juice, and joined her father on the deck for breakfast.

"Any squirrels yet?" she asked him as she slid into the chair to his right. Her eyes went slightly wider with implied humor, and she smiled at him.

He gave her a wry smile in return. "Not yet. They knew I had my secret weapon today."

"Oh," she replied, "Which secret weapon is that?"

"You." He smiled at her. In that moment, he looked more like his old self than he had in weeks. There was a light in his eyes that she hadn't seen in quite some time, and for that Kaitlynn was eternally glad. Perhaps she'd get one last good deck memory out of today after all.

2

T he day of the funeral was cold and rainy. It was the kind of rain that would make you wish it was just a couple degrees colder outside so that at least it would snow, and you wouldn't be both cold *and* wet. The wind was not howling but was stiff enough that no umbrella would really do the job properly. Kaitlynn stood shivering in the cold at her father's graveside dressed in a long black dress under her long winter topcoat that she hadn't bothered to button up. Her cousin, Mark, stood in silence next to her, holding an umbrella for the both of them. Though it wasn't doing a whole lot of good, Kaitlynn appreciated the sentiment. The rest of the family was already dispersing and heading back to their vehicles, the funeral service concluded. But Mark had stayed behind to keep Kaitlynn as dry as possible in the wind and rain as she hovered behind at the freshly dug plot, saying her last goodbyes to her father.

Some of the rain on her face was salty as the tears she'd held back for her father's benefit over the last couple of months flowed freely now. Her father was gone. She'd spent so much of her life on the other side of the country away from him, coming to visit him usually for a weekend or two every summer. But she'd missed out on so much by not having him truly in her life, and now it was too late to make up for lost time.

Only a little over a month had passed since that perfect day on the deck. The short Indian summer in the middle of January had lasted only two days and then winter had returned in full force. There had been another named storm whose name she had chosen not to learn, this one dumping frozen rain on the roads and trees instead of snow. They had lost power for a couple of hours during that storm as an ice-laden tree branch down the street had punished the powerlines for daring to get in its way as it plummeted to the ground. There had been a couple of dustings since then as well, and in places the ice still lurked just below the surface of the freshly fallen snow, waiting to claim an unsuspecting victim or two.

"You ready?" Mark asked her quietly. He was tall and handsome with the same dark hair as Kaitlynn, though his was curly and bobbed slightly on his head in the gusting wind. He had the same dark eyes that her father had had as well. He was a couple years younger than her, but they had always been close as kids.

She nodded silently and gave him a smile. "You didn't have to stay out here in the rain for me," she said, grateful that he had.

"Yeah, I did," he said, forcing a smile. "That's what family is for."

They took their time as they plodded back to the edge of the cemetery where all the cars were parked. Mark led Kaitlynn over to her father's car with his hand on her arm to protect her from the treacherous ice that might be hiding anywhere. She'd been driving the three-year-old Camry since she'd come out a little over 3 months ago, and she figured that it would just be one more thing that she'd have to sell before heading home to her old life in Arizona.

The last month had been particularly brutal. Her father's decline had been steady and rapid. In the end, his death had been a blessing. The cancer had been eating him alive from the inside out. The fire had been drained from his eyes long before his body gave up its fight and seeing him lose the last of the hope that he had been clinging to had hurt her most of all.

Mark opened the car door and held it for her as she slid behind the wheel. "I'll see you back at Mom and Dad's. You remember how to get there?" he asked her.

"It's been a while, but I think I can manage." She gave him a half smile and closed the door. She watched him in silence as he made his way back to his own car before she turned the key and fired up the ignition.

Twenty years away from a place can change a lot of things. The landmarks change, even when they're the same as they used to be. Nothing prepares you for how much the trees will grow over the course of time. But despite making a couple of wrong turns (and with the help of the woman with the soothing British voice on her GPS), Kaitlynn made her way to her aunt and uncle's house where the rest of her family had gathered. Luckily, by the time she had arrived the rain had let up a bit. She was grateful for that at least. Rain, especially cold rain with a biting wind, was not something she was used to anymore. A lifetime of desert living had thinned her blood out considerably.

As she stepped inside, her aunt greeted her at the door with a warm embrace. "Katie dear, how are you doing?" She hated the old nickname from her childhood but decided to let it go. Today had been a hard enough day without letting the little things get to her.

"I'm coping," she said with a faint smile. "The last few months were tough. I'm just glad he's at peace. Thank you for having us all here Aunt Jo."

Her aunt shushed her. "No, it's no trouble. He was my brother as much as he was your father. And it's good to have everyone here again."

Her Aunt Jo was a lively woman in her late fifties, about three or four years younger than her father had been—Kaitlynn could not remember specifically. She had the same dark hair and eyes that ran through that entire side of the family, but the slight frame that she used to have when Kaitlynn was a child had grown somewhat with time and the occasional meal. She gave Kaitlynn one last hug and then motioned for her to come in out of the cold.

As her Aunt Jo headed off into the kitchen to finish dinner for everyone, Kaitlynn looked around the room. Her Uncle Dave (Jo's husband and Mark's father) sat in a leather recliner in front of the fireplace with a glass of whiskey in his hand while Mark stoked the fire in the beautiful stone fireplace and contemplated throwing another log on. Uncle Dave had been her father's best friend; that's how he met Aunt Jo. He had blonde hair and blue eyes, a rather large sized anomaly in both of those regards on her father's side of the family. His good looks and once athletic frame had changed over the years, but he was still a good man. He had been there with her at the end of her father's life with his hand on her shoulder and had hugged her when her father had finally stopped breathing. She'd cried all over his shoulder as they had taken her father away and his shirt had still been damp when he finally left to go home later that night.

Her father's older brother, James, sat on the couch nearby reminiscing about her father with his son, Jeff. Uncle James was taller than her father and a year or two older as well. His dark hair had long since gone a peppery gray along the temples and back of his head, but the rest had thinned out considerably until only a few wisps still perched upon the top of his balding dome. Despite that, it was clear that he still took care of himself physically; he was still in very good shape for a man in his mid-sixties.

Jeff looked up at Kaitlynn and forced a smile. He was her age. In fact, they had only been born a few days apart, with Kaitlynn just beating him into the world. He was tall like Mark but broader in the shoulder. He had been the starting quarterback of his high school football team and still looked the part to a certain extent with his biceps showing out from under the short sleeve dress shirt he had worn under his suit jacket.

In the kitchen, Kaitlynn heard Jeff's mother, Aunt Barb, chatting with her Aunt Jo. If she remembered correctly, Kaitlynn figured that Aunt Barb might possibly be helping with dinner but would be far more likely to be getting in the way than doing any real good. Barb was about ten years younger than her husband, James, and was still slim and fit. Her long red hair made her look even younger than her age, but Kaitlynn knew that her natural color was a slightly lighter brown than the chocolate that had been spread throughout the rest of the family's hair.

Aunt Jo stuck her head out of the kitchen and said, "Mark dear, can you get the table set up. Dinner will be ready in about fifteen."

Mark dutifully headed to the dining room, and Kaitlynn joined him. "I'll help," she said, forcing a smile.

"No, it's okay, I've got it," he said. "I mean…" he trailed off and glanced away for a second before he could bring his eyes back up to her face.

Kaitlynn looked him in the eye with a solemn look on her face. "It helps to stay busy," she whispered. She looked down and tried to wipe away a tear, hopeful that he hadn't seen her do it.

Mark nodded, handed her a pile of plates and said, "I'll get the silverware." He trudged off towards the kitchen, came back a few moments later, and followed Kaitlynn around the table finishing the settings that she had begun.

Eventually, the whole family settled down for a nice dinner together. Aunt Jo had kept things relatively simple, choosing to go with lightly seasoned chicken breasts and a few different veggies as sides. Everyone talked and reminisced about Kaitlynn's father (or Uncle Danny to the two boys). Kaitlynn was quietly working on her third glass of wine and just trying to get through it all without breaking down again when her Uncle James turned to her.

"Have you thought about what you're going to do with the house? I know Danny—I'm sorry—your father left everything to you," he paused, apprehension in his voice. "Were you thinking of staying here in Connecticut?"

Kaitlynn sighed a little more heavily than she would have liked to and replied, "I'm going to have to sell everything. I have an apartment back in Scottsdale, and a job to hopefully go back to. They let me take a leave of absence under the circumstances, but I know I'll need to go back soon if I want to keep it." She gulped down the last of her glass. She was a paralegal working for one of the larger law firms in Arizona, and she was grateful for the understanding they had shown her under the circumstances. But she knew there was really only so far she could push things before they'd have to find someone to replace her. "I have a life there—friends. I feel guilty selling it all, but I haven't lived here since I was fourteen. That was—a long time ago," her voice dropped as she finished. She reflexively reached for the wine bottle and refilled her glass.

She didn't like to think about that last year in Connecticut. There were all the fights between her parents followed by the ugly divorce. Then the long move across the country that pulled her away from her family and friends. She didn't really want to contemplate those memories with everything else already pulling at her heart.

"Well, Jeff's in real estate now," Uncle James said, shifting his gaze away from her. It was clear that the topic was making her uneasy, and she could tell that he didn't want to push it. "And the Salvation Army will take the furniture and stuff. If you want any help, we can stop by to help you pack some things up. Just let me know, okay?"

Kaitlynn gave her uncle a smile and thanked him. She knew that she was going to need all the help that she could get to make it through the next few days. Sorting through all her father's things was probably the last thing she wanted to have to do, but she knew under the circumstances she wouldn't have much choice but to do it.

After dinner, Kaitlynn insisted that she help with the dishes, again making herself busy to keep her mind as clear of thought as possible. She thanked her family again for having come, and her Aunt Jo and Uncle Dave especially for hosting the family afterward. She assured her Uncle James that she would call him and got one of Jeff's cards so that she could get the house on the market. After a few more goodbyes, and a few tears, she hopped into her father's car and headed back to his place. "Her car and her place," she thought before shaking the idea out of her head. She really didn't want to think of these things as hers, because then she would have to face the fact that he was really gone. And she was not ready for that yet. Not by a long shot.

3

The day after the funeral it hit Kaitlynn hard; her father was gone. She'd looked around at the empty house for hours wanting to let out a scream. Finally, she decided to get out and go for a walk in the woods.

Her father's house had a decent sized yard; the lot was almost two acres in all. Roughly half of the property was overgrown with the woods that went off into the distance behind the house. When she had been younger, the woods had been her sanctuary long before things had gotten toxic at home. She would slip out and spend half the day roaming between the evergreens, oaks, willows, red maples, and the white birches that made up the back half of the yard. Today she felt like she could stand to get away into those old woods again.

Her father hadn't kept up the trails that she'd used to walk through, and the thickets had overgrown much of the woods. But Kaitlynn didn't let that stop her. She delved deep into the woods, ignoring the occasional thorn that made it past her jacket or her jeans and drew a little trickle of blood.

About three-quarters of the way back to the old stone wall that marked the property's edge, she noticed that some of the wood underbrush had been cleared. And in one of the taller trees, a tree stand had been erected.

"Strange," she thought, "Dad's not—wasn't—a hunter." She strolled over to the stand, wiping away a fresh tear, and saw that the stand was quite new. The nails holding the planks together were still shiny, and the wood was completely un-weathered. There were a few two by two's nailed directly into the trunk of the tree, creating a makeshift ladder as well. She brushed what little snow there was left off them with her gloved hands so she wouldn't slip, and then climbed up into the tree stand.

She stood there in silence looking out into the woods, her breath crystallizing in the frozen air around her. She wondered if the hunter that had erected the stand had gotten permission from her father, or if they had put it up on their own hoping that it wouldn't be found. "Regardless, it will have to come down when the house goes on the market," she thought to herself. Either way, she was happy she'd found it now and could account for the expense of having it removed.

Just then, Kaitlynn heard a rustling off in the distance. She held her breath and stood still as a doe stepped out into the clearing. It stood motionless, almost acutely aware for a moment that it was being watched. Kaitlynn slowly exhaled, hoping not to spook the deer. But the doe seemed to relax and started eating some small plants at the edge of the clearing that had been protected from the snowfall by the canopy of trees above. After about five minutes, or an eternity, Kaitlynn wasn't entirely sure, the doe pranced away and jumped over the stone wall separating the property from the farm that bordered the back of the properties along roughly half the street.

Kaitlynn smiled. It was the first true smile that had crossed her face since getting the news of her father's health. "No view like that in Scottsdale," she thought to herself. Certainly, she knew that if she wanted to see evergreens and snow this time of year, she only needed to drive up to Flagstaff for the day. But it didn't feel like home the way these old familiar woods still did, even after all this time away.

As she stood there lost in her thoughts, the wind kicked up and Kaitlynn felt a shiver come over her. She didn't remember home feeling this cold. "Blood's thinned out," she reminded herself again. She let the wind gust pass and then decided to climb down. She reached the bottom and hopped the last few feet down, landing with far less poise than she'd hoped for, but graceful enough for a woman who hadn't jumped out of a tree for well over a decade. She looked around and decided against heading directly back to the house, but instead decided to follow the length of the stone wall and avoid the thickets that were just under waist high along the property's edge. Just out of sight of the clearing she began to hear the babbling stream that ran alongside the property as the border between her father's house and the neighbor's.

When she arrived at the break in the old stone wall where the small brook passed over onto the farm on the other side, she headed upstream towards the road. When she was younger, she would have jumped from rock to rock back and forth across the water. But with most of the stream covered with a thin sheet of ice, Kaitlynn decided that discretion was the better part of valor, and that maybe she would just stick to the banks this time.

As the brook wound its way hither and fro through the underbrush, eventually Kaitlynn arrived at the drainpipe that took the stream below the road. "Smaller than it used to be," she thought to herself. "Or I'm bigger." She stifled a laugh and thought for a moment about going through the drainpipe and running off into the woods on the other side of the road like she had so many times in her youth. But instead, she grabbed a tree root that was sticking out of the ground and climbed up the steep embankment on the side of the ditch that the stream had cut out of the ground over the long length of time that it had wound itself through this patch of earth. She walked a few steps and took the mail from the box by the side of the road (three days' worth, she noted to herself), and headed back to the light brown raised ranch that had been her childhood home.

Once inside, she sorted out the junk mail and various grocery flyers and tossed them directly into the trash without further appraisal and left the bills on the kitchen counter unopened. "Not today," she thought to herself, "there will be time enough for that later." She walked over to the now-cold coffee pot, poured herself a fresh mug, and then put it in the microwave for thirty seconds to heat it up. After doctoring it in her usual way (cream, two sugars), she sat down at the kitchen table and looked around at the house that she had grown up in; the house that would soon belong to someone else, and she cried until the tears wouldn't come anymore.

4

The brown cardboard boxes were already starting to pile up on the reddish-brown carpet in the common room. Kaitlynn had been packing up her father's old things for three days now, but she had found it hard to work for too long at one time. Emotionally, she was completely drained, which made her feel physically weak as well. Thankfully her Uncle James and her cousin Jeff had come over to help today. They were already making more progress than she had managed to on her own since the funeral service.

She was emptying the drawer on her father's nightstand when she came across a pile of old pictures of her as a child in a plastic sandwich bag. They were faded from time and exposure, and she didn't remember many of the events that were captured within them. There was one of her in a white floral Sunday dress from when she was about eight or so that she didn't remember at all, but she assumed that it must have been from a trip to church. There was another one with her wearing a tank top and overalls with her ponytail sticking out of a Yankees cap while sitting on a picnic blanket with her two cousins. She guessed it was probably taken at Kent Falls, but she couldn't remember for sure. There were a few more of her with her childhood friend Candice from down the street that was taken before they went to a middle school dance. Kaitlynn smiled as she thumbed through them. She hadn't thought of any of her old friends in years.

At the bottom of the pile, she found one that stuck out to her as specif ically odd though. There was no one in it at all, only a picture taken in the woods somewhere at what appeared to be the foot of one of the many rolling hills in the area. But going up the hill was a set of wood stairs. The wood was clearly weathered and old, and there were dead leaves on the ground. She wasn't sure if it was part of one of the many trails in the area or not. It was an odd thing for her father to have taken a picture of and stored in such a place. She shrugged to herself and decided to keep the photographs.

She walked into her bedroom, and she stuffed the bag into the front pocket of her suitcase. As she was walking back into her father's room, the doorbell rang. She hadn't been expecting anyone else today and as she made her way back into the hallway, she saw her uncle turn out of the kitchen and head down the steps to the door. She stayed in the hall and listened intently.

"Hello, can I help you," her uncle asked politely as he opened the door.

"Oh, I'm sorry. I must have the wrong address," a woman replied, her voice pensive. "I was looking for an old friend, Katie Jenson. Is she here?"

Kaitlynn made her way down the hall and looked around the corner. In the doorway was a pretty, blonde-haired, blue-eyed woman about her age and height. She looked at her for a moment before the slight recognition set in. Without the photos she had just found, she wasn't sure she would have recognized the woman at all. "Candice?" she asked, her voice sounding unsure, before taking an anxious step down the stairs.

"Oh, Katie!" Her friend gasped. "I'm so sorry about your dad. I read the obituary in the paper, and I thought I'd see if you were here."

Her uncle stepped aside and let Kaitlynn pass as she went to embrace her childhood friend. She hadn't seen Candice Winters since she was a girl, right before she'd moved across the country. They had been thick as thieves as young girls, and it was good to see her despite the circumstances. She thought about how odd it was that she had just come across those pictures of them together a few minutes ago. "It's good to see you, Candy," she whispered as she held her friend tight against her.

"I'm so sorry that it's under these circumstances, Katie," Candice replied and returned the embrace. "I wanted to come to the funeral, but I had to work. I'm so glad you're still here."

"I'll be here for another couple of weeks," Kaitlynn replied. "I need to get things in order." She looked around the room at all the boxes and suddenly remembered the two men standing in the room. "Oh, let me introduce you. This is my Uncle James and my cousin Jeff. They're helping me with the packing."

They all exchanged greetings and shook hands. Kaitlynn silently noted how her cousin tried not to stare at her friend and smiled a little bit. He was single, and Candice had always been a good-looking girl. It was clear that she'd grown into her body as a woman as well because Kaitlynn thought she looked like a knockout, even in the gray sweater and pair of blue jeans she was wearing.

"Well, I'd be happy to stay and help with anything you need," Candice said with confidence. "And then tonight you have to let me take you out for dinner. It's been years, and you look like you could stand to get out for a bit."

Kaitlynn smiled at Candice's suggestion. "Yeah, I think that's a good idea."

5

Kaitlynn's uncle and cousin had gone, and an immense amount of progress had been made. All her father's clothes had been packed, and most of the drawers around the house had been sorted through as well. Pretty much all that was left in the kitchen was a handful of utensils and some paper plates. Kaitlynn looked around the room at the piles of boxes to be donated. She decided that she would rent a truck on Monday morning and take it all down to the Salvation Army building the next town over. Jeff had given her a quote as to what the house was worth in its current condition and suggestions for what work could be done to increase the value. He also recommended leaving all the furniture until the house sold for staging purposes. It was a lot for her to think about. One thing Kaitlynn knew for sure though, she wanted to get rid of the hospital bed in which her father had died as soon as possible; there were too many unhappy memories associated with that thing. But for now, it was Saturday night and she wanted to try to have a good time, and hopefully get her mind off of things as much as possible.

Candice had left to get herself "prettied up," and told Kaitlynn that she'd be back in about an hour or so. In the meantime, Kaitlynn grabbed a quick shower and then went through her suitcase looking for something other than the collection of sweatshirts and jeans that she had hurriedly packed. The only dress she had with her was the black one that she had bought and worn to the funeral, and she'd decided on that day that she would rather burn that thing than ever wear it again. Eventually, she settled on a pair of jeans and a flowing red top she had packed and hadn't worn yet. She had bought it a few days before her father had called her and the tags were still on it. "Must have grabbed it by accident when I was packing," she thought to herself as she cut the tags off and slipped it on. She pulled on her favorite boots and then went back into the bathroom.

After applying a light layer of blush and some eyeliner, she tied her dark hair up in a bun and looked in the mirror. She decided to go with some gloss to make her lips look a little fuller, and then deemed that that was enough. At thirty-six, she was still a very good-looking woman. There were the occasional lines by her striking emerald green eyes trying to sneak through, and her perpetual Arizona tan had faded from being in Connecticut for the last few months. She couldn't remember the last time her skin had been as pale as it was. She let her hair down again and decided that that was a better look after all.

She walked downstairs and grabbed her coat just as Candice's car pulled into the driveway. She locked the door behind her and walked over to the car, a brand-new looking SUV. She pulled herself up into the passenger seat and suddenly felt like she might be underdressed for the occasion. Candice had changed into a tight miniskirt with heels and black stockings and was wearing a low-cut blouse under her jacket. Her makeup was far more pronounced than Kaitlynn's as well. "Sorry, I didn't realize we were getting that dressed up," she stammered out, a little bit taken aback.

"Oh, it's ok Katie," Candice replied, her face showing slight embarrassment. "I didn't think about the fact that you probably didn't bring much in the way of dress up. We can swing by my place if you want to borrow something. It's not that far."

"Um, if you're okay with it, sure." Kaitlynn blushed. She wasn't entirely sure that she and Candice were the same size, but they looked like they might be close enough. It had been months since she'd been able to dress up and go out, and she was looking forward to it even if it meant borrowing clothes from a friend she hadn't seen in twenty plus years. They chatted on the short drive to Candice's house. It was only a few miles away, but it was nice for the two of them to catch up.

Candice had apparently gotten a job in New York City and spent most of her week in Manhattan working at a brokerage on Wall Street. She usually drove across the New York border to Brewster and took the train into the city every morning, and then did the reverse late every evening. The idea of that kind of daily commute blew Kaitlynn's mind. She hated her twenty-minute drive to work back home as it was.

When they arrived at Candice's house, Kaitlynn was surprised by how big it was. It was a large colonial style house with a huge lot. "All this just for you?" she asked, trying to hide the look of surprise on her face. "You must be doing well."

"Yeah, the job pays *really* well," Candice replied. "I have a guy who takes care of the yard for me, and a lady who does the cleaning. It's nice to get away from the city and relax on the weekends even if the commute is hell." There was warmth in the way she smiled at Kaitlynn. "Come on Katie, let's get you something to wear."

"Can I tell you something honestly?" asked Kaitlynn. "I hate that nick-name. I've gone by Kaitlynn for almost twenty years. I just didn't have the heart to correct my family this week with everything going on. It just didn't seem that important."

Candice smiled at her. "No problem, *Kait-lynn*," she said, over-enunciating the name for comedic effect. Both women laughed at that. "Come on. I have the perfect skirt to go with that top."

6

About forty-five minutes later, Candice pulled the car up in front of an Irish bar simply called The Pub. The two ladies walked in and strolled up to the bar, turning a few heads along the way. The black skirt that Candice had let Kaitlynn borrow had a billowy quality to it to match her top and it ended just above her knees. Additionally, her boots ended just below the knees, showing off just a slight bit of leg between them and the skirt. For the first time in months, she felt attractive.

"Scotch on the rocks," Candice said with an air of confidence to the bartender when he came over to them.

"And for you miss?" he asked as he turned to Kaitlynn.

"Screwdriver and menus please," she said, blushing a bit. She was pretty sure the bartender had been checking her out as they walked up, and she hadn't been the only one who had noticed.

"Looks like I have some competition tonight," Candice joked while nudging Kaitlynn with her elbow. "*Somebody liiiiiikes yoooouuuu.*" The sing-song nature of the way she said it made both of them chuckle.

"Well," said Kaitlynn, stifling a laugh, "I'm not exactly gonna be here for more than another couple of weeks. So, I don't think it would work out. He's all yours."

Candice looked at her with a smirk. "You don't have to have a relationship with him you know. I mean, you could pick any guy in here and take them home. Have you seen yourself? It'd be the luckiest night of their life, guaranteed."

"Oh, is that how you do it?" Kaitlynn asked playfully, returning the smirk.

"Damn right." There was such a confidence in the way that Candice said it, that Kaitlynn didn't believe it was a joke.

"Well, I guess I won't mention that I caught my cousin checking you out then," Kaitlynn joked. "I mean since you've got all the men in the world to choose from," she added slyly.

"He was cute," Candice responded coyly. "But he seemed a little tame for me."

"So, no serious relationships then?" Kaitlynn asked, digging a little bit deeper.

"I don't have anything against them," Candice replied with a sigh. "But I work in the city and live here. The commute is brutal. Guys in the city would want me to move closer to the city, guys out here would want me to work closer to home. I love my job, but I like living close to my parents. They're still right down the street from your dad's house. I'd have to give up too much either way." Candice paused and smiled. "Besides, I like to play with my food." They both laughed at that. "What about you? Is anybody waiting for you back home?"

"Not right now," Kaitlynn explained. "I've had serious relationships, but nothing that's worked out."

"Sounds like a story," Candice inquired. "So, what's the deal?"

"Well, I was engaged to a guy. But it didn't work out," replied Kaitlynn with a dour expression on her face. "I came home early one day because I wasn't feeling well and found him in our bed with some girl he'd met somewhere."

Candice winced. "Oh, I'm sorry Katie...er...Kaitlynn." She shook her head for a second as she realized her mistake. "Sorry, that's gonna take some getting used to. But you're better off without a guy like that."

"Yeah, it's been a while at this point," Kaitlynn explained. "I've kinda been taking a break from dating for a while. And then everything with Dad happened, so my personal life has been on the back burner for months."

"Then it sounds like the perfect time for you to pick a guy tonight and let loose," Candice said with a sly smile. "No need for a walk of shame when you're hopping on an airplane." She raised her eyebrows at Kaitlynn in an exaggerated joking manner.

"Yeah, I think I'm good. But thanks," Kaitlynn replied, but the idea sounded better to her than she wanted to admit to herself. "I'm just not in the right place for that right now."

"I understand. Just trying to lighten the mood." Candice smiled at her. Then she downed her scotch, turned and looked at the bartender, and pointed to her empty glass. He nodded at her, and she turned and picked up the menu. "So, what are we having before I kick your ass at pool?"

"Oh, you think so?" Kaitlynn said, raising an eyebrow at her friend.

Candice shrugged. "Honestly, I suck at pool. But I find that bending over a pool table in a skirt tends to attract guys, and I haven't given up on getting you laid yet."

Kaitlynn spat part of her screwdriver back into her glass, and the both of them laughed. It was the best that she had felt in a long time.

7

Candice pulled her car into Kaitlynn's driveway. They'd had a great time reminiscing about the old days, trading stories about the parts of their lives they'd each missed out on and flirting with a couple of guys at the pool table. As she put the car in park, she turned and gave Kaitlynn a hug. "It was great to see you, we need to do that again before you leave," she said.

"Absolutely," Kaitlynn agreed. "That was a lot of fun. Besides, I'll need to return this skirt."

"Hang on to it for next weekend then. I've got ideas of where I can take you next," Candice said while flashing an evil grin at her friend. Both of them laughed again. Kaitlynn hadn't laughed this much in months.

"All right, sounds good," she said. They traded phone numbers and social media accounts before Kaitlynn got out of the car. She waved at her friend as she pulled away, and then took a deep breath before turning up the steps and heading into the house.

At the front door, Kaitlynn turned the key and stepped inside. She'd left the hall light on for when she got home, but she wasn't expecting it to be quite so late. Even still, she wasn't tired. For the first time in months, she felt alive. She kicked off her stylish knee-high boots at the door and headed into the kitchen. In the freezer, she dug out a pint of mint ice cream from underneath a few frozen dinners and then grabbed one of the last remaining spoons from a drawer.

She went downstairs to the living room (which was slightly below ground level except for the windows) and sat down on the couch. It occurred to her that in the months she'd been here since her father had gotten sick, she couldn't remember coming downstairs for anything other than to do the weekly cleaning.

Kaitlynn turned on the television and dug into her ice cream while she flipped through the channels. It was well after midnight on a Saturday— "Sunday now," she thought—so she wasn't expecting to find much on. Her father barely had anything other than the basic cable channels, and anything above that was just the sports package so he would have been able to watch the Yankees games. She would have loved to have some movie channels to pick through. After a while, she gave up and switched over to one of the music channels instead and just sat back with her ice cream and listened. She'd settled on the classic rock station and AC/DC was currently saluting those about to rock, which she thought would have very much appealed to her father.

After a while, she looked around the living room and saw the various pictures placed around the room of her and her father together from a number of her different visits home. There was her high school graduation picture on one end table, a picture of her and her father together from that same summer before she had started college on the other one. There were also various pictures of them together on the mantle above the fireplace from throughout the years. She regretted that she hadn't been home as often over the last few years, as work and her life back home had kept her busy.

Her father had been a good-looking man, and a little bit taller than she was. She'd gotten her rich, dark hair from him, but not his brown eyes. She'd gotten her dark green eyes from her mother instead. They both had the same soft features though. It was hard for her to believe that the man she had watched wither away over the past few months was the same person in the photographs that she was staring at now.

It was then that she noticed for the first time the painting above the mantle of the fireplace. It had a gold embossed wooden frame that made it stand out slightly from the dark brown paneling on the wall. She gasped, put her ice cream down and ran upstairs to her room and grabbed the plastic bag of pictures that she had stuffed into her suitcase. She ran back down the stairs and held the picture up to the painting and stared at them both. It was uncanny. It was the same random set of weathered stairs, going up the wooded incline into the distance. Everything was the same: the trees, the rocks, the fallen leaves, and the slight hanging fog in the air.

Confused, she put the picture down on the mantle and stepped away. Had her father always owned that painting? Had he taken the picture and then had the painting done of it? It was too much of a coincidence, but unfortunately, she couldn't ask him. It was just one more thing she'd never be able to talk about with him again. She felt the all too familiar lump in her throat returning, so she sat down on the couch and ate her feelings, one minty spoonful at a time.

8

Kaitlynn woke up the next morning on the couch, her eyes still red from the tears she had cried the night before, to the sound of knocking on the door. She looked at her phone and saw that it was a quarter after ten in the morning. She rose up off the couch and grabbed the empty carton of ice cream and spoon and walked up the stairs to the landing halfway between floors where the front door was. She quickly brushed her hair out of her face and opened the door a crack. On the other side was her cousin Mark.

"Oh, hey," She stammered out as she opened the door the rest of the way. "I forgot you were coming over today." She ushered him inside and closed the door to the biting cold outside.

"No problem," He replied. "I'm sure you've got a lot on your mind." He motioned towards the empty ice cream container in her hand. "Breakfast?" he asked her with a smile.

"No, from last night," she chuckled. "I just forgot to bring it upstairs."

"Looks like maybe you forgot to bring yourself upstairs too," he said. "Everything okay?"

"Yeah, I'm fine," she replied, forcing a smile. "I met up with an old friend last night and got home late. I must have fallen asleep on the couch."

"Must have been some friend," he said. "You look good."

Kaitlynn realized that she must have fallen asleep with her makeup still on as well and blushed a bit. "*She* let me borrow her skirt," Kaitlynn replied. "I didn't come all this way to go on a date," she added, a slight tone of defensiveness slipping out.

"Okay, no problem," he said, clearly not wanting to upset her. Changing the subject, he asked, "Anyways, you needed some help with Uncle Danny's stuff? How can I help?"

"Uncle James and Jeff were here yesterday, and they got a lot done," Kaitlynn replied, relieved to be moving on. "My friend Candice helped a lot too. But I don't think we touched the attic or the garage yet."

"I see. So, I get the cold patrol, huh?" Mark joked. "I see how it is."

"I appreciate your help, Cuz," Kaitlynn replied, giving him a hug. "But if you don't mind, I'm going to go get changed before we get started."

She excused herself and bounded up the stairs and into her room. She grabbed a pair of jeans and a baggy sweatshirt and tossed them on as quickly as she could. She moved into the bathroom to brush her teeth and wash off her makeup, and then came out and started to make a pot of coffee. She stepped out of the kitchen and looked around the rest of the upstairs area, but Mark was nowhere to be found.

"Mark?" she called out. "Did you want some coffee?"

"Yeah, sure," he called back to her from downstairs.

Kaitlynn got the pot brewing and then started back down the stairs to see what Mark was doing. She saw him standing in front of the fireplace, staring at the painting above the mantle. Seeing him staring at it reminded her of the events of the night before.

"Has Dad always had that painting?" she asked him as she slid up next to him.

Mark shrugged his shoulders. "I don't remember," he said. "I was just kind of looking around while I was waiting."

Kaitlynn tried to hide her disappointment, but she was really curious about these mysterious stairs now. "Here, look at this," she said. She walked over to the mantle and picked up the picture that she had left there the night before. "It looks like the same place. I found it in a drawer upstairs. It must have meant something to Dad, but I've never seen it before."

Mark looked at his cousin. Her face was scrunched up in frustration, and he couldn't help but laugh a little. "I wish I could help you, Katie," he said. "But I've never seen it before."

Kaitlynn nodded. "Well, thanks anyway," she said. "I guess we should get started." She took a deep breath and let it go slowly. "Pick your poison, garage or attic?"

"Garage," replied Mark. "I don't know how tall it is in the attic and I'd rather not throw my back out at the beginning of all of this." They both chuckled at that. Kaitlynn went back upstairs to the kitchen and grabbed their coffee before they headed out into the garage to begin packing her father's things.

9

Kaitlynn closed the hatch to the attic as Mark placed the last cardboard box on top of the pile in the upstairs common area. Luckily the attic hadn't been too bad, and the garage was mostly just tools and yard supplies. Despite the bitter cold that had rolled in overnight, the day hadn't been too stressful at all.

Mark stared at the pile of boxes that had taken over much the common room and blocked the big bay window looking out upon the front yard. He took a deep breath and asked, "So what's the plan for all this stuff?"

"I was gonna rent a truck tomorrow morning and take it all down to the Salvation Army in Danbury," Kaitlynn replied. "Better to donate it all than to throw it away," she added. She reached up and swept a cobweb full of vicious dust bunnies off the shoulder of Mark's sweater with her right hand. Then she turned and looked at the pile of boxes, immediately regretting the fact that she would likely have to move them all by herself.

"Do you have anyone to help you?" Mark asked her. "I work until around three, but I could help after that." Mark was a seventh-grade social studies teacher at the local middle school, a fact that Kaitlynn found somewhat ironic since it had been the same school that she had gone to as a girl. She imagined having her cousin as a teacher would have been better than the overweight mouth breather that she'd had in seventh grade. She couldn't remember any of what she had learned that year in class, other than how to cover up and hide her freshly budding breasts so that Mr. Nielson wouldn't leer at her the way he did so many of the other girls in her class. The memory made her shudder involuntarily.

"No, it's okay. I want to get it done early," Kaitlynn replied, trying to shake the image of Mr. Nielsen out of her mind. "And Jeff's coming over tomorrow night to go over a few things before we put the house on the market," she added. "I want to be home and done before he gets here."

"Well, I have a buddy who has a truck. I can see if he's willing to lend it to me on Tuesday afternoon," Mark said. "That way you don't have to waste money on renting a truck and you can definitely be here for Jeff tomorrow night."

"Are you sure it'll be okay?" Kaitlynn asked. She didn't really want the pile of boxes to linger for an extra day, but she didn't want to move them all by herself either.

Mark pulled his cell phone out of his pocket and said, "I'll call him now and let you know." As he slipped off into the kitchen to call his friend, Kaitlynn decided to go downstairs and give him some space rather than hover.

At the bottom of the stairs, she paused for a moment and then walked over to the fireplace. She stared at the painting, her mind trying to decipher the riddle of the mysterious stairs in the unfamiliar forest. As she looked at it, she felt like the painting looked different somehow, as if the colors had muted somewhat since last night. It was almost as if the fog in the painting seemed thicker than before. She blinked her eyes a couple of times and then looked again, squinting her eyes this time. She was sure that through the fog she could see the outline of a person near the top of the stairs, but something wasn't quite right about it. The shape was all wrong somehow, but she couldn't quite figure out what was out of place.

"We're good for Tuesday night," Mark said from behind her. She hadn't heard him come down the stairs at all and she jumped almost a foot in the air at being startled. Mark gave her a second to compose herself and then said, "I'll get the truck after work and meet you here."

She looked back to the painting, and it looked to her as it had the night before when she first noticed it. The shape in the fog was gone. "Must be seeing things," she thought to herself. It was possible that the stress of the last few months might be getting to her. She turned to her cousin and said, "Great, thank you. I really appreciate it."

Mark looked at her. "Are you feeling okay?" He asked her. "You look white as a sheet."

She nodded her head and forced a slight smile. "I'm just drained," she said. "It's been a long couple of months, and I think it's catching up with me. I think I just need to get some rest."

Taking his cue, Mark gave her a hug, wished her a good night and left. She watched him walk to his car and waved to him from the door as he pulled away. Once he had pulled out of the driveway and had driven out of sight, she walked back downstairs to the painting and looked at it again. It looked exactly as it had the night before. She closed her eyes, shook her head and turned away. "You're going nuts, Katie," she said to herself under her breath. She winced at the fact that she had used the old nickname that she hated so much. She walked upstairs and went to her room and decided to sleep the rest of the afternoon away.

10

"In its current condition, you're talking about two hundred and fifty thousand," Jeff said. Kaitlynn listened to him repeat what he had told her on Saturday afternoon about the house. "If you're willing to put in about twenty thousand on the kitchen and the two bathrooms, I'm pretty sure we can bump that up to three hundred thousand dollars," he continued. "The place is in great shape overall, and what I'm talking about would just be modernizing as opposed to repairs. New appliances, new fixtures, that sort of thing. Biggest project would be knocking out this wall in between the kitchen, dining room and common area and opening up the concept. Worst case scenario, you'll have to leave a post for support, but the open concept really drives up prices."

Kaitlynn listened to her cousin's suggestions, as the steam from their coffee mugs drifted up between them at the kitchen table, but frowned and said, "I appreciate what you're saying Jeff, but I don't have that kind of money. I had to go through a lot of my savings to stay here these last few months. And staying for renovations may test the limits of my leave of absence from work." She shook her head and scrunched her face. "I just don't think it's realistic to put that kind of work in under the circumstances."

Jeff nodded his understanding before responding. "Okay, so how quickly are you looking to sell then? Because I can put it out at under market value and see if we can get a quick offer."

"Well, I want to get a fair price if I can," Kaitlynn replied. "But at the same time, I was hoping to be home in a couple of weeks."

"Okay, so here's my suggestion then. Let's put it on the market for two hundred and thirty-five thousand," Jeff explained. "That's fifteen grand below market value. That should generate some interest quickly, and you might even get a bidding war."

Kaitlynn nodded her approval. "I like it. But what about any work that needs to be done?" she asked. "I don't know if I can afford to pay for anything that comes up in an inspection. And there's a tree stand in the woods that probably has to come down too," she added.

"Well, if anything comes up, we can make a price concession and let them deal with fixing it," Jeff explained. "The tree stand I can probably take down, but I say leave it up for now. Someone may want to keep it, or maybe someone will convert it into a tree fort for their kids. If we have to take it down, we'll cross that bridge then."

All of this sounded good to Kaitlynn. "Okay, so I think I'm good to go then."

"All right then," Jeff said. "I will get the house on the market first thing in the morning. I'd like to do an open house this weekend if we can. So, the place will have to be clean, and you'll have to take off for a few hours."

"No problem there," Kaitlynn said. "My friend Candice and I were going to go out again on Saturday, so if that works for you, that works for me."

"Saturday it is then!" Jeff exclaimed. "I will get everything set up." He paused for a moment and finished his coffee, before standing up and asking, "So how long have you known Candice?"

Kaitlynn covered her mouth and chuckled. "I knew you were checking her out the other day," she said while standing up and then giving her cousin a playful punch on the shoulder. "Careful, she's a man-eater. We're talking a real praying mantis type. But I'll put in a good word for you if you sell the house quickly," she said raising her eyebrows at her cousin.

"Well then, I will do my best," he said with a smile. "I will talk to you in a couple of days to make sure everything is set up for Saturday." He gave her a hug and added, "It's good to see you again Katie, and I'll get this done for you." Despite his muscled physique, Jeff had wrapped his arms around her gently. He stepped back and smiled at her with his hands still on her shoulders for a moment before grabbing his briefcase and jacket.

She started to walk him to the door, but at the landing by the door she stopped short and asked, "Can I show you something?" She headed downstairs to the fireplace without waiting for a response and pointed at the painting above the mantle. "Do you know where that is, or how long Dad's had that painting?"

Jeff considered the painting above the mantle for a minute. "Could be any number of trails in the area here, or really anywhere else," he said. "As far as how long he's had it, I don't know," he added. "Why?"

She showed him the picture and explained where she found it. "It must have meant something to Dad," she said, echoing what she had said to Mark the day before.

"Maybe so Katie," Jeff said sympathetically, "but what's this really about?"

She took a deep breath and sighed. "I've missed so much of his life," she said, the dejection heavy in her voice. "And here's this thing, this strange thing that clearly meant something to Dad and I'll never be able to ask him about it."

At this, the floodgates opened, and the tears flowed freely from her eyes. Jeff put his arms around her and let her cry on his shoulder for as long as she needed to.

11

It was Friday, the day before the open house and Kaitlynn was cleaning up and preparing for the rush of people that she hoped would take an interest in buying her father's old house. Mark had helped her get rid of all the boxes of her dad's things on Tuesday night. It had taken two trips to get rid of everything and they had made it to the Salvation Army just moments before they had closed on the second trip. She'd felt bad showing up so late, but she knew that it had to be done. It had made for a long day though, and she'd spent most of the following day sleeping or just putzing around the house.

She looked out the bay window in the common area and smiled. There had been another fresh dusting of snow overnight and it looked beautiful outside. She could see the snow blanketing the grass and icicles clinging to the branches of the large evergreen tree in the center of the front yard. She figured she would take a push broom to the driveway and the deck a little later when it warmed up a bit if it didn't just melt off those surfaces on its own by then.

Jeff had recommended that she take down as many personal items as possible before the open house the following day, so she was picking up the various picture frames around the house and boxing them up. She planned on sending the pictures back home to her apartment to keep, but she felt rather sad taking them down. They were reminders of her father and the times she'd spent with him, and she liked having them around the house. In a way it made her feel like he was still there watching over her.

She worked her way through the upstairs with the box in her hand, wrapping the picture frames with care in a couple of layers of tissue paper each, and then headed downstairs to do the same to the photos in the living room. She cleared off the end tables and then began taking the pictures off the mantle. As she was picking up one of the frames, she accidentally knocked the strange picture of the stairs in the woods that she had left on the mantle down to the floor. She bent down to pick it up and saw that it had landed face down. For the first time, she noticed that there was writing on the back of the picture.

Follow the Instructions on the back

It was her father's handwriting. "Instructions on the back?" she thought to herself. "This is the back." She flipped the picture over again to see the photo on the other side of the strange staircase in the woods, and then flipped it over again and reread the message on the back.

Follow the Instructions on the back

Frustrated, Kaitlynn sat down on the couch with the picture in her lap and rubbed her temples with the forefingers of both hands. "What the hell does that mean?" she asked herself under her breath. She sat there brooding for a few minutes while turning the words over in her head. She kept flipping the picture over in her hands as if she expected some new clue to appear.

Eventually, she sighed and tossed the picture down on the end table and laid back on the couch. She looked around the room until her eyes fixated on the painting above the mantle. Intrigued she got up, walked over to the fireplace, and picked the painting up slowly off of its hook above the mantle. It was heavier than she had anticipated, and she put it down carefully in front of the wall to the side of the fireplace. She then flipped it around and looked on the back. There was an inscription that had been carved along the top of the frame on the back of the painting.

Into the forest take me.

Kaitlynn read the inscription over and over, trying to understand what it meant. She walked back over to the end table and picked up the picture again and read her father's message one more time.

Follow the Instructions on the back

"Wait, I'm supposed to bring the painting into the woods?" she asked herself, her voice rising as she spoke. She threw up her arms in frustration. "*That doesn't make any sense!*" she yelled at the empty room, and then went back to the couch and threw herself down on it. As she sat there, she stared at the back of the painting, rereading the inscription on the back as it balanced itself against the wall.

Into the forest take me.

Kaitlynn took a deep breath and said, "Oh fucking hell." She stood up and went upstairs to her room. She threw on a baggy maroon sweatshirt with the old Arizona State University logo in block letters on the front over her t-shirt, and grabbed her boots, putting them on over the pant legs of her jeans. She grabbed her wool gloves and winter jacket from the hall closet and went downstairs. She picked up the painting with care, walked out through the garage and headed for the woods behind the house.

She was careful while walking through the woods to hold the painting high enough to avoid the overgrown thickets as she didn't want to damage it. Eventually, she reached the clearing by the tree stand she had found the week before. Her arms were starting to get tired from carrying the painting, but she didn't know what to do next. She looked at the two by two's nailed into the tree and hung the painting on one of them, then stepped back and looked at it.

"Okay, now what?" she asked, looking right at the painting. Kaitlynn threw her arms out with her palms up and shrugged with frustration. She stared at it for a minute and then decided that she had had enough of this and turned to go back to the house. The damned thing could stay there for all that she cared.

She started to walk away, but after she got halfway through the clearing, she heard a twig crack behind her. She stopped, and slowly turned around and looked back. The painting had fallen off the crude wooden ladder and had landed on the ground, snapping the twig. It was still standing upright, but amazingly, it had grown bigger. Much, much bigger.

Kaitlynn's eyes went wide with wonder. Before her, the painting was now life-sized. She guessed it was roughly six feet tall by eight feet wide, though she didn't have a tape measure to pull out and check it. The trees in the painting were moving as if stirred by the breeze. The slight fog in the painting seemed to move slightly in the air as well.

She walked back over to the painting and looked at it. The closer she got to it, the less it looked like a painting at all; it looked real. She reached out to touch it, and her hand passed directly through it. She pulled it back quickly, and then walked around to the right of the painting and looked behind it. She could see the back of the painting leaning up against the tree. To her right was the stone wall separating the property from the farm behind it. She shook her head again, completely incredulous, and then walked back around to the front of the painting again.

Kaitlynn stood there looking at it for a full five minutes, unsure of what to do. She could see the fog from the painting slowly drifting through into the real world. She passed her hands through the fog trying to see if it was real, as if she could actually grab the mist in her hands like a tangible thing. She shook her head at this realization and cursed her own stupidity. After staring at it for another minute without any clue as to what to do, she walked right up to the painting and exhaled into it. Her breath froze in the February air and then passed into the painting—where it disappeared. This close to it she could feel that there was a bit more warmth coming from inside the painting. She reached out and watched her hand pass directly through it again. Kaitlynn held her hand there for a minute and noticed that the sun on the other side was casting the shadows of her fingers in a completely different direction than on the ground in front of her. She took another deep breath and then pulled her hand back out of the painting again.

Kaitlynn took a few steps back, then took a long, deep breath and put her hands over her face. She looked out at the painting from between her fingers. "This is crazy," she said out loud, though the sound was muffled by the wool gloves on her hands. She looked around and saw a small stick on the ground, picked it up, and tossed it at the painting. It passed through and she could hear it crash land as the stick skittered across the wood of the second step.

She paced back and forth for a few minutes, unsure of what to do. Finally, she took off her right glove, unbuttoned her jacket and reached up under her shirt and pinched herself hard to make sure she wasn't dreaming. It hurt quite a bit as she dug her nails into her side trying to wake herself up. Eventually, she stopped and accepted the fact that she really was awake, and this really was happening, as hard as that was to believe.

"What do I do?" she thought. She looked at the painting. How could her father have had something like this? Had he known what it could do? "He must have known," she remembered, thinking about his handwriting on the back of the picture. "He must have taken the picture from the inside!" she thought, her eyes going wide.

She looked over her shoulder, brushing her hair back over her ear to do so. She could see the path back through the woods and towards the house, but the trees and the underbrush were too thick to see the house from here.

She looked back towards the painting, took a deep breath, steeled herself, and walked through it into another world.

12

K aitlynn looked around at the strange woods she had entered. The trees here were similar to those in the woods back behind her house, but they were thicker here, more robust. There was a misty haze in the air, and the lush canopy of branches and leaves let very little sunlight through. The spots where the rays of light came through shone like beacons against the deep forest backdrop. The air felt cool, yet far warmer than it had been on the other side of the painting. She could still feel the cold winter air at her back, and the frigid breeze behind her brushed her hair ever so slightly. She looked up the stairs and saw that they seemed to go on for an eternity before the fog claimed them.

Kaitlynn turned around and looked back the way she had come. She could see the woods she had just left, the dusting of snow upon the ground, and her footprints emerging from the underbrush along the path back to the house leading her into the clearing and right up to the edge of the painting. On this side, the frame of the painting looked exactly the same as it had where she had come from, as if the paintings were mirror images of each other. She walked around the painting and saw that the woods seemed to go on as far as the eye could see. The trees were tall, thick, and old, and there was a path that wound its way between them. Not too far from where she stood, she could see that a white birch had fallen across the path with its roots pulled out of the ground.

She glanced at the back of the painting and saw it leaning against a makeshift wooden post roughly five feet high. On the top of the painting, inscribed along the frame just as it had been back on her side, was the same message.

Into the forest take me.

Kaitlynn shook her head in disbelief as she walked back around to the front of the painting. She stuck her ungloved right hand back through the painting and could instantly feel the chill in the air upon it. She pulled it back to the relative warmth on this side of the painting. She took off her other glove, stuffed both of them into a pocket on the interior lining of her coat, and then turned and looked at the steps again.

She walked over, picked up the stick she had thrown through the painting and examined it. It was about a foot long and an inch and a half thick. It was still slightly damp where the snow that had lingered on it before she had picked it up and tossed it through the painting had melted slightly in the warmer air. She turned and tossed it back through the painting, watching it land in a slight puff of snow on the other side. She sat for a moment on the second step and tried to calm her frenzied thoughts.

"This is impossible," she thought to herself. "How the hell did I walk through a painting? Why the fuck did Dad have this thing in his house?" The more she tried to calm herself, the more frantic her thoughts seemed to become. She started taking a number of deep breaths in an effort to fight back the building panic. Eventually, she began to calm down and re-collect herself.

She stood up and turned towards the staircase. This was the focal point of the painting from her side, these stairs in the woods. With a sense of trepidation, she put her left foot on the first step, and then slowly shuffled her right foot on to the one she had been sitting on. After about a dozen steps, she turned around and looked back at the painting. It was still there, but from this distance, the other side looked less real and more like the strokes of a paintbrush. She wondered if this painting, too, shrunk down to normal size and if her world looked this fake through it like it had on her father's mantle.

"The answers are this way," she thought to herself, returning her attention back to the staircase. One cautious step after another, she made her way up the strange wooden steps. The farther up the steps she went, the thicker the fog became.

13

The stairs seemed to go on forever. Kaitlynn had been climbing the steps for what she thought must have been at least an hour (she had forgotten her phone and couldn't check the time), and her legs were weary. Off to her left, she could hear the raging sounds of a waterfall in the distance. She had seen no evidence of water at the bottom of the stairs and wondered if it must be falling in a different direction. She hoped that she might finally be getting closer to the source, but the fog was as thick as pea soup now and her visibility was down to only a few feet ahead of her. Unfortunately, the more of the water she heard, the more her bladder began to ache. She was beginning to think that soon she might have no choice but to go back. Luckily it seemed like the stairs had been going in a relatively straight line up the never-ending hill, rather than weaving to and fro, so she figured it would be a pretty straight shot back down.

Without warning, as if nature had pulled back a curtain, she stepped through the fog and reached what appeared to be a large plateau on the top of the hill with a clearing in the trees. In the clearing, she saw an open field of tall grass, about as high as her chest. The path seemed to enter the center of the grass and then disappear within it as if the grass had grown and covered the trail over a long period of time.

The sound of the waterfall was closer now and her bladder wouldn't wait much longer. She glanced around to make sure she was alone and then stepped over to the tree line by the edge of the clearing. Quickly she undid her belt, lowered her jeans around her ankles, and then propped her back against a tree. She squatted down with her legs out in front of her and relieved herself, the pressure releasing from her lower abdomen. She felt disgusting like this, pissing in the woods, but she knew that she hadn't had much of a choice.

Kaitlynn stood and pulled her pants back up, then walked over to where the path entered the tall grass all the while buckling up her belt. She stood there for a moment, transfixed as she watched the tall grass sway back and forth in the wind. She reached out her hand flat above the grass and felt it sway against her palm for a second before gently pushing it aside and passing into the field. As she passed through the grass, small bits of golden pollen stuck to her jacket. She decided to keep walking straight ahead, hoping that the path didn't wind its way through the open field, as she couldn't actually see where it had once been before the grass had swallowed it up.

After a few minutes, the trickle of the water had grown loud enough that Kaitlynn was sure she was about to come upon the source of the waterfall. She stepped out from the grass and almost fell directly into a fast-moving stream that was about fifteen feet across and looked like it might just be just deep enough to cover her head at the center. She looked to the left where the water was flowing towards, and in the distance she could see an opening in the woods with blue sky and small tufts of clouds. The water seemed to head right towards it, and there was a slight mist rising into the air. "Must be the waterfall," she thought to herself, before turning her attention back to the small river that blocked her path. "I don't want to swim it," she thought. She looked to her right and about thirty feet down she could see a small stone bridge arching its way over the stream.

Kaitlynn made her way along the embankment, careful not to step in and get her favorite boots wet until she made it to the bridge. On the other side the path immediately disappeared into the tall grass again, but from the top of the arch in the bridge, she could see the part in the trees where she guessed that the path would enter the woods again on the far side of the clearing. She looked to her right and saw that the woods got dense where the hill started to rise again. She could see the stream came down through the woods and down the hill, but she couldn't see where it began in the distance.

After crossing the bridge, Kaitlynn brushed the first bit of the tall grass away and stepped into it, hoping to make a straight line to the gap in the trees in the distance. "If I get that far and I still can't see anyone, I'm going back," she thought to herself, yet still she pushed on through the tall grass.

About halfway to the other side, Kaitlynn heard a rustling in the grass. She looked left and then right but couldn't tell where the sound had come from. She began walking again when suddenly she saw the grass was being displaced ahead of her. Something was passing through the grass at an impressive pace and was heading directly towards her. She panicked and turned to run when something slammed into her side and knocked her to the ground. Dazed, Kaitlynn did her best to brace her fall, but she landed hard on her left shoulder. "Ow!" she cried as she hit the ground. She rolled instinctively onto her back and reached across her body to rub her shoulder, when she saw someone, or something, standing over her.

It stood about five feet tall and had the upper body of a man. But the lower body was covered in some sort of dark brown hair-like fur from the waist down and its animal-like legs ended in some sort of hoofs. She could see a tail like a horse's flick in the grass behind it. Upon its head, it had dark brown hair that matched the color of the fur below, with two small ivory-colored horns protruding from underneath. Its eyes were emerald green and seemed to shine slightly in the sun. It looked down at her and gave her a toothy grin and she could see that its teeth were sharp and triangular, like fine points perfect for ripping and tearing. She also noticed that it had a kind of spear strapped over its back. Kaitlynn screamed, a mix of terror and surprise, as she tried to back away, pushing with her legs as her backside trailed across the ground.

"*Vartu ka!*" the strange thing said, calmly. "*Ach lor hanata du-ka.*" He put his hands out, palms up. The nails were sharp and claw-like, and Kaitlynn couldn't take her eyes off of them. She kept scooting backward away from it, shaking her head, her left hand out in front of her as if guarding herself while her right hand held her injured shoulder. The strange thing strode forward and took her hand gently, squeezing softly. There was a warmth and gentleness to the way it touched her and she stopped backing away. "*Fala itar vo-ka,*" he said, its voice softening, and then it placed the palm of its left hand on her forehead.

Kaitlynn saw a bright light before her eyes but could not pull away. There was no pain from the light, but it was as if she was stuck to this strange creature's hand. After a few moments, he let go of her and the light faded. She fell backward into the grass and rubbed her eyes with her left hand.

"What was that?" she asked out loud without realizing it.

"Twas unlocking your mind to my tongue," the strange thing said to her, its voice deep and masculine.

Kaitlynn looked up at it, surprised. "You can understand me?" she asked. "But what...where...how...." The world began to swim before her eyes.

"Slowly, child," the creature said to her. "Breath deep, calm thyself." Kaitlynn took a series of deep breaths until after a time, things started to come back into focus. "I am Faljon, Keeper of the Gate," he said, bowing low. "I take it you stumbled upon the Gate from the other side?" he asked her.

"Um, yeah you could say that," Kaitlynn replied. "There was a painting and..." she paused mid-sentence, her thoughts crashing together like waves. "Wait, Keeper of the Gate? What do you mean?" she asked.

"Yes child, I am the Keeper of the Gate," he replied. "'Tis a title passed down for generations to one who is worthy on both sides. We are protectors, keeping our worlds separate since the days of old." He paused, looked at her as if studying her and asked, "How is it that you are here? Where is your Keeper of the Gate?"

Kaitlynn shook her head. "I don't know what you're talking about. I found this painting in my father's house and now I'm here," she explained with a shrug. A bolt of pain shot through her left shoulder at the slight exertion, and she grimaced. She was pretty sure that a deep bruise was growing there.

"Your father," Faljon paused, and then asked, "Daniel?" There was an inquisitive look on his face.

"He was," Kaitlynn responded, her voice turning solemn. "He died about a week and a half ago." Emotionally spent, her eyes filled with tears as she fought to hold them back.

Faljon looked at her with pity in his eyes, "Much sorrow I have for his passing. 'Twas a good man. May he rest eternal, Keeper of Souls." He reached out his hand to her, palm up. "Rise, Keeper."

She reached out for his hand to allow him to help her up and then stopped. "Wait...why did you call me 'Keeper'?" she asked.

"For 'tis your title now by birthright," he replied. "Your father was Keeper. With his passing, you are now Keeper." He said this matter-of-factly, with a sharp nod for emphasis.

"Whoa, whoa, whoa," Kaitlynn said, her tone incredulous. "I'm still not certain this isn't some sort of hallucination. What is this place? What are you?"

"You are in Keeper's Wood. This world is called Somalie," Faljon replied. "I am a satyr."

"A satyr?" Kaitlynn asked, her mind filled with doubt. "Like from ancient mythology?"

"What is a myth, except for the truth long forgotten?" Faljon asked. The question seemed rhetorical to Kaitlynn. "Daniel should have told you all of this before he passed the Gate to you."

"Well, he didn't," Kaitlynn replied, her tone flat. "And I doubt I would have believed him," she mumbled under her breath, turning her head and looking away.

"Then why are you here, Keeper?" he asked her.

She then told him the story of how she had found the picture of the steps in a drawer, and then the painting above the mantle. How she had put things together on her own and had stumbled into the fact that the painting seemed to be some sort of gateway.

"I came here looking for answers," she finished. "I don't know anything about this place, or why my father had this painting. I just knew it must have meant something to him." The tears were flowing freely now down her cheeks, like the waterfall in the distance. "I just wanted to know him better," she said, staring down at the ground and away from the strange creature standing above her.

Faljon was quiet for a minute, contemplative. "How did Daniel die?" he asked after a while.

"Cancer," Kaitlynn replied.

"What is this 'Cancer'?" Faljon asked.

"It's a disease where your body basically eats itself from the inside," Kaitlynn explained. "It's a horrible way to die," she finished, her voice trailing off at the end.

He placed his hand gently on her right shoulder and patted it twice. He then extended his hand to her again, took her hand in his own, and pulled her up to her feet. He was strong for his size, she thought to herself. She stood about six inches taller than him, and from this angle, he looked far less menacing.

"You have a name?" he asked her, his voice low.

"Kaitlynn," she answered, as she wiped away a fresh tear.

He looked up at her and said, "You are Kaitlynn, Keeper of the Gate of Earth. I am Faljon, Keeper of the Gate of Somalie. Tis our sacred duty to keep all others from passing between our worlds. We are the protectors of both. Since Daniel did not prepare you, I shall try to do so in his stead." Faljon began walking back the way Kaitlynn had come from. "Come," he said. He headed off through the tall grass towards the stairs, back towards the painting, and she followed him.

14

Faljon and Kaitlynn did not speak as they made their way back through the tall grass to the other side of the clearing. As they started back down the stairs, Kaitlynn turned to the satyr to ask a question, but he raised a single clawed finger to his lips. He paused and cocked his head slightly to the side as if listening for something off in the distance. A moment passed before he lowered his finger and motioned her onward.

"Thousands of moons before I was born, there was but one world," the satyr began as he started down the steps. "Twas a great cataclysm and the world was split in two. Some say the Gods went to war with themselves. All creatures mundane now live on Earth, all creatures born of magic now live on Somalie. Those that believe that the Gods were at war also believe that these were the sides that were chosen. They believe that the world split as a result of this war, but no one knows for certain. The two worlds were linked together by the Gate, as they had once been but one world. Tis but one Gate and we satyrn have guarded it from both sides for generations. Well, until one of the Keepers of the Gate on Earth abandoned her post and your father took over."

"Wait, hold on," Kaitlynn interrupted. "Are you saying there's one of your kind running loose on Earth?"

"Indeed, many more than one most likely," he said. "Generations ago, the first Keeper of the Gate of Earth underwent the change."

Kaitlynn looked at him confused. "The change?" she asked.

"He became a human," he replied matter-of-factly. "He married a human, and the line continued from there until your father took over."

"Wait, so you're saying my father was a regular old human?" She asked. "Why did he take over as the Keeper then?"

"It was his wife that abandoned her post," Faljon replied.

Kaitlynn froze. "Wait, hold on. Are you saying that my mother is a *satyr*?" she asked, her tone incredulous again. "That I don't believe."

The satyr turned and looked at her. "Green is not a natural eye color for humans," he said to Kaitlynn, pointing to his own eyes. "You have our eyes." He turned and started back down the steps. "I unlocked my tongue in your mind. I did not place it there like I had to with your father."

"Hold on, I call bullshit," Kaitlynn replied. "Lots of people have green eyes. Are you saying everyone with green eyes are satyrs? That's not possible."

"Tis been generations," Faljon replied with a shrug. "The blood has likely spread and thinned. Only the darkest of green has the purest of blood. Pure like Rebecca's. Pure like yours," he finished.

Kaitlynn gasped. Her mother's name was indeed Rebecca. "Wait, why would my mother abandon her post as Keeper? She's never abandoned anything in her life!"

"Did she not abandon your father?" asked the satyr, his point digging deep into Kaitlynn's heart.

"No, they got a divorce," replied Kaitlynn. "It just didn't work out between them."

"Call it what you will," he replied. "But tis lucky that you are Keeper of the Gate now. I liked your father, but the Gate belongs in satyrn hands."

"And I don't get any say in this?" Kaitlynn asked, her frustration clearly mounting with the situation.

"It tis how it tis," the satyr replied with a certainty to his voice that seemed to make the point moot to him.

"But what if we just destroyed the painting?" Kaitlynn asked. "Wouldn't that keep everyone on their own sides?"

"The worlds are linked," Faljon said, "and the Gate connects the worlds. If the connection is broken, no one knows what would happen to the worlds. It might create another great cataclysm. Both worlds might be destroyed." There was silence between them then as the satyr let his words sink in.

The silence held for most of their long journey back down the steps. As they neared the bottom and the fog began to thin, Faljon stopped short and Kaitlynn almost collided with him, barely avoiding knocking him down the steps. Her gaze carried itself down the steps and Kaitlynn saw why the satyr had stopped so suddenly. The oversized painting that had been at the bottom of the steps was nowhere to be seen.

15

No longer conscious of her weary legs and sore shoulder, Kaitlynn raced to the bottom of the steps as fast as she could while her mouth hung agape. Amazingly, despite being six inches shorter than her, Faljon beat her to the foot of the stairs. When she reached the spot where the painting had been, Kaitlynn fell to her knees and put her head in her hands. "Oh crap, how will I get home?" she asked, her voice cracked as if on the verge of tears again.

"More important question, who has the Gate?" Faljon asked. "These woods have been guarded by my people for generations. Tis why the gate was safe here." He nodded his head as if to punctuate the point. The satyr hunched over and began examining the ground around the makeshift post to which the painting had been hitched. After a moment he said, "Footprints, small ones," and pointed to the ground. "Goblins, most likely. Could be much worse."

Kaitlynn looked up at him, disbelieving. "Now there are goblins?" she asked, a condescending tone in her voice. "Next you'll tell me there are centaurs too," she added with a snort.

"And much worse," he replied, not picking up on her obvious sarcasm. "We must find the Gate. We are Keepers. Tis our sacred duty." He paused and looked her over from head to foot. "You will need a weapon," he said almost as if it were obvious.

"A weapon?" she asked? "To fight goblins? This is insane."

"Tis our..."

"Sacred duty," she interrupted, "yeah, I got that." She stood up and slowly walked over to the stairs and sat on the second step for the second time today. "I don't want any of this," she said to the satyr. "I just want to go home." Kaitlynn was becoming dejected. Her head had dropped into her hands again, and the tears had started flowing freely once more.

She reached up under her shirt and pinched herself one more time, this time harder than before, hoping against hope that she just needed to shake herself from this nightmare. Once again, it didn't work.

Faljon pursed his lips as if in contemplation. He walked over and sat down on the step to her left. "You did not ask for this burden," he said, his voice barely audible over her sobs. "But without the Gate, tis no way to Earth that I know of. We must find it in order to send you home." He put his hand on her shoulder and patted it twice a second time. The pain in her left shoulder returned then and she winced, but the shock of it managed to shake her from her delirium. Faljon seemed oblivious as he stood up and checked the tracks on the ground again. "Did you close the gate?" he asked.

"I'm not even sure how I opened it, never mind know how to close it," Kaitlynn replied.

"The gate was open when they arrived," he stated, his face rife with concern. "Hopefully they just took it and none of them passed through."

"How would they take it at that size?" Kaitlynn inquired. "It was huge!"

"The weight of the Gate is always the same," Faljon replied. "Once they picked it off the ground, it would shrink again, to be able to move it and protect it."

Kaitlynn looked at him, a look of disbelief crossing her face. "So, you're telling me that the magic portal to another world just needs to be put on the ground to open, and picked up to be closed? No magic words, no special sauce, nothing?"

"What is 'special sauce'?" the satyr asked her.

"Never mind," she said. "Just a gate to another world, sitting in the forest, no one around to watch it," she stammered out, her voice dripping with sarcasm. "Did it really seem like hanging it here was the safest place in the world?"

"Only my fellow satyrn should know that it is here, and they guard the Keeper's Wood to keep intruders out," he replied. "And the Gate needs to be opened from both sides. I do not know how it came to be open here."

"So, what happened to the guards then?" asked Kaitlynn him pointedly.

"I fear that answers lie this way," said Faljon, pointing down the path into the woods that Kaitlynn had glanced down when she first arrived through the painting. "We should go," he added, as he started down the trail. Kaitlynn stood up and trudged slowly behind, feeling like all her options were gone except to follow the satyr and try to find her way back home.

16

Kaitlynn and Faljon followed the path through the woods for at least an hour before the sunlight shining through the trees seemed to find more cracks for the light to break through. Kaitlynn's stomach had been rumbling for about thirty minutes, but she wasn't even sure that anything here was safe for her to eat at all.

Faljon paused and held up his hand as if to tell Kaitlynn to stop. She did, and he cocked his head to the side and listened. "Tis quiet," he said. He brought his fingers to his lips and let out a shrill whistle. Nothing happened. After a few moments, he repeated the noise. Again, nothing.

"The guards should have responded," he said turning to Kaitlynn, concern in his voice. She nodded her understanding and continued down the path, more cautiously this time.

Eventually, Kaitlynn could see the sunlight breaking through the trees ahead, illuminating the edge of the woods as if they were wreathed in flames. It made it hard to see anything too close to the edge of the forest. But as they got closer, they could see a grisly scene unfold before them.

Dead on the ground were two satyrs, one male and one female, both with numerous arrows protruding from them. It seemed like they had been caught by surprise in an ambush and left where they had fallen. Sticky red blood had covered their skin as it had poured out of the entrance wounds of the arrows and their lives had spilled away on the forest ground. Kaitlynn felt her stomach do a somersault inside of her, and she looked away before the gymnastics routine in her gut could continue.

Faljon walked cautiously over to the bodies, reached down and quietly closed their lifeless eyes. "May they rest eternal, Keeper of Souls," he said as he crouched over the second satyr, the female. He reached down and unfastened a scabbard from her belt, stood up and handed it to Kaitlynn. She took it with reluctance and pulled the blade from within it. It appeared to be a sword of some kind, with a blade about two feet long. It shone brightly in the sun, as it had clearly been polished with much care. She sheathed the blade and then attached the scabbard to her belt, hoping she would never have to use the thing. She looked up and saw that Faljon had taken the sword from the other body and put it on, belt and all.

Faljon stepped to the edge of the woods and looked out. Kaitlynn followed him without saying a word. Once Kaitlynn's eyes adjusted to the blazing sunlight beyond the boundary of the forest, she could see lush green plains rolling off into the distance for miles. To the left, Kaitlynn saw a mountain range in the distance which stood out as brown and rocky with snow-covered tops against the foreground of so much green from the rolling fields. It was more beautiful than anything she had ever seen before. To the right, the plains continued until they reached a part of the forest that seemed to curve out and block their path. She looked down the length of the forest and saw it disappear far off in the distance. She looked up and couldn't see a single cloud in the clear blue sky. She was completely lost in the amazing view around her when she heard the satyr speak off to her left.

"Golkan and Lillia are dead, and the gate is stolen," Faljon said. His voice was almost a whisper. "We must inform the other satyrn." He paused and looked around. "I can call them to meet from my burrow on the other side of the mountain," he finished as he pointed back the way they had just come.

Kaitlynn was exhausted and hungry. Her shoulder hurt and her leg muscles throbbed. She turned to Faljon and said, "So we've got to go back through the woods, up the stairs and back down the other side? That could take hours."

"Yes," he replied and then turned to go, leading her back into the woods towards the trail.

"Wait," Kaitlynn said. "I'm tired and I'm starving. I don't think I can make that kind of trip."

Faljon paused, taking in what she said. "I forget, you are part human and untrained. Wait here, I shall return," he said before making a hard right off the trail and deeper into the woods. It wasn't long before he was lost to Kaitlynn's view.

Kaitlynn watched him go, unsure of what to do next. "I'm all human," she thought to herself. She was alone again now in a strange world and the bloodied bodies that lay naked on the ground nearby made her feel uneasy.

She gripped the hilt of her sword in its scabbard and looked around in every direction. The light cascading through the trees created a halo around one of the dead bodies on the ground, and she shuddered. She heard a rustling in the underbrush between the trees and she pulled her blade in a clumsy motion, only to see Faljon return with a handful of red berries.

"Eat," he said, "There will be real food at my burrow, but this should keep the hunger at bay." Feeling sheepish, Kaitlynn put the blade back in its scabbard and then took the handful of berries. She examined them for a moment, uncertain. They were simple, round, and a bright shade of red. She popped one in her mouth with some trepidation, hopeful that it wouldn't poison her. She bit down and the taste was unfamiliar but pleasant. She finished the rest of the handful in a matter of minutes, and she felt strangely refreshed; her muscles were noticeably less sore, and her shoulder had stopped throbbing. She looked at Faljon and raised an eyebrow at him.

"Gorkaberries," he said as if it answered her unasked question. Without another word, he turned and headed off down the path back towards the stairs in the woods. Gathering herself as quick as she could muster, Kaitlynn followed.

17

They made good time scurrying back through the woods and then up the long staircase in the fog. At the top of the hill, Faljon moved without a word into the tall grass. Kaitlynn followed him, keeping an infinite number of questions to herself for now. Like magic, the satyr seemed to know exactly where the path was despite the tall grass, as he came out right in front of the stone bridge over the fast-running stream. She looked off to her left hoping to catch a glimpse of the waterfall but couldn't see any more than she had when she had passed this way previously. On the other side of the bridge, Faljon again weaved her through the grass on the other side and came out right in front of the opening in the trees that marked the other end of the clearing and the path back down the hill on the other side.

"How do you do that?" Kaitlynn asked. Faljon turned his head and raised an eyebrow at her. "It's like you know exactly where the trail is even though the grass has overgrown it."

The satyr smiled a toothy grin at her, which she found somewhat disturbing because of how pointed and sharp his pearly whites looked. "I have walked these paths since I was but a satyrling," he replied, holding his hand out, just below his waist. She looked down and blushed when she realized for the first time that he was completely exposed down there. "I know them by heart," he finished, not noticing her reaction to seeing his penis flapping in the breeze.

They headed down the path on the opposite side of the hill, and there was another set of stairs there as well. Though it was hard to tell in the thickening fog, this set did not seem to go down the hill in a straight line like the ones on the other side. These steps seemed to have a slow turn to the left the entire way down. It made the trip down seem to take a bit longer than the steps on the other side. Like the side where Kaitlynn had first entered the painting, the woods here were thick and dense with a canopy that kept too much sunlight from coming through. Unlike the steps on the other side, however, the sound of the waterfall never really seemed to go completely away. The fog made it difficult to see anything beyond a few feet off in any one direction. Still, many of the trees looked familiar, harboring a similar appearance to the trees she was used to. However, every once in a while, Kaitlynn would see a bush or a tree that looked unfamiliar to her. She passed one bush that was just taller than her waist that had large flowers with blue petals, some of which seemed to be in the middle of sprouting into some sort of strange fruit she'd never seen before. She stared at it in wonder until she had passed too far to crane her neck around to look at it and still maintain her balance.

After about a half an hour into the trip on the way down, she saw a bush that seemed to have more of the strange berries she had eaten earlier. She reached out to grab one when suddenly Faljon's spear was placed solidly across her path level with her chest. She stopped suddenly even though the tip of his spear was all the way past her body, still afraid that she'd somehow manage to impale herself on it. "Not gorkaberries," he said to her, his eyes serious. He stepped over and manipulated one berry up using the tip of his spear without pulling it off the branch. On the bottom of the berry was a sickly yellow spot that didn't match the red of the rest of the berry. "If it has this spot, tis poisonous," Faljon said. "Gorkaberries are all red." He let the berry drop off his spear and began walking back down the steps without another word, slinging his spear back over his shoulder in one smooth motion as he walked.

Kaitlynn took a deep breath and released it slowly. It took a moment to get her moving again, like a car engine that had trouble starting up in the cold, but eventually, she managed to get herself moving back down the steps as they continued their slow trek to the left, picking up the pace to catch up with him again. "Thank you," she said to Faljon. He simply nodded and continued on.

The sun was getting dimmer in the sky and the sound of the waterfall was getting closer and closer as they neared the bottom of the stairs and reemerged through the thick fog once again. They stepped out into a clearing when they reached the bottom. There was a fast-moving stream directly to the left of the path and a large clear pond before it. Kaitlynn looked over to the left and she could see the waterfall coming out of a hole in the cliff face and cascading into the large pool. The waterfall seemed to come down the cliff face in stages, slowly turning to the right around the side of the hill as if it was trying to meet up with the path at the bottom of the hill for a secret rendezvous deep within the forest. The path and stream seemed to mirror each other like a pair of lovers holding hands as they walked together into the depths of the woods beyond the clearing.

Faljon turned right off the path at the bottom of the steps and skirted the bottom of the hill for about twenty yards. Here he stopped and pulled back a blanket of grass and leaves to reveal an open doorway slanted into the side of the hill between two large rocks. The door was wooden and heavy, yet somehow the leaves and grass seemed to be attached to the outside of the door like a natural camouflage. He stepped inside and bade Kaitlynn enter. Faljon closed the door behind them and then placed his spear down against the wall by the door.

Kaitlynn could not stand upright in the burrow as the ceiling was about two or three inches too low for that. She hunched over a little and looked around as best she could with what little light slipped through the cracks around the door. The room before her was almost a perfect square, maybe ten feet wide in each direction. The walls, floor, and ceiling were all made of wood and the scent of cedar filled the room. There was one wooden pillar in the middle of the room for support. In one corner lay a pile of hay just large enough for Faljon to sleep on. On the far side of the room, there was a table that was just tall enough for the satyr to sit on the floor and eat at. On the wall between them there was a small circular hole in the roof.

As Kaitlynn was trying to figure out its purpose, Faljon walked over to the hole with a short wooden cylinder in his hand. She hadn't seen where he had produced it from, but he snapped the cylinder open, and a green mist came out. He lifted the canister up to the hole allowing the mist to flow into it, took a deep breath, and then blew it out into the mist as hard as he could, sending almost all of it up into the hole where it disappeared. He turned to her and said, "I have called the others. They will be here in the morning. For now, we should eat."

Faljon walked back over to the door and grabbed his spear. He opened the door and walked out. Kaitlynn followed him, not sure what else to do. He closed the door again behind them and made his way over to the large pool at the bottom of the waterfall. He stepped into the water until he was about waist deep, spear poised to strike in both hands above water.

Kaitlynn sat on the shore and watched the waterfall, and she could see a rainbow as the setting sun cast itself through the prism of the falling mist. While it was warmer here than it had been back on her side of the painting, there was still a chill in the air. She put her hand into the water and cupped it to get herself a much-needed drink of water, wondering to herself how the satyr wasn't freezing in the water even if he hadn't submerged below the fur that ended at his waist.

There was a quick movement and a splash and Faljon lifted his spear into the air triumphantly. Impaled upon it there was a strange type of fish that Kaitlynn had never seen before. It was yellowish with little flecks of orange along the tips of its scales, and almost a foot long. The satyr waded his way back out of the water and made his way back towards his burrow. Kaitlynn stood up gingerly. Her legs were feeling sore again after all the walking she had done today. She made to follow him back to his home under the hill, but he walked just past his burrow and into the woods to the side of the hill.

As Kaitlynn followed him, just beyond the tree line there was a small clearing with a small stone stove in the middle of it and a pile of small twigs next to it for kindling. The satyr put the fish down on the edge of the stove and began preparing a fire. Once the fire was burning, he picked up a rock that seemed to be shaped like a knife and started cleaning the strange fish before tossing it onto the stove and preparing it for them. It smelled unlike any fish that Kaitlynn had ever eaten before. There was almost a fruity scent in the air as the fish cooked. Faljon went back in the direction of the burrow, but Kaitlynn remained behind, transfixed by the luscious aroma filling the air that was emanating from the stove. He returned a few moments later with two wooden plates and a half-filled bucket of water. He took the fish off the stove and put it on the plates, handed them to Kaitlynn momentarily, and then doused the fire before grabbing one of the plates back from her and making his way back towards the burrow. This time she followed him. Her stomach had begun rumbling again, and she thought that it sounded much angrier with her this time.

In the burrow, Faljon sat down at the table and motioned for Kaitlynn to join him. She sat cross-legged across from him and put her plate down on the table. She watched as he picked the fish up with his claw-like hands and bit directly into it, his teeth ripping and tearing into the filet. Kaitlynn looked around but saw no utensils or tools of any kind. She touched the fish with one finger, making sure it wasn't too hot and picked it up with her fingers. She bit into it with some trepidation. It had a taste as if combining a freshwater lake trout with some kind of unknown citrus that she found quite pleasing. She tried to maintain some semblance of civilized manners in these strange circumstances as she could. She finished off the rest of her filet, but the juices ran down her chin and hands. Forgetting for a moment where she was, Kaitlynn looked around for a napkin to use and then settled on the sleeve of her sweatshirt once she realized that the rules of etiquette didn't mean diddly squat out in the middle of nowhere. "Very good," she said to Faljon after she had finished cleaning herself up as best as she could. The satyr seemed to blush at the compliment. "I've never had anything like this," she added.

"Tis called klempfish," the satyr replied. "Tis a famous satyrn delicacy. Tis only found in the waters of Keeper's Wood." He took the two empty plates and headed for the door. Kaitlynn stood in the doorway and watched as he walked towards the stream this time and washed the plates off in the water. She ran over and did the same with her face and hands, and then dried herself off with her sweatshirt again before returning to the small burrow.

As she stood in the door, she turned and took a look around at the clearing. The sky was starting to turn a shade of midnight blue now, and Kaitlynn could see the full moon rising above the trees. She looked at it and wasn't sure whether to be surprised or not that it seemed to have the same features as the moon from her side of the painting. But the more she studied it, the more she realized that its image was reversed. The familiar crater formation, the "man in the moon" if you will, was backward. She gasped at this realization, unable to remove her gaze from it until Faljon touched her lightly on the arm. She hadn't even noticed that he was standing directly in front of her.

"Tis late," said Faljon, letting his hand fall to his side. "You need rest. In the morning, the others will come, and we'll find the Gate." He stepped inside and motioned her to the small bed of hay in the corner. "Take the bed, you need the rest."

She looked at him, shook her head, and smiled, "No, I couldn't. That's your bed," she said.

"You will need your strength for the trials ahead," he said, his tone flat and unwavering. "Rest." He gave her a toothy grin again, which she once again found unsettling. He sat down in the corner opposite the bed and propped his head against the wall. Within moments, he was snoring lightly.

Kaitlynn walked over to the small bed and took her coat off. She folded it over a couple of times to make a makeshift pillow, took off her boots and then curled up on the bed of hay. The wooden floor was hard beneath, and the hay pricked her skin through her clothes in spots. She didn't think that she could ever fall asleep like this, but in moments her weariness claimed her, and she drifted off to sleep.

18

Kaitlynn awoke as if in slow motion from the deepest sleep of her life. "What a strange dream," she thought as she rubbed the crust of sleep from the corners of her eyes. She opened her eyes and looked around, saw the small burrow with the wooden walls, faint sunlight seeping in around the cracks in the door, and sighed deeply. "Fuck, its real," she thought to herself. She looked around for Faljon, but the satyr was nowhere to be found.

Kaitlynn sat up and pulled her boots on. There was hay stuck to her clothes and she did her best to wipe it all off back into the makeshift bed on the floor. She ran her fingers through her hair and more of the hay fell out, but she wasn't sure if she'd gotten it all or not. She grabbed her jacket off the bed, undertook the same ritual to it as she had to her clothes and put it on before opening the door and stepping outside.

The sun was just starting to rise above the tree line down the path. She looked around for a couple of minutes before she saw Faljon bathing in the waterfall, the water cascading down around him. Once again, she wondered how he could stand that water without freezing. She closed the door carefully behind her and then walked out into the clearing.

At the path at the base of the stairs, she paused and looked both ways. She didn't see anyone else coming yet. She looked back at the waterfall and saw Faljon wading through the pool and back towards her. He climbed out, drenched from horns to hooves.

"Aren't you cold?" Kaitlynn asked him, bypassing any morning formalities. He shrugged at her and walked off dripping all over the grass.

"The others should be here soon," he said to her, "then we will track the goblins and retrieve the Gate. Pray that none of them passed through to your world, for that will make our mission even more difficult."

He walked over and picked up his weapons, fastening his belt with his sword and slinging his spear over his back. He drew his sword and stepped towards her. "Can you use that?" he asked, pointing his blade at the sword on her waist. She looked down at the hilt and realized that she must have been so exhausted that she had slept with it on.

"I've never used one before," she answered, "and I hope I never need to." Kaitlynn wasn't the type of person who liked the idea of having to hurt anyone or anything.

"You will," he replied, his voice full of certainty. "Come, we'll train while we wait." He motioned for her to join him in the center of the clearing.

"Are you sure this is a good idea?" she asked. "Shouldn't we use sticks or something?"

"No, the weight is all wrong," said Faljon. "Strike with the flat of the blade for practice," he said, turning his sword and showing it to Kaitlynn. "Turn it like this for a real fight," he finished, holding the sword with a more traditional grip. He beckoned her into the clearing again.

Nervously she gripped the hilt of the sword and unsheathed it. She did her best to mimic the stance that the satyr took opposite her. Without any warning, he lunged at her in a flurry of strikes. Droplets of water flew off him and landed on her coat and jeans. She blocked a few swings and managed to dodge a couple of others before he landed a blow with the flat of his blade against the point of her left hip.

"Good!" he exclaimed as he stepped back and nodded at her. "You defended yourself well."

"Not well enough," she said as she rubbed the point of her hip with her hand. Between her left hip and her left shoulder, she was beginning to feel rather bruised and battered. But overall, she had surprised herself with how well she had reacted to the satyr's attacks.

"With practice, you will improve," he said. "I did not hold back though. I wanted to see what I was working with. From here, we will take it step by step."

For the next little while, Faljon worked with Kaitlynn, teaching her how to defend herself with her sword, when to parry and when to dodge. After about half an hour, two other satyrs (one male and one female) arrived, and they stopped sparing and put their swords away. Eventually, others arrived until there were a dozen satyrs in the clearing other than Faljon. All of them seemed to Kaitlynn like they were eyeing her with suspicion. She wondered if she was the first human that any of them besides Faljon had ever seen before.

She stood next to Faljon and looked around at the group of strange creatures as they formed a circle in the clearing. There were now five new males and seven new females in the group. All of them bore some sort of weapon on them, be it swords like Kaitlynn and Faljon now carried, spears like Faljon's, or bows with quivers full of arrows that a couple of the females carried. All of them had the same dark emerald green eyes. Most had the same brown fur and hair as Faljon. The exception was one of the females, who was a blonde both above the neck and below the waist. Kaitlynn felt somewhat self-conscious about the fact that she was the only one in the entire circle wearing any clothing and tried to keep her eyes at head height as much as possible.

Faljon introduced her to the group and explained who she was and how she had come to Somalie by accident. He then explained what had happened to the Gate and to the two satyrs who had been guarding the entrance to the woods. There were many troubled murmurs from the group at this news. A few added in the same blessing to the Keeper of Souls at the mention of the deaths of the other satyrs that she had heard Faljon utter a couple of times before. Kaitlynn would have to ask what that meant at some point.

Eventually, Faljon asked for volunteers to accompany the two of them to search for the lost Gate. Even though many of them had the wide-eyed look of fear, every single one of the satyrs volunteered. Kaitlynn was surprised by this apparent dedication; it was a thing she didn't understand and found quite bewildering. Even if it was becoming more and more clear to her that this was not her imagination, it was obvious to her that all of the satyrs saw the threat of the missing painting as dire.

Eventually, it was decided that half of the group (three males and three females) would come along with Kaitlynn and Faljon, and the other half (two males and four females) would stay behind and defend the woods from any further incursions. The six satyrs that were staying behind gave their well wishes to those that were going and then moved off back into the woods in various directions. After they had left, Faljon began introducing Kaitlynn to the others who were coming along.

The three males were named Delok, Hammel, and Peton. Both Hammel and Peton carried spears and Delok carried a sword. The females were called Shanja, Uliah, and Jali. Shanja carried a sword and the other two carried bows. Uliah was the blonde that had stood out to Kaitlynn earlier, and she seemed to be the youngest of the group. Kaitlynn also realized that it was Delok and Shanja that had been the first two satyrs to arrive while she and Faljon were training with their swords.

It was decided that they would head off after breakfast. Hammel and Peton strode off into the pool with their spears to catch some klempfish, while Uliah and Jali prepared the fire at the small stove in the woods. Faljon asked Shanja to continue Kaitlynn's sword training while he and Delok talked about the trip ahead.

"What do you know?" Shanja asked her. The female satyr's long dark hair was tied back into a braid that reached all the way to the middle of her back. Kaitlynn assumed that hanging free, it might actually reach down to her tail. She had the hardened features of middle age, but her eyes were soft and warm.

"Not much," Kaitlynn replied. "We just worked on a little bit of defense before the rest of you showed up."

"Very well," she replied. "We will continue."

They took to their ready stances, and Shanja struck in a whirlwind of flurry, much as Faljon had in his first attempt at training her earlier. Again, Kaitlynn managed to parry a few strikes and dodge a couple more before the satyr managed to clip her with the flat of her blade, this time in the upper thigh just below where Faljon had hit her earlier.

"Dammit!" Kaitlynn yelled as she stepped back. She rubbed her upper leg with her left hand and said, "By the time I'm done my whole left side will be black and blue."

Shanja chuckled. It was an odd sound as she hadn't heard any of the satyrs laugh before. There was a slight clucking sound to it. "Your coat restricts your movement," she said.

Kaitlynn nodded, took it off, folded it neatly, and put it down in the grass. "As long as that's all I have to take off," she said. "I don't know how you fight with your tits flying all over the place."

"What are 'tits'?" Shanja asked with a puzzled look on her face.

Kaitlynn blushed and pointed to her own breasts. The conversation made her feel a bit sheepish. She hadn't meant to say that out loud, it had just sort of slipped out.

"Ah, yes," Shanja replied. She turned the lips on one side of her face into a half smile and said, "They make a great distraction when I spar with Delok."

Both of the women laughed at that. "At least that's familiar," Kaitlynn thought to herself, shaking her head. Somehow it was comforting to Kaitlynn that even in this place where everything was so different apparently the men still liked looking at breasts. The thought made her laugh even harder. It was a hearty laugh, the first Kaitlynn had had in this strange place. Shanja smiled at her, but both Faljon and Delok turned and looked at her with their eyebrows raised as if questioning whether or not she had gone completely mad before they returned to their discussion.

After a breakfast of klempfish, Kaitlynn and the seven satyrs set out up the steps and over the hill to follow the goblins who had stolen the painting. Faljon took the lead and Kaitlynn fell in right behind him, with the other six following along behind. "There's got to be a quicker way around this thing than this," Kaitlynn said to Faljon as they started passing into the fog and climbed. He simply shook his head and said nothing in response.

By the time they had climbed up the stairs on the one side of the large hill, crossed the clearing with the tall grass at the top, climbed back down the steps on the other side and followed the path to where the two dead satyrs lay at the edge of the forest, it was midday and the sun was shining down from directly above them all through the dense canopy of the trees. The group stopped and the satyrs all paid their respects to their fallen brother and sister, as well as to the Keeper of Souls.

After a while, Faljon led Uliah and Jali off into the woods in the direction of the gorkaberry bush he had found the day before and they each brought back a couple of handfuls for the entire group to share. Kaitlynn was grateful for the food, but she felt odd sitting and eating so close to the bodies of the two dead satyrs.

"Shouldn't we bury them," she asked Shanja, motioning discreetly towards the two bodies. She kept her voice low. The male, the one Faljon had called Gorkan was lying on his back with four crude arrows piercing him in his chest, his legs splayed, and his fur covered genitals exposed in her direction.

Shanja shook her head. "Tis the cycle of things," she replied. "They will feed the beasts of the forest." She downed the last of her gorkaberries and said, "When you finish, we will train again."

Kaitlynn had not been looking forward to training anymore. She had felt bruised all over her body and her legs were tired from all the stairs she had climbed. But once again, the gorkaberries left her feeling refreshed. The sensation was strange and unexpected.

She finished her last berry and then grabbed her sword. Facing off against Shanja, she positioned herself so that the bodies of the two satyrs were behind her, making sure that she didn't have to look at them anymore and entered her ready stance. She and Shanja sparred for a few minutes with Kaitlynn still focusing entirely on defense. She felt like she was getting the hang of it a little bit, even if it was clear that Shanja had gone easy on her after the initial flurry in the clearing by Faljon's burrow.

After a while Faljon called them all over, telling them it was time to go. They gathered up their belongings and left through the path out of the woods and into the vast rolling plains beyond.

As the last satyr, Uliah, passed beyond the borders of the forest, a large black raven landed on the body of Lillia, which was pierced with three crude arrows. One of them had hit her square in the face and shattered her skull in a gory mess at the point of the left cheekbone. The raven plucked the left eyeball out of her lifeless skull, gobbled it down whole, and then flew up into one of the trees on the edge of the forest.

From its perch, the raven watched the group quietly, the seven satyrs and their human companion, as they walked off into the distance. Once they were out of view, the large black bird squawked once and then flew off in the direction of the mountains to the south.

19

Candice had been waiting on the doorstep for about half an hour when Jeff arrived to set up for the open house. She had been pacing back and forth, and her footprints were a crisscross of trampled snow on the concrete of the small front porch. As Jeff's car pulled into the driveway, she walked down the path over to the driveway and waited for him.

He got out of the car and started to smile and looked her up and down as discreetly as he could. She was wearing a knee-high skirt and black pumps under her coat, which she had bundled around herself to keep as much of the chill out as possible. He made as if to greet her until he saw the look of concern clouding her face.

"Is everything all right?" he asked her.

I've been ringing the doorbell for half an hour," she replied. "And I've tried calling a few times too. She's not answering at all. I'm worried that something's happened to her."

Jeff pursed his lips and then walked over to the front door. He opened the realtor box hanging off the handle and unlocked the door, letting himself and Candice into the house. "Katie?" he called out to the empty dwelling. He headed up the stairs with Candice shadowing him. He checked Kaitlynn's bedroom first, and then methodically checked the rest of the house starting with the other bedrooms and eventually working his way downstairs.

In the living room he found a cardboard box on the floor with all of the personal pictures from around the house packed carefully within it. "She was decluttering like I asked her to," he thought to himself. He folded the lid of the box closed and put it in the garage for now. He saw that the car was still in the garage, and then came back out into the living room.

"The car's still here," he said. "Maybe she just went out for a walk?"

Candice shrugged at him. "Maybe, but why didn't she answer her phone at all then?"

Jeff had no answer for that initially, but then he saw her cell phone sitting on the end table by the couch. He pointed it out to Candice, and she frowned. She walked over and tried to open the phone to see if she'd called anybody, but she didn't know Kaitlynn's passcode. She handed it to Jeff, but he didn't have any idea how to open it either.

'Jeff knew that the open house started in half an hour and people were going to start arriving soon, but he had to admit that these circumstances seemed damn peculiar. He stepped back outside and looked around. The only footprints he saw in the snow were his and Candice's on the walkway. He decided to go back inside, get the push broom out and sweep the walkway before the first open house guests arrived. He began sweeping, and when he got to the end of the walkway, he saw another set of footprints headed off from near the keypad at the garage door and into the woods behind the house. He jogged back to the front door and called inside to Candice, "Hey, I think I may have found something."

She followed him out to the driveway where he showed her the footprints. They looked at each other, and without a word, they followed the trail off into the woods. Jeff went first and took the worst of the thorns from the various bushes since Candice was only wearing a skirt. After a short walk, they came to the clearing with the tree stand and they saw a painting leaning against the tree. The footprints seemed to go right up to the painting and then they disappeared into thin air.

Jeff went around to the other side of the tree, looking for signs of where Kaitlynn could have gone and saw nothing. Candice stood in front of the painting, bundling herself against a gust of wind that caused her to shiver. She examined the painting. It was a landscape of lush rolling green hills as far as the eye could see.

Jeff came back around to the front of the tree and saw Candice staring at the painting and he glanced at it too. "Strange place for this thing to be," he said, bending over to get a closer look. The painting didn't look familiar to him at all, not recognizing the gold embossed frame that had been above the mantle in Uncle Danny's house. He looked over at Candice and saw her shiver as another gust of wind blew through the trees around them. "Come on, we'd better head back," he said to her. "You look like you're freezing." He put an arm around her to try and help warm her up and led her back down the overgrown path back to the house.

20

The sky was beginning to threaten a sunset and Kaitlynn was exhausted. She couldn't remember walking this much before in her entire life, and her boots weren't meant for stomping across rough country trails as much as they were designed for the cobblestone streets of Old Town Scottsdale. They had been traipsing across the rolling green hills since they had left the Keeper's Wood at midday. The forests to the right had fallen away and the rolling fields seemed to go off into the distance forever now, but to the left, the large snow-covered mountains kept their vigil on the vast plains from afar. Faljon had led the group, tracking the goblins across the lush fields. They had a full day's head start on Kaitlynn and her seven horned companions, and she was pretty sure that despite being six inches taller than them all (and with longer legs to boot), she was the one slowing the rest of them down.

She had thought of herself as a pretty fit woman, or still as shapely as she'd been in her early twenties at least. But she thought to herself that if she ever got out of this alive, she was going to have to step up her cardio regimen at the gym back home. But as she looked around at the foreign landscape around her, she doubted very much that she would ever find her way back to her side of the painting again, never mind reopen her long-expired gym membership at L.A. Fitness.

In fairness, it had been roughly three and a half months since she'd been able to work out at all. She usually liked to go for walks around her apartment complex at night and tried to keep up with a routine of sit-ups every morning before work. But such things fall by the wayside when you are forced to become the primary caregiver to a dying parent on the other side of the country. The memory of her father slowly deteriorating and drifting away deepened the sadness that had gripped her and threatened to bring the tears again.

The group rounded a small hill and saw that the path ahead dropped into a gully with a small ridge on either side. Faljon and Delok conferred for a moment before deciding that the ridge would give them sufficient cover for the night. Uliah and Peton were sent off to hunt for food, Hammel and Jali to retrieve whatever they could find for a fire. The rest of the group made for the gully.

Kaitlynn was glad to finally get some rest. Her legs ached and the bruises she had picked up over the past two days had begun to throb again. She sat down in the grass just off to the side of the dirt path, put her legs out in front of her and stretched. She could feel the muscles straining against their stiffness, so she pushed herself down gingerly so as not to pull anything. She looked up and saw Faljon, Delok, and Shanja watching her with inquisitive looks on their faces. She ignored them and kept trying to stretch out her legs as best as she could, eventually reaching all the way down to her boot tips. She normally wouldn't have had such a hard time reaching down that far, but it felt like every muscle in her lower body was rebelling against her.

It wasn't long before the other satyrs returned with their various bounties. Hammel and Jali had found a small grove of trees just past one of the rolling hills ahead and had brought back as much firewood as they could carry. Shortly thereafter, Uliah and Peton returned carrying what looked like a rabbit that was nearly as large as a medium-sized dog. The rabbit had antlers, which reminded Kaitlynn of the jackalope myth she'd heard so many times after moving to Arizona. She thought to herself that the fourteen-year-old girl inside of her that had once believed in those tall tales would have shit herself at the sight of the thing. But after everything else she had seen over the past two days, she thought to herself, "Why the hell not," and let it go. It turned out to be pretty tasty in the end either way.

After they had eaten, Shanja came over and motioned for Kaitlynn to grab her sword. She wasn't certain she could even stand after how long this day had been, never mind train. She thought about protesting but decided against it. She stood up slowly, took off her jacket, grabbed her sword, and reluctantly walked over to where Shanja stood waiting for her.

Kaitlynn was surprised to find that once her training began in earnest that her legs seemed to find new life despite their weariness. She continued to work on her parries and dodges while Shanja methodically attacked with the flat of her blade. After a few minutes, the two picked up the pace a little bit. Before long Shanja was nearly attacking at full speed and Kaitlynn was parrying and dodging almost all of her attacks. The few that managed to slip through her defenses slapped her lightly on the side, as it was clear the satyr was being careful not to hurt her. But for a novice swordsman, Kaitlynn felt like she was doing herself fairly proud.

When they stopped sparing, Shanja bowed to Kaitlynn, her arm across her chest with her left hand in a fist. The motion had the unintended effect of supporting her bare breasts rather than letting them hang as she bent over. Kaitlynn suppressed a chuckle and mimicked the bow.

As they turned to return to the fire, Kaitlynn saw that Faljon had been standing nearby and watching them. He gave her a silent nod and walked over to her.

"You learn well," he said. "The blood is pure in you."

Kaitlynn took a deep breath. "Look, I'm not saying I believe you that I'm part satyr or whatever..."

"You are," he interrupted. "The speed at which you learn is proof enough. The magic is in your blood. In time you will learn how to use it for other things."

"Magic," she asked, doubt far more than a mere shadow across her face. "You're saying I can use magic?" She shook her head at him. "This is getting crazier by the minute," she thought to herself.

"You will learn," he said with confidence. "For now, your belief is not necessary. When the time comes, you will believe."

He walked back to the fire then, and after collecting herself for a moment Kaitlynn followed. Watches for the night were decided, with four groups of two each. Kaitlynn and Faljon were paired together for the last watch in the early morning. In the meantime, Kaitlynn took off her coat, made a makeshift pillow out of it again, and laid herself down in the soft grass just below the ridge. Despite her sore body's protest, it wasn't long before she drifted off to sleep.

21

A clawed hand gently shook Kaitlynn from her slumber. She looked up and saw that it was Shanja. She and Delok had finished their watch, and it was time for Kaitlynn and Faljon to take over. She rubbed the crusts of sleep out of the corners of her eyes and stood up. Her movement was slow and deliberate, and her body ached from sleeping on the ground. She saw that Faljon was already up and watching the path from the direction in which they had come.

The rest of the satyrs were asleep. Kaitlynn noticed that most of them slept alone. But Shanja went over and lay down next to Delok, throwing her arm over his chest and curling up next to him. Kaitlynn smiled at that. She liked Shanja and was happy for her. It also explained why she had always seen the two of them together for the most part.

The rest of the morning watch passed uneventfully. When the sun started to unveil itself to the world from back the way they had come, most of the other satyrs began to wake up; though Uliah had to shake the sleep away from Jali. Once she was awake, the two female satyrs headed off together with their bows in search of food for the group.

While they waited, Faljon came over to Kaitlynn and drew his sword. He began teaching her a few thrusting and slashing attacks, which he had her practice until the two women came back with what looked like two good sized crimson furred squirrels. Delok stoked the fire and brought it back to life while Shanja skinned the two animals. Eventually, after breakfast, the party set out again across the open plains with Faljon in the lead.

It was warmer today than it had been the last two days. Kaitlynn took her coat off and threw it over her shoulder. Her clothes were covered in dust and grass stained. She thought that they looked almost as roughed up as she felt both physically and emotionally. This was her third day in this strange new world, and she missed her friends and family back home.

Her thoughts drifted to her mother back in Arizona, and she wondered if she'd ever see her again. She had a lot of questions for her that she needed answered, some of which were ones she'd spent her whole life avoiding, others were brand new thanks to the situation she now found herself in.

The group had made their way along the trail for a couple of hours when they came upon the remains of a campfire on the side of the path. Delok went over and checked the remains of the burnt wood and declared it quite cold, at least a day old. Faljon went and looked at the trail continuing into the distance, shook his head and began circling the abandoned campsite. To the left of the camp, he stopped and stooped down on his haunches for a minute. He looked down, and then his eyes slowly rose, and he stared off into the distance.

"They left that trail," he said, standing and pointing to the trail that continued along in the direction they had been going. "They went this way." The group filed in behind him as he led them off the main trail and onto a smaller one that took them in the general direction of the mountains in the distance.

Kaitlynn settled into the marching order beside Shanja. The two of them walked in silence for a while. Eventually, Kaitlynn looked at her and said, "So, you and Delok, huh?" The satyr nodded and a slight smile passed her lips. "You two been together long?" she asked.

"Many seasons," she replied. Her face seemed to glow as she thought about it.

"Any kids?" Kaitlynn asked.

"Our satyrlings are grown now. We left them back at Keeper's Wood," she replied. A shadow passed over her expression as if the moon had blocked the sun. "With luck, we will see them again," she said, a sullen tone to her voice.

Kaitlynn swallowed hard. She had been scared for her life for a good part of the time since she'd come through the painting. The idea of potentially having to use her newly acquired sword training terrified her as well. But she hadn't considered that the group of satyrs she was traveling with were also putting their own lives on the line, that they might not see their own families again. The stark realization hit her hard; they didn't know if they would come back from this adventure either, yet they had volunteered anyways. All of them had. Even the ones that had been told to stay behind had stepped forward, while only she had protested. She felt very ashamed at this realization. They continued in silence for hours. Kaitlynn kept her head down, unable to look any of her companions in the eye.

22

The large raven picked at the bones of one of the squirrels that the party had eaten before heading off that morning. The small morsels of meat clinging to the bones were still slightly warm, but there wasn't quite enough substance to sate its appetite. When it had finished, it took to the air and flew off towards the west in the direction that strange woman and the satyrs had gone.

After a while, it came across the party at the abandoned campsite and watched as they turned south towards the mountains. It circled a few times before landing and searching the abandoned campsite for any scraps without any luck. Discouraged, it took to the air again, flying south towards the mountains in the distance. It passed over the group without pausing, heading off as quickly as it could to report to its master. It stopped only once in its trip as it dived to grab an unsuspecting mouse and gobble it down while it still squirmed and fought for its life, before taking flight again.

Its large wings carried it through the air, and it made unnaturally good time. It arrived at its master's keep, a tall tower made of shimmering black obsidian hidden deep in the snowcapped mountains, just before nightfall. The snow covering the parapet that encircled the top of the tower was thick and frozen in some places, more of a wisp in others. A strong gust of wind swept through the mountains and kicked some of the lighter powder up into the air.

Fighting the high winds, the raven flew through a window and landed on a perch in its master's workshop on the top floor of the tower. There was a small bowl next to the perch with water in it; a thin layer of ice had begun to form on the top. The bird pecked once and shattered the ice, and then it lapped up the water until it was all gone. When it was done it squawked, announcing its presence, and then waited. Soon its master would come, and it would tell him all that it had seen. It hoped that it would be rewarded with a worthy meal for all its effort. The raven was always hungry, and the hollow pit in its stomach never stopped craving more.

23

The sun hung low in the sky, and Kaitlynn was exhausted. As bad as her muscles had hurt her the day before, the pain was nothing like today. They had marched on for most of the day, stopping only for a quick lunch and then continued as quickly as they could. They had passed the remains of another campfire about an hour before, and Faljon seemed to think they were gaining on whatever had stolen the painting. Kaitlynn wasn't quite sold on the idea of "goblins," but after everything she'd seen so far, she wasn't willing to completely discount the possibility.

They cleared another rise and the sun started to dip below the horizon in the distance. Kaitlynn figured they must be going south since they'd been walking towards the setting sun the day before. This morning they'd turned left towards the mountains. She assumed that the directions were the same in Somalie as they were on Earth but tried not to give it much thought. Things had been confusing enough as it was without having to figure out a new name for "west" or "north."

Despite the creeping darkness, the party continued until they came across a stream frolicking its way through the far-reaching plains. The path seemed to go into the water and come out the other side. They would have to ford the stream. By then the light had nearly left the sky, and they decided to stop for the night and cross in the morning. When they finally did set up camp, Peton and Hammel went downstream with their spears to look for food while Jali and Uliah looked for fuel to start a fire.

Kaitlynn went over to the stream and cupped her hands to take a drink. The water was cool but not as cold as she thought it would be. She desperately wanted a shower. It had been three days in this wilderness, and she felt like she was covered in an ever-thickening layer of dust. She settled for washing her face and running some water through her hair. She wasn't quite ready to give up on her modesty yet.

Eventually, the satyrs all returned with fish and wood for a fire. These fish were brown and bland in taste compared to the klempfish that she had eaten by Faljon's burrow, but after yet another long day on the march, Kaitlynn decided that she would take what she could get when it came to food and not complain.

After dinner, most of the satyrs took turns bathing in the stream. It was not particularly deep as it only came up to each of their waists, but they were all happy to clean up as best they could. Kaitlynn was slightly jealous of how comfortable they all seemed to be with their own nakedness. But she stayed and stoked the fire with a long branch, pretending not to be paying attention to her companions. After each took their turn in the stream, they came over and sat by the fire. Kaitlynn assumed that they were drying off and warming up.

After taking his turn in the stream, Faljon grabbed his sword and pulled Kaitlynn aside and began working with her on her attacks again, this time parrying her attacks while she practiced. For the second night in a row, despite her legs feeling like gelatin after the long march, once she had gotten into a rhythm, she felt pretty good. However, as the sun fell behind the horizon to the west, Kaitlynn put up her hands and took a step back.

"I think I'm done," she said. It's getting too dark for me to see."

Faljon looked at her for a moment in silence. "Come with me," he said and walked slowly away from the campsite. The further they went, the darker it got with only the moonlight to guide them. Faljon stopped, turned, and looked at Kaitlynn. His emerald green eyes seemed to be reflecting the moonlight as they shone brightly in the dark. Kaitlynn let out a slight gasp. "Darkness is not your enemy," he said to her. "Concentrate and you will see."

Kaitlynn didn't understand. "Are you saying that I can do that too?" she asked. "I don't think so," she added, shaking her head in protest. The idea seemed completely ludicrous to her.

She heard Faljon take a deep breath as if trying to find his patience, and then he said to her, "Look for the outlines of everything. Concentrate on them and they will become clearer. It will take a few moments; do not let yourself get discouraged."

Not quite believing what she was hearing, Kaitlynn looked off into the distance. She could barely see the rolling hills and grassy plains that stretched for miles in every direction, but she did as the satyr had told her to do and concentrated on the outlines of the objects. After a couple of minutes, things did start to become clearer. The world looked colorless and washed out, like shades of gray across the landscape, but her eyes seemed to be adjusting to the dark.

"Now look at me," she heard Faljon say. She turned and looked back at him. He was holding his sword up horizontally at her eye level. There was a green reflection in the blade that stood out as a stark contrast to the various grays that surrounded it. Kaitlynn gasped. Her eyes were glowing just like Faljon's had. She shook her head in disbelief. "The magic is in your blood, Keeper," he said to her, his voice hushed. "You are learning to use it." He lowered his sword and looked at her, his own eyes shining in the darkness at her.

He steadied his sword before her in his ready stance and motioned to the scabbard on her belt. She pulled her own sword as well, marveling at how crisp and clear the world had become. She saw the reflection of her eyes in the blade in her hand and smiled. Faljon returned her smile with a toothy grin of his own. With a flurry, they sparred back and forth then, nothing more than a glimmer of light and clash of steel in the moonlight to any observers without the emerald eyes of the satyrn.

# 24

Kaitlynn and Faljon had drawn the last watch again, and she was sitting by the banks of the stream looking off into the distance. It had taken a few moments after Shanja had gently shaken her out of her sleep for her eyes to adjust, but she was amazed at how well she could see in the dark now that she had managed to tap into her satyrn blood. After a little while, her eyes turned to the stream in front of her. The water moved quickly through the plains, surprisingly so for how flat this particular area was. Kaitlynn wished she could slip away and wash off. She couldn't remember feeling this dirty before. She cupped her hand and put it in the stream. The water had chilled considerably once the sun had gone down, and it cold made her whole body shiver. But she scooped up a handful of water and took a quick drink before drying her hand on the outside of her coat as best she could. She considered reaching into her coat pocket and getting her gloves out for a moment but decided against it.

She heard a rustling behind her and looked back over her shoulder. Faljon was standing next to her, his tail flicking the air by her right ear. He sat down on the grass next to her with his back to the stream, looking off in the other direction.

"Go ahead," he said to her in a whisper. "I have the watch."

"What do you mean?" she asked him, keeping her voice low as well.

"You've been looking at the water since we got here last night," he stated. "Everyone else is sleeping, and I will not look."

Kaitlynn nodded, understanding his meaning. "Yeah, but it's too cold," she said. "I don't have all the fur you guys have."

"That is not what keeps us warm," he said, "tis the magic in our blood."

Kaitlynn looked at him, her eyebrows raised. It was clear that she didn't understand. Faljon reached out his hand to her.

"Here," he said. "Feel my skin." She took his hand in hers, careful to avoid the sharp claws on his fingertips. His hand was like a furnace in hers, and far warmer than her own. He pointed to his heart with his other hand. "Feel the warmth in here, and it will spread."

Kaitlynn closed her eyes and focused her attention on her chest. She felt her abdomen rising and collapsing with each breath and could almost hear the beating of her own heart in the silence around them. She focused on trying to feel warm, but nothing happened. She opened her eyes and shook her head. "It's not working," she said, disappointment evident in her voice.

Faljon pointed back over towards the campfire. "Not warm like the fire," he said, before pointing off in the direction of Shanja and Delok spooning with each other in the grass. "Think warm like that," he said. "You need to feel the love in your heart."

Kaitlynn smiled at the two satyrs as they slept peacefully in each other's arms. "I wish I had somebody like that to think of," she said. She looked back at Faljon and shrugged.

"Do you love yourself?" the satyr asked her.

The query was perhaps more pointed than he had intended, and Kaitlynn was taken aback a bit by the question. "I...I guess so," she stammered out. "I guess that I've never really thought about it."

Faljon nodded. "I have no one, but I love who I am. I am Keeper of the Gate. My title brings me much pride. I have *earned* this place among my people." He reached out and put a finger over her heart. His touch was gentle. "Think of whatever warms your heart, and your body will follow."

She nodded, understanding his meaning. She closed her eyes again and concentrated. She thought about that day with her father on the deck, their breakfast together and laughing with each other as they watched the squirrels trying to climb into the bird feeder. She could feel warmth growing in her chest, slowly at first, but soon it spread throughout her entire body. She realized self-consciously that she was sweating a little despite the nighttime chill in the air. She opened her eyes and looked at Faljon. He was smiling that toothy grin of his at her again.

"When you fight, you use the blood without thinking," he explained. "Tis why you don't feel tired. Tis why you react so quickly. You don't have to learn this, tis instinct." He paused, thinking about his words before continuing. "Other things will require thought to use the blood: seeing, warming, and giving a language for example." He paused again. "There are other things you will learn in time as well. In the meantime, go clean up. I will stand watch."

Kaitlynn nodded and smiled. "I would never have believed any of this a few days ago," she said.

"You would not have believed it a few hours ago," Faljon replied. "We all change when we have to, not a moment before." With that, he stood and headed back to the other side of the camp to keep watch and give her some privacy.

Kaitlynn focused on the memory again and slipped out of her clothes. She waded into the water feeling its coldness on her skin, but not bothered by it. She was more than warm enough. She sat down in the middle of the stream and submerged herself to just below her shoulders. The rushing water was peaceful and felt good against her skin. She could feel the very last tips of her hair being pulled lightly in the current. She lay back, propped herself up on her arms, and dipped her head into the water. She had to arch her back slightly to keep her face in the open air, but even still her ears and chin were submerged. She could feel the occasional trickle of water rush over her lips. She sat back up and brushed her hair back with her fingers so that it wouldn't cling to her face and looked around. The water was pristine and clear, and she caught a glimpse of one of those brown fish the likes of which they had had for dinner swimming against the current. It looked gray to her eyes in the darkness, but she recognized its shape. She smiled and waved her toes at it playfully as it swam by, chuckling lightly to herself.

She glanced over at the campsite and saw that the satyrs were still sleeping. The only exception was Faljon, who stood watch on the far side of the campsite and was looking the other way as he had promised. Kaitlynn thought about staying in the water a little longer but decided against it. The others would start to wake soon enough. She stood and walked over to the edge of the water where it was only ankle deep and grabbed her coat. She slid it on and buttoned up the front, letting it soak up the water before she put her clothes back on. She was grateful that her jacket went down to the middle of her thighs and that at least everything sensitive was covered if the others started to rouse themselves.

She kept her focus on the memory of her father and her on the deck, and she found that she dried off in only a few minutes. When she was mostly dry, she slid her panties and jeans back on, then turned her back to the campsite and finished getting dressed. She left her jacket on the ground and opened it up to the air, hoping it would help to dry it out as quickly as possible. She imagined she would have to replace all of these clothes if she ever got back to her own world, but in the meantime, they were all she had and she didn't want to ruin them completely.

She walked over to Faljon and stood next to him for a few moments in silence. "Thank you," she said to him eventually, and he simply nodded. The sky was starting to turn orange in the east, and the other satyrs had started to rise. "I have a question," she said to him. "You said that one of your kind, my ancestor, was a satyr but became human. How is that possible?"

"The change is a ritual we can perform," he replied. "It takes many satyrn, and quite a bit of magic." He paused, drawing a deep breath. "'Tis not been performed in generations."

"So, with enough satyrs, you could make any one of you human?" she asked him.

"Or any other intelligent creature of their choosing," he replied. "The change is permanent." He took another deep breath. "'Tis a great sacrifice that your ancestor undertook for the good of all. We honor him, and all of his line." He turned his head and looked at her then. She could see there was a tinge of admiration in his eyes. "Your father understood your mother's duty, even if she did not. He was worthy of the same honor, though he was only human." He reached up and put a hand gently on her shoulder before adding, "And so are you."

Kaitlynn blushed and looked away embarrassed. "I hardly understand any of what's going on," she said.

"Yet you are strong," He replied. "You are learning to use the magic in your blood. Understanding will come with time."

She nodded, though she wasn't really sure she believed him despite the confidence in his voice. She turned back to the camp and saw that all the satyrs were up and about except for Jali. Apparently, she was not an early riser by nature. This thought made her smile to herself.

Kaitlynn took a step as if to head back to camp but paused before turning her head and looking back at Faljon. "You didn't peek, did you?" she asked him. He blushed and looked away. As realization set in, Kaitlynn felt the color rising in her own cheeks as well. She covered her mouth with her hand and chuckled a little bit. "Men really are the same everywhere," she said, trying not to laugh too hard. He lowered his head, trying to hide his embarrassment. "That's a good thing," she said, leaning down and giving him a small peck on the cheek. "I need a little consistency at this point."

25

After a breakfast of two more of the strange brown fish (Kaitlynn secretly wondered if one of them was the one she had seen while bathing in the stream), the group set out again, fording the stream and then trekking to the south towards the mountains. Kaitlynn had taken off her boots and socks and carried them above the water at least, and then kept the memory of her and her father on the porch in her mind until her jeans had dried off. When they had, she paused long enough to put her boots back on and then caught up with the rest of the group. She walked next to Uliah and Jali, deciding to try and get to know some of her other companions. She figured she'd start with the other two women first.

Uliah tied her long blonde hair into two pigtails which she let flow down over her shoulders, almost all the way down to her breasts. Kaitlynn thought that if she let it grow just a little bit longer, she might actually be the only woman in the group other than herself to have covered herself up at all. Her features were soft and beautiful, and she had no age lines around her eyes. Kaitlynn thought she must be fairly young indeed.

Jali kept her brown hair short in a messy kind of look. She looked a little older than Uliah but younger than Shanja. She had a scar on her left side just above her waist that looked like she might have been gored by an animal at some point. "Greetings, Keeper," she said to Kaitlynn as she fell in line next to them.

"Just Kaitlynn is fine," she replied with a smile. "If you call both Faljon and me 'Keeper', we're apt to get confused as to who you're talking to."

Both satyrs smiled at her warmly. They seemed to be happy to be rid of the sense of formality. It felt good to be accepted by them, unlike the way they had all eyed her with suspicion when she had first met them all.

"What did you do to yourself there," Kaitlynn asked Jali, motioning to her side.

"I got that while I was hunting boarfrog," She replied. "I was much younger, and still learning to hunt at the time."

"Boarfrog?" Kaitlynn asked, raising one eyebrow and peering over at the satyr.

"You don't have those?" Uliah asked.

"Well, we have boars, and we have frogs," replied Kaitlynn. "I'm just gonna assume that it's some sorta mix of the two," she added with a shrug.

Jali shrugged as well, unsure. "To the east of Keeper's Wood is a swamp," she continued. "There's very good boarfrog hunting there. I got too close to one and it leaped at me. Tusk got me, but I got it too." She smiled at the memory.

"Ouch," said Kaitlynn. "How young were you?" she asked.

"Seventy," she replied, offhandedly.

Kaitlynn flinched at that. "Did you say seventeen or seventy?" she asked.

"Seventy," Jali said again with a quizzical look.

Kaitlynn shook her head. "That's not possible, you look like you're my age," she said.

"You are one hundred and thirty-two?" Jali asked.

Kaitlynn's jaw dropped. "No, no..." she stammered. "I'm thirty-six."

This time it was both satyrs who looked surprised. They glanced back and forth at each other and then turned back at Kaitlynn.

"How can you be thirty-six and be fully grown?" Uliah asked. "Or are adult humans even taller?"

Kaitlynn shook her head. "No, I am an adult," she said with a smile, "most of the time anyway." The joke seemed to be lost on them. Disappointed, she let it go and moved on. "Most humans live to their seventies. Some might make it to a hundred, but that's really rare."

The two satyrs' eyes went wide. "Your people are very short-lived," Jali said, a tinge of sadness in her voice. "Uliah is ninety-three. Most of your people don't see her age, and she is barely an adult among us." Uliah nodded along as Jali spoke as if to give additional credence to her words.

Kaitlynn bit her lower lip, and said, "We're considered adults at eighteen. I would be considered to be in the prime of my life, I suppose."

The two satyrs glanced at each other and seemed to come to a mutual decision to change the subject. "Why do you wear strange animal skins?" Uliah asked her.

"You mean my clothes? Pretty much everyone in my world wears them," she replied. "It's kinda considered indecent if you don't where I'm from."

The two satyrs exchanged a bemused look among each other and then turned back to Kaitlynn. "We don't offend you, I hope," said Jali.

"Huh? Oh no," she said, waving her hand, slightly embarrassed at the implication and hoping that she hadn't offended the two satyrs. "After all the other strange things I've seen in the last few days, a little T and A is nothing." She saw their confused expressions and said, "But yeah, this whole trip has been an experience."

"Is it much different where you are from?" asked Uliah.

"Very," replied Kaitlynn. "I can't remember ever seeing this much open space on Earth. We'd have passed tons of houses and people by now. We also have indoor plumbing, which is much nicer than squatting in the tall grass. The animals are all very different, but it's like a bunch of the animals from my world got mashed up together here to make yours. The moon here is the same, but it looks backward to me compared to home. Not to mention we don't have satyrs in my world. A little nudity is pretty minor compared to all of that." She finished and glanced at the two satyrs. Their eyes were wide with amazement and their mouths hung open. "That must have been how I looked to them at first," she thought to herself, suppressing a chuckle.

Kaitlynn and the two women talked for a few hours as they marched along to the south until the group stopped for lunch. They found themselves learning much about the differences in their two worlds but discovering that in many ways the three of them were much more alike than not.

A few hours after they had stopped for lunch, they passed the remains of another abandoned campsite. Faljon seemed to think that they were gaining on whatever they were following, which Kaitlynn took as a mixed blessing. While catching up meant retrieving the painting and going home, it also likely meant having to test her new skills with the sword. She was in no hurry to actually enter a life-or-death situation.

As they walked along, Kaitlynn spent most of the afternoon talking to Delok and Shanja. She found that she liked them both and she saw why they had ended up together as a couple. While they were similar in a lot of ways, Shanja seemed a little bit more lighthearted while Delok was the more serious of the two; they balanced each other out well.

As they walked along, Kaitlynn asked them, "I've heard you mention the 'Old Gods' and the 'Keeper of Souls' a few times. Can you tell me about them?"

Shanja looked at Delok and said, "Go ahead," with a waving motion of her hand, and her mate smiled at her before regaling Kaitlynn with his tale.

"In the old days, there were many gods," said Delok. "The two most important were Raeyl, the Keeper of Life, and Qyr, the Keeper of Souls. They were twin brothers, and they created the old world and the afterlife to which we return at our life's end. Raeyl ruled over the old world, and Qyr ruled over the afterlife. Our ancestors named the protectors of the Gate 'Keepers' to honor them. They each married, and their wives and children became other gods as well. Their wives, Yaleen and Feway joined them in the rule over the world and the afterlife respectively."

"Like Raeyl and Qyr, all of their children were twins. But it was always one male and one female, and the things that they ruled over would always be connected in some way. There was a Goddess of Rain and a God of Thunder. A Goddess of Truth and a God of Lies. A Goddess of Peace and a God of War. And so, on it went for eons."

"But as time went on, Yaleen and Feway grew jealous of their husbands. They began planning to overthrow them and claim the rule of the old world and the afterlife for themselves. They began picking some of their children that they knew would be loyal to them and plotting a war."

"In the end, the war between the Old Gods caused the Great Cataclysm that separated our two worlds. Raeyl and Qyr created the Gate, using their own blood to paint it. Not knowing which of their children they could trust, they cast their wives and all of their children through the Gate and into what became Earth, and they stayed here in Somalie to rule it and our afterlife alone."

"But we don't have 'Gods' like that on Earth," said Kaitlynn. "Most people believe in one God, and they can't even agree about how to worship him. I mean, they used to believe in multiple Gods, but they were all different in different parts of the world if I recall. My recollection of ancient mythology isn't very good."

"Perhaps you do not have multiple gods anymore," replied Delok. "But in time, even Gods can die, especially in battle with each other. Perhaps your one God is the only one of the Old Gods left. I hope for the sake of your people, that he is one of the more merciful ones."

Kaitlynn contemplated all of this quietly. She had never been religious herself (at least not since she was a kid and hadn't had any choice in the matter) and wasn't sure that any of what Delok had said was true. But it was clear that the satyrs seemed to believe it. And the idea of all of the old mythological gods having been real and that the one God that most people believed in now was just "the winner" made her blood run cold inside. She decided that she didn't want to think about that anymore and found other things to talk about while they marched ever onward.

When they made camp for the night again just after dark, Shanja pulled Kaitlynn aside and sparred with her while the others tended to gathering food and fuel for the fire. Kaitlynn could feel herself getting better at defending and began adding some offensive thrusts and slashes into her repertoire to surprise Shanja. All of her attacks were blocked with ease, but Shanja was pleased with her progress overall.

After practicing for a while, they ate a dinner of more of the red-looking squirrels and set up watches for the night. Kaitlynn bedded down and waited for her watch. She felt restless. For the first time since coming to Somalie, she had real trouble falling asleep. She was bone tired, but everything she had learned so far kept turning over in mind. The constant stream of thought eventually got the better of her and she got up and sat by the fire for a while. Peton and Uliah were on the first watch, and Uliah came over and sat down next to her.

"Can't sleep?" she asked.

Kaitlynn shook her head. "Too much on my mind I guess," she replied with a shrug.

They sat together in silence for a while. Finally, Uliah asked, "You miss your home?"

Kaitlynn nodded. "The last few months have been pretty shitty," she said. "I was really looking forward to going home, and I ended up here instead."

Uliah pursed her lips. "What was so bad back home?"

Kaitlynn explained her father's slow deterioration to Uliah, speaking softly and with sadness in her voice. Uliah nodded along while listening to her. When Kaitlynn was done, she sat in contemplation for a couple of minutes.

"I am glad you are here," Uliah said. Kaitlynn turned and looked at her. "I am glad to have met you."

Kaitlynn smiled at her, glad for the kind words. "You all seem really nice," she said. "And everything here is so different. It's exciting and scary at the same time."

Uliah nodded. "But tis not home." Kaitlynn nodded again, a somber look painting itself upon her face.

Uliah stood up and motioned to Kaitlynn to follow. She led her back over to the place in the grass where she had left her coat as a makeshift pillow. "I can help you get some rest," she said, pointing to the ground. Kaitlynn shrugged her shoulders and lay down. Uliah bent down over her and put her hand gently over Kaitlynn's eyes and murmured something that sounded incoherent. Suddenly Kaitlynn felt her mind become foggy. Within moments she had drifted off to sleep.

<h1 style="text-align:center">26</h1>

It was dark, but the raven didn't dare risk getting too close to the camp. It circled quietly above, careful not to draw any attention to itself. It could see the discarded bones of the squirrels with small morsels still clinging to a few spots. But its instructions were clear; follow the satyrs, but don't get too close. Report back to its master about their movements.

Its master had been particularly intrigued by the news that there was some other type of creature with the satyrs. It was a bit taller, and a female. But the raven had never seen its like before. It was not slight enough to be an elf, nor did it have the pointed ears or bronze colored skin of their tree-loving kind either. It had been unable to correctly identify her like to its master, and Master had found this fact to be highly frustrating. It watched this strange woman closely, looking for any detail it could give its master about her origin and get back in his good graces. The quality of its meals depended on every detail it could remember and pass along.

Additionally, the satyrs were closing in on the goblins carrying the Gate to its master, and its master was not pleased by this. Measures were going to need to be taken to assure the Gate's safety. The raven knew that it had until the first rays of sunlight rose in the east before it would have to fly to its master's keep if the master was going to be able to intervene before the satyrs made up the distance. It looked with longing at the scraps again, contemplated diving for them as quietly as possible, but decided against it. The two satyrs on watch were waking two of the others, and the raven decided instead to fly off and look elsewhere for food while the rest of the satyrs and the strange women slept.

27

Shanja shook her gently awake, and Kaitlynn sat up. She smiled at her friend and took up her position on the watch for the night. She felt strangely refreshed and wondered what it was that Uliah had done to her to help her fall asleep. Whatever it was, it was the best she had felt in days.

The morning came without incident, and the group set off shortly after breakfast. As they walked, Kaitlynn looked back at the camp in the distance and saw a large black bird picking at the remains of their food. She didn't think anything of it and marched on to the south with her companions.

28

The sun was beginning to set in the west, and Faljon was cresting a ridge at the head of the line when suddenly he dropped and laid flat on his stomach and peered over the top of the rise. The rest of the group stopped and crouched down and began moving forward and spreading across the top of the small hill as well. Kaitlynn dropped to her hands and knees and crawled up next to them, ending up between Peton and Jali. Ahead in the distance, they could see a campfire burning with the smoke rising against the fading sunlight. They were still a ways away, but it was clear that the group of goblins they had been chasing was up ahead. Faljon slowly slid back down the hill, and the others followed. He looked back and forth at the rest of the party and said, "We wait until dark before we advance. No fire."

Hammel slithered back up to the top of the rise and kept watch on the camp in the distance while the rest of them planned their attack. Kaitlynn listened as best she could, but she could feel her hands shaking. Shanja gently put a hand on her shoulder as if to try to reassure her. Quietly she whispered to her, "We all have our first. You will do fine." Kaitlynn nodded and clenched her fists, hoping it would stop her body's uncontrollable quaking.

Slowly the sun slid down in the west, and the sky bled red against the clouds until the darkness finally claimed them. The group spread out with the two archers, Uliah and Jali making up the flanks. The two spearmen, Peton and Hammel were next, and Delok, Shanja, Faljon, and Kaitlynn with their swords made up the center of the line. They advanced as quickly as they could while staying as quiet as possible. In order to maintain the element of surprise, they all made sure to focus on the light ahead rather than let their eyes adjust to the night. The last thing they needed was their glowing emerald eyes giving away their advance.

They closed the distance until they were only a few yards away from the edge of the light, and then hunkered down. The two archers continued to fan out to flank the campsite, staying low to the ground. The plan was for the archers to quickly take out any guards, and then the others would advance in the confusion and take care of any goblins that were left.

In the firelight, Kaitlynn could make out the strange creatures ahead. They were small, shorter even than the satyrs she had been traveling with. Their faces were misshapen and grotesque, like gruesome Halloween masks. Some of them seemed to have tufts of hair on the tops of their heads, and there was a sickly green pallor to their skin as well. She counted twelve of them in total. Most of them seemed to be sleeping, but there were three of them up and on watch set in a triangle around the camp. One was looking directly the way they were coming from, and the other two were set almost equilaterally around on the other sides. They all seemed to be armed with bows and daggers. Kaitlynn noticed that none of them seemed to have the strange glowing eyes that she and her companions had, and she hoped that that meant that they couldn't see as well in the darkness as the satyrs could. She prayed quietly that this gave them an advantage despite being outnumbered as she continued clenching and unclenching her fists to try and stop herself from shaking.

Out of the darkness, arrows descended on two of the goblin guards, killing them both instantly. Kaitlynn saw the one on the right take the arrow directly through its neck and a fountain of blood sprayed out into the darkness beyond the fire from the wound. As their bodies hit the ground, the satyrs were already charging at the camp. Peton ran forward with his spear poised and took out the third guard, stabbing it in the back as it turned and watched one of his comrades fall, a scream of warning lost forever in its throat. The others fanned out and attacked the other goblins as they tried to rouse themselves from their slumber.

Kaitlynn ran in behind the satyrs, her sword clutched in her hand. She watched as Faljon ran in and beheaded one of the goblins with a single stroke while it was still trying to get to its feet, and then ran past its falling corpse to take down the next one. While she stood transfixed at the scene in front of her, an arrow flew past her right side close enough for her to feel the tug on her clothes as it put a hole in her sweatshirt. She looked in the direction the arrow had come and saw a goblin pulling another arrow from his quiver. She charged the goblin and struck it down with a single swipe of her sword, instinctively slicing it from chin to groin. Kaitlynn looked around for another target as the goblin screamed and fell to the ground with its innards spilling out, landing in a puddle of its own blood and organs. As she scanned the battlefield, she saw no other goblins left standing.

Their surprise attack appeared to have been a rousing success. After only a few moments and a flurry of action, the goblins had all been defeated. Kaitlynn looked around and started counting satyrs to make sure that they'd all come through the fight unscathed, and then took a deep breath. They were one short. She looked around quickly checking faces and then said, "Where's Hammel?"

The other satyrs looked around and saw that they were missing their companion as well. They fanned out and started searching. It wasn't long before Jali called out, "I found him." There was a morose sadness in her voice.

The rest of the group all went over to where she stood and saw Hammel laying on the ground, a single crude arrow sticking out of his chest. He had been hit in the heart and looked like he had died instantly with a look of surprise on his face. Faljon bent down and closed his eyes. "May he rest eternal, Keeper of Souls," Delok said. The other satyrs nodded and repeated the blessing, and Kaitlynn joined them. She wasn't sure if this "Qyr" was real or not, but Hammel had been one of them and she figured that he had believed in their gods. She hadn't even had a chance to get to know him at all yet though, and she instantly regretted that fact.

Faljon reached down and picked up Hammel's spear and handed it to Shanja. She took it with a slight nod and slung it over her back. She reached down and patted Hammel's body softly on the shoulder, and said, "I will treat it well, friend," before she stood up and walked away with her head down. She stood silently on the edge of the light of the campfire. Delok walked over to her and wrapped his arms around her quietly to comfort her, and she held his arms tight around her chest.

Kaitlynn walked slowly back to where she had left her coat outside the circle of firelight and sat down in the grass. She put her head in her hands and wept for the dead satyr. It took her a few minutes before she realized that she had killed one of the goblins herself. She shuddered suddenly at the memory of its guts spilling out as it died and felt the contents of her stomach gurgle up to the back of her throat. She swallowed hard and put a hand over her mouth, barely managing to keep herself from vomiting. Then she grabbed her coat and tossed it over her shoulder before she headed back to the campfire.

The satyrs were searching the campsite with a frantic energy that she found unsettling when she got back. Faljon walked over to her, a look of grave concern on his face. He looked up at her to meet her eyes and said, "The Gate is not here."

Kaitlynn tried to take a deep breath, but her stomach wouldn't hold anymore. She felt a hot rush lurching up her throat and bent over and retched all over the ground between the two of them. She took a couple of steps back and fell to her knees, wiping her mouth with the sleeve of her sweatshirt and trying not to look at the former contents of her stomach lest she give back anything else in the same manner. Faljon put his hand gently on her shoulder. She looked up at him and asked, "What do we do now?" The color had drained from her face, and she looked far paler than he'd ever seen her.

He looked down at her, a look of concern on his face. "Are you ill?" he asked her.

She shook her head. "I've never..." she began but couldn't finish for a moment. She collected herself and said, "I've never killed anything ... anyone before. I didn't even think about it; I just did it." The tears started flowing down her cheeks again in torrents, like flood waters washing away the sandbags that tried to deter them.

He nodded, beginning to understand what she was feeling. "The first is always hard," he said quietly. He patted her shoulder gently with his hand. "Let it out, I'm here for you." He stayed there with his hand on her shoulder, quietly letting her cry for as long as she needed to.

The other satyrs had gotten to work moving the dead to take over the camp for the night. They started by piling up the bodies of the dead goblins away from the fire. Suddenly Peton called out, "This one's alive!"

Shanja and Delok ran over and checked on it. The goblin was indeed still breathing. Shanja motioned with her head towards Delok, and he went over to where Faljon and Kaitlynn were. Kaitlynn's tears were finally drying up when Delok arrived. "Keepers," he said quietly, not wanting to disturb them, "We have one to question."

Faljon nodded without looking away from Kaitlynn. "Are you all right?" he asked her gently. She nodded and stood up slowly. Faljon nodded at her before heading off with Delok, and Kaitlynn followed the two satyrs over to where the goblin was laying on the ground.

"Is she okay?" She heard Delok ask Faljon as they were walking over.

"First kill," he replied to the other satyr, his voice low. Delok nodded his understanding, and then he led them over to their captive.

They arrived at the wounded goblin, and by then the rest of the satyrs had gathered around. It snarled incoherently at them with vicious looking fangs, but Kaitlynn thought it looked more like a wounded animal than anything else. She could see a large slash mark across its upper chest, and there was inkish black blood seeping from a wound above its left eye as well. Peton and Shanja held it still as Faljon walked over to it and put his hand on its forehead. The goblin went silent and there was a white light that lasted a few moments around his hand. When the light had faded, Faljon looked it in the eyes and quietly asked, "Where is the Gate?"

The goblin's eyes darted back and forth between all of them. "It's gone," it said with a snarl. There was a gargled sound to its voice as if it was trying to talk while underwater.

"He won't last long, there's blood in his lungs," said Shanja. Faljon nodded his agreement to her.

"Where is the Gate?" Faljon asked again, this time with a bit more force to his voice. "You are dying, drowning in your own blood. Tis a painful way to die." He held his sword in his hand and glanced at it, and then back at the goblin.

The goblin nodded. "The Master sent for it. A great winged beast carried it away just before dark."

Kaitlynn took a deep breath. They had just missed it.

"Where did it take it?" Faljon asked it.

"To the obs...." It began before suddenly a large black raven swooped down and attacked him. The raven pecked the goblin with its beak directly in the goblin's throat. There was a bubbling sound as the goblin's scream was cut off and blood began spouting out of the open wound. The raven began to take flight when suddenly an arrow pierced through the firelight right at it, but the raven disappeared in a cloud of black smoke and the arrow flew out the other side and landed in the distance just beyond the light of the campfire. Kaitlynn turned and saw Jali standing there slowly lowering her bow. She turned back and saw the goblin was bleeding profusely from the throat and gagging on its own blackish blood. Faljon stepped forward and sliced its head clean off sparing it the misery of a torturous death, but not before the spray of black ichor covered his face and chest.

Kaitlynn looked at the black cloud as it dissipated where the arrow had struck the raven. "Nevermore," she thought to herself and suppressed a chuckle with a slight cough. She was a little bit embarrassed by her instinct to turn to gallows humor under the circumstances, but she considered it a coping mechanism. If she was going to get through this, she figured that she would need to do it in any way that she could and still stay sane.

29

Well outside the circle of the firelight and high above in the air, the raven reappeared in a puff of black smoke. It had managed to become incorporeal just in time, but it knew just how close it had come to being killed. It circled for a minute to get its bearings before flying south towards the obsidian keep in the mountains to inform its master of everything it had seen. It had stopped the last goblin from talking, and it hoped that its master would reward it handsomely for its actions. Using the magic its master had imbued it with had made it hungrier than usual, which was very hungry indeed.

30

Kaitlynn and the group of satyrs sat quietly around the fire eating dinner, though she found that she was only just picking at her food. Peton and Jali had gone out into the darkness and returned with another of the large-antlered rabbits. Kaitlynn's vacated stomach still gargled and roared at her, and she didn't want to take too many risks with it.

There was an uneasiness in the air around the fire. The pile of dead goblins just outside of the light of the fire and the body of their fallen comrade gave everything an ominous feeling. Kaitlynn could still smell her vomit in the air as well. And then there was the matter of the missing painting; Kaitlynn had no idea how she would get home without it.

She broke the silence first, turning to Faljon and asking, "So what's our next move?"

He sat there quietly for a moment before responding, "The goblins were taking the Gate south along this path. I say we continue, see where it leads."

"That's pretty thin," replied Delok. "We don't know where they were going at all."

"We can't just give up though," chimed in Uliah. "We need to retrieve the gate and get Kaitlynn home." Faljon gave her a stern look. "Get the Keeper home, I mean."

"It's okay, Faljon," Kaitlynn said, putting a hand gently on his shoulder. "I'd rather they call me by my name than my title. We're all in this together." She glanced quickly in the direction of Hammel's body, and then back at Faljon. The satyr looked at her for a moment and then nodded in acquiescence.

"You are correct," he said, his voice sullen. "'Tis no more need for formality here. We have spilled blood together, and we have mourned together." The satyrs around the fire all nodded in agreement. Faljon paused for a few moments before continuing, "I know that we don't have much to go on, but I refuse to give up. The answers lie somewhere to the south."

Shanja put her hand gently on Delok's upper leg and said, "Everything is uncertain, except the danger. The Gate must be found, and we will follow." Delok paused for a moment, looked at Shanja, and then nodded his agreement. The rest of the group nodded as well.

The decision made; the party chose to get some rest. Short one man, the group set up a new watch schedule. It was decided that Jali would join Peton and Uliah on the first watch of the night, and they would cut down from four watches to three. Kaitlynn quietly walked over to where Faljon had laid himself down for the night and set her own place not far away from him. After everything that they had gone through tonight, she didn't want to be alone and felt more comfortable having him nearby. She looked over and saw Delok and Shanja bedding down together and wished that she had someone that she could turn to like that after a day like this. Exhausted, it wasn't long before she drifted off to sleep, though this night her sleep would come in fits and starts and be filled with memories of the battle that had taken place this day.

31

The rental car pulled into the old familiar driveway. Rebecca hadn't been here for over twenty years. The day after the divorce had been finalized she had packed her and her daughter's bags and moved them across the country. She swore she would never come back to this place. But she hadn't been able to keep her daughter away from her father and the dangers that resided in this house no matter how hard she had tried.

Rebecca got out of the car. Her former brother-in-law, James, had called her when Kaitlynn had been missing for a full forty-eight hours. The police had been here, looking for her. They'd scoured the entire neighborhood but hadn't been able to find her. But Rebecca instinctively knew where her daughter was. It was the one and only reason she had left, and it had been exactly what she had feared the most; the family business that she had always hated had taken her daughter from her. Her fears were almost immediately confirmed when her nephew Jeff had told her over the phone about how he had followed her footprints in the snow into the woods, and how they had just disappeared. He didn't understand it, but she did. She had been to Somalie before. She had asked him if there had been anything unusual in the area where her daughter had disappeared, and he mentioned in an off-handed manner about a painting that someone had left in the woods. She thanked him, hung up the phone, and then booked a plane ticket right away.

Rebecca walked over to the keypad on the garage door and punched in the same old code the door had always had; zero nine twenty-seven. September twenty-seventh was Kaitlynn's birthday. She knew Danny would never change that, he loved his little girl too much. Shame washed over her' it hurt her to remember what she had done to her ex-husband. She had done it for her daughter's safety, and she knew in her heart that it had been the right thing for her to do. However, it still hurt her to know how much she had hurt him. She had always loved Danny, but everything changed for her when her own father had passed on the secret of the Gate to her right before he had died. She didn't want the responsibility and the danger, and she sure as hell didn't want it for her daughter either.

She pulled the car into her old spot in the garage, and then went back outside. Without hesitation, she walked into the woods behind the house. The old paths had been overgrown, but there had been enough activity recently that the thorn bushes had been mostly trampled over. She walked directly to the new clearing by the old oak tree that had been there for as long as she could remember and saw the painting leaning against it on the ground.

Rebecca took a deep breath and walked over to it. Gone was the old staircase in the woods. Instead, she could see what looked like the inside of a strange room. The walls were a blackish gray, and there was an open window. She could see mountains and snow in the distance through the window as well. But in the foreground, there was a perch with a large black bird sitting on it, and it was staring directly at her with its blood red eyes. She found the creature completely unsettling and looked away quickly.

She understood all too quickly what had happened, and her blood ran cold. Kaitlynn had gone through the Gate, and then something on the other side had stolen it. That something was a danger to this world, and Rebecca couldn't let it through, even if it meant losing her daughter. Tears formed in her eyes and started streaming down her cheeks. She knew her duty as Keeper, but her duty as a mother would always, always come first to her. She picked up the painting and carried it back to the house. Inside, away from the woods, there was no way that anything could come through unless she brought it back outside and let it through. She walked into the house for the first time in over two decades, and immediately put the painting back on the mantle. She sat on the couch and watched it, waiting for any sign of daughter. Only then would she take the painting back into the woods and open the gate.

32

In the morning, the party set off to the south along the path. They made their way quietly, not talking much as they made their way through the wide fields. After they had stopped for lunch and moved on again, Kaitlynn fell in line next to Peton. He was really the only satyr left in the group that she hadn't had a chance to talk to at all, and she'd missed out on that chance with Hammel before he had died. They made some small talk, but the satyr seemed lost in his own thoughts. She wondered if he and Hammel had been close, and perhaps he was dealing with the grief. Kaitlynn left him alone after a while, and they continued along in silence.

As midday started to turn into late afternoon, Kaitlynn could see a large forest coming into view up ahead. As they got closer, she could also see that a stream seemed to come out of it and track off to the west. She wondered to herself if it was the same stream they had forded the previous morning. By the time they made camp, they were almost right outside the forest as it stretched to the west of the path as far as the eye could see. The path they were on, however, passed by the forest and continued to the south.

Peton and Faljon headed off together towards the stream to hunt for dinner for the group, while Uliah and Jali made their way into the forest to find fuel for the fire. Shanja pulled Kaitlynn aside and began sparring with her while Delok stood watch at the camp. After a while, Peton and Faljon returned with two large, brown fish from the stream, and Faljon began to clean the fish and prepare them for the fire. But as darkness began to fall, Uliah and Jali still hadn't returned from the woods. Kaitlynn was worried, and it looked like the others were as well. She was looking at the forest, waiting for any movement that might signal the return of the two satyrs, when Faljon finally spoke.

"We need to go looking for them," he said, and the others nodded. They all grabbed their weapons and prepared to head out.

These were the thickest woods that Kaitlynn had ever entered. The trees were large, and the air hung heavy around them. Any light left from the setting sun did not make it through the canopy of the trees, and Kaitlynn and the satyrs all let their eyes adjust to the darkness. The greens and browns that she had seen from the outside of the forest were a pallet of grays now as they made their way deeper into the woods.

After passing through the thickening woods for about ten minutes, there was a surprised yelp from behind Kaitlynn and a loud rustling above and behind her. She turned around and looked up, and she saw Peton hanging upside down from a rope that had caught around his ankle.

Faljon looked up at him and sighed. "If only we had the archers to shoot him down," he said. Kaitlynn wasn't sure if he was being sarcastic or not. She hadn't heard that type of humor from any of the satyrs so far, so she thought he might have been being literal.

Kaitlynn walked over to the tree that the rope was tied from. The branches were high, but she figured she could get a handhold. She reached out and pulled herself up and continued climbing until she was level with Peton's waist. The branch he was tied to was higher up, but from here she could reach the rope and cut him down. She did her best to look up at the rope as his fur covered testicles and smooth flaccid penis bounced in the air right in front of her face while she worked. Once again, she wished silently to herself that the satyrs had worn clothes instead of all running around with their junk hanging in the breeze. "Catch him," she said as she cut the rope, holding onto it above where she cut it to help maintain her own balance. Even still, the snapping of the rope as the branch above attempted to lift back up at the change of weight pulling against it almost sent her flying. Peton fell and the other satyrs cushioned his fall, but his weight and the momentum of his fall knocked them all down to the ground. Kaitlynn tried to stifle a chuckle as she watched the scene unfold below her and it ended up sounding like she was having a coughing fit instead. Once she managed to calm herself down sufficiently, she started working her way back towards the trunk of the tree where she could climb down more safely. As she was reaching the trunk, she heard a voice below call out.

"Don't move!" he said. The voice had a slight melodic quality to it but was in perfect Satyrn. "You are surrounded, satyrn. This is not your forest."

Kaitlynn pressed herself against the trunk of the tree and looked down. The group of satyrs had been surrounded while they were still picking themselves up off the ground. There were about half a dozen human-shaped creatures around them with bows drawn. They were tall, slight of frame, and all had a bronze hue to their skin. Their ears were long and pointed, and they were dressed in dark greens and browns to match the surrounding forest.

"Mighty elf kind," replied Faljon. "No disrespect was meant. We were passing by on the trail and set camp. Two of our own came into the forest looking for wood for a fire. They hadn't returned and we were searching for them."

"Your fellow satyrn have been taken to the King of the Elfwood," the elf responded. "And you will join them."

Kaitlynn looked down. It was a little bit farther than she would like to fall, but she thought she might be able to drop onto one of the elves and surprise them long enough for the satyrs to get up and defend themselves. She slowly stepped out onto the branch and prepared to drop when there was a cracking sound and the branch started to give way. She balanced herself as quickly as she could and grabbed the trunk again, but the noise attracted the attention of the elves. The leader looked up and pointed his bow directly at her.

"What manner of creature is this?" he asked

"She is with us!" replied Faljon, a panic in his voice. "She is a human."

A murmur swept through the elves. Their leader turned to Faljon and said, "Lies! There have been no humans since the Sundering five millennia ago!"

"Let her down safely and take us to your King," Faljon replied. I will explain everything to him." He paused for a moment before saying, "The fate of two worlds may hang in the balance."

The leader of the elves looked up at Kaitlynn again. He had piercing blue eyes and dark hair. There was an exquisite grace about him. He motioned for her to come down, and she did. Once she was on the ground, she looked around at the group of elves that had descended upon them. Five of them were men, all taller than Kaitlynn and there were two women, who were about her height. She could see once she got closer that they all appeared to be wearing armor made of leather or hides. The leader walked over to her, looked her over quickly, and then pushed her into the group with the satyrs. All of them were disarmed, had their hands tied behind their backs, and were forced to walk together in the middle of the group of elves.

They trekked through the woods in the dark for about half an hour before they came upon an area with wooden houses and large walkways built up among the branches of the trees. A platform was lowered down from above at their approach, and they went up in two separate groups. In each group were half of the elves and satyrs. Kaitlynn went up with the second group, along with Faljon and the leader of the elvish guards.

When the platform reached the walkway among the trees, the group regained the formation they had taken in the woods. It was brighter now, as there were lanterns hung along the path that burned with a strange blue light, and Kaitlynn could see that other elves had come out of their homes within the trees to see what all the commotion was about. Most of these elves wore the plain gowns or tunics of commoners, but they all had a grace of movement that Kaitlynn couldn't help but notice. She found herself taken by the fact that the elves were all beautiful in a way that could not be said about her own kind. Some people were just plain ugly, unfortunate as that might be, it was an undeniable fact. She wondered if all the elves were born this way, or if they just killed off the ugly babies at birth.

They followed along the path to a large building that seemed to almost be suspended between two large, sprawling trees. Guards opened the double doors at their approach and the leader of the party of elves led them inside. Against the far wall of what looked like a great hall, there were two thrones, one slightly larger than the other. They were made of branches of trees and the leaves were still on them and growing. Kaitlynn looked at them and thought perhaps they had grown that way through the floor. On the smaller of the two thrones sat a female elf with dark hair, dark eyes, a long green gown, and wooden tiara upon her head. In the larger throne sat a male elf with hair so blonde it was almost white, dark blue eyes, and he was wearing a dark green tunic and a wooden crown. There were a handful of attendants dressed in brown gowns and tunics moving throughout the hall. In the middle of the room sat Uliah and Jali, bound in the same manner as the rest of the party, with two guards standing over them. Their weapons were in a pile on the floor against the wall. They were herded into the center of the room along with Uliah and Jali. The two satyrs looked happy to see the rest of the group and concerned about the situation. Two of the elves that had captured them added the rest of their weapons to the pile along the wall.

The leader of the patrol stepped forward and said, "My King, we have captured more of the satyrn invaders," he said. "And they claim that this woman with them is a human!" There was an air of incredulousness in his voice.

The King of the Elfwood stood up and slowly walked over to the group. He eyed them all suspiciously but paused before them and looked directly at Kaitlynn. "Bring her forward," he said, his voice soft but filled with authority. One of the elves pushed her forward gently and she went without a struggle. The King looked at her, eyeing her up and down for a full minute. "Look at me," he said to her, his voice gentle. She looked him squarely in the eye. He nodded and stepped back. "Who among you is your leader?" he asked.

Faljon stepped forward and said, "Lord King Delavon of the Elfwood. I am Faljon, Keeper of the Gate of Somalie."

King Delavon looked at him, an inquisitive look in his eye. "And what brings you here, Keeper?" he asked. "Should you not be in Keeper's Wood, protecting the Gate?" There was a hushed murmur from the other elves throughout the room.

"The Gate was stolen," Faljon replied. "Goblins killed two of our guards and took it, under orders from one I do not know. We tracked them, one day's march south of here and killed them, but the Gate was gone." He paused before he added in a hushed tone, "Another of ours fell there." He continued again in his normal voice, "Send out riders if you must to verify my story."

"And the human, when did she undergo the change?" he asked, pointing at Kaitlynn.

"She did not," replied Faljon. "Her ancestor did, many generations ago, to guard the gate from the other side. She is Kaitlynn, Keeper of the Gate of Earth. Finding the Gate is her only way home."

"You know, Keeper, that the change is forbidden since the Treaty of the Sundering," King Delavon said.

"'Twas shortly after the sundering itself when the Gate appeared, before the treaty was signed my lord," he replied. "Regardless, none here are responsible for the actions of the past. Those satyrn are long gone my lord, even if you are not."

King Delavon nodded, and his face was solemn. He turned to the leader of the guard that had brought them in. "Release them, Derrith. They are our guests. They may have their weapons back when it is time for them to leave."

The elf paused for a second, and then said, "Yes, my lord." He motioned for his patrol to untie the satyrs.

To one of the attendants, the King said, "Prepare a feast in their honor. We have two of the most important beings in our two worlds here with us tonight; we shall treat them as such." The attendant bowed her head and left the room.

After being untied, Kaitlynn and the other satyrs all hugged Uliah and Jali, happy to see that they were all right. Faljon looked at King Delavon and said, "My lord, you are a gracious host."

"You must excuse Derrith and his patrol," The King replied. "They are sworn to protect our borders and they take that oath seriously."

"I understand oaths, my king," replied Faljon. Both nodded at each other.

The Queen rose from her chair, and walked over to Kaitlynn, her long silk gown trailing on the floor behind her. She motioned for one of the attendants to join them. "Take the Keeper's measure and get her some proper armor," she said. "The satyrn may prefer to go without, but humans do not. Least not those humans I remember." She smiled at Kaitlynn. "I am Queen Reliara, I have not seen one of your kind in over five thousand years," she said.

Kaitlynn shook her head in disbelief. "Five thousand years?" she replied, and the queen looked at her with curiosity.

"The Keeper has only recently inherited her title," Faljon said to the elven queen. "She still has much to learn, but she is learning well."

Queen Reliara nodded and said, "Then while she is our guest, we shall do our best to further her education."

"Thank you, my Queen," replied Faljon. He looked at Kaitlynn and nodded to her. She nodded back and then smiled at the queen. She would be happy to learn whatever she could if it helped her get back home.

A large wooden table was brought into the hall and shortly thereafter was covered with fine linens and bowls of food. There were fruits and vegetables the like of which Kaitlynn had never seen before. The only thing on the table she recognized was a bowl of gorkaberries. There were glasses of wine poured for all, blood red in color and sweet of scent. One side of the long table was lined with elves, on the other sat Kaitlynn and the satyrs.

Kaitlynn and Faljon were seated across from the King and Queen at the center of the table in a place of honor.

Kaitlynn leaned towards Faljon and asked, "Did my ancestor do something wrong by undergoing the change?"

Faljon shook his head. "The change was forbidden because of how it had been used in the past," he replied. "Once there were great nations of elves, men, centaurs, goblins, and other creatures. Many of these nations would hire satyrn to undergo the change and act as spies. This led to many wars between these nations. After the Cataclysm, the change was forbidden by the Treaty of the Sundering."

Kaitlynn nodded and listened intently. "The Sundering...is that what the elves call the Cataclysm?" she asked, and he nodded at her. "How do we understand them? Do they speak the same language as you?"

"They speak every language," replied Faljon. "The elves are the only creatures in Somalie whose magic surpasses ours."

"So, are they King and Queen of all of Somalie then?" asked Kaitlynn.

"They are King and Queen of all of the elves of Somalie," Faljon replied.

"Queen Reliara said she was over five thousand years old," Kaitlynn said. "Jali is a hundred and thirty-two. How long do you all live?"

"Elves are the longest living creatures in Somalie," he replied. "I know that the King and Queen are older than the Cataclysm, more than that I cannot say." He paused, and then continued, "we satyrn can live as long as three hundred years."

Kaitlynn took all this information in. "So how old are you then?" she asked him.

"One hundred and thirty-four," he replied. "Tis why we honor your ancestor. He sacrificed his long life for the duty of protecting the Gate." She could see a hot flash of anger in his eyes. "And tis why we signed the Treaty of the Sundering which forbade the change. Those satyrn who wasted this gift on fortune betrayed all we satyrn stand for. The change was designed for two purposes only. Duty and love. No others."

"Love?" she asked.

Faljon took a deep breath and looked at her. There was something gentle in his eyes. "There are stories of Satyrn who gave up their long lives for the love of another of a different race," he said. "But the last to undergo the change was the first Keeper of The Gate of Earth. It has been forbidden since." His gaze lingered on her for a moment, and then he looked away.

Kaitlynn looked up and saw that the King and Queen had been listening intently. The glanced at each other, and then King Delavon stood and raised his glass. The room became quiet slowly at first, and then those who had still been speaking saw King Delavon and silenced themselves.

"Friends and honored guests, welcome to our hall. Though it has been many generations since we have had the courtesy of the company of your kind, we are pleased to see that your company remains true. We know that your mission is of great importance, and we hope that tonight you can find rest. On the morrow, we shall bid you farewell with our best wishes, and whatever aid we can offer in your quest. In the meantime, feast, drink, and be well!"

Everyone around the table applauded and they drank from their glasses. Kaitlynn was surprised to find that the wine tasted like gorkaberries, and while she got a slight buzz from it, she also felt strangely refreshed as well. After the toast, they all dug into the food. Kaitlynn decided she would try a little bit of everything and found that she was quite full by the time she was done.

After dinner, two of the Queen's attendants pulled Kaitlynn aside into a separate room and began measuring her. Once they were done, one of them ran off with a list of numbers and the queen entered. She looked at Kaitlynn and gave her a warm smile. "Walk with me, Keeper," she said and bade Kaitlynn follow. The attendant that had remained followed along behind them at a respectful distance.

They left the great hall and walked further down the walkway in the trees. As they weaved through the streets high above the ground, Kaitlynn looked down. She could see the stream that had come out of the forest was down below snaking its way between the trees that the elves had made their homes in, and she could hear what sounded like a waterfall in the distance that was getting closer as they walked. Eventually, they came upon a small hill with a wooden structure at the top, and the waterfall was coming out below the building. The Queen led Kaitlynn inside.

Inside the building was a small pool of water with the rocky ground of the hill exposed all around it. The water seemed to be bubbling up from below the surface and there was steam in the cool air. On the north side of the building, there was an opening in the floor to allow the waterfall to cascade down. The Queen's attendant walked up behind her and untied her gown at the back of her neck and upper back. The gown slid down around her ankles and Queen Reliara stepped into the water. Kaitlynn was convinced that the Queen was the most beautiful woman she had ever seen, elf or not, and tried not to gape at her. She certainly felt more than just a tinge of jealousy as she watched the queen enter the water. She sat down near the center of the pool where the water was just below her neck and bade Kaitlynn join her.

Slightly embarrassed, but not wanting to insult the Queen, Kaitlynn slid out of her clothes and joined her in the water. The water was quite warm and was clearly being heated somehow from below. Kaitlynn sat down near the center, but far enough away from Queen Reliara to give them both some space. She knew that she was a good-looking woman herself but did her best not to think about how little she measured up to Queen Reliara sitting naked in the water across from her. She could feel the current of the waterfall pulling the water over the rock face behind her. The Queen's attendant gathered up her clothes and carried them away from the edge of the water.

"So, Lady Keeper," began the Queen, "I would hear of Earth. We have not seen your people since the Sundering. How have they fared?"

Kaitlynn paused and thought for a moment. There was much of human history she did not know, and not all of which she did know was pleasant. Finally, she said, "We've made great strides in technology, medicine, and culture. But we still have our struggles with each other. Wars, crime, that sort of thing. We are far from perfect."

Queen Reliara smiled. "There is no perfect society," she said. "Even we elves have our issues." She looked at Kaitlynn, her face more serious. "Whoever has the Gate could do much harm to both of our worlds. You understand this?"

Kaitlynn lowered her eyes. "I don't know," she replied honestly. "I came through by accident. My father was the previous Keeper and he had just died. I really don't understand much about what's going on. I'm just beginning to learn how to fight and use the magic in my blood. But mostly I just want to go home."

The Queen nodded slowly. "You do have much to learn then, as the Keeper had said."

"Yes, my Queen," Kaitlynn replied. There was a long pause between them, and Kaitlynn could hear the water bubbling up to the surface around her.

"Tis clear to me that you speak truths," said the Queen. "Tis difficult to hide behind lies when so exposed." She motioned around at the pool of water. Kaitlynn nodded her understanding. This had been a test of sorts, and she had passed.

The first attendant joined them then, a bundle of items in her hands. "I beg your pardon, my Queen," she said, "I have found some new attire for the lady Keeper."

The Queen nodded at her attendant, and then stood and walked to the edge of the water. Her other attendant wrapped her in what appeared to be a silk robe, and then went and grabbed another one for Kaitlynn. She stood up and walked to the edge, allowing the attendant to wrap her as well. The Queen walked over and sat on a wooden bench along the northern wall of the building and bade Kaitlynn join her.

"Please allow me to present these gifts to you," said Queen Reliara. "These clothes and armor will help you blend in more in our lands and protect you in your battles ahead."

"Thank you, my Queen," replied Kaitlynn. She was happy to be out of the clothes she had worn since she'd arrived in Somalie. She was fairly certain they were beginning to reek.

The attendant handed her the new clothes, and she could see they were dark green and brown, as well as a leather cuirass with a leather skirt attached that covered her thighs to just above the knee. There was also a backpack for her old clothes. She grabbed her panties and bra from the pile of her old clothes and then began getting dressed. The tunic and tights fit her well, and one of the attendants helped explain to her how to put the cuirass on. There were four buckles across the front from just above her breasts to her waist. She grabbed her socks and boots along with her belt and put them on as well before examining the rest of her clothes.

Her favorite ASU sweatshirt had a hole in it where an arrow had pierced it on the right side. She counted herself fortunate that the arrow had missed her. It and her jeans were covered in grass stains and dirt, as was her coat. Her t-shirt was still in pretty good condition if not covered in sweat, but just about everything else might as well have been burned or tossed in the trash. She sighed, stuffing the rest of her clothes into the backpack. She felt comfortable despite the stiffness of the leather armor.

She turned and looked at the Queen and took a bow before her. "They fit wonderfully, my Queen."

"Perfect!" she said, much cheer in her voice. "Now you look like you belong in the trees with us."

"Not hardly, my Queen," Kaitlynn replied, "though you honor me with such a compliment." She wasn't sure if she was doing all of this royal formality correctly or not and just hoped that by mimicking the tone she had heard from Faljon that she was pulling it off close enough so as not to offend.

Queen Reliara stood, and her attendant took her robe. She walked back over to her gown and her attendant helped her back into it and tied it again. She smiled at Kaitlynn and bade her follow, and they made their way back to the great hall.

By the time they entered, there were elven minstrels playing music, and many of the elves and satyrs were dancing. Kaitlynn looked around and saw Delok and Shanja arm in arm, lost in each other. Uliah and Jali seemed to be tossing Peton back and forth between each other and Kaitlynn couldn't tell if he was enjoying himself or consumed with dread. The thought made her laugh to herself either way.

The Queen entered the room and walked up to her husband on the throne and offered him her arm. He stood and took it, and they joined in the dancing. Kaitlynn stood on the wall and watched. Seeing all her friends happy made her smile. It took her a minute to realize Faljon wasn't dancing with the rest but was instead standing by the wall on the other side of the room watching the others. He had seen her come in and smiled at her and nodded his approval of her new attire once she noticed him. Slowly he moved his way around the crowded dance floor and made his way over to her.

"You look as if you belong here in Somalie now," he said to her with his toothy grin. She was beginning to find it less disconcerting with time.

"Thanks," she replied with a warm smile. "It's more comfortable than I thought it would be too."

He stuck his arm out to her. "Then you should dance," he said. She took his arm and let him take her out to the dance floor with the other satyrs and the elves. They danced for hours, laughing and enjoying themselves until finally, the minstrels ran out of songs to play. The various elves began to disperse and King Delavon and Queen Reliara came over to the group of satyrs.

"My attendant will show you to your quarters for the night," said the King. "Rest and be well, for your journey continues on the morrow."

"We thank thee for your hospitality, my King and Queen," replied Faljon. "I have questions that I hoped you might be able to answer before we leave."

"On the morrow," replied King Delavon. "For now, rest. For it is late, and you have a journey ahead of you." He smiled and beckoned to his attendant.

The attendant bade Kaitlynn and the satyrs follow him. He led them out to a row of three small unoccupied houses near the outskirts of the town. Delok and Shanja claimed one, Peton, Uliah and Jali another, leaving the third house for Kaitlynn and Faljon. Inside there were two beds, "about the size of a full-sized bed back home," Kaitlynn thought to herself. She imagined that in the other houses, beds were likely being shared and chuckled involuntarily.

Faljon looked at her. "What is it?" he asked.

"Nothing," she said, before bursting into full-blown laughter. Faljon looked at her as if she might be going mad. She finally got a hold of herself and said, "it's just that I imagine Delok and Shanja are enjoying finally having some privacy. And the way Uliah and Jali were passing Peton back and forth on the dance floor, I'm sure they're probably having a great time tonight too."

Faljon raised his eyebrows slightly and chuckled himself. "Yes, well..." he began before looking away. "They've earned the right to a little pleasure," he finished. She could see that his cheeks were turning bright red. This only made her laugh harder.

When she finally settled herself down again, she started trying to get her leather cuirass off. After a few moments of struggling with it, she felt a clawed hand gently touch hers, and then Faljon undid the straps on the front of her armor for her. She slid it off over her shoulders and placed it down on the ground. "Thank you," she said, looking at him. She bent down and kissed him on the cheek. She could feel his skin flush warmly against her lips. She stood up with her eyes wide, realization suddenly setting in.

Faljon looked away and headed over to one of the beds. Kaitlynn thought that she had seen the embarrassment on his face before he had turned and walked away. "Rest well, Keeper," he said to her before climbing onto the bed above the covers.

Kaitlynn walked over to his bed and pulled at the covers. They were silk, like the robe she had worn in the bathhouse with the Queen. "Help me a little here," she said, and he lifted himself up enough for her to pull the covers down. She then pulled them back up, tucked him in under them, and leaned down and kissed him on the cheek again. "It's nothing to be embarrassed about," she said quietly, before standing up and walking over to the other bed.

She pulled off her boots and slid the covers down. She felt the soft silk sheets in her hands and glanced over her shoulder at Faljon. He was laying on his side with his back to her. She took her tunic and tights off and slid under the covers wearing only her underwear. The sheets felt amazing against her skin, like being wrapped in pure comfort and ecstasy. She could hear Faljon's breathing slow and turn into a light snore, and she found the sound strangely peaceful. It wasn't long before she drifted off to sleep herself.

33

Kaitlynn heard Faljon get up and rolled over and looked around the room. She was so grateful to have slept in an actual bed that she was pretty sure she could stay bundled up in the exquisite comfort of the silk sheets forever. She looked over and saw the satyr sitting on the edge of the bed, his hooves hanging just an inch or two above the floor. He was rubbing his temples with the palms of his hands, which made him look like he had a crown of claws around his horns.

"Good morning," she said to him, and he looked up at her. She held the sheets up against her chest as she sat up and smiled at him.

He smiled back at her, and then looked down at her pile of clothes on the floor. "I can step out," he said, looking away and turning red.

"Its fine, you can look. I'm covered," she said. "No need to be embarrassed. But yes, when I get up, I wouldn't mind a little privacy. I may need your help with that armor again though."

He nodded at her. "Just open the door when you are ready. I'll be happy to help," he said to her, before stepping out into the morning sunlight. The light was brighter than Kaitlynn had expected considering the dense canopy of trees in the forest that they had seen when they had arrived the night before.

She stood up and got dressed quickly. She threw her armor on over her shoulders and worked at the buckles on the front. After struggling with them for a few minutes, she finally got them to work. She opened the door, stepped out, and saw Faljon looking over the railing at the forest below. He turned when the door opened and looked back at her.

"I got it," she said with a smile, and he smiled his toothy grin back at her. "Are the others up yet?" she asked him.

"Not yet," he replied. "We should wake them. We need to get moving."

"Okay," Kaitlynn replied. "You get Delok and Shanja up. I'll get the other three."

Faljon paused for a second, and then said, "Are you sure? After what you said last night..." he trailed off.

Kaitlynn giggled a little bit. "I went to college, I've probably seen worse," she said. "ASU was a bit of a party school. My roommate sophomore year was into some freaky shit, and she never locked the door. You wouldn't believe some of the things I walked in on."

Faljon looked at her, his face twisted in puzzlement, and shook his head. He walked over and knocked on the door to the house Delok and Shanja had taken. Kaitlynn smiled at him and then walked over to the house that the other three were in, braced herself, and knocked. She could hear some movement on the other side, and eventually, Uliah opened the door. Kaitlynn could see that one of the beds had not been used and that Peton and Jali were a tangle of limbs under the sheets on the other one. The sheets had been pulled down just enough to allow Uliah to get up and answer the door. She looked up at Kaitlynn and blushed slightly before looking down and apparently examining her hooves with much interest.

"No worries, no one's judging anyone," said Kaitlynn quietly. "But Faljon wants to get a move on." Uliah nodded quietly, and then closed the door to rouse the other two satyrs. As soon as the door was closed, Kaitlynn covered her mouth to stifle a laugh. She looked over at Faljon at the other door and nodded at him with glee in her eyes. She saw him swallow hard, trying not to laugh himself.

After a few minutes, all the satyrs were out on the walkway. The elves had begun to rouse themselves as well, and a few of them passed the party along the wooden streets above the forest floor. After a few minutes, one of King Delavon's attendants came and brought them back to the great hall. The King and Queen sat on their thrones, and the leader of the patrol that had brought them in the night before stood there as well.

Kaitlynn and the six satyrs filed into the room and stood in a line across from the King and Queen. Faljon stood at the center of the line with Kaitlynn to his right and Shanja to his left. Delok and Peton filled out the line to the left, while Jali and Uliah finished out the line to the right of Kaitlynn.

King Delavon and Queen Reliara rose from their thrones and stepped down in front of the party. Kaitlynn and the satyrs all bowed before them.

Delavon motioned for them to rise. "You had questions Keeper. Speak, and we shall answer as best we can," said the King.

Faljon nodded. "We were tracking the party of goblins that had stolen the Gate. They had been heading south. What can you tell us of the lands to the south of here?"

"Once you exit the forest, it is miles of mostly green plains," the King responded, "until you reach the Frostspire Mountains."

"The mountains are treacherous, as are the creatures that live there and beyond them," added the Queen.

"Treacherous enough to steal the Gate?" asked Faljon. Both the King and Queen nodded. Faljon thought for a moment, and then said, "One of the goblins that we questioned mentioned that a great winged beast had taken the Gate back to their master. What kinds of beasts live in the mountains that match that description?"

"There are wyverns in the mountains. They make their nests in the peaks," said the King. The satyrs looked taken aback by this revelation. Kaitlynn had no idea what a "wyvern" was but decided not to ask until they were back on the trail.

Faljon nodded, and then said, "The goblin we were questioning was killed by a large raven. When Jali shot it, it disappeared in a cloud of smoke. Have you heard of such a thing before?"

The King and Queen looked at each other for a moment, and then slowly turned back to Kaitlynn and the satyrs. "It is the messenger pet of Uligart, the Lord of the Obsidian Keep in the mountains," said King Delavon. "Uligart is the King of the Frost Elves."

Faljon looked confused. "Frost Elves?" he asked.

"They are much like us, though their skin is pale, almost white," replied the King. "The Frost Elves used to be a part of our kingdom. However, about three hundred years ago, Uligart rose to power and declared himself their King. There was a war between our peoples, but the mountain snows were to their advantage, and the forests were ours. We fought to a standstill."

"We lost many a good soldier to the frost elves," said Queen Reliara. King Delavon nodded in affirmation.

"Eventually we came to a truce," continued the King. "The mountains and the Frost Elves belonged to Uligart, and we would maintain our rule over the rest of the elves."

"We do not know why Uligart would want the Gate," added the Queen, "or why he would employ goblins to do his work for him."

"But if he has gained control of the goblins, and the wyverns…" the King trailed off.

"He is preparing for war," finished Faljon. "Perhaps not with Somalie, but with Earth."

"No offense," said Kaitlynn, "But humans have some pretty absurdly devastating weapons technology. We're well past using swords and bows. We could wipe ourselves out in about fifteen minutes if we were feeling stupid enough to do it. They wouldn't stand a chance attacking Earth."

"Then maybe that tis what he needs," said Shanja. Everyone turned and looked at her. "If he had those weapons here, he could slaughter us all and rule over our dust and bones."

The great hall went as silent as a tomb, and the air was heavy with dread as they all pondered the consequences of advanced human weapons ending up in the hands of an army in Somalie. Even if they didn't understand exactly how disastrous that would be, the certainty with which Kaitlynn had spoken had grabbed their attention. Finally, King Delavon turned to the leader of his patrol and said, "Derrith, you are to go with them and help them secure the Gate."

The elf paused for a moment with uncertainty in his eyes and then said, "Yes, my King," with a bow.

To Faljon, King Delavon said, "Derrith is the best of my guards. He will serve your party well. I will do all I can to rally an army to defend Somalie from attack. I will send messengers to the centaurs, dwarves, and the other nations of elves. We will rally on the fields to the south of Elfwood as soon as I can gather what forces I can persuade to join us."

Faljon held his left arm across his chest and bowed, and all the satyrs followed suit. Kaitlynn looked around for a moment, and then matched the salute.

"Before you leave," said the Queen, "you will need your weapons back. And we have taken the liberty of improving on some of what you carry."

The Queen's attendants entered the room carrying two bows with intricate carvings on them both above and below the handles. They also brought full quivers of elven arrows and handed both them and the bows to Uliah and Jali. They also handed the two satyr bowmen a small dagger each. They then brought in the satyr's spears and handed them to Faljon,

Shanja, and Peton. Next, they brought the satyr's swords in and handed them to Faljon, Shanja, Delok, and Peton. Kaitlynn and Peton looked at each other, confused.

Finally, the Queen herself brought forth a sword that was about a bit longer than the satyr's swords and handed it to Kaitlynn. There were intricate carvings on the blade. She held it in her right hand, and despite its additional length, it felt lighter and more perfectly balanced than the sword she had been carrying. The King then handed her a round metal shield that was just as light with similar carvings on it. Kaitlynn strapped it around her left forearm and bowed to the elven royalty. "Thank you," she said. The other satyrs echoed her.

"The threat is dire, and we shall stand as one against it," replied King Delavon. "Our hopes go with you to retrieve the Gate before any harm can be done to either world. But we shall prepare for war against Uligart and the frost elves regardless. For their treachery brings peril to all Somalie, and this we cannot abide."

The King and Queen of Elfwood bowed then to Kaitlynn and the party of satyrs. Then they turned and bowed to Derrith. It was clear that the patrol captain was uncomfortable with his lord and lady bowing to him, and he returned the bow quickly. The King called over his attendants and had them begin sending out messages to the other nations of Somalie.

Derrith turned to look at the party of satyrs. He was wearing armor similar to Kaitlynn's, except instead of a leather skirt attached to the bottom, he wore leather greaves. He carried a bow much like the ones given to Uliah and Jali, as well as a sword much like the one given to Kaitlynn. He looked at Faljon and said, "I can lead you out of Elfwood, and I've seen the Obsidian Keep. It is many days march from here, and the Frostspire Mountains are steep and covered in snow. It will be dangerous."

"We trust in your knowledge," replied Faljon. "You are most welcome among us."

After the party was lowered down on the platform from the walkway to the forest floor, Derrith took the lead and led them south through the forest.

34

The raven had watched the group of satyrs enter the realm of Elfwood but hadn't dared to follow them. The elves there would have certainly sensed the magic within it and recognized it. That was something that could not be risked. Its master had already been displeased by the fact it had been forced to show itself to kill the goblin that had almost talked. Luckily the raven had been spared its master's wrath on the account that it had, in fact, silenced the goblin before it could do so.

The raven had waited for hours, but after the satyrs and their strange companion had entered Elfwood, they had not come back out. Finally, it had decided to fly back to the Obsidian Keep and inform its master what it could. It was almost all the way through the mountain pass now, fighting its way through the brutal winds.

The Obsidian Keep was a large castle nestled up against the side of the mountain and surrounded by a large wall on its other three sides. There were about a hundred frost elves manning the wall with bows in hand, and a few catapults behind the walls. In the center of the walled fortress stood a single large tower made of the same black stone as the walls below. The tower was a perfect square of at least ten floors that looked down across the Frostspire Pass for miles in either direction.

As the raven neared the keep, it could see its master barely more than a white outline against the sky, standing at the top of the tower. The raven closed the distance and landed carefully on the parapet. Its master looked at it and said, "Speak."

Its master had pale white skin, white hair, and ice blue eyes. He wore a heavy white cloak with the hood up to protect himself against the wind. He was tall, even for an elf, and there were slight age lines around his eyes. His left hand was gnarled and black and hung limply by his side.

The raven squawked a few times, and the frost elf listened. Eventually, it replied in disgust, "Elfwood! Are you certain?" The raven appeared to nod and then squawked again. "We cannot take any further chances," he said to the raven. "Find Golash and bring him here. I have need of his goblins."

The raven took off and headed south towards the swampy lands beyond the mountains. It hoped that it could find suitable food along the way, as it flew past the large frost elven village nestled along the side of the mountains in the pass just a few miles past the keep. The mountain passes beyond there would be desolate and it hadn't eaten in hours. It did not want to have to wait as long as the goblin's swamps on the other side of the pass. Strange things festered there that weren't suitable for eating.

35

The elven patrol captain led them through the forest, weaving in and out of the thick trees and dark underbrush for many hours. It was just before dark when they finally emerged from the tree line and found themselves just off the path they had been following to the south, though the campsite they had left behind the night before was far to the north and out of sight. The Frostspire Mountains still seemed impossibly far away to the south, and now that Kaitlynn knew what waited for them there, they seemed far more ominous against the horizon than they had before.

As they got back onto the path, they could see the sun starting to fall behind the trees of Elfwood to the west, and Faljon called a halt to the party to set camp for the night. Derrith took Peton with him back into the forest to grab fuel for a fire, and Uliah and Faljon went off to hunt for food for the group. Kaitlynn sat down next to Jali, who along with Uliah and Peton had been especially quiet throughout today's trek.

"Are you all right?" Kaitlynn asked her.

"Too much Gorkaberry wine," she replied, her eyes down.

"Look, no one has anything to be embarrassed about," said Kaitlynn. "Everyone needs to blow off a little stress sometimes. Hell, if there had been a human male around last night, who knows what I would have done to him. I've got months' worth of stress I'd like to get rid of."

Jali looked at her and gave a half smile. "Maybe the elf would suit you," she said.

"Honestly, I'm not sure if the mechanics are all the same or not," she replied with a chuckle. "Besides, I think Faljon's a bit smitten and I wouldn't want to hurt his feelings like that," she thought to herself. "Anyway, it's one thing to do it all behind closed doors. It's another to go for a roll in the grass in front of everyone," she said to Jali. Their eyes met and the two of them laughed for a while at that.

It wasn't long before the others returned with food and fuel. Derrith had grabbed some fruit from one of the trees in the forest as well as bringing back fuel for the fire with Peton. He declined any of the meat the from Faljon and Uliah's kills and sat on the outskirts of the campsite eating his bounty instead.

Uliah and Peton sat down next to Jali, and they both had their heads down. Kaitlynn looked at Jali and said, "I'll let you handle those two." They both chuckled a little and dug into their dinner.

Watches were set for the night, and Derrith joined Uliah on the first shift. With their number back to eight, they were able to go back to four sets of two for watches. As the others began bedding down for the night, Kaitlynn began unbuckling her armor. Derrith walked over and said, "You're better off sleeping in that."

Kaitlynn nodded at him and redid the one buckle she had undone and then laid down in the grass. She used her backpack as a pillow and laid her sword and shield on the ground next to her. She was surprised to find that she was able to get quite comfortable in her armor, far more comfortable than she had been when she slept on the ground in her clothes previously. She looked up at Derrith and asked, "How is it that I'm more comfortable in this than I was without it?"

"Elven enchantments," he said, before walking off to take his side of the camp for the watch. Kaitlynn shrugged and lay back down on the ground. It wasn't long before she had drifted off.

36

Kaitlynn had been awoken for her watch by Shanja and was standing by the edge of the firelight looking south towards the mountains in the distance. They were a dark gray outline against the black sky of the night, even with her eyes adjusted to the dark. She couldn't imagine how far away they still were. After a while, she looked around at the other satyrs sleeping around the fire, and the elf who seemed to position himself just outside of the rest of the group. Faljon was standing watch looking back down the path to the north from which they would have come if they hadn't taken their trek through the forest. She walked over to him and stood next to him, looking back towards the south to keep an eye out.

"I didn't want to ask in front of the King and Queen, but what's a wyvern?" she asked.

Faljon glanced at her. "Large, winged beasts," he said. "Like a dragon, only two legs instead of four."

"I'm guessing it breathes fire too," Kaitlynn said, her voice sounded heavy with dread.

"No," responded Faljon, "but they have a poison stinger on their tails as well. Very dangerous nonetheless."

"And this Uligart has at least one of them under his control. Greeeaaat," she said.

Faljon shook his head. "Not great. Very, very bad," he said.

"They don't have sarcasm on this side of the painting, do they?" she asked.

"What is 'sarcasm'?" he asked.

"How do I do that thing where I teach you my language? Maybe that'll help explain the concept," she said.

"You put your hand on their forehead and bring all of the warmth to your hand," he said. "You can then pass a tongue to another."

"All right then, do you mind?" she asked. He shook his head no and turned to look at her.

She placed her hand on his forehead and remembered the memory of her and her father on the deck again. Soon the warmth spread from her chest throughout her entire body. She focused on her hand and felt all the warmth go there. There was a white light coming from her palm. She could see inside the language portion Faljon's mind almost like looking at a picture and saw that English was not there. Like reaching in and touching two wires together, she put her language in his mind, and then took her hand away from his forehead. For the first time in days, she spoke English. "Do you understand me?" She asked.

There was a moment where it looked like Faljon was trying to process the strange sounds he was hearing, and then suddenly it was as if the light went on inside. "I do understand," he said in perfect English. He smiled his toothy grin at her. "Tis the first time someone has given language to me. Tis an odd feeling."

"Yeah, I know what you mean," replied Kaitlynn. "I had no idea what you were doing to me when you taught me Satyrn. Imagine never having seen one of your kind before, and then next thing you know there's a glowing light right in front of your face. I thought I was dying."

Faljon nodded and looked away. "I'm sure it was quite an experience," he said quietly.

"I ... I didn't mean..." Kaitlynn stammered. "Look, you've all been fantastic to me. Like I said, it was just the initial shock, you know?"

Faljon nodded silently. "I forget that we must be strange to you," he said.

"You're getting less strange all the time," she said with a smile. "Look, on my side, sometimes people treat others who look different as if they're somehow inferior. They judge each other by their skin color, their religion, or their nationality. It's wrong. Most people just want to live in peace and have the same opportunities as everyone else. It's sad that some people still try to divide us over something so superficial." She paused and took a deep breath. "You may be different than I am, but you are all good people. It was just a little bit more of a shock to the system than something like different skin color at first. But I couldn't have made better friends in either of our worlds."

She put her hand on his shoulder and squeezed it gently, and he turned and looked at her. There was a look in his eyes that she couldn't quite identify. "Thank you," he said. "You are a good friend too."

She smiled at him and leaned down and gave him a kiss on the cheek again, before wandering back over to the other side of the camp to resume her watch. She looked back over her shoulder and saw Faljon glancing over his own shoulder at her. He looked away as soon as she saw him. Without realizing it she smiled and returned to her watch silently beaming to herself.

When the rest of the party awoke in the morning, Kaitlynn and Shanja stepped away and sparred for a while as the others dealt with hunting for food. Kaitlynn didn't want to admit it, but she was looking forward to trying out her new sword and shield, as well as seeing how well she could move in her new armor. She and Shanja bowed to each other and began circling one another. She noticed over Shanja's shoulder that both Faljon and Derrith had taken an interest in their duel and were watching the two of them closely.

Shanja attacked in a vicious flurry, and Kaitlynn dodged and parried as she had practiced. After a few passes, it occurred to her that she wasn't using the shield at all and was reacting from the habit of only having the sword in her right hand instead. She waited and with Shanja's next attack, she blocked with the shield, pushed back into her with a sudden charge, and swiped with the flat of her blade into the satyr's side. Shanja went down in a heap on the ground and looked up with surprise in her eyes. It was the first time Kaitlynn had scored a blow on either of the satyrs that had been training her, and she had done so decisively, sending Shanja down to the ground with force.

"Are you okay?" Kaitlynn asked, sheathing her sword and offering her hand to the satyr.

Shanja looked up at her for a second before taking her hand and pulling herself up. "Your new weapons suit you," she said. She sheathed her sword and pulled her spear off her back instead. "Let's see how you do against a different weapon."

She thrusted with the spear quickly, and Kaitlynn blocked it with her shield. The two repeated the motions a couple more times. Then Shanja stabbed low below her shield. Kaitlynn angled her shield down to knock the spear away and swipe with the flat of her blade again, but instead found herself catching air with her shield as the butt end of the spear slammed her hard in the stomach, just below the rib cage. She bent over in a heap involuntarily and gasped for air.

"Are you all right?" asked Shanja. Kaitlynn put up a hand and took a couple of steps backward before falling onto her backside. Her chest felt like it was on fire and the air wouldn't come for a couple of minutes until slowly her breathing became normal.

"Yeah, you just … caught me … pretty good," she said between breaths as the air came back. "I guess … we're even."

Shanja gave her a half smile. "Remember, the spear has two sides," she said. "The end with the tip is only one of them."

"Yeah, I think I got that now," replied Kaitlynn, starting to feel better again, though the recovery was slow. She hadn't had the wind knocked out of her in a long time and had forgotten how miserable it felt. She wondered how much worse that blow would have been without her armor on.

"Different weapons require different defense," said Shanja. "But remember, even with the sword, there is always the other hand. Be aware of where both hands are. Both are weapons, armed or not."

Kaitlynn slid her sword back into her scabbard and forced herself up off the ground. "Well, I think for a while we should stick to theory until I can breathe normally," she said. She tried to give Shanja a smile, but a groan came out instead as she slipped back down to one knee. "Okay, maybe we're not ready to stand yet," she said under her breath.

Derrith walked over to her and looked down at her. "May I?" he said, pointing at her shield. She slid it off her arm and handed it up to him. He put it on, pulled his sword, and began circling Shanja. He waited for her to strike, and when she did, he blocked the spear out wide with his shield and swiped with the flat of his blade across her arm right at the point of the elbow. She dropped the spear and grabbed her arm.

"What did you do?" she asked him, rubbing her elbow. "I can't feel anything in my arm!"

"Give it a moment and the feeling will return," he said to her, before turning to Kaitlynn. "A spear is a weapon that requires two hands. Take one off." He dropped her shield in front of her and walked off without another word.

Faljon watched the elf walk off, and then came over and checked on both Shanja and Kaitlynn. Kaitlynn finally felt strong enough to stand, and Shanja was shaking her arm vigorously trying to get the sensation to come back into it. "He's right, even if he was kinda a dick about it," said Kaitlynn, glaring over her shoulder at the elf. "We call that 'hitting our funny bone,' because it feels kinda weird. But it goes away in a few minutes."

"I deserved it," replied Shanja. "I hit you about as hard as I could. I was embarrassed that you knocked me down. I apologize." She kept shaking her arm as she spoke.

"Nothing to apologize for," replied Kaitlynn. She was still a bit out of breath, but she was starting to feel better. "I appreciate his help," she said quietly while nodding towards the elf, "but I could do without his attitude."

"We are all in this together," replied Faljon. "He knows the risk is dire and will do what he must."

"I wasn't suggesting we send him home or anything," Kaitlynn said, a somewhat defiant tone to her voice.

Faljon simply nodded and looked back towards the camp. Peton and Jali had come back with breakfast, and they had begun cooking at the fire. "We should go. We have a long day ahead," he said. He headed off towards the fire and the other two followed.

After breakfast, they headed off to the south again. The giant Frostspire Mountains in the distance seemed no closer than they had been days ago when they had first turned south towards them. But they were beginning to see some terrain that was more than just rolling fields. They could see a rock formation ahead to the southeast and could smell some sort of bog off in the distance as well.

Kaitlynn and Shanja walked together for most of the morning bringing up the rear of the line. Both of them were feeling better now that they'd had a chance to recover and eat. They could see Derrith and Faljon out ahead of the rest of the group leading the way, and the other satyrs had filed in behind.

"So, tell me, was that all of the satyrs when I met you at Faljon's burrow?" Kaitlynn asked.

"No," replied Shanja. "We satyrn are the guardians of Keeper's Wood. Many other satyrn live in the wood, and elsewhere in Somalie."

"Are they all like you guys?" Kaitlynn asked. "I don't remember much of the mythology I learned in school, but usually satyrs were depicted much different."

"How so?" asked Shanja.

"A lot less duty and honor, and a lot more music and dancing," replied Kaitlynn. "Lots of drinking wine and chasing women ... that's what I remember anyway."

"Well, I believe there was plenty of that in Elfwood," replied Shanja with a glint in her eye. "But duty has always been important to our people. So has love. Both are important." She paused and smiled at Kaitlynn. "But you know this already."

"What do you mean?" Kaitlynn asked, raising an eyebrow at the satyr.

"You and the Keeper. You look at each other," she replied, her voice low so that it would not carry to the others.

Kaitlynn chuckled slightly. "Well, I will say ... I think he's got a crush, that's true," she said echoing the satyr's tone of voice. "But I ... he's not ..." She blushed slightly while searching for the right words. This reaction surprised her somewhat. "I'm human," she finally said, her voice flat. "And he's a friend." Shanja quietly raised an eyebrow again as if to protest but said nothing more on the subject as they continued walking and making small talk.

As midday approached, they found the path weaving slightly towards the southeast, and the rock formation was quickly approaching. Kaitlynn looked at the strange rocks and wondered how they had gotten there, so far from the mountains. One of them looked like it might be as tall as fifteen feet, and thirty feet long in an oblong shape that rose higher on one end than the other. It looked like about half of it might still be buried underground. There were a number of other large boulders here as well, and Kaitlynn wondered if there had once been large glaciers and an Ice Age here on Somalie like there had once been on Earth. She saw Derrith and Faljon stop up ahead, and the rest of the group quickly caught up with them.

"Are we stopping?" asked Uliah.

Faljon shook his head. "Not until we check that out," he said, pointing at the large pile of rocks just off the path. "Good place for an ambush. Wait here," he said, as he and Derrith started to head off.

"Keeper, wait," said Jali. "You are too important to risk, I will go."

Faljon tried to wave her off, but the other satyrs chimed in, each offering to go in his stead. Finally, he relented and allowed Jali to go in his stead, though he seemed somewhat put out by everyone else worrying more about his wellbeing than their own. Jali and the elf made their way over to the rock formation, staying quiet and low to the ground.

They reached the edge of the rocks, and Derrith looked quickly over the top of one before ducking quickly back down. He went to grab Jali by the shoulder, but it was too late. She had gone around one of the rocks and started to enter the formation. He reached out and grabbed for her belt and missed, catching her tail instead and pulling her back hard. She looked over at him with a fierce gaze, but she froze when she saw the look of terror frozen on his face. He motioned to her to go back, and they headed back towards the others. About halfway back he turned and said something to Jali, and her face went white.

"No ambush, but a nasty pit of vipers," said Derrith when they got back. "We'd better move on just in case." Faljon nodded and they continued down the path.

Kaitlynn couldn't help but notice Jali looking back over her shoulder at the rocks as they passed them and put them in the distance behind. She quickened her pace to walk next to Jali, put an arm around her shoulders, and gave her a quick hug. She could feel the satyr shaking. "You're okay," she said quietly. Jali nodded wordlessly, and they continued until the rocks were far behind before stopping for lunch.

37

The large raven landed on the highest rock of the formation and watched the party continue off into the distance. The addition of the elf to the party boded ill, and it would have to report that to its master.

It had spent a day and a half circling near the forest of Elfwood looking for the group of satyrs and their strange companion. It had finally caught a glimpse of them in the distance and flown to catch up. It was tired and hungry, but it couldn't let them out of its sight. It needed to let its master know if they fell into the trap he had set for them ahead.

It looked down and saw the pit of venomous snakes nesting inside the rock formation below. It eyed a smaller one and dove quickly, plucking it out of the group with its claws and flew off before any of the other vipers could react. It had grabbed the small snake right behind the head with one of its claws, and it tore through it with its talons and ripped the head clean off. It then sucked the rest of the snake down whole as it flew off to the south.

38

After walking quite a ways past the rock formation, Kaitlynn could see the ground starting to fall away ahead and the wretched scent of the bog was getting stronger. As they crested the top of the short hill and looked down the other side, the rolling grasslands gave way to a large swamp that looked like it would take a couple of hours to cross.

Faljon turned and looked at the rest of the group. "We'll stop here." Per usual, some of the party went off looking for food, and others went off looking for fuel for a fire. Faljon pulled Kaitlynn aside and sparred with her for a bit while they waited for the others to return. After lunch, they started down the hill towards the path through the middle of the swamp.

As the last of the party entered the swamp, there was movement on either side of them. Suddenly strange creatures that looked like six-foot-tall lizards that could stand on two legs rose out of the waist-deep water. They seemed to be a variety of colors, from shades of green, to brown, to black. The creatures all seemed to be carrying large spears and began advancing on all sides. With lightning speed, Jali and Uliah pulled their bows and started firing at the strange lizard creatures. They each took down one with their first shots, one arrow impaling a creature in the eye with a wretched popping sound, and they prepared to fire again. Kaitlynn and the others drew their own weapons and prepared for battle.

Kaitlynn looked over to her left and saw Derrith reach out with his left hand with his palm up, make a fist, and then pull it back down again. She saw some of the swamp vines come up from below the murky water, completely entangle one of the lizardmen, and then pull it back down under the water as it thrashed wildly against them.

Kaitlynn turned her head and saw one of the lizard creatures charging directly at her. Taking what she had seen Derrith do earlier that morning in sparring to heart, she slammed its spear away with her shield and lopped the lizardman's left arm off just below the shoulder. Blood poured from the wound, and she felt the spray hit her in the face and arms. With her next attack, she stabbed it in the center of its chest, impaling it all the way through. The lizard tried to chomp down on her with its massive jaws, but it seemed to have no fight left in it, and she kicked it off her sword as its body went limp.

She turned and saw another one bearing down on Delok, who slid down under the lizard's spear attack and swiped at its legs. It went down in a heap, and with a single motion Delok stood up and stabbed it through the back of the neck. There was a loud hissing sound as its life expired.

Kaitlynn turned around again just in time to see another one charging at her from her right. She got her shield up just in time to block its spear, but its massive jaws opened at her. It was like staring down the throat of a crocodile. She reached out quickly and stabbed the lizardman directly in its open mouth and out through the top of its head. Its teeth dug into the meaty part of her forearm and its blood mixed with hers all over her right arm, but the light left its eyes and it slumped over. She pulled her sword out as it fell. Ignoring the pain in her arm, Kaitlynn turned and saw another one of the creatures bearing down on Uliah, who fired her bow, hitting it in the midsection. It slowed, bending over involuntarily upon impact, and then another arrow from her bow pierced it directly through the eye and it dropped.

Behind Uliah, Kaitlynn saw Jali turning with her bow in hand and grabbing for another arrow, but one of the lizard creatures was charging her from behind. Kaitlynn charged the distance yelling for Jali to move, but the satyr turned and saw the lizardman a moment too late. She tried to dodge, but the spear pierced her side. Kaitlynn charged in and bashed the lizard in the face with her shield and then sliced its head clean off while it was dazed. Its blood poured out of its neck like a fountain as its body fell to the ground. She looked back at Jali, who was on the ground holding her side and positioned herself over the injured satyr to protect her from further attack.

Kaitlynn took a quick look around the battlefield and saw Faljon with his spear impaling one of the lizardmen through its throat. He let his spear go as the lizard's blood poured down it, pulled his sword, and ran behind another one that Peton was fighting, slicing it across the back of its legs. It went down and Peton's spear impaled it through the chest as it fell, killing it.

As Kaitlynn continued to scan the battlefield, Derrith ran over to her and Jali, the elvish runes on his own sword obscured with blood and knelt down by the injured satyr. He looked up at Kaitlynn and yelled, "Cover us!" before turning back to Jali. He dropped his sword on the ground and put both of his hands over the wound. He closed his eyes and began chanting something in elvish. Kaitlynn turned and saw another lizard charging at her. She braced herself for its charge but saw Shanja run in from its side and impale it with her spear just under the arm. Kaitlynn ran up and stabbed it through the heart to finish it off, kicking it off her blade as it fell. She turned back to look at Jali and saw that the wound on her side had stopped bleeding, though she still looked far worse for wear than Kaitlynn would have liked.

The battle had raged but ended in only a matter of minutes. The rest of the lizards had fallen, and it looked like other than Jali, the rest of the party had suffered only superficial wounds. Looking around, there were at least a dozen reptilian bodies littered around the group, and blood seemed to be forming lakes all around them. She watched as Faljon walked over to the edge of the water where the one lizard had been pulled under the murky water by the vines that Derrith had controlled and was thrashing about. He stabbed it through the chest twice to make sure it was dead, and then turned back towards the rest of the party, reclaiming his spear along the way. "Is Jali all right?" he asked as he walked over and knelt next to the injured satyr.

Derrith nodded. "She'll recover, but we shouldn't move her today," he replied. "I exhausted the rest of my magic stabilizing her. I'll need to meditate."

Faljon nodded, and then looked around at the rest of the group. Peton had a small cut above his eye, and Shanja was bleeding from a gash on her upper arm. Otherwise, no one else had been hurt. Kaitlynn slipped her backpack off and pulled out her t-shirt. She sighed, as it had been the only piece of clothing that she thought might have been salvageable. "Let me see one of those knives," she said. Uliah handed her dagger to her, and Kaitlynn began cutting pieces of the shirt into long strips. She handed three of them to Uliah, and one larger strip to Derrith and stuffed the remains of her shirt back into her bag. Uliah began by bandaging the bite wound on

Kaitlynn's forearm and then moved on to take care of Shanja and Peton. Derrith bound Jali's wound tightly to make sure it didn't start bleeding again.

"Is it safe to move her back to the campsite at least?" asked Delok. Derrith nodded and lifted the injured satyr carefully into his arms. Any negative thoughts Kaitlynn had had about the elf earlier this morning were gone now.

While Derrith took Jali back up to the campsite, the rest of the party worked to toss the bodies of the lizardmen back into the swamp where any predators could get them without coming up onto the path. There had been fifteen of them in all. Uliah went around retrieving whatever arrows could be recovered from the corpses and retrieved Jali's bow off the ground. The murky swamp had a horrible stench to it, but everyone used it to get as much blood and grime off of themselves as they could without having to actually enter the still waters of the bog.

Eventually, they all made their way back up to the campsite. From the edge of the rise, Kaitlynn looked back down towards the swamp and the bloodstained path; she had killed four of the lizard creatures herself, and yet she felt completely numb about it. She wondered if the fact that they looked so much less like humans made a difference in her reaction but dismissed the idea. The goblins hadn't exactly looked all that human either. "I guess it does get easier," she thought to herself. She turned to go back to the rest of the group and saw Faljon walking over to her. He was looking at the makeshift bandage on her arm.

"Are you well, Keeper?" he asked.

She looked down at her arm and said, "Yeah, a bit of a bite wound but I'm fine." She looked back at the camp. "I'm far more worried about Jali."

Faljon nodded and looked back at the camp as well. "Derrith says she will be all right. He should be able to heal her further once he rests."

"Well, she's gonna have matching scars now," replied Kaitlynn, forcing a smile.

Faljon forced a smile at her as well. It was not his usual toothy grin, but far more serious. "We'll have to be careful from here on out," he said, his tone serious. "Uligart likely set this trap. There will be more of them to come, I would expect."

"What were those things?" asked Kaitlynn.

"Lizardmen," he replied. "Not unusual to find in a swamp, but that many together at once?" He shook his head, finishing the unspoken thought.

She nodded at him, and then looked back towards the swamp. "I'll keep watch for a while then," she said. "Let me know how Jali is doing though."

Faljon nodded at her. "You fought well," he said.

"Thanks to you and Shanja," she replied with a forced smile.

He took another glance at her injured arm with concern in his eyes and then walked back towards the camp. Kaitlynn watched him go, and then turned back to the swamp below, watching for any additional movement.

39

It was nearly nightfall, and the elf had been meditating for a few hours. Kaitlynn had maintained the watch for most of that time, but Shanja had come over and relieved her within the last hour. She was grateful for the chance to rest. She sat down on the grass next to Jali and held her hand. "How are you doing, champ?" she asked, forcing a smile.

"I've felt better," the satyr responded. "I have you to thank. If you hadn't charged in, I might not be laying here, but down there instead."

Kaitlynn blushed and looked down at the makeshift bandage across the satyr's abdomen. There were some small blood spots where the wound had reopened a bit. "Well, I couldn't let that thing turn you into a kabob," she said. "Besides, Derrith is the one that healed you."

"I have already thanked him," replied Jali. She closed her eyes, and her voice sounded tired.

The elf finally stirred from his meditation and came over to them. "Keeper, I'll need to see the wound," he said.

Kaitlynn skirted around to the other side of the wounded satyr and held Jali's other hand while the elf knelt and examined the wound. "How bad is it?" Jali asked through gritted teeth.

"I've seen worse," replied Derrith, "but that was on a corpse." He gave her a smile. "In all honesty, you're very lucky to be alive. If it had managed to hit you a little bit deeper, there wouldn't have been anything I could have done. It got you good, but the worst of it is already healed. I should be able to heal the rest of the damage now. You'll need to rest through the night though. No watch for you."

"Don't worry Derrith, Jali's a good sleeper," Kaitlynn joked. The satyr glared at her and then rolled her eyes. "She should be fine by morning then."

Derrith nodded without a word. He put his hands on the wound, closed his eyes, and began chanting in elvish again. Kaitlynn watched as the remaining damage started to slowly heal itself. After a few minutes, the elf took a deep breath and opened his eyes. There was a nasty pink scar on Jali's side where the wound had been, but the wound itself was completely closed.

"You'll need to rest for the magic to finish repairing your body," he said to Jali. She nodded.

Kaitlynn turned and looked at Uliah, who had been sitting a few feet away, watching. "Can you do that thing you did that helped me sleep?" The satyr nodded and walked over, put her hands over Jali's eyes, and a moment later, she was deep in sleep.

The elf looked at them a moment before standing up. "I'll let you look after her for a while, Keeper. I need to recharge my magic again."

"Thank you," Kaitlynn said to him, and he nodded. "And not just for what you did by healing her. That shield thing you taught me this morning saved my life in the fight earlier." He smiled at her then and nodded again before walking away and positioning himself to meditate once more.

Eventually, Faljon replaced Shanja on the watch, and she and Delok went off to search for food while Peton and Uliah looked for more fuel for the fire. Kaitlynn stayed by Jali's side and kept an eye on the satyr to make sure she stayed asleep and recovered her strength. Peton and Uliah returned after a while with an armload each of more wood. It was a bit longer before Shanja and Delok returned. They brought back what looked like a fox, but it had a greenish color to its fur. Kaitlynn had never seen anything like it before but imagined it must help it blend into the environment. The satyrs began preparing it for the fire. As dinner got closer to being ready, Derrith roused himself from his meditation and came over to them.

"She'll need to eat," he said to Kaitlynn.

"I was wondering that," she replied. "I'll make sure she gets taken care of."

He nodded at her and began heading away from camp. Delok saw him start to head off and then yelled after him, "Derrith!" The elf turned around and Delok threw a strange fruit to him. The elf caught it with one hand, looked at it, and then nodded his approval at the satyr before returning to the camp and eating with the rest of them.

Kaitlynn turned to the elf and asked, "Do you not eat meat?"

He shook his head. "Elves do not eat animals at all," he replied. "We take from nature only that which we can give back." He paused for a moment. "I'm sure that seems strange to you."

"No, I have friends who are vegetarians," she replied. "I just love a good burger too much for that myself." She smiled at him, but he just nodded and looked away. "Not much for conversation, that one," she thought to herself.

She looked at Jali, who was sleeping peacefully. She felt bad about it but roused her so that she could eat. After she ate some of the fox, she laid back down. Kaitlynn turned to Uliah who came over and put her hands over Jali's eyes again, putting her back to sleep. "You'll have to teach me how to do that," she said in a whisper to the satyr after she had finished.

Uliah smiled at her and nodded. "We usually use it to help our satyrlings sleep," she said, "or help our elders sleep when they are ill, so they pass in peace." She gave Kaitlynn a wry smile, and then sat down next to Jali and said to Kaitlynn, "Go eat. I've got her."

Kaitlynn went off and tried some of the fox meat. It wasn't great, she thought, but she was hungry and would take what she could get. Faljon sat down next to her, as Peton had eaten and replaced him on the watch.

"How is it?" he asked. She shrugged at him, and he nodded. "How are you?" he asked her.

She looked down at her arm. The makeshift bandage had soaked through and would need to be replaced soon. "I'm okay," she replied. "It got its teeth into me a little bit."

"I mean after the fight," he said quietly. "You had a hard time after the last one."

"Yeah," she said her voice turning somber. "I'll be honest, it bothers me that I kinda took this one in stride. I killed four of those things." She shrugged. "I don't know," she said finally.

Faljon nodded. "It gets easier," he said. "I don't know if that's good or bad, but it does."

She looked at him. There was a sadness in his eyes that she hadn't seen before, and she decided that she didn't like seeing him like that. She put her arm around his shoulders, gave him a light squeeze, and left her arm around him to try and comfort him. She could feel his skin against her arm, and there was something soothing about that for her as well. After a couple of minutes, she looked over at him and saw her blood running down his back from her bandage. "Shit," she said, reaching for her backpack and pulling out what was left of her t-shirt.

Faljon looked at her and then down at her arm. "Let me see," he said. He removed the bandage and looked at the wound. "Tis deep," he said, raising his eyes to meet hers. He grabbed the t-shirt from her and used it to put pressure on the wound. "Derrith!" he called over to the elf and pointed at her arm.

Derrith came over and took a look at the wound. He immediately knelt down next to Kaitlynn and took her arm in his hands. "This is pretty bad," he said, looking at her. "Why didn't you say anything?"

"Jali was much worse off that I was," she replied.

Derrith nodded his understanding at her, and then closed his eyes and began chanting in elvish again. She watched as the wound on her forearm slowly closed. She felt like her energy was being sapped away from her though, as she felt very tired all of a sudden. Eventually, Derrith let go of her arm and she saw that the wound had closed. There was a nasty pink scar there in the shape of a bite mark with three distinct imprints where the teeth had dug into her flesh. Turning to Faljon, he said, "She's off watch for tonight as well, Keeper. She'll need to rest."

Faljon nodded at him. "Join me on the last watch," he said. "That should give you more time to recharge your magic." Derrith nodded and walked off to meditate again.

"Sorry, I got blood on you," said Kaitlynn, her voice sounding like a distant echo even to herself. She laid back into the grass, and Faljon propped her backpack under her head.

"It's fine," Faljon responded. He looked at her, eyes full of concern. "Get some rest." He bent down and gently stroked the hair out of her face, and then placed his hand gently over her eyes. She felt herself drifting off to sleep almost immediately.

40

The raven had circled high above and watched as the satyrs had cleared the bodies off the path. One of them had been injured, but overall, the lizards had failed and paid for their failure with their lives. However, the raven had watched the fight and had much to report regarding the elf joining their party and leaving Elfwood with them. It hoped that what it had to tell its master would spare it any reprisals for the lizards' failure.

It flew off while there was still daylight and made its way towards the Obsidian Keep in the mountains to the south. It searched for food as it flew, the hunger a deep everlasting pang in its gullet, but saw nothing for miles. It would have to hope that its master was feeling generous enough to reward it when it arrived back upon its perch.

41

Kaitlynn felt a light shaking sensation and slowly opened her eyes. Shanja was kneeling next to her and looking down at her. "Time to get up," she said quietly. "Breakfast."

Kaitlynn slowly sat up and looked around. The sun was still low in the sky to the east, and the other satyrs were already up and about. She could see that some of them were already eating, and Uliah was currently working on waking Jali as well. Derrith sat off to the side eating a strange fruit that she had never seen before that looked like some sort of red pear. She looked down at her forearm. The wound was completely healed, but the pinkish scar remained. She figured she'd have to pass it off as a nasty dog bite if she ever got home.

She stood up slowly, taking her time to find her legs. She had felt far more drained the night before than she had expected after Derrith had healed her, and it took a minute for her to steady herself. She looked over and saw Jali finally sitting up as well. She walked over to her and offered her a hand, helping her get up. She had a large pink puncture scar on her right side, slightly higher on her abdomen than the one on her left that she had told Kaitlynn the story of. The new scar still looked gruesome, but Jali seemed in good spirits overall. They went over and joined the others by the fire and ate.

After breakfast, Kaitlynn walked over to Derrith and sat down next to him. "Thank you," she said to him, her voice low but appreciative.

He nodded. "Do you feel well, Keeper?" he asked her.

"Tired, but otherwise I'm good," she replied.

"That is understandable. The healing magic drains both of us," he said. "I can meditate to regain what I have lost, but rest is the only way for the injured." He looked around at the rest of the group, and continued, "Rest is not a real option, unfortunately. We must move."

She nodded to him. "Yeah, I understand. I'd like to get home as soon as possible." She looked at him, but he said nothing. "I'm sure that's not much of a concern to everyone else though."

"Uligart is trying to take over, or destroy my world," he said. "You'll forgive me if your desire to go home seems insignificant to me." There was no anger in his voice, only a flat admission of the facts as he saw them.

Kaitlynn looked down as a wave of embarrassment flowed through her. She knew that her desire to get back to her own world was selfish, but she hadn't really thought much of the greater purpose that the others were fighting for. They weren't fighting for her; they were fighting for their world. She promised herself that she would be more mindful of this fact in the future. "Well, again … thank you," she said as she stood up and prepared for the group to move onward through the swamp again.

It took a little over two hours to clear the swamp, and Kaitlynn was happy to be past it. There were no further incidents, but the stench was still strong. The terrain had changed considerably as well. Gone were the rolling grasslands that they had spent days walking through, replaced now by flat and rocky ground. The Frostspire Mountains finally seemed less like ghosts in the distance. They were larger and somehow more solid to Kaitlynn the closer they became. But even from this distance, they looked far bigger than either the rolling Appalachians where she had grown up or the various peaks around the greater Phoenix area where she had spent most of her adulthood. She hadn't seen the Rockies, or any real mountain range up close before, so she wasn't sure how they compared to what she was facing before her now.

For the first time in days, Kaitlynn's legs felt weary. She wondered if it was the aftereffects of having been healed by the elf in the wake of the battle with the lizardmen in the swamp. She had started to feel like she had been acclimating to the increased physical activity, but today she felt bone tired. She looked over at Jali, and the satyr seemed to be dragging a bit as well. She forced a smile at her and said, "Hey, we're doing okay for the walking wounded, right?" Jali smiled at that and seemed to pick herself up a little bit. Kaitlynn's smile became more natural as well and kept her legs churning despite the soreness in her muscles. Her calves in particular, felt like they might rebel against her at any minute.

They passed a rare clump of trees and Peton and Uliah grabbed as much deadwood as they could find rather than risk stopping later and not having fuel for a fire. After another couple of hours, they came to an area with a little bit of grass instead of being all rocks and dirt and decided to stop for lunch. It was still a bit before midday, but Kaitlynn was happy to give her legs a break.

Delok and Shanja went off looking for food in the sparse landscape. It took them quite a while but eventually came back with a couple of handfuls of gorkaberries each. They had found a bush with the fruit growing just as they had been getting ready to turn back and give up. Kaitlynn took some of the berries and ate them happily. Shortly after finishing her portion, she could feel the ache in her legs starting to dissipate a bit. She looked over at Jali and saw that she looked better as well.

Their break for lunch was longer than they would have liked due to the lengthy search for food, so the party moved out without further delay. Kaitlynn felt genuinely refreshed and moved up to the front of the line and walked next to Faljon. The satyr looked over to his left at her and smiled his toothy grin at her.

"You look well, Keeper," he said. "I ... we were worried about you." He tried to pass the slight slip of the tongue off nonchalantly, but Kaitlynn had noticed it. His concern warmed her heart. She smiled at him and put a hand on his shoulder. "How is your arm?" he asked her.

"Well, it's gonna scar," she said, turning it over and showing off the pinkish bite mark. "I'll have to come up with an interesting story of how it happened," she added with a chuckle. "But otherwise, it feels good."

Faljon reached over and touched the wound gently. Kaitlynn noticed that his fingers felt good on her forearm. He pulled his hand away slowly, letting the tips linger for a moment, and said, "I am glad you are well." He was looking at her, and Kaitlynn suddenly felt like she could get lost in his eyes. She turned away, blushing slightly. She had known that the satyr had feelings for her. He didn't hide it well, much as he tried. But she hadn't realized until now that she had been developing feelings for him as well. She felt slightly embarrassed, as he wasn't even human like she was. "I'm only part human," she thought to herself. She wasn't sure if that made her feel better or worse. She glanced over at him with just her eyes. He was handsome, despite the fact that he clearly wasn't human. His features were chiseled in a way that she had to admit that she found attractive. His arms and chest were well defined if not overly muscular. She glanced down and saw what he was working with down below. The coarse hair-like fur around his genitals snapped her back to reality somewhat, and she brought her eyes forward. "I'm letting my loneliness get the better of me," she thought to herself, and they continued walking in silence for a while.

It was almost dark, but the rocky landscape didn't seem to be letting up at all. Finally, Faljon called a halt to the party, and they set up camp. The search for food and wood for a fire was fruitless, and the ground was hard and uncomfortable. But they needed whatever rest they could get. Hopefully, the ground ahead would improve in the morning.

Kaitlynn sat down on a rock and flexed her tired legs. She could hear her stomach growling but tried to ignore it. She had watched as Shanja and Delok had come back empty-handed and knew that there would be no sating her belly tonight.

She sat for a while in silence and watched as everyone else tried to find decent places to sleep with little luck. Eventually, Derrith and Uliah took up the first watch, but nearly everyone else was still awake. Only Peton seemed able to fall asleep in the rough terrain.

"Tis only going to get worse when we arrive at the Frostspires," said Faljon, who had sat down next to Kaitlynn without her noticing. "It will be rocky, cold. There will be wind and snow as well. Food will be scarce. You should rest while you can."

"Not sure if I can, but I'll try," she replied. "At least we'll have water though, even if it's frozen. Do you know if it'll clear up between here and there?"

Faljon nodded his head. "Derrith says it will," he replied. "I take him at his word."

"If we can find some fruit and vegetables, I can carry those in my backpack instead of my old clothes," she said. "I can keep my coat and gloves, but everything else is basically ruined anyway and it'll be better to be prepared once we get in the mountains."

Faljon nodded his approval and made like he was going to stand. "I'll go check on the others," he said.

"Hey, you need rest too," she said to him and flashed him a smile.

"I will try," he replied. "But you and Jali especially need to finish healing and regain your strength."

"I'm well enough to join you on watch tonight," she replied. "The gorkaberries helped a lot. Whenever we have them, I feel like all my aches and pains go away."

He nodded at her. "There is a healing magic in them," he conceded. "Fine then, I'll wake you when it's time. For now, rest." He stood up and walked over to Jali. Kaitlynn assumed he was going to give her the same message.

Kaitlynn kicked away as many small rocks as she could to give herself space to sleep. She took her sweatshirt out of her backpack and laid it down on the ground to lie on, and then used the rest of its contents as her pillow as usual. It was hardly comfortable, but she lay down and tried to rest as best as she could.

42

I t was morning, and Shanja was gently shaking her awake. Kaitlynn blinked a couple of times and looked up. "Time to go," said the satyr to her.

"Did I sleep through my watch?" she asked her voice full of confusion.

Shanja smiled at her. "We let you and Jali sleep. You needed it," she replied.

Kaitlynn frowned. She didn't like people making special accommodations for her; it made her feel guilty. She imagined that was how her father had felt those last few months. He had always been a self-sufficient man, but in the end, Kaitlynn had had to take care of his every need. She knew he hadn't liked that, even if he was happy to have her back home again.

She brushed off her sweatshirt without thinking and stuffed it back into her backpack, threw it on over her shoulders, and grabbed her weapons. She made her way over to the rest of the group, who were already prepared to move out. They headed out again, weaving in and out of the rocks and sticking to the path as best they could. After a few hours, they could finally see some green in the distance ahead, but Kaitlynn figured it would be most of the day before they reached it. They continued through midday, skipping their normal lunch break, and Kaitlynn could see the rolling fields in the distance getting closer. The mountains appeared to be creeping closer as well, and she wondered how much longer it would take to get there.

As the sun started to creep about halfway down in the west, the rocky terrain finally started to give way and the grassy plains returned. They continued for another couple of hours before stopping and setting up camp for the night. Kaitlynn and Jali both insisted on doing their part after two days of being on rest duty. They volunteered to go search for wood for a fire, while Uliah and Peton went looking for food.

Kaitlynn had remembered seeing a small grove of trees off to the west about half an hour back, and they made their way back along the path until they saw it again. They left the path and headed for it. As they got closer, Kaitlynn could see that there appeared to be a small pond next to the grove.

"We should have had the others come here," she said. "There might be fish in the pond too."

As they got closer, Jali looked at the water longingly. "I don't know about you, but I could use a bath," she said to Kaitlynn. "Wash some of this blood off."

"The others are waiting for us," said Kaitlynn, though she knew exactly how Jali felt. "We can come back after dinner. There's still a bit of sunlight left."

Jali nodded, and they began searching around the trees for anything that had fallen recently that they could bring back. After a few minutes, they each had an armload and headed back to the camp. Peton and Uliah had already returned with what looked like two large black beavers, but each had a pair of small horns on their heads. Kaitlynn told everyone about the pond by the clump of trees they had been to and suggested that they go in shifts to get cleaned up. Looking around, she saw that they were pretty much all covered in dirt and dust with blood caked on in places. Everyone seemed to be in agreement with the idea, and that pleased her.

After dinner, Jali and Uliah headed off first towards the pond. They came back a little over an hour later, and Derrith and Peton headed out as soon as they saw the others coming in the distance.

Shanja turned to Kaitlynn and said, "Did you want me to go with you when they come back?"

Kaitlynn looked at her, and then over to Delok. "No, it's okay," she said smiling. "I'm sure you two wouldn't mind some time alone."

Shanja smiled back at her, and silently raised a single eyebrow. "I'm sure you wouldn't either," she replied in a sly tone of her voice. Kaitlynn blushed a little bit and waved her off.

When Derrith and Peton became visible in the distance, Delok and Shanja headed off hand in hand. Kaitlynn glanced over at Faljon and while suppressing a chuckle said, "They may be a little bit longer than the others."

Faljon smiled his toothy grin and nodded. "I imagine so," he replied.

It was dark by the time Delok and Shanja returned. They had been gone about half an hour longer than the rest, but they both seemed to have a glow about them as she and Faljon passed them on the path. Kaitlynn chuckled to herself, as Shanja silently mouthed "your turn" to her as they passed. She shook her head and rolled her eyes while simultaneously trying not to blush.

It wasn't hard to find the grove in the dark now that Kaitlynn could adjust her eyes to it. She led Faljon over to the side of the clump of trees where the pond was. The water was clear but didn't look too deep. Faljon walked into the water, and by the time he got to the middle of the pond it was up to just below his chin. He kept his back turned to Kaitlynn and began running the water through his hair with his hands.

Kaitlynn took off her armor and placed it down next to her weapons, which she had leaned against a tree. She then slipped out of her clothes and waded into the water. It was cold, but she barely noticed. There were warm thoughts in her heart, though they were not the ones she had expected to find there. She stood in the water looking at the satyr's outline against the night sky and approached him slowly until she was right behind him. The water only covered about halfway up her breasts and she knew that if he turned around now he would get an eyeful of her. But she found that she didn't care if he did or not. No, she decided that she wanted him to see her, and her skin seemed to flush with even more warmth than before.

Kaitlynn bent down slightly, reached out and wrapped her arms around Faljon, her hands slowly gliding across his chest. The muscles in his chest and arms were firm beneath her fingertips. She pressed herself into his back and put her chin on his shoulder. "Gotcha," she whispered into his ear.

Faljon tensed slightly at her first contact with him, and then slowly relaxed as she wrapped her arms around him. "I did not think…" he started, but she gently placed her hand on the side of his face, turned him to face her and put her lips on his. He turned his whole body to face her and put one hand behind her head. She could feel him running the tips of his claws gently through her hair. His other hand cupped her lower back firmly, holding her against him. He was strong, far stronger than he looked at first glance.

Kaitlynn felt her body temperature rise even more as she wrapped her legs around Faljon's waist and lowered herself down onto him. She pulled away to look at him, but he held her close to him for a moment, his eyes closed, his hands on her hips. He opened his eyes slowly and looked at her as if seeing a work of art for the first time—with awe and wonder. She leaned back, her fingers interlocked around his neck, and they both started to move with each other. Their body temperatures continued to warm until steam started to rise from the once cold water that engulfed their bodies.

43

The large raven sat in one of the trees in the grove, watching the scene below. Two by two the party had come and bathed in the pond. The last two groups had done far more than it seemed. If some of them had connections of the heart, it would be easier for its master to tear them apart. It would need to tell its master of these developments. It would surely be rewarded for this information.

It watched as the final two stepped from the water, hand in hand, and the strange female slowly put her clothes and armor back on. They laughed a few times, a hideous sound to its ears. It wanted to cry out in pain, but held its beak shut, maintaining its silent vigil. It waited until they had made their way down the path to their camp before flying off to the south.

44

Kaitlynn and Faljon walked back down the path to camp hand in hand until they saw the campfire in the distance. Kaitlynn let go then, and Faljon looked at her. "I just don't want to make anyone uneasy," she said, giving him a smile. He nodded at her and they continued.

By the time they got back to camp, Derrith and Jali were already on watch, and everyone else was asleep. Faljon and Kaitlynn took two spots near each other (but not too near) and prepped themselves to bed down for the night. As she lay her head down on her backpack like a makeshift pillow, Kaitlynn felt genuinely happy for the first time since she had arrived in this strange place.

45

Shanja gently woke Kaitlynn again. She was kneeling beside her in the grass as she looked up, smiling down at her. "Hey," said Kaitlynn. "Is it time for my watch?"

Shanja just kept smiling down at her, and finally said, "So?" She raised a single eyebrow at Kaitlynn.

"No," she replied, trying to brush it off. "We took turns. He was a perfect gentleman."

"Liar," said Shanja with a smile. "You mumbled his name in your sleep. I was standing right here when you did it."

Kaitlynn's face turned a deep shade of crimson as panic set in. Her ex-fiancé had told her that she talked in her sleep sometimes and had even recorded her once on his phone to prove it to her. She'd watched the video with a mix of horror and embarrassment, as she'd rambled on in her sleep about spiders and how he wouldn't kill them for her. She stared up at Shanja and blurted out, "Promise not to say anything. I don't want anyone to get wind of this and make things weird."

Shanja looked at her with her eyes wide, put her hands over her mouth, and laughed while Kaitlynn looked at her with pleading eyes. "I lied," she said finally once she calmed down. "I wanted to see what you'd say."

Kaitlynn sat up and punched Shanja in the arm all in one motion. "You bitch!" she whispered, before stifling a laugh herself. "I swear that's the sort of thing one of my friends back home would do to me."

"So?" Shanja repeated, letting the question hang in the air.

"Oh no," replied Kaitlynn. "You don't get details after that stunt you just pulled." That sent them both off into a tizzy again. The two women sat there for a while laughing as quietly as they could. Faljon was already standing guard and looked over at them quizzically for a moment before going back to his watch. None of the others stirred. Eventually, Shanja and

Kaitlynn calmed down, and the satyr went over and lay down next to her mate.

Kaitlynn waited until she was sure Shanja was asleep and walked over to Faljon. "Shanja knows," she said, in a matter-of-fact tone in English.

"I assumed as much by the laughing," he replied in her native tongue. "But I didn't think I was that bad." He gave her his toothy grin again.

"I'll punch you too," she said, rolling her eyes and raising her fist at him. They both laughed then, covering their mouths so that the sound wouldn't carry and wake the others. "She's suspected us for a while, actually, kept pushing me to go for it."

"I'm glad that you did," replied Faljon. "But I thought that you weren't interested."

"Yeah, me too," she said, looking at him. He was keeping his glowing eyes on his watch but took her hand in his. "But I guess I was just scared. I still am a bit, I think." She looked away, turning to the horizon herself. "There's not really a playbook for this sort of thing."

"I understand," he said. "You've had a strange week." He turned and gave her a grin again.

She stifled another laugh. "Yeah, yeah I have," she said, smiling. She bent over and kissed him on the lips, and then went back to the other side of the camp to maintain the watch. Her mind filled with thoughts of her and Faljon making love in the pond, and she began warming herself up without even realizing it. She barely felt the wind pick up or the light rain that started to fall just before morning.

46

By the time the party had prepared to head out for the day, the rain was coming down in buckets. It was a cold rain too, the kind Kaitlynn normally hated, but she managed to keep herself warm despite it. She figured she should probably be glad that it was the first time it had rained since she had gotten here, but the muddy path made the day's march more difficult. Her hardened leather cuirass took to the weather well enough, but she decided to go ahead and toss her coat on if only to try and keep her clothes from soaking through. The clouds in the sky were dark and ominous, and they seemed to stretch on for miles. The idea of stopping and starting a fire in this weather was pointless, so they counted themselves fortunate when they came upon another small grove of trees with fruit on them. Kaitlynn and Derrith climbed up and raided the branches, gathering enough to feed the party. Before climbing back down, Kaitlynn stuffed whatever she could into her backpack. She wrapped her sweatshirt around everything and then tossed her old jeans aside so that she could carry more food. She hated just leaving them there but didn't really know what else to do with them.

They all sat under the trees in the small grove while they ate and then headed out again. Kaitlynn's backpack was significantly heavier than it had been before, but she took on the burden without complaint. They wouldn't get far without food, and somebody had to carry it. They made their way out to the path again, trudging along in the mud. Kaitlynn looked down at her boots and cursed silently to herself. They were caked in muck, and she was afraid that they wouldn't survive this trip to Somalie anymore than her clothes had.

It was some time in the late afternoon when the rain finally started to let up. The road ahead was still a sludge-filled mess for miles, but the rain downgrading from a pour to a drizzle was at least a good sign. They were closing in on another small grove of trees as well, and Kaitlynn hoped that the others would want to stop and get out of the rain for a bit. As they closed on the small grove the sun finally started to peak out from behind the clouds. There was a rainbow on the horizon and Kaitlynn smiled at it. She looked over at the grove and something caught her eye. She thought she saw some sort of glare coming from just inside the edge of the tree line.

"Hold up!" she said, and everyone turned and looked at her. She pointed towards the trees and said, "I saw something over there in the trees, like light shining on metal. It might be an ambush."

Faljon turned back around and looked at the trees. "Everyone get down," he said quietly. The entire party dropped to a knee, Kaitlynn slid off her backpack and coat. "I'll go look."

"No, you won't," said Jali. "I will go."

Faljon shook his head. "Not this time. You are just getting over being hurt. I'll go."

Uliah stepped forward then and said, "No, Keeper. You are too important. I'll go."

The other satyrs all nodded in agreement, and Faljon looked around at them with slight frustration. "I won't keep risking others to protect me," he said.

"We make our own choices, Keeper," responded Shanja as she softly put a hand on his shoulder. "You are our Keeper. Of all of us, you, we cannot lose." The other satyrs nodded agreement again.

"Fine," he demurred. Turning to Uliah, he said, "Stay close to the ground. Get back if you see anything." She nodded and then headed off.

They kept low and watched as she closed the distance to the grove of trees. She bent low to the ground until she got closer, and then dropped. Kaitlynn couldn't make out what she was doing, as the drizzle obscured her vision slightly. She put her hand on her forehead to shield her eyes from the rain, and then she saw the gleam of metal from the trees again. Uliah seemed to see it as well and notched an arrow on her bow. Almost on cue, a row of goblins came pouring out with swords drawn, some tossing rocks, all charging at Uliah as fast as they could in the mire that had accumulated throughout the day. The satyr stood with her bow in hand and fired off a quick shot taking down one of the goblins with a clean headshot before turning and running back towards the group. The mud kicked up around her hooves, slowing her down considerably. Kaitlynn and the others were already on the move towards her as fast as they could go. Derrith managed to get out in front of everyone else as if somehow running on top of the soft ground without sinking into it and passed Uliah. She turned around behind him with another arrow notched just as the elf rammed his sword into one of the goblins, spun quickly and took another one's head clean off. Two more dropped around him, arrows protruding from their chests. Jali now stood at Uliah's side, and she was pulling out arrows as fast as the younger satyr next to her. After they managed to get off another quick volley, a rock flew and slammed Uliah square in the chest, knocking her down to the ground. She sat up, her back completely covered in mud. Jali helped her up, and the two bowmen moved back a bit farther before they resumed firing.

Kaitlynn charged forward and bashed one of the goblins in the face with her shield. It staggered backward and she sliced it across the throat. It dropped, clutching the gaping wound as its life expired, and she moved onto the next one. She parried a quick sword attack with her own and then kicked the goblin in its nether regions. As it buckled over in pain, she stabbed it through the back. As she pulled her sword free of it, the goblin dropped into the mud with a loud thunk.

She looked around quickly and saw Shanja and Delok fighting back-to-back and chopping down goblins all around them. Peton had slammed his spear into a goblin's face and pulled the sword that used to belong to her. He was dueling with another of the goblins as the first one was being propped up on his discarded spear, slowly sliding down its shaft towards the muck below, its eyes completely glazed over. Uliah and Jali stood just far enough away that they could shoot their arrows at anything that they had a clear shot at. Uliah was filthy and had blood running out of an open wound on her left breast where the rock had hit her.

Kaitlynn turned around again and saw another two goblins charging at her. She parried one's attack with her sword and the other with her shield. The one to her left dropped suddenly, an arrow sticking out of its neck. She made short work of its companion, and then looked over at where Derrith stood, bow in hand; she never saw the rock that hit her in the back of the head, only felt the abrupt pain before she descended into darkness.

47

It was dark out when Kaitlynn awoke, her head throbbing like the double bass drums on the latest Metallica album. She opened her eyes and saw Faljon looking down at her. "What happened?" she asked, her voice sounded farther away than it should have.

"You took a rock to the head," he replied, his expression filled with concern. He turned and motioned to someone, and Derrith walked over.

"So, here we are again Keeper," he said, a wry smile forming as he spoke. Kaitlynn was amazed how much different his bedside manner was from his normal personality. It appeared that the only way to make Derrith pleasant to be around was to get injured. She wasn't sure that she wanted to keep getting hurt, however. She preferred to keep all her limbs attached to her body if she could help it.

"Yeah, we need to stop meeting like this," she said, wincing. She touched the back of her head softly and could feel the dried blood and mud caked in her hair. "At least that scar will be covered," she said, giving them both a fake smile. "Is everyone else okay?" she asked, suddenly remembering the battle that had felled her momentarily.

"Everyone's alive," Faljon responded. "Your injury was the worst."

Kaitlynn tried to sit up, and Faljon and Derrith helped her. "Slowly," said Derrith, "You took a good knock. Don't rush it." She nodded to him and stayed seated. The world swam around her for a second before coming back into focus.

She looked around and saw everyone else sitting by the fire. Uliah had a fresh pink scar on her left breast where she had been hit with the rock, but there was surprisingly little bruising in the area. "Must be Derrith's healing magic," she thought to herself. In her mind's eye, she pictured the elf with a handful of Uliah's breast as well as a goofy grin on his face and suppressed the desire to laugh. Everyone else looked relatively normal.

"How many were there?" she asked. "It's like they were everywhere."

"About two dozen," replied the elf. "We were lucky you saw them in the trees or else they might have done worse to us."

The compliment from the elf lifted her spirits, and a smile touched her lips without her realizing it. "How bad was it?" she asked, motioning to the back of her head.

"Not bad," replied Derrith. "You may be dizzy, but the damage was minor."

She nodded her head in understanding, and said, "Thanks again Doc," with a slight smile. "Send the bill to my insurance." The elf gave her a quizzical look and then glanced over at Faljon. The satyr shrugged his shoulders and shook his head, also unsure of her meaning.

"Well, I will leave you in the Keeper's very capable hands for now," replied Derrith. "I need to get ready for my watch." Turning to Faljon he said, "She should be okay," and gently patted the satyr on his shoulder before walking away.

Kaitlynn sat in silence for a moment, and then looked up at Faljon. "I take it everyone knows now," Kaitlynn said, her voice low.

Faljon gave her a sheepish look. "I may have reacted somewhat when you went down."

She nodded as if in contemplation and sat silent for a moment before responding. "You know what, I'm fine with it," she said. "I'm shit at keeping secrets anyway." She reached up and touched his face and let her fingers slide along to the back of his head. She gently grabbed a handful of his hair, pulled him down to her, and kissed him on the lips.

48

They let Kaitlynn and Uliah sleep through the night to rest their wounds (though Uliah argued that she was fine and didn't need any special treatment), and in the morning they headed off again. The Frostspire Mountains loomed large now, no longer a distant shadow, but a real looming threat. Kaitlynn figured it would only be a couple of days at most before they reached the foot of the mountains. She wondered if there was a pass, or if the path simply ended at the foot of the mountains.

They made their way along for a good portion of the morning and stopped just before midday. After a quick lunch, they moved on again until nightfall. At night they made their camp and set their regular watches.

"How much longer until we reach the mountains?" Peton asked, turning to Derrith. There was a serious look on the satyr's face.

"Not long now," replied the elf. "We might reach the base of the mountains by nightfall tomorrow. But we will be climbing for a couple of days before we reach the Obsidian Keep."

They all sat pensively and ate their dinner. An uneasy silence had settled over the group. Their journey was coming to a close, and they were uncertain as to what they would find when they entered the looming Frostspires. Despite the worry that laid heavy on their minds, most of the party eventually turned in for the night while Derrith and Uliah took the first watch.

49

The raven sat on its perch and looked out the window at the snow-capped peaks that surrounded the Keep. There was a stiff wind that came through the window, and it could feel its feathers flutter in the breeze. It squawked at the wind in vain as if insolence alone would hold back the bitter chill.

It turned on its perch and saw its master's ominous form standing in the doorway. He motioned to the raven and said, "Come." The raven flew over and landed on its master's shoulder and rode on it as he walked up the stairs to the roof of the tower. Against the parapet was a dead goblin. Its innards had been spilled all over the stone as if it had been sliced from its shoulders to its groin. The raven looked at the body and recognized Golash, the goblin chieftain. Apparently, his master had not taken his trap's failure well.

"Feast," Uligart said to the raven. It needed no further command and swooped off of his master's shoulder and began ripping and tearing at the goblin's intestines. "Leave his face intact. I want to send a message to the rest of his men when I return the body to them." The frost elf turned and walked to the parapet on the opposite side of the keep. He looked far above to the nearest peak to where his greatest weapons nested and decided that it was time to turn one of them loose.

50

King Delavon looked around at the assembled armies camped just south of Elfwood. The centaurs had come in full force, giving them a large cavalry force. The dwarves had also answered the call, though not in as great a number as the centaurs. There was also a small contingent of satyrn, who had come as well once they'd heard that their Keeper was a part of the mission. But the largest contingent of forces came from the armies of the elves. The elves had emptied all the nearby forests at their king's call and were prepared to lay down their lives if necessary to stop Uligart once and for all.

Time was running out, and Delavon knew it. They would have to begin their march soon and hope that any forces still coming would join them on the way to the Frostspires. He turned to one of his attendants and said, "Send for King Halcor and King Garoth." The attendant went off and grabbed a courier, sent him to find King Halcor of the centaurs, and went off to deliver the message to King Garoth of the dwarves himself.

It wasn't long before Halcor arrived with a handful of soldiers in tow. Halcor was a majestic multicolored centaur, with a light brown and white body like that of a paint horse. His long hair matched the color pattern of his body, and he wore a crown made of many intertwined rose stems that were still sharp with thorns. "King Delavon, you wished to speak?" he asked as he trotted up. Delavon had to look up at the centaur, whose height was quite imposing.

"Indeed, King Halcor," he replied. "We must have a council of war before we move out. Once Garoth is here..." Delavon began, but almost at once he saw the dwarven king making his way over to them. "Ah, here he is now."

King Garoth was tall for a dwarf. He was almost five feet tall, had long red hair that he tied in braids and a beard to match. He wore a suit of chainmail that seemed to shine in the evening's last sunlight, and his crown was made of pure gold and encrusted with rubies. He grunted as he walked up with several of his own soldiers following closely behind. "What's all this about then?" he asked as he joined the other two kings. He had a dour look on his face, and Delavon was beginning to believe that it was a permanent fixture there.

"We need to begin our march," replied Delavon. "We head out at dawn."

"Not all of my people are here yet," said Garoth, his voice hard. "If we leave now, we will not be at full strength."

"I understand your concern, King Garoth," replied Delavon. "But the longer we wait, the more entrenched Uligart's forces can get in the mountains."

"The mountains are no concern for dwarves," responded Garoth, defiantly. "What is a concern is the numbers!"

"Your people may be adept at fighting in the mountains and the cold, King Garoth," said Halcor, "but mine are not used to such conditions. The sooner we strike, the more effective my people can be in the battle ahead. We can't let them dig in."

"King Garoth, if King Halcor will agree to send riders to meet your forces and direct them to meet us at the Frostspire Pass instead of here, do you think that they can make it there in time to be of use?" asked Delavon. He knew the short-legged dwarves would slow the movement of the entire army as it was.

"Aye, they might," he responded. "If there's enough open ground for them to move the siege weapons upon. If not, it may slow them down further."

"How are we getting siege weapons through the mountains?" asked Halcor, an immense amount of doubt flooding his voice.

"How do you think we got them out of the mountains that we came from?" responded Garoth harshly. Delavon thought he detected quite a bit of pride in the dwarf's tone. "We dwarves have our ways that you tree folk wouldn't understand."

"Let's not let this devolve into a squabble," said Delavon sternly. "We need to trust each other and work together." He paused and thought for a moment. Assuming they hadn't been delayed, Derrith and the party of satyrn would be in the mountains by now. "I believe that time is of the essence, King Garoth. I believe it will be in our best interest to arrive at the

Obsidian Keep as quickly as possible. If that means moving without your full complement, I am prepared to do so. But if we can redirect them, they may be able to reach us in time. If we wait for them, there may not be a Somalie left to save."

Halcor and Garoth nodded grimly. "Very well," said Garoth after a few moments of silence. "Send your riders. We will do what we can with what we have."

"I will see to it at once," replied Halcor as he turned and trotted off towards his army's camp with his company of centaurs.

"I don't know how much help those beasties will be in the Frostspires," said Garoth, watching the centaurs ride off. "If this were an open field of battle, aye. But in the mountains and snow..." he trailed off and shook his head. "We shall see."

"That we shall," replied Delavon. He understood the dwarf's concerns well, but their options were limited. He knew he did not have to explain this to Garoth. The dwarf seemed to have a keen mind for warfare. "We need those siege weapons," stated Delavon. He turned and looked down into the dwarf's eyes.

"We'll have them," replied Garoth, "hopefully soon enough to make a difference." The dwarf turned towards his troops and headed off with a wave.

Delavon looked off at the looming Frostspires in the distance. Somewhere in those snowcapped peaks were the captain of his guard and a party of satyrn that he was certain he had sent to die. He hoped that was not the case and they would succeed in their mission to retrieve the Gate, but his hopes diminished daily. They marched tomorrow whether the siege weapons had arrived by then or not.

51

Most of the following morning had passed, and Kaitlynn could see where the base of the mountains met the edge of the grassland up ahead. She was surprised by how quickly the landscape ahead appeared to change. It looked as if the rolling grasslands simply ended at the edge of the large mountain range. The path seemed to continue and wind its way between the first two mountains, after that she couldn't see where it went.

"We'll be there by nightfall," Derrith said, turning to Faljon. "We'd better camp outside the pass and enter in the morning. Food will be scarce once we enter the pass."

Faljon nodded his approval, and said, "We might as well stop for lunch now." He held up his hand and the party slowed. "Let's break for lunch; we'll reach the mountains by nightfall," he said, loud enough for the rest of the group to hear him.

Uliah and Jali headed off to find wood for the fire, and Derrith and Peton headed off looking for food. Kaitlynn turned to Derrith before he left and said, "If you want to take my backpack go ahead and load it up with whatever fruits you can find. We'll need them in the mountains." He nodded and threw the straps over his shoulder.

While the others were off, Kaitlynn and Shanja spent the time sparring with each other. Kaitlynn was amazed at how much better she had gotten in such a short time, as she was parrying and blocking with relative ease. Breaking down Shanja's defenses, on the other hand, was a far more difficult task. Each of them managed to land the occasional blow, but more often than not they found themselves at a relative standstill. The fact that she had picked up her skills so quickly gave her a confidence she hadn't had even just a few days before.

When the others began returning, she and Shanja put their weapons away and helped in any way that they could. Derrith and Peton had returned with her backpack weighed down heavily with fruits, as well as another of the strange jackalope type creatures for lunch. Derrith took what looked like a large yellowish apple from the bag and sat down while the rest of them prepared the meat.

When the food was ready, Uliah and Jali sat down next to Kaitlynn. She noticed that both of the satyrs kept looking at her, smiles barely contained on their faces. Finally, she whispered to them, "Look, we've all gotten laid at some point on this trip. Let's not make a big deal out of it." Both of them busted out in laughter then, and Kaitlynn rolled her eyes.

"If you're trying to get details out of her, I'm in," said Shanja as she sat down with the rest of them.

"You're all just as bad as my girlfriends back home," Kaitlynn said, trying to hold back a laugh. "Let's just say that everything works the same for me as it does for you." She paused and looked around to make sure none of the men were listening in. "And it was very good," she finished with a smile.

The women spent the rest of their lunch trading stories of their various escapades. Kaitlynn appreciated the conversation as it kept things light-hearted. She didn't want to think too much about the gigantic mountain range lingering over her shoulder and the hardships that they were likely to endure once they entered them.

As they prepared to head out, Delok came over to Shanja, put his arm around her waist and asked, "So what was all that about?"

"Just girl talk," replied Kaitlynn, giving Shanja a wink and a smile. The women all started laughing again.

Once she was able to contain her giggling fit, Shanja whispered something into Delok's ear, and his face went bright red with embarrassment. "I shouldn't have asked," he said, walking away and shaking his head. This sent all the women into a tizzy again.

"What did you say to him?" asked Jali. Shanja whispered something into her ear and they both lost it again.

"I don't think that I want to know," said Kaitlynn with a smile as she tossed her backpack over her shoulder and picked up her weapons. "I think it's time we get a move on," she added. She tried to fake a smile at them, but they all nodded in silence. It was as if a shadow had suddenly passed over them all. Kaitlynn wished she could take the words back, she liked seeing them all laughing together. But they grabbed their gear and prepared to fall in line and head out.

They made their way onto the path again, and about halfway through the afternoon dark rain clouds began to block the sun. Kaitlynn could feel the temperature of the air dropping against her skin and the clouds thickened above. "Didn't we just leave this party?" she asked to no one in particular as the first raindrops fell on her, but she heard a slight chuckle from Peton behind her.

"On the bright side," he said to her, "tis not snow. Not yet."

She looked up at the mountains and saw how the snow seemed to cover at least the top half of all of them. She was certain that it would be snowing once they entered the mountains, assuming it didn't let up by then. "You've got a point," she said, flashing Peton a quick smile. She adjusted her backpack a bit to take some of the pressure off her shoulders and kept scanning the horizon for a break in the clouds.

It was dusk when they arrived at the base of the mountain range. The light drizzle had kept up but hadn't gotten worse. The snowy peaks seemed to go on as far as the eye could see to both the east and west. They began assigning tasks to set up camp when Kaitlynn felt rather than saw a large shadow pass over them. She looked up and saw what looked to her like a large black dragon swooping down at them from the mountains. "What the hell is that?" she asked, turning to Derrith and pointing at the beast.

The elf looked up and his eyes went wide. "Wyvern!" he yelled at the top of his lungs. "Aim for the wings!" he added, pulling his bow out. Jali and Uliah pulled their bows as well and a volley of arrows flew at the beast. Everyone ducked as it flew overhead and snapped its massive jaws down at them. Kaitlynn could see a few arrows sticking out of its hide.

"Aim for the same wing!" Faljon yelled out to the archers as it turned and prepared to swoop down on them again.

"Left!" yelled Derrith, and the two women nodded. As it dived at them again, Kaitlynn could see that two of the arrows had already hit it in the left wing. All three archers aimed for its left wing this time. The three arrows all hit, and the arrows tore a hole right through the skin. The wyvern seemed to do a barrel roll out of control to its left and crashed heavily to the ground. Screeching in pain, the wyvern stood on its two legs, and its height seemed to dwarf all of them. Its left wing had crumpled upon impact with the ground and hung broken at its side. Despite its injury, the wyvern stood defiantly before them and screeched at them again before advancing.

Derrith, Uliah, and Jali kept firing their arrows at it, but they seemed to bounce off the thick hide of its torso. Faljon, Shanja, and Peton all pulled out their spears and charged the large beast, while Kaitlynn and Delok pulled their swords and followed. All three of the satyrs impaled its chest with their spears, but it seemed relatively unfazed by their attacks. In one smooth motion, it chomped down and took off most of Peton's body just above the waist. His legs and what was left of his torso fell to the ground in a bloody mess. It raised its head back up and Kaitlynn could see what looked like part of an intestine hanging from the creature's crimson painted jaws.

Enraged, Kaitlynn swept her sword at the wyvern's other wing, mangling it as well. There was no way the beast could fly now, and it reared up in rage and pain. Looking at Kaitlynn, it flailed its large tail at her, but she managed to step out of the way. It pulled it back and swung at her again, and she dove quickly to avoid it again. She popped back up expecting the tail to have been pulled away again, but unfortunately, it appeared to have struck something other than her. Kaitlynn turned with dread and saw that the pointed stinger on the end had impaled Delok in the chest. The satyr's face was racked with pain. He dropped his weapon and slowly started slinking over onto his side towards the ground.

"No!" screamed Shanja as she pulled her spear out of the wyvern's hide and stabbed repeatedly in its chest. Kaitlynn turned back to the beast and sliced down with her sword at the thing's tail with all of her might. Her sword made it about halfway through, and she pulled it out and sliced down again with all the strength she had left in her body. Her second swing took the tail clean off at about its midpoint, and blood sprayed from the stump where she had hacked it off. The creature screeched in pain again, its large head rearing up into the air once again.

Kaitlynn happened to look over to her right in time to see Derrith drop his bow and jump up on what was left of the wyvern's tail. He leaped and clutched at its mangled wing to pull himself up, and then grabbed a hold of its neck. Getting a foothold on the thing's back and holding on with his left arm, Derrith reversed the grip of his sword and stabbed downward through the wyvern's massive head. It let out a final screech of pain and began to teeter on massive legs that were suddenly devoid of strength. Kaitlynn and the others scattered as best they could before it collapsed down upon them, and Derrith leaped from it as it toppled to the ground with one final grunt. The large draconian head fell lifeless right next to

Delok's prone body, and Faljon ran over and slammed his spear through the top of its head to make sure it wouldn't rise again.

Her face already drenched with tears, Shanja dropped her weapons and ran over to Delok and grabbed his hand. There was a large hole in his chest just above his heart and below his collarbone. The others ran over as well, all looking down at him with anguished looks on their faces. Shanja looked up at Derrith, her eyes pleading with him. "Do something," she said, her voice weak and cracking with grief. "Please."

Derrith shook his head, his face solemn. "I can heal the wound," he said, his voice quite low. "But the venom…" he trailed off. It was clear by the look on the elf's face that there was nothing that could be done, and he lowered his head, closed his eyes, and began saying something under his breath in elvish. If Kaitlynn had to venture a guess, she would have thought he was praying.

Delok began to choke, and frothy white foam was coming up out of his mouth. All around the wound, his skin had started to turn a sickly shade of yellow-green. His eyes locked with Shanja's for the last time as his body convulsed once … twice … and then his labored breath stopped with one final, slow exhale.

"No!" she screamed and began shaking his lifeless form. "Delok, please…" her voice trailed off as she began to sob uncontrollably. She collapsed on top of him and held him in her arms. The others stood quietly around the two of them for a moment, and then slowly started backing away, leaving her to her grief. Kaitlynn saw Jali and Uliah walk over to what was left of Peton's gnarled remains and give each other a hug while the tears rolled down their faces.

Kaitlynn walked over and put a hand on Shanja's shoulder with care. "I'm sorry," she whispered. Shanja turned her head and looked up at her, her face streaked with tears. She was blubbering, and there was snot coming out of her nose. She reached out, still on her knees and hugged Kaitlynn as hard as she could around the waist. Kaitlynn reached down and held her tightly. "I'm here for you," she whispered. "We all are."

"May they rest eternal, Keeper of Souls," she heard Faljon say behind her, his voice low and full of sadness. The prayer voiced finality to it. Delok and Peton were gone. Shanja continued to sob in Kaitlynn's arms, and everyone else seemed to be trapped in a daze as they tried to process what had just happened to them all and the losses they had just suffered.

52

Kaitlynn and Shanja sat next to each other by the fire. Kaitlynn had her arm around the satyr and let Shanja lay her head on her shoulder. She had stopped crying for now, but it was quite evident that she was still in a state of shock. She kept repeating, "I have lost my mate. My children have lost their father," over and over again under her breath. Kaitlynn felt at a loss for how to console her friend, so she just sat there, with her arm around her shoulders letting her vent her grief however she needed to.

At Faljon's suggestion, they had made their way into the pass just out of sight of the remains of the dead wyvern and their friends. No one seemed to be in any mind to argue the point. It was late, but none of them felt like sleeping or eating. They all sat around the fire in stunned silence.

After some time, Faljon broke the silence, his voice low. "Gorkan, Lillia, Hammel, Peton, and Delok," he said. The others looked up at him, and fresh tears came to Shanja's eyes at the mention of her mate's name. "I swear this upon my vow as Keeper, we will avenge them. We will retrieve the Gate. We will kill Uligart." There was a certainty to the way in which he spoke, and the other satyrs all nodded.

All of them, except for Uliah.

The youngest satyr of the group with her sprawling blonde hair looked at each of them in turn, then back to Faljon. She took a deep breath, and then whispered, "Keeper, I am with child." There was a new stunned silence around the fire. Even Shanja seemed to snap out of her daze for the first time since Delok's death.

"How long have you known?" Faljon asked her quietly.

I was not certain until today," she replied. "I was feeling sick the last few mornings. But now, I can feel the satyrling growing inside of me. I can feel the warmth of its life inside of me." She paused and looked around at the group before her eyes settled on Jali. "It is Peton's," she said, her voice heavy. Jali lowered her head, and Kaitlynn could see fresh tears forming in her friend's eyes.

Faljon said nothing for a few moments, his face contemplative. When he finally spoke, he did so with sadness in his voice. "You must go back," he said. "We cannot bring an unborn satyrling into the battles ahead. Plus, this terrain, this weather in the mountains would be a danger alone to an unborn."

Uliah nodded her head, her face downtrodden. "Keeper, I want this child," she said, "but I do not want to abandon you all. Especially now." She glanced back through the pass in the direction of the battle earlier that evening. "If it cannot know its father, I should be able to help avenge him for it." There was a fire in her eyes as she spoke.

Jali stood up and walked over to the other side of the fire and sat down next to Uliah. She put her arm around the younger satyr, wiped a tear from her cheek, and said, "I will notch my arrows and fire true for the both of us. For Peton." She paused and wiped away a tear. "You have all that remains of him inside of you. You must protect that now." Uliah threw her arms around Jali, and the two of them wept in each other's arms.

After a long pause, while the two satyrs composed themselves, the silence was finally broken by Derrith. "Return to Elfwood," said the elf. "The King should be rallying forces to the south of the forest by now. Hopefully, they may even be on the march by now. Return, explain the circumstances. They will make sure you are kept safe there." He paused for a moment, before adding, "Until we return." The final words hung heavy in the air as if he didn't quite believe them.

"You'll be safer with us tonight," added Faljon. "We shall part on the morrow." His voice was heavy with grief.

Uliah nodded to him. "I'm sorry, Keeper," she said, tears rolling down her face. "I can't help feeling like I let you down."

Faljon stood, walked over and knelt down in front of her. He put both of his hands on her shoulders and said, "Feel no sorrow, Uliah, you have acted with honor befitting of any satyrn I have ever known. But you have a new duty now, as a mother." She nodded but kept her head down. She didn't seem to be able to meet any of their eyes. The tears continued to roll down her face until she fell asleep almost an hour later, still locked in Jali's arms.

53

When morning came, Uliah gave each of them a hug, in turn, lingering longest with Jali and Shanja, sharing their grief for an extra moment or two. She took off her quiver of arrows and handed enough to Jali and Derrith to refill their own before slinging the rest back over her shoulder and heading out. As she was about to round a corner and exit the pass, she turned back to the others and waved. There were tears streaming down her face again. She wiped them away with her hand, and then turned and headed back for Elfwood. The others watched her go until she was out of sight.

"Our numbers continue to dwindle," said Derrith, his voice low. He had turned to face Faljon. Kaitlynn silently acknowledged that the elf was right. They were down from a party of eight to five. "This will make our mission that much more difficult."

"Yet we will complete it," replied Faljon, his voice confident, yet defiant. Kaitlynn looked at him, taking in his full presence. He was a natural leader, and it was clear to her that the other satyrs looked up to him because of it. She couldn't help herself from becoming more attracted to him the more of this side of him that she saw but felt cautious of expressing her feelings in front of the others under the circumstances. She was particularly afraid of the reaction Shanja might have after losing Delok. So, she took a deep breath and resisted the urge to go to him and flung her backpack over her shoulders for the journey ahead.

They headed out, the five remaining members of the party that had left Elfwood. Faljon took the lead, with Shanja and Kaitlynn following behind. Kaitlynn kept a careful watch of Shanja to make sure she was all right ... or at least as well as possible considering the loss she had just suffered. Derrith and Jali brought up the rear. They followed the path as it wound over the side of one of the mountains, though it stayed far from the snowline before it started to descend back down again. Even still, as they got higher, the winds picked up and the occasional gust carried some of the crystal white power upon it. It was well past midday as they crested the other side and Kaitlynn could see the path winding its way over the next mountain, crossing much closer to the peak above the snow line before disappearing on the other side. The long trek they had been on was only going to get more difficult from here.

54

Uligart stood by the parapet of his Obsidian Keep and looked out into the distance, staring at his forces as they passed through the mountains. The lizards were at the front of the line, moving slowly through the mountain pass. The goblins would make much better time, but they weren't cold-blooded like the lizards were. They had come a long way from the swamps on the other side of the mountain, but they still had a ways to go. Getting an army of them through the frigid air of the Frostspires was going to be a challenge and the goblins would need to be on the other side of the pass for a day or two by the time Delavon and his allies arrived if they wanted to be able to dig into a fortified position.

Uligart knew that Delavon was amassing an army just south of Elfwood. The elves were being joined by dwarves, centaurs and a small contingent of satyrn. His own frost elves, goblins, and lizardmen would have to hold them long enough for him to learn the secret of the Gate.

But the lizards brought their own unique problems. The frost elves and Goblins could fight in the cold of the mountains, but the lizards had to be where it was warmer, on the other side of the mountains, to be effective. But placing them there alone left them exposed, or if he placed his entire army there it would leave his frost elves exposed rather than being able to use the mountains to their advantage. He had decided to place his army in stages. The lizards would be just inside the mountain pass, where it was warm enough for them to fight, but not exposed to the open fields before the mountains or the frigid snow behind them. The pass would force Delavon to narrow his lines. The lizards would fall, but they'd at least take as many of Delavon's forces with them as possible. Those losses would be acceptable in his opinion, for he had no love for the lizardfolk. They would make excellent cannon fodder though, and he imagined that the goblins wouldn't mind being able to expand their territory into the lizard's swamps once this was all over. The goblins and frost elves would be far more valuable to his plans and would be placed much closer to the tower with his own people hiding high up in the mountains. They would have the advantage there, even if they might not have the numbers of their enemies.

He turned then and looked back to the north and saw his raven fighting the stiff, cold winds of the mountains. It came down and landed on the parapet in front of him, kicking some snow off to get a better grip against the winds. It seemed to have a reddish blood stain over its beak and chest. It squawked at him a couple of times, and Uligart turned away and closed his eyes. His face started to flush with anger and his blood began to boil.

The wyvern was dead.

The raven squawked again then, and Uligart turned back and looked at it with interest in his eyes. Two of the satyrs were dead, and a third had left the rest of them and turned back. They had entered the mountain pass, but there were fewer of them. He nodded and said to the raven, "You have done well. And I see that you have feasted on the satyrs." The raven seemed to nod at him. He smiled, a dark malevolence seeming to advance across his pale face. "Come," he said, and the raven landed on his shoulder as he began walking.

Uligart walked down the steps into the tower and through the hall to the workshop at the top of the tower where the raven's perch was. He turned and faced the painting that hung on the wall there. It had changed since the wyvern had taken it from the goblins and brought it here. Instead of showing a snow-covered forest, it now appeared to be inside a strange room of a strange building. There was a long chair of some sort, and there was a woman laying on it sleeping. The brushstrokes of the painting were crisp and clear, and Uligart could see every detail of the room. He pointed at the woman on the chair and asked the raven, "The woman traveling with the satyrs, does she look like this type of creature?"

The raven appeared to nod and then squawked something again. A dark smile spread across Uligart's face again. "Fly to Nalidur. Tell him that in a few days, there will be a party of satyrs, an elf and a human woman who will approach the tower. I want the woman taken alive. Kill the rest." The raven squawked and then flew off to deliver the message to the Uligart's lieutenant and the Captain of his Obsidian Guards.

Uligart stood there in front of the Gate, staring at the sleeping form of Kaitlynn's mother, Rebecca. She seemed peaceful for now. She had hardly moved from the chair in days, except when she was pacing back and forth in front of the painting or staring into it with pleading eyes. He finally understood why she was doing this. She was keeping a vigil, the way a parent does when they fear for their child. And now armed with this knowledge, he knew how he could get her to open the gate from the other side. He smiled his malevolent grin again and ran a finger from his good right hand over the canvas. He could feel the texture of the paint that made the image against his fingertip. The Gate was a marvel of ancient magic; the magic of Raeyl and Qyr themselves. He would have its power, and then challenge the Old Gods themselves for dominion over Somalie. If he could master the magic of the Gate, he could control the power of creation itself.

55

They had reached the bottom of the first mountain, and it was already getting late. The snowy peaks in the distance seemed even taller from here and Kaitlynn wasn't sure how much progress they would make once they actually got above the snowline. The air was cold here, and the wind whipped through the mountains. There was no wood for a fire however, and they all sat together and ate the fruits in Kaitlynn's backpack in silence. Kaitlynn felt lucky that she had been taught how to use some of her magical gifts because she couldn't imagine being up in these mountains without being able to warm herself up at will. She sat there and looked at Faljon, letting her memories of their night together fill her heart. After a few moments, the cold mountain wind was barely more than a nuisance against the few parts of her skin that were exposed to it. Even Derrith seemed unaffected by the cold, and Kaitlynn wondered if elves had a similar power to the satyrs or if it was something different entirely.

Kaitlynn looked over at Shanja and saw that she was shivering, and she could even hear the satyr's teeth chattering. It took a moment for Kaitlynn to realize what the problem was. With Delok's death, Shanja couldn't feel the love in her heart to keep herself warm. Kaitlynn reached into her backpack and slid her coat out, walked over to Shanja and draped it over her shoulders. She reached into the inside pocket and pulled out her gloves and put them on over Shanja's claws as carefully as she could and then buttoned up the front of the coat for her. Shanja looked up at her, tears in her eyes, and mouthed the words, "Thank you," to her, before putting her head back down to try and hide the waterfalls streaming down her cheeks.

Kaitlynn went back to her spot and glanced over at Faljon. He was staring at Shanja, a worried expression on his face. He glanced over and noticed Kaitlynn looking at him and flashed her a smile, though it was far more discreet than his normal pointy tooth grin. She looked over at

Shanja and thought that she looked like she was almost swallowed up in the oversized (for her) winter coat, but Kaitlynn decided it was better for her friend to look a little strange than to freeze to death.

With their party down to five members, Jali volunteered to take the first watch and let the others sleep, giving each of them a chance to rest (and giving herself a chance to sleep in a little bit later, Kaitlynn thought to herself with a wry half-smile). Kaitlynn took the last watch, with Faljon taking the one right before hers. As she bedded down for the night, she realized that for the first time she was going to have to try and get by without her coat as a pillow out in the wilderness. She looked over at Shanja and saw the satyr lying on the ground with her horse-shaped legs curled up under as much of the coat as she could. Kaitlynn got up and went over to Shanja and curled up next to her, keeping warm thoughts in her heart and trying to pass her body heat along as much as she could. She thought about that last porch day with her father though, lest she forget who she was cuddling with, and things start to accidentally get awkward. Shanja looked over at her, a grateful expression on her face once again, and the two of them drifted off to sleep in each other's arms

56

The morning seemed to come later than usual the following day. It took Kaitlynn a little longer than she would have liked to admit that it was because the mountains were hiding the sun a longer than she had gotten used to. When she had gotten up for her watch, Shanja had gotten up with her and the two had sat next to each other quietly until the sun crested over the mountain peaks. Shanja looked up at the next mountain they would have to climb, the path disappearing up past the snow line. There was fear in her eyes for the first time that Kaitlynn could remember. Seeing her friend like this pulled at Kaitlynn's heartstrings and she had to fight to keep a happy memory in her own heart to keep the chill out. She put her arm around her friend and did her best to keep her warm as well.

Once the others were up and about, Faljon came over and knelt next to them to check on Shanja. "Can you continue?" he asked her, his voice low so as not to carry to the rest of the camp. She simply nodded once, her eyes looking down instead of at him.

"Shanja, no one will think less of you," whispered Kaitlynn. She couldn't hide the worry on her face as she looked up at Faljon and pursed her lips.

"The Gate..." Shanja croaked, trailing off before taking a deep breath and finishing her thought. "It's more important than ... how I feel." Each word was a struggle for her to express, Kaitlynn saw.

"Do you have any happy memories that you can focus on that don't involve him?" Kaitlynn asked keeping her voice low again. "Maybe trying to think about something else will help with the cold."

Shanja nodded and said, "I can try." She closed her eyes and wiped away her tears with the back of her hands. Kaitlynn could see the wet spots on her gloves from her tears as she put her hands down on her lap. She took a few slow, deep breaths and a little color came back to her cheeks. It wasn't much, but Kaitlynn thought that it was a good sign, nonetheless.

"What are you thinking about?" Kaitlynn asked her quietly.

Shanja let out her breath nice and slow, and then responded, "My satyrlings." She paused, and more color returned to her cheeks.

"Good," replied Kaitlynn, looking up at Faljon and forcing a smile, before turning back to her. "You keep that memory right here," she said, placing her palm over Shanja's heart. Shanja opened her eyes and looked at her, nodding. "In fact, I want you to tell me all about them today. Everything you can think of."

Faljon smiled at her. It wasn't his normal toothy grin, but it didn't look forced either. He put one hand on each of their shoulders and gave them both a soft squeeze. He stood up and headed over to Derrith and Jali, both of whom had already started eating, and joined them.

Kaitlynn motioned to him to toss them some food, and one at a time he lobbed over what looked a little bit like more of the large yellowish apples to them. She managed to catch both of them and handed the first one to Shanja. She sat with her and listened to her talk about her two children, both of whom were grown adults now. Her son Junis was a musician and loved playing the flute. He would perform whenever all the satyrn would get together. Kaitlynn couldn't help but think of the myths she had heard of satyrs as a child and this image of Shanja's son was more like what she expected from those stories. Her daughter Heya was pregnant with her first satyrling of her own, and Shanja was looking forward to meeting her first grandsatyrling soon. The thoughts brought a sad smile to her face, and Kaitlynn could tell that she was thinking about Delok. But the color didn't leave her face, and Kaitlynn decided it was all right so long as Shanja didn't start shaking again.

After breakfast, they headed out again in the same formation as the day before. Kaitlynn let Shanja keep her coat and it was almost hilariously long on her. But as long as it kept her warm and Kaitlynn could keep her focused on the happy memories of her children, it didn't matter.

After climbing the trail until after well after midday (and eating some of the fruit from Kaitlynn's backpack as they climbed), they finally crossed over past the snowline. The path became invisible under the snow and their footing was quite treacherous. The wind whipped through the mountains, and the loose powder stung their exposed skin. Faljon and Jali looked like they had turned bright red from the waist up, and Kaitlynn saw the same color on her arms, as they were exposed from the mid-bicep down. Only Derrith seemed immune to the effects of the elements. The sun was halfway down in the west by the time they crested the top of the peak and saw the largely frozen pass below.

It seemed like the mountains didn't descend nearly as far on the other side of the mountain, and the pass was about four times wider than it had been on the other side of the mountain they were currently on. The wind blew large drifts of snow through the pass, and the mountains on either side of it seemed even taller than the one they were just now cresting.

Faljon stopped and looked down at the pass. The others came up next to him and looked down as well. "Tis not going to get any warmer, is it?" asked Shanja, her voice heavy.

Faljon shook his head and said, "I'm afraid not."

"If we can make it to the pass by tonight, it'll be about a day and a half until we reach the Obsidian Keep," said Derrith, his voice nearly drowned out as he fought against a sudden gust of wind.

"We won't be able to hide out there," said Jali. "What about staying in the mountains?"

"It'll take longer," replied Derrith, "But I'm not against it. We'll be horribly exposed out there."

Faljon looked over at Shanja, and his brow furrowed. She glanced over at him and said, "Tis no better in the pass than in the mountains. I will follow your lead, Keeper."

He nodded, collecting his thoughts. "Then we stick to the mountains," he said after a few moments. "If we can, we should stick to the other side away from the pass."

"It will more than double our time," replied Derrith. He turned and looked at Faljon. "I believe it's the most prudent thing to do, but I wanted you to be aware of everything."

Faljon nodded. "Thank you," he said, his voice almost blown away by another sudden wind gust. He waited for the wind to die down, and then continued. "If the Gate tis at the Obsidian Keep, then Uligart cannot open it. Not there. This buys us time. If tis not there...." His voice trailed off and he swallowed hard before continuing. "If tis not there, then none of this matters."

They went silent, and Kaitlynn heard nothing for few minutes except the wailing of the winds through the mountains, the sound cresting and falling again like waves in the ocean. And then Faljon began walking back down the other side of the mountain. One by one, they followed him as he veered to the east towards the next peak among the mountains and away from the sprawling snow-covered pass down below them.

57

It was getting dark as they started to cross the peak of the next mountain. Kaitlynn didn't think it would be a good idea to stay all the way up here once night fell; they would be far too exposed to the elements. She started looking around to see if there was any cover to be found, and her eyes tracked down to the mountain pass below. It was then that she saw Uligart's army entering the pass in the distance.

"Look, over there," she said, placing her hand on Faljon's shoulder. The satyr looked off into the distance and saw exactly what she had pointed out. The others paused and looked off into the distance as well.

"Tis a good thing we stayed out of the pass," said Jali, her voice low and almost carried away by a light gust of wind.

"They're moving awfully slow," said Faljon, his eyes squinted as he peered off into the distance.

"Lizardmen," replied Derrith. "The cold slows them. But there are goblins behind, and more coming around the bend in the distance. Uligart's frost elves are likely bringing up the rear of the line." Kaitlynn turned and looked at the elf. Most everything in the distance was little more than a speck on the horizon to her, but Derrith seemed to be able to see quite clearly well past what her own eyes could see.

Faljon meanwhile, was looking over at Shanja. She was shaking visibly, and her teeth were chattering. "We need to keep moving," he finally said, loud enough for everyone to hear, and began marching back down the other side of the mountain. It was just after the sun had slipped behind the mountains to the west that Faljon held up his arm calling for the group to stop. As the mountain ran down-slope, there appeared to be a natural opening on the side of its twin going back up on the other side. Faljon turned and motioned to Derrith. "Can you see what's in there?" he asked, pointing to the opening on the side of the slope ahead.

"It too dark," he replied, but he glanced back at Shanja before continuing, "But I'm not sure it matters much. We may not have much choice."

Faljon nodded his understanding. "Then we'll make our way there. Hopefully, at least we'll be protected from the wind." The satyr led the group down the rest of the mountain as quickly as he dared in the darkness.

Even with her eyes adjusted to the dark, the howling wind and the snow that it carried upon it made visibility difficult for Kaitlynn. She tried to keep an eye on Shanja as much as she could while still trying to navigate the difficult footing herself. The waning moon was high in the night sky before they reached the bottom of the slope, and they were still looking up at the opening of the cave on the next one.

As they started to head up the next slope, Kaitlynn heard a thud in the snow behind her. She turned around and looked back to see that Shanja had collapsed face down into the snow. She ran over to her friend as quickly as she could, and the others all followed. "She's freezing," said Kaitlynn, as she rolled Shanja over and touched her face.

"How soon can we make that cave?" asked Jali, the concern evident in her voice.

"It might be almost daylight by then," replied Faljon. His lips were pursed as he looked down at Shanja. The constant and frigid wind had burnt her exposed skin raw, and it was probably thanks to Kaitlynn's coat and gloves that she was still alive at all.

Shanja's eyes fluttered open in a slit. "Leave me if you must," she said, her voice hoarse. "The Gate..." Her voice trailed off into a series of hacking coughs.

"Like hell, we will," said Kaitlynn, and she reached down and tried to lift Shanja up off the ground. "Give me a hand here," she said, and Derrith stepped in and helped her pull the satyr up. She slipped her backpack off and handed it to the elf, who looked at her with a quizzical glance before putting it on. She got down on her knees and wrapped Shanja's arms around her neck and said, "Whatever you do, don't let go," and then stood up. It took a tremendous amount of effort, however. The satyr was heavier than she had expected, and her knees almost buckled under the weight. "Wrap her legs around my waist," she said, straining under the dead weight on her back. Jali grabbed Shanja's legs and wrapped them around Kaitlynn, and she felt like she could control the weight on her back now at least. "Okay, let's go," she said to Faljon with a nod and a look of determination.

She wasn't sure how long she could carry her friend, but she was going to give it everything she had to keep her alive. She'd seen enough death as it was.

The group set out again, moving as quickly as they could through the knee-deep snow. Kaitlynn thought about the night in the pond with Faljon as she trudged through the snow, keeping herself as warm as possible and hoping that some of her body heat was transferring to the satyr on her back. The warmth seemed to give her legs a boost and her back seemed to strain less under the weight than she feared that it would. But it was still almost dawn before they reached the mouth of the cave.

Faljon went in first with Derrith right behind them, weapons drawn. Kaitlynn didn't wait for them to report back whether it was safe or not, she simply followed them in out of fear that Shanja might not make it outside in the wind and cold much longer. She glanced at Jali, who had followed her in as well, and she helped Kaitlynn put Shanja down. Faljon and Derrith continued deeper into the cavern, which was much larger once they had passed through its opening than they had expected from the outside.

Kaitlynn and Jali carried Shanja far enough away from the opening of the cave so that the wind outside didn't find its way within before they put her down. Kaitlynn looked around the cave and saw the two men coming back. "Anything back there?" she asked as they returned with their weapons away.

The cave continues deep within the mountain," replied Faljon. "We may be able to cross to the other side and avoid the elements."

"Not now," she replied, her voice emphatic. "We need to warm Shanja up before we try to move her." Kaitlynn considered her modesty for a moment and then cast it away before stripping off her armor and her tunic but leaving on her tights and her bra. She gently pulled the coat off Shanja and curled up next to her, letting their skin come into contact before tossing the coat back over the top of them like a blanket. "Jali, toss my tunic over her legs please," she said and watched as the satyr did as she had told her while she pulled herself as close to Shanja as possible, until they were on their sides, face to face with each other. She kept the thought of her and Faljon making love together in her head and heart (awkwardness be damned) and gently kissed her friend's forehead. Then she turned her face and let her cheek lay against Shanja's, trying to pass as much body heat along as she could.

Jali looked down at the two of them and began nodding, and then she curled herself up on the other side of Shanja, pulling the open coat over herself as well to keep as much of the body heat as she could muster beneath it and into Shanja's weak form. She wrapped her arm around Shanja's back and it reached over to Kaitlynn's side, and then she pulled the three of them as tight together as possible. "We're here for you," she whispered into Shanja's ear before laying her head down on the hard ground next to her.

"I'll take first watch," said Derrith. His voice was haggard, but he looked down at the women on the ground and understood what they were trying to do. He respected that and would do whatever he could to help them. Faljon nodded and then curled himself up behind Kaitlynn, hoping to add whatever he could to the warmth beneath her coat to help save Shanja from freezing to death.

58

The light outside the cave had come and gone again. Derrith, Faljon, Kaitlynn, and Jali had all taken turns on watch while the others had curled up with Shanja while sleeping to keep her as warm as possible. Even Derrith had joined in the effort despite not being able to supernaturally warm himself the way Kaitlynn and the satyrs could. He was simply immune to the cold, but he added what body heat he could to the effort regardless.

It was after the sun had set and darkness had claimed the cave again that Shanja finally opened her eyes. At the time, Derrith was back on watch and Faljon was eating some fruit from Kaitlynn's backpack. She turned herself over slowly, her side sore from lying on the ground for as long as she had and sat up. Kaitlynn sat up with her, though Jali was fast asleep yet again.

"Good evening, Sunshine," said Kaitlynn as she lopped an arm around Shanja and gave her a peck on the cheek. Her skin had lost its horrible chill, and this pleased Kaitlynn immensely.

"What happened?" Shanja asked as her eyes darted around the cave and she tried to take the scene in.

"You collapsed," replied Faljon, as he came over and knelt in front of her. "You've been out for a full day." Her eyes went wide at that, and she looked over at Kaitlynn, and then back to Jali sleeping on the ground next to her.

"And you all…" she trailed off, tears welling in her eyes again. She shook her head and sighed deeply.

"We would never leave you behind," replied Kaitlynn, her voice just more than a whisper. "But if you're feeling better, I'd like my shirt back," she said, a little louder this time. Faljon smiled at her and picked up her tunic. He made to hand it to her, pulled it away playfully when she reached out for it, and then gave it back to her with a big toothy grin. She glared at him, not really meaning it, and then put her tunic back on over her head.

Shanja had taken the playful exchange as an opportunity to wipe the tears out of her eyes. She stood up, her legs a little unsteady at first, and then walked over towards the entrance of the cave. She could hear the wind bellowing outside, but as luck would have it, it was blowing away from the entrance to the cave rather than towards it. She peered out into the darkness at the tracks in the snow.

"How did I get here?" she asked. "Last I remember we were down at the bottom of this slope."

"The Keeper carried you up the mountain," replied Derrith.

She turned and looked at Faljon, but he shook his head and motioned to Kaitlynn with a slight nod of his head. She turned and looked at Kaitlynn, the strange human woman who had come from another world, become her friend, who had apparently saved her life. "Thank you," she said, her voice cracked and barely a whisper. Kaitlynn simply nodded and gave her a slight smile that really only showed on the corners of her mouth.

"This cave appears to go deeper into the mountain," added Faljon. "We are hoping we can cross below and stay out of the elements." He paused, and then said, "We aren't certain, however, how far it goes. But unless you think you can bring love back into your heart, it seems the only way we can go."

Shanja looked at Faljon and smiled. "I've been surrounded by much love here, and it burns within me." She dropped Kaitlynn's coat on the cave floor and stood there, truly unburdened for the first time since Delok has died in her arms. "I will follow wherever you lead, Keepers." She looked back and forth between Faljon and Kaitlynn as she said this, her eyes meeting both of theirs in turn.

"Well," said Kaitlynn with a cough, slightly embarrassed by all the praise she was getting. "Some of your love is still sleeping," she said, motioning with her head towards Jali. "Should we wait until morning, or test the caves tonight?"

Faljon looked at Shanja, and then down to Jali still dozing on the cave floor. "We should move as soon as we can," he said, "but I don't want to rush it if Shanja tis not fully recovered."

"I'm ready," she replied with a smile. Kaitlynn thought it was very good indeed to see her friend smile again.

"Very well," replied Faljon. He motioned towards Jali and said, "Good luck waking her. We leave when she's ready." He smiled at Kaitlynn, and she felt her cheeks flush and her heart race, but she reached over and started gently shaking Jali awake.

After everyone had gotten a chance to eat and collect themselves, the party moved on deeper into the cave. Faljon took the lead, and they all followed behind him. Kaitlynn could see that after a time the rough cave walls began to smooth out as if they had been cut through the mountain rather than the tunnel being just a natural formation. "I wonder if this was a mine at one point," she said as they passed the first of what turned out to be many wooden support systems along the cave walls and ceiling.

"The frost elves that inhabit these mountains usually live above ground. These may be old dwarf tunnels," replied Derrith. "Or worse, goblin tunnels," he added, his voice a bit darker.

"Well, let's hope for the former then," replied Shanja. Her voice sounded much stronger than it had in a couple of days, which made Kaitlynn glad. The fact that it felt warmer down beneath the mountain didn't hurt either.

They continued for what seemed like a few hours. The tunnel seemed to steadily slope downward as they went and with a slight curve to the right the whole way down. A bit ahead of them, Kaitlynn thought she could see a dim greenish light and hear the sound of running water. As they approached the light, she saw that the tunnel opened into a large cavern. Growing out of the dirt floor along the walls of the cavern seemed to be a number of large mushrooms, which seemed to be what was giving off the strange green light. These strange glowing mushrooms came all the way up to Kaitlynn's waist and had to be at least two feet in radius. In the middle of the cavern, there was a pond, the water of which was bubbling slightly in the middle, and there was steam rising above the water. Kaitlynn thought that it might be a hot spring like the one Queen Reliara had taken her to in Elfwood. There were a number of stalactites above the water, and Kaitlynn thought she saw the point of at least one stalagmite poking its tip out of the water. Heading out of the room on the other side was another tunnel, but the water went out that way as well, taking up much of the cave as it went. "Looks like we're all going to get wet on this ride," Kaitlynn thought to herself with a wry smile. She hoped that the water was at least decently warm, for Shanja's sake.

"I've never seen anything like this before," whispered Jali as she entered the room, bringing up the rear of the group. Despite how quietly she had said it, her words carried throughout the room.

"Yeah, me neither," replied Kaitlynn, the awe clearly audible in her voice. Even though this world was strange to her, she had come to expect the unexpected. But to find out that there were things that were still strange and wondrous to the inhabitants of such a world surprised her. She considered this and realized that it probably shouldn't. She remembered watching one of those marine biology documentaries and seeing all the crazy sea life on Earth that she'd never known had existed, and the satyrs didn't even have the benefit of the Discovery Channel.

Derrith walked over to one of the mushrooms, cut a small piece off with his sword, and tossed it back to Jali. "Try it," he said, cutting another piece for himself and popping it into his mouth. "We have these deep in the Elfwood, and they are delicious." In turn, each of them tried some of the strange glowing mushrooms. Kaitlynn found that with even just a little bit of it she felt full, but also felt like she was more aware. The world seemed to have sharper edges somehow.

"So, there are some mushrooms on Earth that can cause hallucinations," she told them. "These aren't like those are they?" she asked Derrith, her face scrunched up in concern.

"They do have some effects," he said, "but they are helpful ones. Things seem to come more into focus. They can be very helpful on a long patrol when I start to get tired."

"Yeah, I noticed," she replied with a chuckle. "That's why I asked. I was just making sure these weren't *that* kind of magic mushroom is all. Somalie is different enough as it is without me seeing things that aren't there." She heard Jali chuckle at her joke and turned and gave her a smile.

Faljon walked over to the hot spring and bent down to run his fingers through the water, testing its temperature. With a nod of approval, he stood and walked into the water and began cleaning himself off. The other satyrs followed along and did the same, taking the opportunity to clean off as much of the dirt and grime from the trail as possible. Kaitlynn and Derrith stayed at the water's edge keeping a watch until the three satyrs were done, and then they both stripped down and took their own turns while the satyrs took over on watch. Kaitlynn had considered passing on the opportunity for a minute. But after so much time with them all, and then lying next to Shanja as they had to keep her alive, her modesty didn't seem to matter as much anymore. She did, however, stay on the opposite side of the spring as Derrith, though not without stealing a glance in the elf's direction once or twice. She could feel herself falling in love with Faljon, but she wasn't going to pass up a good view if she could see it discreetly enough. The elves were all beautiful in her opinion, and despite his sometimes gruff exterior, Derrith was no exception to that rule.

The water was warm, and it felt great on her skin. Despite her ability to warm herself from within, her skin had gotten a bit of frost burn from the wind and cold as they had crossed the mountains. She wished she had some soap and shampoo with her to truly get all the grime out but figured that the warm rinse would have to do. She dipped her head back until her hair was submerged and ran her fingers through it a few times trying to get all the knots that had accumulated out of it. She did a quick inventory of her body and noticed that her arms and legs were more muscular than they had been before she had come to Somalie. The walking, in particular, had done her a lot of good and tightened up her lower body; her biceps were a bit more pronounced as well. She smiled to herself, wondering if she'd ever been in as good of shape as she was currently, and if she'd ever be able to maintain it if she managed to get back home after all. She did wish that she had a razor though, as things had started to get a little bit out of hand in some places. She started to worry about what she would do if she got her monthly visit while in this strange world as well but pushed those thoughts away. Hopefully, she'd manage to dodge that particular bullet.

When she was done, she climbed out of the water, pulled her coat out of her backpack, tossed it on and looked over at Faljon. He had been watching her, and he smiled his toothy grin at her. She filled her head with thoughts of him and found herself drying off in no time. Once she was dry, she pulled her clothes and armor back on and put her coat back into the backpack. She noticed that the provisions she had stored in there were starting to look a little bit thin, so she took her sweatshirt out of the bag, tossed it aside, and cut one of the mushrooms up with her sword and stuffed it into the backpack. "That oughta be enough," she thought to herself as she tied it closed.

They headed out again down the tunnel with the water running through it. The water was only about ankle deep here, and Kaitlynn carried her boots and stuffed her socks inside of them to keep them dry. It wasn't long before the water cooled considerably as it flowed further and further from the hot spring beneath the mountain. She began warming herself from within once the water got below a certain threshold and discovered that the air temperature was dropping at a significant pace as well. About an hour after they left the large cavern the water started to get a thin film of ice on top of it. Kaitlynn waited until the ice was thick enough to hold her weight before putting her boots back on. It wasn't much longer before they could see the proverbial, light at the end of the tunnel, as well as hear the wind howling outside again.

Once they came to the cave mouth at the end of the tunnel, they discovered that they were much lower on the mountain than they had been when they'd entered it on the other side. The stream was completely frozen here and flowed down the side of the mountain in an icy pirouette back and forth before it fell off to the east behind the mountains, away from the large mountain pass to the west.

Kaitlynn carefully stuck her head out of the cave and looked to the west. In the distance below they could see Uligart's army marching past. From here she could see the lizardmen, who walked almost as if in slow motion through the snow. They were a rainbow of colors, various shades of green, red, yellow, black, and blue among them. They looked just as menacing as the ones they had fought in the swamp, only there were far more of them this time. She unconsciously caressed the scar on her right arm where one of them had bitten her as she had stabbed it through the mouth. Faljon joined her at the mouth of the cave and after glancing at the passing army looked up at the sky. "It's still early," he said. "We'll have to move fast to stay out of sight."

"I have an idea," Kaitlynn said, flashing him a mischievous grin. She backed up into the cave and then got a running start before dropping down onto her backside as she exited the cave, using the momentum and the ice of the frozen stream like a slide. She managed to suppress the desire to scream with delight as she slid, leaning from side to side as she approached each curve of the iced-over waterslide of the stream, and rode it all the way to the bottom on the far side of the mountains away from the large pass to their west. From the bottom, she looked up and couldn't even see the cave mouth that she had just left a few short minutes before. It wasn't long before the three satyrs followed her down, flopped over on their sides together as if they were driving a makeshift bobsled that had toppled over. "And taking last place, the team from Jamaica," Kaitlynn thought to herself while trying to suppress a chuckle. She helped them all to their feet just in time to get them out of the way as Derrith came barreling down the frozen stream after them. He appeared to have done much better at keeping his balance than the group of satyrs had.

"That was crazy," said Shanja as she dusted the snow out of her hair. "What made you think to do that?"

Kaitlynn smiled. "On Earth, when I was a kid, when it would snow my dad would take me sledding," she replied. "We had this circular sled with straps called a flying saucer that I would sit in and hold onto as I would slide down the hill behind my school on top of the snow. It was the best." The memories of her youth came flooding back to her and filled her heart. She hoped that Shanja had understood her story. She wasn't sure if the satyrs understood even what the concept of "school" was.

"The wind's not as bad down here," Derrith said, looking off into the distance as the frozen stream continued to the south and wound its way around the next peak. "If we can stay down in this ravine and go around the next mountain, we might make better time, and perhaps find shelter."

"Indeed," replied Faljon. "We'll have to watch our footing on the ice, but I agree."

Kaitlynn looked over at Shanja. The satyr wasn't shivering anymore and seemed to be doing well. This made Kaitlynn even happier than she was already feeling. "Well, what are we waiting for, let's go," she said with a smile and gave Faljon a playful nudge with her elbow. They all filed into a line to work their way through the thin ravine, continuing to the south.

59

The raven had lost them in the mountains. It had seen them enter the cave, but it had made sure not to get too close to its opening where they could see it. For a few moments, it had thought that it was going to get a meal when it saw one of the satyrs fall over in the cold. But then the human had carried her into the cave, spoiling its opportunity for fresh meat. It had thought about following them in its incorporeal form, but it didn't know how long it could hold it. So instead, it had circled. But they hadn't come out of the cave, and now it feared what would happen when its master found out that it had lost them.

After it had circled for almost two days and the satyrs had not yet emerged from the cave, the raven decided to take the risk. It flew down into the cave mouth and became incorporeal. It turned out it needn't have bothered; the satyrs and their companions were gone. It screeched a loud curse that only its master would have understood and then flew out of the cave. It began flying in ever-widening circles, hoping that it could find them again and not have to risk its master's wrath.

60

Uliah had made great time since she'd left the others on her way back to Elfwood. She loathed herself for leaving them, but she could feel the seed of her satyrling growing within her, and she had to protect that life. Even still, she was surprised to have already come upon the marching armies of dwarves, elves, and centaurs heading in the opposite direction. King Delavon had sent messengers to the other kings, and they had come forward to meet her as soon as word had gotten back to him that one of the satyrs was coming back the other way.

"Well met, satyrn," he said as he stepped from the ranks. Kings Halcor and King Garoth stepped forward with him. Uliah bowed low to the three of them. "What news do you have?" he asked her after beckoning her to rise.

"The others have reached the mountains. We had two members of our party fall in battle with a wyvern," she replied. "The Keepers are well, as is Derrith. But Delok and Peton..." she trailed off and wiped away a tear before it managed to flow down her cheek.

"Why are you here then?" asked Garoth, his voice gruff. "Why would you abandon your mission?"

"I am with child," she replied. "They sent me back. The father is one of the ones who fell." She wiped away another tear with the back of her hand.

"Wait, why would they send a pregnant woman on a mission like this in the first place?" asked Garoth, his quick temper clearly rising.

"I'm guessing she wasn't with child when they left," replied Halcor quietly. The dwarf's eyes seemed to go wide with understanding, and Uliah simply nodded while looking down at the ground and examining her hooves again.

"I understand," replied King Delavon. "King Halcor, can you spare a rider to take her back to Elfwood? My people can watch over her there."

"Aye," the centaur replied and then motioned to one of his attendants. "Take the satyress here back to Elfwood. Present her to Queen Reliara." The attendant nodded and reached a hand down to help Uliah onto his back. She threw her legs over him and wrapped her arms tightly around his midriff, careful not to let her claws accidentally dig into his skin.

"As I said, my King, they have entered the mountains," Uliah said, looking at Delavon. "How they fared from there, I do not know. But we encountered two ambushes before we fought the wyvern: goblins and lizardmen. Be careful."

Delavon nodded to her. "We shall be wary," he replied.

The attendant rode off then with Uliah on her back, leaving the three kings behind them. Uliah looked around at the sheer size of the army. She saw a contingent of satyrn in their midst as well and smiled. She hoped that they would find glory and victory and hoped that her friends in the mountains would be able to complete their mission and retrieve the Gate. However, she feared what they might run into in those mountains. The wyverns weren't the only beasts that resided there, never mind the threat of Uligart and his armies. They traveled at a high gallop past the rest of the vast grasslands and into the rocky terrain. At this pace, Uliah thought that she might actually be able to see the vast forests of Elfwood in the distance just before sundown.

61

"Five of them against Uligart's army," howled Garoth. "They're as good as dead." He had waited until the satyr had ridden well out of earshot before speaking his mind. All three of the Kings had stood in silence until that moment, but now Halcor and Delavon were looking at the dwarf. "Assuming the cold doesn't kill them first, that is."

"We must step up the pace then," replied Delavon, his voice steady. "King Halcor, can you spare a rider or two to scout ahead for further ambushes?"

"Indeed, I shall do so," replied the centaur. "My riders returned earlier from tracking down the dwarves who were still on their way and had them reroute to meet us at the Frostspire Gap. I can send them forward as scouts."

"Very well," replied Delavon. He had quietly assessed the odds of the small party of satyrn's success as low to begin with, but now that their number had been almost halved, he shared the dwarven king's concerns. "We keep moving, for now, move until well after sundown, and move again before sunup. We need to make up as much distance as we can." He nodded at the other two kings and then walked off to return to his men and began issuing orders.

62

The wind wasn't as bad down in the ravine that the frozen stream had cut between the mountains, but it was still brisk and constant even if the worst of the gusts were being blocked by the peaks on either side of them. Kaitlynn was finding herself more and more grateful for the magic in her blood the more time she spent in this place. She looked up and saw the clouds above were gathering; there would be more snow soon. She glanced over at Shanja again, her new hourly ritual to make sure that the satyr was doing all right, and she seemed to be managing much better than she had before they'd had to keep warm her in the cave for an entire day.

The ice of the frozen stream was slippery, and they'd all had minor spills as they'd made their way along since they'd emerged from the tunnel earlier that morning. They'd wrapped their way around the first mountain in about half the time it would have taken to go over it, and the occasional downward slope of the stream had allowed them to slide down it again to gain some additional distance. But as they rounded the mountain, they could see a straight shot through to the pass on the other side. There they could see the massive army on the other side passing by. It was nearly dark, and they decided to wait until the cover of darkness before passing along to the other side of the gap and the cover of the next peak.

Kaitlynn dug into her bag while they waited and brought out some of the mushroom she gathered. She noticed that in the sunlight, it didn't glow the way it did in the darkness of the cave. She wondered if that was because she had cut it out of the ground, or if its phosphorescence was a natural reaction to the lack of light. She took Jali's dagger and cut small pieces off for everyone and handed them out to the rest of the group. It didn't take long before they all had their hunger completely sated.

Faljon went over to the gap and hid against the rocks while peering at the passing army. The lizardmen were off in the distance now, and it was the goblins that were in this part of the Frostspire Gap now, moving off towards King Delavon's army gathering to the north. Faljon hoped that the elves had managed to assemble a sizable force and that they were on their way here by now. He stayed there and kept a watch on the passing goblins, making sure none wandered off their lines and came towards them.

The clouds above had grown dark and filled the sky before the sun had had a chance to settle behind the mountains. The wind picked up and the first flurries began to drift slowly to the ground. Kaitlynn thought they might be able to move out before night if the weather could give them enough cover, but the snow stayed light, dropping only a new dusting on top of the snow already frozen on the ground. It wasn't until after nightfall that they finally made their move.

Kaitlynn looked off towards the west where she could hear Uligart's army still passing as the sound was carried on the winds, but in the darkness, she couldn't see them. Still, the satyrs had all decided not to let their eyes adjust, lest they any attract suspicion. Besides, it turned out that Derrith could see in the dark without making his eyes glow, so they followed him while holding hands to make sure no one strayed from the path. It was dangerous to walk on the ice in total darkness, but the freshly falling snow gave them a bit more traction than they had had earlier, and they took it slowly. It took only about fifteen minutes to clear the gap in the mountains that would have made them all visible to the enemy army, but Kaitlynn felt horribly exposed for that time. Once they'd cleared the gap, she felt like she could exhale for the first time since they had started moving again. She let her eyes adjust, looked around and saw that the other satyrs had done the same. She was glad to be able to see again, though, with the snow falling, it was almost as if instead of seeing shades of gray, almost everything was a shade of white except the black sky above.

They decided to keep moving for a little while, putting a little bit more distance between themselves and the gap. They moved on for another half an hour or so, until the snow started to come down in a much heavier dose than it had up to that point. Kaitlynn feared they might be looking at a decently sized blizzard overnight, and that would certainly slow their progress. The good news was that it would also slow Uligart's army as it tried to pass through the mountains, especially the cold-blooded lizardmen.

They made camp for the night and set watches. In the morning, Kaitlynn passed out more of the pieces of mushroom to everyone and they headed out again. The snow had fallen heavily overnight and was still falling as they headed out. There was at least two feet of fresh powder on the ground, though the wind had blown it into large drifts against the side of the steep slopes to their right as they traveled south through the ravine. After about three hours, the stream turned as if it was going through the mountain they'd been passing on their right, and there was a rocky cliff face covered in snow and ice directly in front of them.

"Crap," said Kaitlynn as she stared at the cliff in front of them and pursed her lips. "We're gonna have to go back."

"Not necessarily" replied Derrith as he walked over to the large snowdrift where the stream appeared to end. He began digging in the snow with his hands. Jali and Faljon joined in, but eventually, they hit rock below. "That's unfortunate," said Derrith, shaking his head.

"What about closer to the waterline?" asked Shanja, and she stepped in and started digging closer to the level of the ice at the base of the slope. It took a few minutes, but eventually, she broke through the snow and discovered and opening a little more than a foot tall at the base of the mountain. The stream continued in under the mountain, frozen as far as Kaitlynn could see into the darkness.

"Can we fit in there?" asked Kaitlynn. "And where does it go?"

"Only one way to find out," replied Faljon as he dropped down onto his stomach and slid his body into the small opening headfirst. It was slow going, pulling himself along on his stomach, but eventually, there was enough room for the next person to slide themselves in. Derrith took his bow off his back and followed Faljon with it in his hand. He managed to just barely fit through the opening, and Kaitlynn saw that if the elf had raised his head at all, he would have hit it on the roof of the cavern. Shanja slid under next, followed by Kaitlynn. She slid off her backpack before sliding into the hole, wrapping one of the straps around her arm so she could pull it through. It barely fit through the opening, and she hoped that it wouldn't snag on anything as she tried to enter the cavern herself.

As Kaitlynn entered the opening, she found that she was just barely able to fit inside. "I've never been so happy to be a B-Cup," she thought to herself with a quiet snicker as she slid her way in. She was not fond of how tight it was inside, and the cold seemed harder to keep out of her skin with the length of her body pressed against the ice. She imagined it must be worse for the satyrs, since they wore nothing at all, and hoped that Shanja would be all right. She had to keep her face low against the ice as well or else she would have cracked her head on the rocks above, and she didn't think Derrith would be able to heal a head wound in these conditions. She heard Jali slide into the opening behind her, and she started to feel like she was trapped, or worse yet, entombed. She stopped, took a couple of deep breaths, and exhaled them both slowly.

"Are you all right, Kaitlynn?" Jali asked from behind her.

"Yeah, just a little tight in here," she replied. She kept her voice steady despite the rising fear and did everything she could to push it to the darkest recesses of her mind. Panic would surely get her killed in here under the mountain.

Kaitlynn started pulling herself forward again, slowly at first, but eventually, she got into a rhythm, and that seemed to help her fears subside slightly. It wasn't long before she heard Faljon up ahead telling them that the cave was opening a little bit. She breathed a sigh of relief at that news and quickened her pace as much as she could until she was practically crawling up Shanja's legs. After a few more minutes, the cave was at least tall enough that she could raise her head and see where she was going, which made her feel a lot better, though she had been hoping that it would open a lot more than that.

"Hold," she heard Faljon say up ahead, though he had kept his voice low. Kaitlynn came to a stop. The cave seemed wider here as well as a little bit taller, and she saw that Derrith had pulled himself up beside Faljon up ahead.

"Scoot over," she said while tapping Shanja lightly on the leg. The satyr slid over to her left and allowed Kaitlynn to pull herself up along-side her. Jali slid up behind as well. "Hey, what's up?" she asked, her voice barely above a whisper. Shanja only shrugged. In the darkness, all they could really see, even with their eyes adjusted to the dark, was their companions in front of them.

Faljon rolled over onto his side and crunched his body down so that he could address everyone behind him. "There's a steep drop off up ahead. I can't see how far down it goes, but I can hear running water," he said. "And voices," he added.

"Frost elves," said Derrith. "I recognize the dialect but can't hear it well enough to understand what they're saying."

"Can you see any farther than Faljon can?" asked Kaitlynn.

"I can't see the bottom if that's what you're asking," he replied. "But the ice is thinner here, and I'm willing to bet that this is where they get the water for the Obsidian Keep."

"So, we're there," said Jali. There was a somber darkness in her voice.

"It appears so," replied Derrith.

A hush fell over the group then. After a few minutes, Kaitlynn asked, "Can we chimney down?"

"What tis, 'chimney'?" asked Faljon.

"Like, press our legs against the rocks on one side and our backs against the other, and lower ourselves down," she replied. "I've gone rock climbing a couple of times. I might be able to do it if it's not too wide." Kaitlynn decided not to mention that she'd never climbed without a rope and her ex-fiancé belaying for her before. She wasn't sure if they would even understand the references, and it wouldn't matter much in any case.

"Come up and take a look," replied Faljon. Derrith and the satyrs slid around like the plastic pieces of one of those little handheld puzzles that kids usually play with for about thirty seconds before they end up confined to the bottom of a toy box for the rest of eternity, giving her room to come up to the front next to Faljon. She peered over the edge into the darkness below. The cave was too wide from side to side for her to be able to reach across with her legs, but from where the water dropped off to the cave wall on the other side was just about the right fit. Unfortunately, it meant that she would have to use the ice for the support on one side, and that would be extremely dangerous.

"Shanja, help me slide my boots off, please," she whispered back behind her. Shanja started working on the zippers on her boots and pulled them off. "Socks too," she said, and Shanja pulled them off as well. She looked over at Faljon and raised her eyebrows as she took a deep breath. "Well, here goes," she said. She untangled the strap of her backpack from around her arm and left in on her shield on the ice next to her before she rolled onto her back and pulled her legs up as far as she could. "Gimme something to push off against," she said, and Shanja repositioned herself and turned her back to Kaitlynn, giving her a flat surface to push off against. Kaitlynn took a deep breath and counted to five in her head, and then she pushed with her legs and shot off the edge of the ice towards the darkness below.

As soon as the back of her neck passed the edge of the ice, Kaitlynn started lifting her head up and bringing her legs back in. Her upper back hit the rock wall on the other side and she stuck her legs out into the ice wall on the side. She hit the rock wall hard, and her feet almost slipped, but she was already thinking about that night in the pond with Faljon. She could feel the ice sizzle beneath her feet as she locked herself in place. She looked up and saw Faljon and Derrith staring down at her, both their mouths slightly agape. She understood exactly how they felt, as she had thought that there had been about a sixty-three percent chance that her legs wouldn't have been able to hold her at first and was hoping that at the very least the fall would either end in a water landing or just kill her outright. To Kaitlynn, the idea of landing on the hard ground, breaking every bone in her body, and still living through it seemed to actually be the worst potential outcome had she fallen.

"Are you going to be able to hold?" Faljon asked her. His arm was extended as if to grab onto her so she wouldn't fall, his reaction had been instinctual as she'd gone over the edge.

"If I move slowly," she replied, her voice low. She looked down, saw only blackness below, and slowly started sliding herself down the rock wall a few inches at a time. Each occasion that she planted a foot, she waited just long enough to melt enough ice to give her a foothold before moving on and lowering herself again. The sound of the running water below got louder with each meter she passed until eventually she went to stick out her foot and the ice started to break underneath it as she pushed. She took it extra slow here, waiting until her foot pressed all the way through to the rock beneath and made sure that her toes wouldn't slip on the wet surface before she moved again. She could feel the water trickling over her feet beneath the surface of the ice. It was cold, but it kept her focused on the task at hand. She paused, looked up, and realized she could still see Faljon and Derrith looking down at her from above. She glanced down and she was just able to see the water running below her. The rock face that her back was against was going to run out about ten feet before the water below, and the thinning ice under her feet was a trickling waterfall for the last few feet as well. There would be no way down quietly; she was going to have to drop. She kept moving herself down slowly until she was just above where the rocks to her back ended. She looked up and she couldn't see Derrith anymore, but she could still see the faint glow of Faljon's eyes above. She looked up at him and smiled, though she was sure he couldn't see it from there. She took a deep breath, pulled her legs away from the cliff face while pushing her back away from the opposite wall with her hands, and dropped towards the water below.

Kaitlynn had her hand on the hilt of her sword and twisted her body in midair to land facing the opening in the cave behind her. She pulled her legs up to try and brace herself for a landing, but she hit the water and dropped right down in with a loud splash, the water was deep enough that it was well above her head and far deeper below her. She kicked herself back towards the surface, and as soon as she managed to get her head above the water, she saw two frost elves staring at her. They were both women with a pair of buckets and heavy white furs for clothes. Their eyes were wide with surprise and fear as they looked at her. One of them yelled something she didn't understand as they started to turn and run from the cavern.

"Drop, the water's deep enough!" she yelled back up as she swam towards the edge of the water where the two women had stood. She heard the first splashes behind her and figured at least two of her companions had jumped at once. She got to the edge of the water and started running, cutting the two women off before they could leave the cave. She was surprised that she'd been able to beat them to the exit but guessed that their heavy furs must have slowed them down. Kaitlynn blocked their path with her sword and motioned for them both to be quiet. Derrith and Faljon were just surfacing behind the two frost elves and swimming towards them when there were two more splashes just behind them. Derrith made his way out of the water first, clearly more adept at swimming than the satyrs were with their hooves and ran over to Kaitlynn. He looked at the two women and then began talking to them quietly in elvish. Kaitlynn didn't understand what he was telling them, but they both seemed to calm down and started nodding and responding in their own slightly different version of Elvish. Kaitlynn imagined that the experience must be like when foreigners who didn't speak the language would be visiting the United States and hear two people from different parts of the country speaking English in different accents to each other.

Eventually, all the satyrs had made their way onto dry land and joined them all. Shanja handed Kaitlynn her backpack and shield. "Your boots are in the bag," she said as she handed it over. Kaitlynn pulled them out and put them on. Amazingly, everything in the backpack was completely dry, even if Kaitlynn's clothes were completely soaked through from the frigid water. Even while keeping warm thoughts in her heart, it still took a minute for Kaitlynn's body to stop shaking. She wondered if it was purely a reaction to the cold, or some combination of fear and adrenaline that had kicked in as she had fallen into the water.

"What did you tell them, Derrith?" asked Faljon as he came up to the group.

"I told them that we are not here to hurt them, we're here to free them," replied the elf. "They've agreed to help us into the Keep."

"Just like that," asked Shanja. She was clearly skeptical and didn't seem to trust the two frost elves.

"Uligart rules through fear. Many of his own people would rather be free of him," the elf replied. Both of the frost elven women shuddered at the mention of their ruler's name.

"We'll follow your lead then, Derrith," replied Faljon. He turned and looked at Kaitlynn. "Are you all right?" he asked?

She nodded at him and smiled. "Yeah, I'm okay," she said. "But I'd prefer not to pull that stunt again." She took a deep breath and chuckled reflexively. In her mind, she was still trying to figure out how she had pulled the stunt off in the first place, and where she had gotten the guts to even consider trying it.

"I agree," he responded, his eyes serious. "All right, let's go," he said, nodding to Derrith to lead the way. The elf turned to the two women, said something in elvish to them, and they led the group out of the cave.

The entrance to the cave looked like it was intricately cut out of the mountain by hand. As they exited the cavern, Kaitlynn looked around and saw that this was just one room in a large complex of caves beneath the mountain. "I thought you said that the frost elves lived above ground?" she asked Derrith.

"I thought that they did," he replied. "I didn't know anything about these caves." He asked one of the women about them, and after a brief exchange he said, "They say that the caves run throughout the mountains to allow them to move troops quickly and use surprise tactics on invaders."

"Why don't they have the lizardmen and goblins moving through them then?" asked Jali. "The lizardmen are slowed by the cold. They could have moved their whole army much quicker underground."

"Wouldn't you hold some secrets back from allies who might one day be enemies?" replied Shanja. Jali considered this and then nodded. Kaitlynn had listened to the exchange and found Shanja's logic sound. She silently admitted to herself that she would never have considered the satyr's idea. It was clear that she spoke with the knowledge that only comes through years of experience.

They moved into a narrow passageway that curved slightly back and forth, but also seemed to slope uphill. As the cave made a sharp turn to the left, it opened into another large cavern. From here there were two exits on the far side of the cavern. The two frost elven women headed towards the exit on the left when a black metal portcullis slammed down through the cavern entrance behind them. Two more of the gates slammed down, blocking the other two doors. They were trapped in the large cavern, all seven of them. The two frost elves ran towards one of the gates and began shaking it, wailing something in their language that Kaitlynn couldn't understand.

It was then that Kaitlynn heard a low growling sound coming from off to their right and above them. She turned and looked up. On a rock outcropping just up above her head, she saw another portcullis that was closing with two frost elves standing behind it. They were looking down and watching them, and the gate slammed shut between them. In front of the gate, she saw two large cats the size of the tigers that she'd seen at the Phoenix Zoo. Both had thick white fur and large overgrown incisors, like the pictures she had seen of saber-toothed tigers in books and museums. The one on the left was growling down at them from above, while the other one was licking its chops, its tongue lolling on its tusk for a moment with a hungry gleam in its eyes.

"Oh shit," she said, her voice low, but loud enough to carry to the rest of the room.

"That's a problem," said Derrith in a surprisingly dry tone, as he slung his bow off his back and notched an arrow from his quiver. He said something to the two frost elven women, and they ran behind the party and pressed themselves against the far wall.

The large snow cat that had been growling leaped in the air and passed right over Kaitlynn's head. Both Derrith and Jali unleashed arrows at it as it leaped over her and came crashing down on Faljon. The satyr had pulled out his spear and impaled the beast as it landed on him. It let out a loud howl of pain and made to bite down on the Keeper, but Shanja had run over and run it through with her own spear right behind its head and out the other side. It tried to roar in pain as it fell over on its side, but there was a gargling sound in its throat. It twitched and coughed a couple of times until finally, it lay quiet and unmoving. Shanja tried to pull her spear out of the large cat, but it was embedded too deeply, and she pulled her sword out of its sheath instead.

Faljon was slowly getting up off the ground and pulling out his sword. There were deep claw scratches on his shoulders and chest which bled profusely, but he seemed otherwise unfazed. Kaitlynn turned back around and looked up at the other large cat above them. It seemed to be looking around at them but biding its time. Kaitlynn was worried that if Derrith couldn't work on Faljon's wounds soon, she might lose him. Despite how relatively short their relationship had been, the thought of facing his loss so soon after her father's death was almost too much for her to bear.

Kaitlynn tried to keep her focus on the battle and watched as Jali let an arrow fly at the beast on the ledge above them. The large snow cat sidestepped it and then leaped down at her while she tried to notch another arrow. Derrith let an arrow of his own fly while the large cat was in the air and it embedded in its side, but it came crashing down on Jali, nonetheless. Its claws dug into her shoulders, and it was biting down on her face before any of the others could spring into action. There was a scream that was lost in something that sounded like water gurgling through a broken faucet. Kaitlynn ran over and stabbed the thing though its back, while Faljon and Shanja attacked it from the side. Another arrow came protruding out of its eye socket with a loud popping sound as Derrith shot his arrow between Faljon and Shanja, landing the killing blow straight through its freshly mutilated eye and into its brain.

The snowcat dropped, its dead weight crushing down on Jali's now life-less form below it. Her pretty face was mostly mauled away, and Kaitlynn thought that she might be sick and might cry all at the same time. "May she rest eternal, Keeper of Souls," she heard herself say while choking back a sob. Faljon and Shanja nodded and repeated the prayer, but she turned away, unable to look anymore as the tears started to fall down her face, cutting a path in the streaks of blood that had flown onto her.

She looked up and saw the two frost elves standing behind the portcullis up above. They were looking down at them all with contempt in their eyes. Through her blurry eyes, she could see now that they were holding chains in their hands. She looked over at the beast lying dead in the cavern and saw a large leather collar sticking out from under the thick fur on one of the snow cat's necks. Kaitlynn looked back up at them again, and her eyes had gone as narrow as slits. She started walking towards the overhang where the cats had been, and then jumped up and grabbed the lip of the ledge, pulling herself up. She pulled her sword back out, and they started backing away from the gate and dropped their chains. "Leashes," she thought, and her blood began to boil. The two frost elves started to look like they might panic, and she was sure that they saw murder in her eyes. She threw her shoulder against the gate as hard as she could, then backed away and did it again. The metal of the gate clanged harmlessly against the supports that were carved into the rock and held it in place. She could see the chain that would raise the gate on the other side of the opening but knew she wouldn't be able to reach through and pull the gate up. She slammed her shoulder against the gate one more time out of frustration, wishing that she knew how to use a bow.

Kaitlynn turned and looked back down at what remained of the group. She saw Derrith tending to Faljon's wounds and could see them starting to close. Shanja knelt over Jali's remains; the snowcat had been moved off her lifeless form. She turned back and stared a hole through the two frost elven beast masters beyond the gate, silently cursing them for unleashing more death upon her friends and swearing that she would make them pay. She would make all of them pay.

63

Word had gotten back to Uligart. His troops were positioned and ready for the coming attack. The lizardmen had filled the mountain gap before the snowline. It was still colder than would be comfortable for them to fight well, but the narrow opening of the gap would give them the advantage. The goblins and some of his frost elves had filed in behind in the gap above the snow line and behind the next series of mountains. The goblins were warm-blooded at least and should be able to fight, and the frost elves would be right at home in the elements. He had more of his frost elves back at the Keep, fortifying it in case Delavon's army managed to break through. However, he did not think that that particular outcome was likely.

Uligart looked at his blackened left hand. It was curled and useless below the forearm, yet as hard as a rock. He had ruined it when he was young and touched the dark magic in his blood for the first time. He had grown wiser and more cautious since then, and it had been a long, slow climb up the ranks of his people until he had been able to take control of them. He ruled them now with his blackened fist from the top of his Obsidian Keep. He had once thought that his hand would be the first thing he would fix once he controlled the power of the Old Gods within the Gate, but now he'd since decided that he liked the way it put fear into the eyes of his people. He would keep it as it was, and rule all of Somalie with this new power.

He'd expected the group of satyrn to come across his troops by now and was disappointed when he found out that the raven had lost them in the mountains. They were in the caves then, and he'd put his men on alert to be prepared for them to attempt to enter the keep from below. For its failure, he had caged the raven without food, which he knew would be the worst punishment the creature could possibly endure. It was always hungry; the price of the magic that Uligart had used to give it its unnatural powers. At first, it had attempted to become insubstantial and fly through the cage but had found that it could not pass through the bars. Uligart had given the bird its magic and wouldn't be foolish enough to not block its ability to escape. Now it sat quietly in the cage, staring out at him. He thought he could detect contempt in the thing's blood red eyes. This pleased him, for the raven would not dare fail him again. Not if it wanted to feed.

As he stood in his room at the top of the keep, his lieutenant Nalidur stepped up to the door and coughed quietly to get his attention. The frost elf was dressed in a heavy white cuirass of furs with a large sword on his back. Uligart turned and looked at him. "Speak, Nalidur," he said.

"My King," replied the frost elf, "We have them. They attempted to enter through the water caves."

Uligart raised a single eyebrow. This approach impressed him slightly. He knew how difficult it would have been to get through the small cave where the water flowed into the keep. "And where are they now?" he asked, sounding far more disinterested than he actually was.

"The four that still live are trapped," replied Nalidur. "We dropped the portcullises around them as they entered the arena in the caves below the keep. There are two peasant women of ours who are trapped with them."

"And the human?" asked Uligart now, his interest no longer hidden.

"She's alive," replied his lieutenant. "The beast masters got carried away and released the frost tigers. They killed them, but one of the satyrn fell as well."

Uligart shrugged slightly. The loss of the two beasts was a minor inconvenience, but they could be replaced. The mountains were ripe with the creatures. Still, the two beast masters would need to be punished for putting the human at risk.

"Bring them all to me at the top of the tower," said Uligart, a dark glow in his frozen eyes. "Unharmed," he added. "I would give these four that survived so deep into our territory and almost made it into my keep the honor of seeing my victory. Kill the peasants and the beast masters for their failures. Publicly." The frost elven village was only over the next rise on the side of the mountain in the pass, and the occasional spectacle was good for keeping the commoners in line.

"Yes, my King," replied Nalidur. He turned on his heel and walked towards the stairs that would take him deep below into the heart of the keep.

Uligart smiled. Soon he would have everything he needed to open the Gate and assume the power that lay within. He took the painting off the wall in his room and carried it up the stairs to the top of the tower and leaned it against the parapet. He looked into the painting and saw the woman. She paced back and forth in the room on the other side, her form like brushstrokes that flowed across the room as if the painting was a work in progress constantly being adjusted by the artist, and somehow erased from her previous place on its canvas. He smiled his poisonous grin and waited for his moment of triumph.

64

The carcass of the dead wyvern and the remains of the two satyrn gave off an awful stench. Delavon watched as a number of the satyrn who had marched with them had gone over to pay their respects to their two dead. It was a grisly scene, especially the one that had been torn in half. It looked like some scavengers had picked much of that one clean as if the once living being were mere carrion on the side of the path south into the Frostspire Mountains.

King Halcor had stridden up to him and was standing and watching the scene quietly at his side. One of his centaurs rode up and bowed low, his forelegs bending as well as his upper body. "My king, there's an army of lizardmen spread out just on the other side of these mountains in the Frostspire Gap," he said. "Our riders were able to get in and out without being attacked, but the entrance to the pass is not very wide. It will be hard to get troops through there without being overwhelmed on the other side."

Delavon turned and looked at the centaurs. His mouth had gone dry. "We'd better send for Garoth," he said, "and devise a strategy."

"Tis a shame they're not on this side of the mountain," replied Halcor, before motioning his man off to find the dwarven king. "My men would run them down easily out here."

Delavon nodded, but he wasn't surprised. Uligart was no fool and wouldn't put his resources in such a vulnerable position. "Can we scout another entrance into the mountains, come around behind them?" he asked. Perhaps if Garoth and I can send our forces in this way and yours could come in behind them, we might be able to take their position and use it against them."

"I will send scouts around in both directions and see what they can find," said the centaur king. "If we can surround them, we may be able to wipe them out. It's cold in those mountains, which works against the lizards."

The elven king nodded again. "If we can attack at dawn, we may catch them particularly vulnerable." He looked around at the size of their army. He was pleased with the numbers, but the dwarves with the siege weapons still hadn't arrived yet. They were still about a day away according to the riders who had been sent back and forth to check their progress. Delavon knew that they wouldn't be overly useful until they reached the Obsidian Keep regardless, but he still didn't like attacking without all of his pieces on the field. Still, the satyress that they had sent back to Elfwood brought grave news of the party that he'd sent ahead, and he feared that time was of the essence. And here before them, lay the grisly evidence of her tale.

Delavon came back from his own thoughts and saw that Garoth was already there and Halcor was explaining the situation and the current plan to the dwarf, who was nodding in agreement. "Aye," he said finally. "But if I may add, my men can flank up the sides of the mountain from here as well. They are used to such terrain. If the elves and satyrn come through the gap, my men can come in from the side and we can hit them from three directions at once. We also have hundreds of men with crossbows; they can hit them from above. They could even lead some of your elven archers up there as well, dropping a bunch of the lizards before any of the three charges hit!" There was a gleam in the dwarf's eyes as he brought his own strategies to the table. It was the first time Delavon thought he'd seen the dwarf in any mood other than either dour or grumpy. "I'll send out a few men and have them look for the best place to cross over the mountains to make it happen," he added, and both Halcor and Delavon nodded their agreement. The plan was set in motion, and hopefully, the scouts would come back with news of favorable terrain. No matter what happened though, they would attack at dawn.

65

A few hours had passed, and Kaitlynn had climbed down from the ledge above and come over to check on Faljon. His wounds had been healed by the elf, but his shoulders and chest were covered in fresh pink scars from the claws of the large white snowcat that had attacked him. Kaitlynn thought that they added a certain amount of character to the satyr's looks but was happy that he wasn't too severely hurt either. Derrith sat meditating, replenishing his magic, while Faljon rested to recover as much strength as possible. Shanja had given up on trying to reclaim the spears out of the large cat that had attacked Faljon, as both of them were lodged in far too deep. Hers had not just gone through the creature's neck but had even gone through the hard leather collar and wouldn't budge at all. Faljon's spear had snapped in half when the creature had fallen over with all its weight on it. Either way, they were both a lost cause.

Kaitlynn walked over and knelt by Jali's body. She couldn't look at what was left of her once beautiful face; the snowcat had made a horrific mess of her. Her shoulders had deep cuts and one of her breasts had been nearly ripped off by its razor-sharp claws. Her bow had been snapped in half by the weight of the creature as it had landed on her. Kaitlynn hoped that she had died quickly because what had happened to her looked absolutely awful. She looked down at the mismatched scars on either side of her body, the one from the boarfrog hunting accident when she was younger, and the other from the spear of the lizardman in the swamp. She thought that it was incredibly sad that Jali had survived both of those unfortunate events, only to be torn apart by the thing lying dead to her left.

Kaitlynn felt a hand come down softly on her shoulder and glanced up to see Faljon staring down at her. She stood up and looked him in the eyes. Her emerald-green eyes were still wet as they locked with his, and she wrapped her arms around him without saying a word. They held each other in silence for a few moments, her chin lying on his forehead. She pulled herself back and noticed that one of his horns had been chipped either from one of the snow cat's claws or massive fangs. Silently, she ran a finger over the fresh mark on it; the color scratched through from beneath was whiter than the worn ivory color on the outside of it. He gave her a quizzical look and felt the spot with his own hand, running his finger over the fresh groove. He sighed reflexively, and his eyes went a little bit wider at the realization of how close he had been to have his own head ripped apart.

"Too close," she said, looking down into his emerald eyes. He nodded, and then glanced down at Jali. He knelt and took the dagger off of her belt and handed it to Kaitlynn, and then salvaged whatever arrows he could that hadn't been snapped under the weight of the giant cat and slid them into Derrith's quiver. Kaitlynn watched him do this, and then quietly stuffed the dagger into her boot. It wasn't a natural fit, but if she needed it in a pinch at least she would know where she could find it.

Kaitlynn reached into her backpack and tossed the last of the yellowish apple things around the room to Shanja and Faljon, and then placed one in front of Derrith for when he finished his meditating. It was as she was standing back up that she saw a dart fly into the room and hit Derrith on the side of the neck. He toppled over right away, falling limply to his left.

She started to turn but felt a sharp pinprick in the side of her own neck almost immediately after. She started to pull her sword, but her eyelids suddenly felt very heavy. She saw Shanja rush past her, a dart sticking out of her shoulder just below the collarbone and heard Faljon drop to the ground behind her. She looked at the door they'd been heading towards before the portcullises had closed on them trapping them in the room, and saw two frost elves with blowguns, and two more at the door to the right of it who were already reloading. Another dart hit Shanja in the chest, and she fell over in a heap.

Kaitlynn dropped to her knees, fought to keep her eyes open, and she then felt another dart hit her in the exposed flesh of her right arm. Her sword clattered to the ground as her hand went numb. She started to fall forward, but the darkness claimed her before she hit the ground.

66

The first light of dawn started to spread over the mountains, and Garoth gave the signal. Hundreds of elven archers and dwarves armed with crossbows began raining death down from the top of the hillsides around the large army of lizardmen. It was cold, and they roused slowly as the arrows fell upon them from above. From near the front of their lines, a large black lizardman that seemed to tower over the rest of them and wearing a bone headdress of sorts began loudly hissing something at the others. Moving slowly, they started arming themselves with their spears and attempted to form ranks.

From the north, the elves began pouring out of the gap and charging at the slowly forming lizards. From the southeast, a stream of centaurs poured from over a ridge and came slamming into the back of the lizardmen's ranks, throwing them into a panic. And then from the west, the dwarves came charging down the side of the mountain crashing into the lizard's flanks. Delavon stood and watched the rout take shape, hardly able to believe their luck. There was no direction for the lizards to run, and the cold and their being caught unawares had slowed them considerably. The last of them fell roughly an hour after the attack had begun.

Walking through the fields of the dead after the battle, Delavon, Halcor, and Garoth marveled at the scene before them. They had lost troops, of course. The centaurs had taken the worst of the casualties. The spears of the lizardmen had caught quite a few of them in the initial charge. But the lizardmen had been slaughtered to the very last.

"Unbelievable," said Garoth. "I've seen battles before, but never such a slaughter!" He let out a loud cackle that sounded almost mad and took a swig from a goatskin flagon on his belt. Delavon could smell the scent of alcohol wafting up from below and suppressed a smile. "And you!" exclaimed Garoth, pointing at Halcor, "I never thought you beasties would be able to maneuver in this terrain! You showed me!" He cackled again and took another celebratory drink. Delavon had never seen the dwarf genuinely happy before, and he was finding the experience somewhere between surprising and unsettling.

"We should have the troops form up again," said Halcor, looking away from the spectacle the dwarven king was making of himself. "We need to make our way to the Obsidian Keep as quickly as possible. I can send out riders to scout ahead."

"Yes, of course," replied Delavon. He nodded, and Halcor galloped off.

"Damn useful those beasties!" exclaimed Garoth. "I never would have believed it!"

"Yes, well," began Delavon with a cough, "I'm not sure he liked you calling his men 'beasties'."

"Ah, you're probably right," replied Garoth, putting his flagon back on his belt. "They're damn unsettling though. I'm not used to their kind in my kingdom."

"After all of this, perhaps that will change," replied Delavon. "If we win this after all, perhaps we can rebuild the old alliances for the betterment of all Somalie. We've proven here today that we can all work together."

"Aye, perhaps," replied the dwarf, eyeing the elven king and stroking his long, braided beard. "One thing at a time, though." He walked off and started rallying his troops to form up and prepare to move out. Delavon gave a final glance across the battlefield, taking in the full extent of their victory and then headed off to muster with his own men to continue the march towards Uligart's fortress.

67

The raven had watched the slaughter of the lizardmen while it circled high above. It had been a masterful attack by the army from the Elfwood, and the lizards hadn't stood a chance. It watched as the enemy forces started to reform, and then it flew off towards the Obsidian Keep. It made excellent time, for it had no desire to displease its master again. It flew over the army of goblins and frost elves in the wide snow-covered gap beyond the battlefield and out of sight of the enemies to the north. It fought the winds in the pass until it landed on the parapet at the top of the tower where its master stood.

It squawked its news to its master quickly, and it could see its master's disappointment. It feared that it might be punished again and flinched. But the frost elven king calmed himself and said, "Go, inform the forces in the pass of what has transpired. They must hold the pass at all costs."

The raven took off, not waiting for any further impetus from its master. It flew back the way it had come and searched for the generals of the frost elven and goblin armies in the mountains and gap below.

68

Rebecca had been pacing in her dead ex-husband's living room (her old living room, she reminded herself), for days now with no sigh of Kaitlynn in the painting. She had seen more than enough that had disquieted her, however, enough that she wasn't sure that seeing Kaitlynn through it would be a good thing at all. She'd seen the strange bird with the piercing red eyes, the old pale elf with the gnarled black hand and evil smile, and now the painting had been moved to another place on the other side of the gate with a new view to behold. No longer was the painting in the room inside the tower, but it was now on top of the tower itself. There were mountains covered in snow as far as she could see into the painting. The snow was billowing on the wind, which seemed to move with constant fresh brushstrokes across the canvas, and there was the pale elf once more, pacing along the tower's parapet for the last few hours as she herself had been doing for days now. She had watched the sky of the painting shift from shades of black and slight hues of midnight blue, to the full glory of crimson sunrise. The days over there were the same length, but it seemed like the sun's position in that part of Somalie didn't match up with Eastern Standard Time as sunrise and sunset in the two worlds seemed to miss each other by a few hours.

She was hungry and exhausted. She had barely eaten and had only slept on the couch in the living room since she had arrived. She missed her bed, and her entire body was sore, but she imagined that whatever Kaitlynn was going through on the other side was probably far worse than the minor inconveniences that she had been suffering. Her stomach growled again, louder this time, like a caged animal trying to break free and devour one of its handlers. With a sigh, she finally gave in, meandered upstairs, and rummaged through the fridge for anything that looked like it still might be good. There were a few eggs left in the carton on the top shelf and Rebecca decided that she would risk them. She pulled out a pan and cracked them directly into it, letting them sizzle until they had formed up enough to flip them over. One of the yokes cracked on her as she flipped them, and she cursed silently to herself. After a few minutes, she slid them off the pan and onto her plate and ate them quickly without really tasting them at all.

She didn't want to spend any more time away from the painting then she had to. She lived with the constant fear of seeing her daughter's dead body lying there, displayed in a series of brushstrokes on the canvas. Or worse yet, she feared never seeing her daughter again. The constant uncertainty, she thought, would be a fate far worse than her daughter's death. At least with certainty, she could grieve. As scared as she thought she might be sitting there in the kitchen, she couldn't even begin to conceive of how much more terrified she was about to feel when she went back downstairs and saw what was waiting for her upon the canvas above the fireplace.

69

K aitlynn started to drift slowly back into consciousness, aware that it was bitterly cold, and the wind was biting hard into her face. She opened her eyes and glanced around as discretely as she could. She was sitting prone against a cold stone wall, and across from her, on the ground leaning against a low black wall with snow and ice on top of it, was a painting with a view of her father's living room, as if it was sitting back on the mantle place where she had found it. Standing next to it was an old, pale frost elf in a white robe. He had piercing blue eyes like little balls of ice, and his left hand was gnarled and blackened.

She tried to stand and noticed that her arms were tied behind her back. She looked to her left and saw Faljon, slowly waking next to her. To his side were Shanja and Derrith, and they both were barely alert as well. On either side of them were a number of frost elven warriors in thick white fur cuirasses with large swords on their backs. Beyond them, she saw all of their weapons piled along the walkway, visible but out of reach as if to taunt them. Four of them stepped forward and yanked Kaitlynn and her fellow captives to their feet.

"Who is the Keeper?" asked the old frost elf in flawless satyrn. His icy gaze never seemed to leave Kaitlynn when he asked the question, but it was clear he was speaking to the two satyrs.

"I am the Keeper," said Shanja, her voice sounded strong and full of fight.

"No, I am the Keeper," said Faljon, with a scowl. "I will not have you protecting me," he added, glancing over at Shanja.

Uligart regarded them both for a second. "Oh, but this is too good," he said, with a raspy laugh. "Two Keepers, are there? And you, elf, are you a Keeper too?" He laughed again, and Kaitlynn shuddered at the dreadful sound.

"I am Derrith of the Elfwood, Captain of the Patrol, and I'm here to bring you to justice in the name of King Delavon, Uligart." Derrith spat the words out more so than he spoke them, all the while regarding the old frost elf with a look of utter disdain.

"Yes, I know who you are, Captain," said Uligart with a wry smile. "And I know who you are as well, my dear," he added, turning to Kaitlynn. "You must be the Keeper from Earth. I've been looking forward to meeting you."

"Pleasure's all yours, I'm sure," replied Kaitlynn. Her heart was thudding in her chest loud enough for her to hear it pounding in her ears, but she was pretty proud of herself for that little comeback. "There could be worse last words than that," she thought to herself.

"Oh, not only mine, my dear," replied Uligart, the smile on his face growing wider and more menacing. He turned and looked into the painting, and then Kaitlynn saw what he was looking for. "It seems that Mother might be happy to see you too." He started laughing again, a raspy cackle that gave Kaitlynn goose bumps. "Bring the human forward."

One of the frost elven warriors grabbed her by the shoulders and brought her before the painting. Kaitlynn saw her mother's eyes go wider on the canvas, almost as if it was being repainted with fresh brushstrokes right before her eyes. Uligart stood next to her and put his good right hand in front of her, just below her chin. She saw what looked like a blue flame in the palm of his hand that flickered into life, but she could feel no warmth from it. The flame gave her a chill, colder still than the frozen winds blowing through the pass. From this spot, she could see that they stood on the precipice of the Obsidian Keep, and she could see Uligart's army amassed in the distance below.

Kaitlynn turned her attention back to the painting on the ground in front of her and watched in horror as her mother peered back at her with pure terror plastered to her face. Slowly she nodded and her arms reached for the painting, lifting it off of the mantle. The scene shifted as her mother held it, her forearm blocking part of the view, as she walked through the garage and out the door. Based on what Kaitlynn could see in the painting, the direction she was heading could only be towards the woods behind the house.

"NOOOOO!" she screamed at the painting, hoping her mother would hear her. "No, Mom, don't do it!"

Uligart laughed behind her again, raising the hackles on the back of her neck. "Child, don't you know that a mother would let the world burn to protect their own offspring?" he said to her, his voice dripping with menace. "Once I had you in my grasp, all else was a foregone conclusion."

"You can't open it, Uligart," said Faljon. "It needs to be opened from both sides, and we will not do it for you. We would all die first."

The frost elf looked at Faljon and the blue of his eyes seemed to gleam for a moment. "Keeper, I know the Gate's secrets. I know what I must do and where I must go," he smiled at Faljon, and Kaitlynn wanted to punch the cretin in his smug face. "In fact, the girl here is coming with me to make sure that her mother follows through. The rest of you, however, your journey ends here."

"My King, should we kill them, or put them in the dungeon?" asked Nalidur as he stepped forward.

Uligart's menacing smile widened even further. "No, I think I like the idea of keeping them up here as trophies." He lifted the blue flame that was still burning cold in the palm of his hand up in front of his face, breathed it deep into his lungs, and then exhaled the blue frostfire all over Faljon, Shanja, and Derrith. The three frost elves holding them let go and stepped back as the three prisoners were covered with a layer of ice that froze them all in place like helpless statues. Kaitlynn struggled to get free and try to stop him, but the frost elf behind her held her tight and smashed the back of her head with his forehead hard enough to stun her into submission. Kaitlynn's head fell, as did her heart. She slowly looked back up and saw her lover and her friends completely helpless before her. She heard the loud screeching sound then, the monstrous pitch high enough to deafen her momentarily, and saw an impossibly large shadow pass overhead. A wyvern twice the size as the one that they had fought at the entrance to the Frostspire Pass landed on the top of the keep and lowered itself down in front of Uligart.

"You're coming with me my dear," he said, grabbing her by the shoulder with his right hand and pushing her towards the large beast. Two of the frost elves helped her up onto the wyvern, and Uligart climbed in behind her. He wrapped his dead, left hand around her and grabbed the reigns of the beast in his right hand. "I'm afraid I can't hold you too well, Keeper. I suggest you don't do anything foolish." He laughed again and whipped the reigns with his good hand. The wyvern screeched again and reared itself up. Kaitlynn had to do everything she could to maintain her balance and not fall off the giant beast. It lifted itself up into the air with one gigantic toss of its wings, circled back and grabbed the painting in its talons before heading north above the large snow-covered pass below.

Kaitlynn looked down and saw the two armies lined up and about to face off in the pass as they soared over them. She was used to flying in airplanes, but the lack of anything other than the giant beast between her and the ground made her almost fall, the height giving her a terrible case of vertigo. But as she regained her senses, she realized that there was one thing she had noticed when she had looked down that Uligart as of yet, had not...

Jali's dagger was still sticking out of her left boot.

The army that had gathered before them was much larger than the one they had fought in the first valley of the Frostspire Pass. But now they were above the snowline in the main pass, and in front of them stood a massive army of goblins and frost elves. Delavon was glad that they'd had so few casualties in that initial battle but feared that this one might be far more devastating to his own men. While his people were immune to the cold, and the dwarves were used to it, he feared what the chill would do to the centaurs.

Halcor and Garoth stood by him as they looked across the gap at the enemy forces. They'd had time to dig in, building long trenches in the snow with the banks piled up behind them. Uligart's army was behind the banks, and Delavon knew his men would have to enter the trenches and then climb up the banks on the other side in order to enter close combat. The archers would have to do much of the heavy lifting to clear those lines for a charge but getting them close enough to fire would expose them to the enemy archers as well, who were positioned directly behind the snowbank and in the mountains above. The whole area before him looked like a perfect killing field with solid cover for their enemies. He shook his head in disgust and turned to the other two kings. "Suggestions, gentlemen?" he asked gravely.

"We charge," replied Halcor, motioning towards his own men. The centaur's front hoof pawed restlessly at the snow as he spoke. "Their archers will concentrate their fire on us, as we would be the most direct threat. Your archers can then fire on them to try and clear them out from above. Hopefully, my men can get through and break the center of their line. If we succeed, then the other armies should be able to follow us through."

"That's suicide for your people, Halcor," replied Delavon.

"That's why I will lead them myself," replied the centaur. "The fate of all Somalie depends on our victory here. Our lives are forfeit for the greater good. We knew that when we agreed to come and fight. Better to fight the battle and fail than to stand here and let our world fall unopposed." Delavon looked up at him. Halcor stood defiant, looking across the snowy fields, a fire blazing in his eyes. Never had Delavon seen a ruler look as regal as the centaur before him now did. "If my men must die, they will do so with their king charging among them," he declared with a nod.

"We will sing songs of the centaur's nobility and bravery for all the ages to come," replied Delavon, his voice loud and strong.

"Aye," replied Garoth, reverence in his voice. "And we dwarves will raise our drinks to honor your fallen along with the greatest heroes of our kind."

Halcor nodded at them. "So, it is settled then," he said. "I will ride to my people and prepare them for battle."

"King Halcor." Garoth looked up at him. "If I have offended you or your people in our time together, I apologize. You are not 'beasties'. You are the noblest of men, and I salute you."

Halcor looked down at the dwarf and smiled. "And you sir, have a great mind for strategy," he replied, "and though you try to hide it, a far greater heart beneath your gruff exterior than I would have expected. I salute you as well." Both men bowed before each other, and then Halcor rode off towards his men.

The other two kings watched him as he galloped away and Delavon felt as if a shadow of sadness had passed over him. He looked up and saw a large wyvern passing far overhead, heading north, and realized it had been an actual shadow that he had felt. He hoped that the giant thing didn't decide to get involved in what was about to happen in the pass, for he didn't know how they'd be able to handle that as well as the army dug in before them.

71

Faljon watched, frozen in place as Uligart flew off with Kaitlynn on the back of the enormous wyvern. The ice that had encased him was the coldest thing he had ever felt, and it might have killed him instantly if not for the supernatural warmth he was able to create within himself. He had seen the attack coming and, in the instant before he had been encased, he had focused everything he felt about the human woman that he'd met only a few short days ago into his heart, hoping that it would be enough to protect himself from Uligart's frostfire spell. As he focused his mind on Kaitlynn's face; the curve of her lips when she smiled, the brilliant green of her eyes, the firmness of her perfect breasts, the perfect hourglass shape of her hips, he could feel the ice begin to melt around him. It hadn't taken long before he could feel enough air around his body to capture a breath or two. By the time Faljon had defrosted himself enough to move, the frost elves had gone below into the keep. He turned his head to look at his companions and saw that Shanja was also almost free, but Derrith was still completely encased in ice.

After quickly brushing and kicking the last of the ice off himself, Faljon pressed his body against the ice around Derrith, hoping that the elf would survive long enough to escape. As soon as she was free, Shanja joined in and pressed herself against the elf's entombed body on the other side. Slowly the ice melted, and Derrith fell over onto the black stone parapet. Faljon and Shanja grabbed his limp body before he toppled off of the top of the tower and put him down on his back.

"He's breathing," said Shanja, her voice barely a whisper. She didn't want to make too much noise, lest the frost elves return and find that they had escaped their icy prisons.

Faljon nodded and touched the side of Derrith's face with the palm of his hand. The elf was warm, and Faljon felt relieved. He knew that like all elves, Derrith was resistant to the changes of temperature of the weather, but he had feared that the elf might have run out of air before they'd been able to free him. As it was, it had been a near thing. It took a minute or two, but Derrith finally opened his eyes and looked up at the two satyrn.

"Are you well?" asked Faljon in the same whisper Shanja had used. Derrith nodded slowly, still recovering from his ordeal. His breath was labored, coming in one large gasp after another for a couple of minutes. Eventually, the elf seemed to stop fighting his own lungs, and the rising and falling of his chest normalized. Faljon watched Derrith carefully, making sure that the elf was okay. But Shanja was looking past him at something else.

"Keeper, look." Shanja pointed off to the left, and Faljon's gaze followed. Piled on the ground not twenty feet away, were all of their weapons.

"They couldn't have been that stupid," Faljon muttered under his breath as he stood up and walked over to the pile. He saw everything was there; his and Shanja's swords, Derrith's sword and bow, and Kaitlynn's backpack, sword, and shield. The only thing missing was Jali's dagger. Faljon smiled. The fools had overlooked it when they'd searched Kaitlynn. She was alone, but Faljon was certain that she wasn't unarmed. His eyes rising to the horizon, Faljon caught himself staring into the distance off to the north and smiled his toothy grin for a moment before his thoughts returned to the pile of weapons on the ground.

He bent down and picked up his and Shanja's swords, putting both sheathes on his own belt and tossed the backpack on over his shoulders as well. He then picked up Kaitlynn's sword and shield and handed them to Shanja. She took them both and slid the shield over her arm. Derrith had managed to sit up and was starting to look far less glassy-eyed. Faljon handed him his bow and sword, and he held one in each hand for a moment, regarding them both with a wry smile, before putting his sword back in its scabbard and taking his bow in hand. He stood up and regarded the two satyrn for a moment, testing his balance and breath.

Faljon unsheathed the two satyrn swords, wielding one in each hand. "Let's go," he said with a calm assurance, and the others followed. He made his way over to the stairs leading down into the tower and found the door locked from below. "Tis no time for subtlety," he said to no one in particular, before stepping back and ramming his shoulder into the door. There was a loud crack, but the door didn't seem to budge.

Shanja stepped up next to him. "Together," she said. They took a silent count of three and slammed their shoulders into the door. It gave under their combined efforts and the wood around the latch snapped off, the latch falling harmlessly to the ground.

Faljon shouldered the door open and stepped inside. Shanja followed him, kicking the fallen debris away from the door and across the large hallway. Two frost elven guards were rushing down the hallway towards them with their swords drawn and one of them jump-stepped over the lock as it flew under his feet. An arrow twanged from just over his shoulder, and Faljon saw one of the frost elves take its fatal blow right in its throat, a geyser of blood spraying out around the wound. The other never stopped charging, but Shanja stepped in front of him taking the attacking blow with the shield on her left arm. With the sword in her right, she ran the elf through its midsection, disemboweling him through his heavy furs. He dropped to his knees stunned, his white armor turning a crimson shade of red as his life spilled out before him. She removed his head with a single stroke, and it bounced once off of the hard obsidian floor before it rolled haphazardly away from them, the body toppling over in a tangle of useless limbs.

Just a few feet from the stairs that they had descended, there was a door to the right which had been left open. Faljon glanced inside and saw that the large room was an opulently decorated bedroom, likely belonging to the frost elven king. Across the hall and around the first corner was another room which appeared to be more of a workshop of sorts. There were powders, potions, and an empty hook on the wall where Faljon guessed that the Gate had once been placed after it had been stolen and brought here. Near the open window, he saw what looked like a large perch and an empty cage. "'Tis where he keeps his pet," Faljon thought to himself, before heading down the hall. Shanja and Derrith followed closely behind. The hall made a series of right turns that led to the staircase that headed down to the level below.

The last room on the floor before they descended the stairs was locked from the outside with the key hanging on a hook nearby. Faljon grabbed the key and opened the door, discovering that the room contained two frost elven women. There was one small bed that they appeared to share, a single chamber pot, and nothing else in the room. Both women had been left completely nude and looked like they had been beaten and scarred many times over. The room's only window had been sealed shut with more of the large obsidian stones, cut like bricks, the shade of which was off just enough for Faljon to be able to see what it had once been. The two women looked terrified, but also seemed to be staring at them with pleading eyes. "Concubines," said Derrith over his shoulder. "Unwilling, most likely. The window was probably sealed to keep them from jumping."

Faljon shuddered. He looked at the condition that the two women were in and thought to himself that he could understand why they might prefer the certain death of the leap than to live the way they'd been forced to. They'd both clearly been raped and tortured, often. "Tell them that we are clearing out the keep and that they are free to go," Faljon said without looking over his shoulder to the elf, trying to make his face appear as sympathetic as possible to the two concubines.

"Tell them that there are two dead guards whose furs they can take down the hall as well," added Shanja. Derrith nodded and relayed the message in elvish to the two women, who nodded frantically and then headed down the hall the way the three of them had just come from.

Faljon watched them go around the corner and then headed towards the final turn in the hall before the staircase that would bring them down to the next level. He could already hear the clamor of footfalls coming up the stairs towards them. The disgust he felt at the way the two captive women had been treated overwhelmed him. He readied his twin swords and smiled his toothy grin, yet it had none of the charm that Kaitlynn usually associated with it. There was something dark in his eyes this time, and he welcomed the killing rage as it filled him from within. "Let the bastards come," he thought to himself and charged down the stairs with abandon.

72

The centaurs had taken up the center of the army, and Halcor looked at his men. They were paraded proudly in rows, their colors a varying array of blacks, browns, whites, and yellowish golds. They were armed with spears, swords, or bows, and there were a few who stood at the head of each column, standard bearers with the flags of his kingdom. His rule had been a benevolent one, and he knew that his men would follow him into the jaws of death itself if he asked them to. But it tore at his heart to ask them to do it. He took a deep breath and addressed his troops as their king for what he assumed would be the last time for many of them, and possibly himself as well.

"My fellow centaurs! Today we charge for battle and glory. But for many of us, this charge will be the last. Honor your brothers and sisters, the ones who gallop beside you, by maintaining your charge if they should fall, and honor me if the same fate should befall your king."

"The frost elven king has control of the one item that could destroy our world. We know he has tried to conquer all the elves before and was held back. Yet with what powers he can gain from the Gate, or the weapons on the other side of it, he could wipe all other races off the face of Somalie or subjugate us all to his rule. But we shall not allow this to come to pass, not so long as we have the breath left in our bodies, and the wind blows strong in our manes!"

A loud roar rose from the ranks of his men, and Halcor couldn't help but smile at them. They were a proud race and would do what had to be done, even facing certain death. They were his men, and they would face their fate like men.

"To battle! To victory!" he exclaimed, and then turned towards the enemy ranks before him and raised his sword straight up above his head before pointing it forward with a single downward slash. "For glory, we *CHARGE!*"

The centaurs started off at a slow trot and steadily increased their pace until they were at a full gallop. They kicked up plumes of snow behind them as they charged the lines ahead, banners flying in the bitter winds of the pass, and their weapons prepared for battle. Behind them, elven archers and dwarven crossbowmen filed into line and rushed forward. The frost elven archers hidden in the rocks of the mountains above began to fire on the charging centaurs, and the archers below returned fire.

Halcor charged alone at the head of his ranks as the goblin archers behind the snowbanks began firing at the charging mass. He heard the yelps of pain and the tangle of fallen centaurs coming from behind him, but his resolve did not waver. He charged ahead; his sword drawn in front of him pointing the way for his men as the arrows flew past him.

As he closed on the enemy ranks, he saw the goblin's bowmen fall back and be replaced by other goblins with spears. They positioned themselves on the top of the snowbank and poised to strike as the charging centaurs dropped into the trench before them. As he entered the trench one of the goblins leaped at him and tried to drive its spear into his chest, but Halcor sidestepped it and slashed the goblin with his sword as he passed. Then his men slammed into the trench behind him, and they all tried to climb up the snowbank and charge through to the other side. Goblins leaped down on them from above, impaling many of them. Some of the goblins landed on the ground and were either cut down or trampled into bloody lumps of diseased flesh beneath the charging hooves of the centaurs.

A volley of arrows passed overhead, slamming into the ranks of goblins farther behind the snowbank. The goblin archers returned fire, shooting blindly from behind the battle, hoping to hit any of the enemies they could. Halcor pranced in the trench, propelling his men forward, whipping his sword in circles in the air and calling out for them to keep charging. He watched as a few of his men began to climb the banks, only to be shot down by the archers behind. But he would not be deterred ... would not let them be deterred. He reached down and grabbed the standard of one of his fallen men and raised it high above.

"Rally! Rally to me!" he yelled as he whipped the banner around in the air, and then charged up the snowbank. The footing fell away beneath him in giant clumps, a minor avalanche of snow falling back into the trench below. But he pressed forward until he had crested the bank and started down the other side. He leaped down from the bank on the other side, slashing a goblin with his sword and trampling another. He felt the sting as an arrow pierced his left arm, forcing him to drop the standard to the ground. But then he saw one of his attendants next to him raising it again. Almost immediately, more of his men were next to him, pouring over the banks and joining in the fight. "Charge!" he yelled, pointing his sword at the goblins in front of him, as an arrow pierced his right shoulder. Then another one hit him in the center of the chest.

King Halcor stumbled and tried to get back up, but three goblins closed in on him while he was down and impaled him upon their spears from all directions. The last thing he saw before his life slipped away was his men charging forward without him, just as he had commanded them to.

The centaur king passed from this life and into the warm embrace of the Keeper of Souls with a smile on his face.

73

Faljon leaped down the stairs and charged shoulder first into the leader of the frost elves. He knocked him backward into the elves that were coming up behind with their swords drawn. They tumbled down the steps together, taking almost all the frost elves down into a chaotic heap. Shanja and Derrith charged down behind, cutting down as many of them as they could before they regained their feet.

Faljon stood up and was face to face with Nalidur, Uligart's lieutenant. The frost elf swung his sword at Faljon, but the satyr blocked the attack with the sword in his left hand. He lunged with the sword in his right, but Nalidur calmly stepped back out of his reach. Another frost elf came at him from his right, but Faljon ducked and spun under the attack, swinging both of his swords around and sending two deep slashes across the body of the elf that had attacked him. An arrow flew over Nalidur's head as he spun, but he sidestepped the shot from Derrith that had meant to end him.

More frost elves came pouring around the corner of the hall, and Nalidur bade them attack before slipping back into their midst. Faljon and Shanja stood side by side covering the width of the hallway, while Derrith stood behind them with his bow aimed over their shoulders. The trio held their ground as the frost elves charged and cut them down as they came at them. As the last one fell, Faljon looked around and saw that Uligart's lieutenant was not among them; he had run.

Derrith looked quickly for any arrows that he could salvage from the bodies of the dead around them, but most had been broken as their victims had fallen. He looked in his quiver and saw that he only had three left. "Hopefully we can find an armory," he said, looking at the two satyrn while fingering his quiver. The two of them nodded back at him silently, and they all headed off down the hallway looking for more of Uligart's men.

74

From their command post, Delavon could see that Halcor's selfless charge had broken through the center of the goblins' lines, but the price had been high, and they were still outnumbered. His archers were firing volleys over the top into the ranks of goblins behind, and his own troops were charging in behind the centaurs to exploit the weakness in the goblins' lines they had created. But the frost elven archers in the mountains above were still raining down death from above.

"Garoth, can you send your men up the mountains and clear those archers out of there?" He asked, turning to the dwarven king.

"Aye, I thought you'd never ask," replied Garoth, a gleam in his eyes. He turned and started giving orders to his men who split into two divisions and started charging towards the mountains on either side of the battle.

Delavon looked out across the battlefield and saw that his elves had finished crossing the open field and were entering the trench on either side of the remaining centaurs. He held a contingent of his own men and the force of satyrn that had joined them in reserve, but he feared that he'd have to use them sooner rather than later. The field between them and the enemy lines were filled with the bodies of dead elves and centaurs, and the dwarves charging up the mountains were beginning to see real casualties as well.

From behind them, a lone centaur rode up to the command post, looked around for King Halcor for a moment, before finally bowing before Delavon and Garoth. "My Kings," he said loudly to be heard over the din of the battle, "the dwarves have arrived with the siege weapons. They can be on the field within the hour."

Delavon smiled, and Garoth gave a full-throated laugh. "Yes!" exclaimed the dwarf. "Now we'll show them what for!"

"Thank you," replied Delavon. "Have them position to fire deep into the enemy lines past our own troops."

"Yes, my lord," replied the messenger. He looked around again, and the asked, "My lord, where is King Halcor." Delavon's smile faded, and then he pointed at the center of the line ahead. The centaur looked ahead his face grim. He nodded and the turned back the way he had come.

Delavon looked past him, and he could see the outline of the catapults starting to come over the ridge behind them. Garoth stood next to him laughing deeply between swigs from his goatskin flagon. They didn't hear the single centaur that rode up behind them, but as Delavon turned to regard the battle in front of them, he saw one of Halcor's attendants coming back towards them at a full gallop. Delavon's face turned sour, and he lightly touched Garoth on the shoulder. The dwarf turned and took on the scene. His laughing stopped abruptly, and he lowered his head in silence.

In the attendant's hands as he rode forward rested the crown of the king of the centaurs.

75

Faljon flew down the next flight of stairs and Shanja and Derrith followed him. Two of the rooms on the floor above had been nothing but empty barracks, but the third had been an armory. Derrith had refilled his quiver and grabbed a second one to keep himself well-stocked before they had continued down the tower. Faljon figured the frost elves could not have been expecting an attack from above when they'd designed their keep, but there was no doubt now that they were aware they were coming now. They'd already worked their way through a number of frost eleven soldiers, and they expected to run into more as they descended the tower.

They continued down one floor at a time. The layout of every floor above the top one was the same; two barracks and one armory. But after the first few floors, they didn't run into any further resistance from the frost elves. They were about to head down the final staircase from the second floor down to the first when Faljon stopped short. The inner ring of the tower opened, and they could see down to the opulent throne room below.

In the throne room, Nalidur and his remaining guards had set up their ambush. There were about a dozen of them, and they were armed with bows and ready to fire at anyone who came down the last set of stairs and into the room. There were large obsidian statues on either side of the large black throne, and there were ice blue banners hanging from the back wall as well. There was no barrier between the steps and the drop in the middle of the tower. As he was taking all of this in, an arrow flew past Faljon's head as he ducked back behind the wall. He kept his eyes forward and listened for any ambushers coming up the stairs and then explained the situation to Derrith and Shanja.

Derrith smiled and asked, "Which direction was the door?"

"Directly across on the other side," replied Faljon.

"Stay here, keep them occupied," said the elf. "When I give the signal, come down." He nodded and then he ran back around the hall. Shanja and Faljon stared at each other with perplexity painted on their faces. They kept themselves just out of view at the top of the stairs and waited. After a couple of minutes, they heard a loud crashing sound downstairs and a gurgled scream.

"I guess that's the signal," muttered Shanja, and the two satyrs nodded to each other before turning the corner and charging down the stairs. As they ran, they saw that all the elven archers had turned to face the door. All of them except for one, that was. One of them was lying in a pool of his own blood in the middle of the throne room with an arrow sticking out of the back of his neck. The door to the throne room was open and hanging off its hinges, and Derrith was letting off another arrow as he was ducking behind the wall outside the door, taking yet another one of them down.

Shanja and Faljon leaped off the staircase and dropped on a pair of frost elves, running them through with their swords as they dropped. Two of the archers wheeled around and fired at them, but Shanja stood in front of Faljon and deflected the arrows with her shield. One of the archers that turned took an arrow from Derrith in the side of the head and dropped. Shanja charged at the other one and rammed it in the midsection with her shield and followed up by cleaving into his side with her sword, cutting his bow in half. Faljon charged in behind her and with an arm crossing motion, removed the frost elf's head with his two swords.

Nalidur and three of the other guards charged at the two satyrn, while the other two covered the door with their bows. Shanja cut the first one down, and Faljon ran and slid between two of the others, slashing at their legs as he passed. They both dropped to the ground howling in pain. By the time he was back on his feet, Shanja was squaring off against Nalidur. He stabbed down quickly with each sword, finishing the two frost elves off, and then ran over to help Shanja with Uligart's lieutenant. Behind him he heard the last two archers drop as Derrith dove past the door firing two arrows at once, killing them both in one stunning trick shot.

Nalidur had his sword in one hand and a long dagger in the other. He was relentlessly attacking Shanja, and she was deflecting his attacks with her shield and sword. The frost elf turned and saw Faljon coming. He flipped his dagger over and caught the blade and then tossed it at Faljon, hitting him in the midsection. The satyr howled in pain and went down to his knees.

Nalidur turned his attention back to Shanja, and never saw the arrow that hit him in the back of the knee. The arrow took out all the ligaments holding his leg together, and he dropped to the ground as his leg buckled beneath him. Shanja stepped forward and with a single motion, removed the frost elf lieutenant's head from his body. She didn't stop to admire her handiwork, instead, ran over to check on the fallen Keeper.

Derrith had run into the room and over to Faljon. He laid the satyr down quickly and pulled the dagger out of his gut, and then closed his eyes preparing to lay his hands over the wound. Shanja stood guard while the elf worked making sure that no one else entered the room and attacked them. She turned when she heard voices on the stairs above her and saw that it was the two concubines they had freed earlier. They were wearing the furs of two of the guards from upstairs, both of which were now painted in large swaths of crimson instead of white and came running down the steps and joined them in the center of the room. One of them said something to Derrith, and he nodded and stepped aside. The other one knelt next to Faljon, closed her eyes, and laid her hands on the wound. After a few minutes, the wound closed in a fresh pink scar, and the frost elf toppled over from exhaustion. The other one knelt next to her, took her hand in one hand and then took Faljon's in her other one. She closed her eyes and began meditating, and Faljon felt the energy that the healing had drained from him start to return to his body.

Shanja looked over at Derrith, whose mouth hung agape. "I take it your people don't know that trick?" she asked in a playful tone. The elf simply shook his head in amazement. "How did you get down here anyway?" she asked him.

Derrith glanced over at her and replied, "Window above the door," before going back to watching the second frost elf revitalize both Faljon and the one who had healed him. After a moment of reflection, he considered the condition that they had found the two women in and came to a realization. "They've been healing each other all this time that Uligart has used them," he said. "The rapes, the beatings; they've been keeping each other alive."

Shanja looked down at the two women with wonder and smiled. They were far stronger in spirit than she had thought they would be when they'd freed them earlier. It was only a few more moments before the two frost elves opened their eyes, and Faljon felt at least strong enough to stand. The one that had been meditating said something to Derrith in elvish and he nodded at her.

"She says that she hopes that this repays the kindness we showed by rescuing them," he said, translating for her.

"I am quite thankful," replied Faljon, running a finger over the fresh scar on his stomach.

"Derrith, you were outside, how many more frost elves are there?" Shan-ja asked the elf.

"There were at least a hundred along the battlements, but the courtyard was empty," he replied.

"Since the Gate is gone, I see no reason to fight our way out through those odds," said Faljon. "Ask them if there's another way out of here, through the tunnels perhaps."

Derrith relayed the message to the two women, and they looked at each other and nodded. The one that had healed Faljon said something and then Derrith grimaced before he turned and said, "They'll show us the way that they were brought into the keep, but they say that will lead us farther south towards their village. We need to meet up with Delavon's army to the north."

"If it gets us out of here, it'll do," replied Faljon. "We can make our way north once we exit the caves. We don't even know where Uligart took the gate."

"I can guess," said Derrith, "Elfwood. What better place to gain his revenge upon my people then in the court of Delavon itself." The two satyrn considered this for a moment and then nodded their agreement. The elf's statement made a lot of sense to the them both. Derrith motioned to the two frost elves to show them the way.

They made their way to a door that was set beneath the stairs they had come down. They opened it to reveal a set of stairs leading deep down within the mountain. The two frost elves led the way, and Derrith and the two satyrn followed them into the tunnels below the keep.

76

The dwarven catapults had made an immediate impact on the battle. Three of them had been set to fire deep into the goblin ranks, and the other two had been set to fire upon the frost elves in the mountains above. The more extensive firepower was more than the goblin army could withstand, and they had turned and run back through the pass towards the keep. The archers and the catapults fired into them as they fled, but eventually, the attack ended. The frost elves in the mountains above had seemed to almost melt away into the mountainsides, and when the dwarves had finally reached the perches above where the archers had been, they had found the tunnels that ran beneath them.

Delavon and Garoth had come forward to survey the battlefield and assess the casualties that their army had suffered. The centaurs had been nearly wiped out, with only about thirty of them remaining in all. The elves that had followed them into battle had fared quite a bit better due to the horsemen's noble sacrifice. They had pushed the goblins back and allowed the elves to use the makeshift battlements against the goblins. The addition of the catapults to the battle had finally turned the tide completely in their favor. Even still, Delavon had lost almost a quarter of the elves that had marched with them between the two battles so far.

Garoth studied his own men and found that he'd lost almost a third of his men in the charges up the two opposing mountains. The frost elves had had the superior ground, and it wasn't until the siege weapons had been deployed that they had been forced to retreat. But Garoth wouldn't wait for the frost elves to pop out of another mountain and had sent roughly half of his remaining men into the tunnels after them on either side of the gap. The rest of his men would be needed for the final assault on the keep.

The two kings looked at each other solemnly and nodded, silently acknowledging the sacrifices made by each other's men. They turned and began issuing an order to their troops to form up and prepare to march. With luck, there would be time for mourning the dead later. Their date with Uligart and the Obsidian Keep waited just ahead of them now, and they needed to strike while the iron was still hot.

77

Faljon, Shanja, and Derrith followed the two frost elves through the tunnels and came out of a cave in the pass to the south of the keep. They looked back to the north and saw the imposing tower glaring down from above upon the mountainside with the walls surrounding it. There were icy blue banners on the corners of the walls and hanging from the tower itself, but everything else about the keep was as black as death. The slope of the mountain was steep, and there was but a single path that weaved up the mountain towards its gate. From down below, they all found it quite intimidating to behold.

Faljon looked into the pass to the north and saw an army of goblins running back towards the south. He wasn't sure if they were heading for the safety of the keep, or if they were going to charge right past them. Regardless, he knew that they couldn't stay where they were and hope to survive.

"Back into the cave," he said, motioning behind him. The others looked where he was pointing and saw the massive retreat moving towards them. "We'll watch and see if they head for the keep, or we wait for them to pass." Derrith and Shanja nodded and followed him back into the cave. The two former concubines followed them, and they waited to find out what would happen with the passing army together.

78

Kaitlynn looked out at the vast countryside below as the wyvern made its way over the same large tracts of land that had taken them days to cross on foot. The sun was getting low in the western sky, and it would be dark soon. They were currently passing over the swamp where Jali and she had been wounded. She thought of Jali, now dead and her face a ruined mess left to rot under the mountains in the distance behind her. The sadness threatened to rise into her throat and choke her, but she pushed it down. She refused to show this monster of a man any weakness.

Kaitlynn could feel Uligart's blackened hand wrapped around her midriff, loosely holding her in place. His arm was as hard as stone from the forearm down. She found it completely and utterly unsettling and was grateful that her armor at least separated her from the touch of his skin. She wished she could toss the wretched old man off the wyvern's back and watch him splatter himself on the ground below. But with her hands tied behind her back and her balance on the beast as precarious as it was, she didn't dare try anything so rash. She hoped against hope that somewhere in the distance behind her, Faljon and the others had found a way to free themselves.

The cold wind billowing through her hair, Kaitlynn looked out into the distance and could see the sprawling forest of Elfwood before her. From above, it seemed to stretch for miles into the distance. She hadn't realized just how vast King Delavon's kingdom had been until she had seen it from this angle. The vastness of the elven kingdom was magnificent. But as she sat perched atop the giant wyvern, she noticed quite suddenly that they were changing direction and heading directly for the giant forest ... and they were descending.

79

Queen Reliara had been quite kind to Uliah when she had returned to Elfwood. They had taken her in and let her stay in one of the small houses in the outskirts that the party had stayed in when they had passed through previously. She sat quietly on the bed in the small house. She didn't know if this had been the bed that Faljon had slept in, or if it had been Kaitlynn's. All that really mattered to her was that it wasn't the bed that she'd conceived this child in. She couldn't bring herself to stay in the same room as before as the memories of that night and what they would mean for her were too much to bear. She hadn't loved Peton, and they'd been quite drunk. All three of them had been: her, Peton, and Jali. It could have just as easily had been Jali who was with child instead of her. She hadn't told Peton that she was with child yet because she had just been becoming aware of it herself and didn't want to distract him from the duty at hand. She hadn't told anyone, in fact. But then she had watched the wyvern rip him in half, and it pained her to know that he had died not knowing that he was going to be a father.

She sat on the bed with one hand on her belly. It would be months before the child began to show, but she could feel its warmth growing inside of her. It was still fragile, yet it would have the strength of both of its parents and would grow to be a great satyr if she could raise it to be so. She ran a finger over the pink scar on her left breast and hoped that it hadn't been damaged too much to serve the purpose for which nature had intended for it.

She said a quiet prayer to Qyr, the Keeper of Souls, for Peton and lay down in the bed to try and get some sleep. She worried about her five friends to the south, searching the Frostspire Mountains for the missing Gate. She knew that all the other things on her mind didn't matter at all if the world itself ended. She didn't know if any of them were still alive at all, but she prayed that they were. She would want Faljon, Jali, and Shanja to know this child, and she would want it to know them as well. She would even want Kaitlynn to know it as well if she could, but she wasn't sure if the human would want to come back through the Gate after finding her way back home.

It was as she was sitting there, contemplating this new uncertain future that laid before her, that she heard a deafening, yet hauntingly familiar screech upon the air outside. "Please no," she thought to herself and thought about pulling the covers up over herself and hiding. She thought about running to protect her child.

In the end, she grabbed her quiver and bow and ran towards the sound.

80

The army of goblins had finished retreating up towards the Obsidian Keep and most of them were inside. They'd been slowed by their ascension up the mountain towards its gate, and the elven archers and dwarven crossbowmen had thinned their ranks as they ran. Garoth was off personally seeing to the placement of the catapults, and Delavon was marshaling up his troops to form a perimeter outside the lines of fire from the frost elven archers raining down fire from above. He pulled his archers back as well, allowing the last of the goblin troops to enter the relative safety of the keep, and watched as the dwarves placed the artillery and prepared to bring ruin down on the fortress above.

As Delavon placed his men, one of his attendants got his attention and pointed south into the pass. He looked over and saw five figures running towards them along the edge of the pass on the side away from the keep. Three of them were taller than the others; three elves and two satyrn. As they got closer, he recognized his patrol captain, Derrith. Running beside him was the satyrn Keeper, and one of his kin. But there were also two frost elven women running along with them, their white furs drenched in blood.

Delavon looked up at the keep and saw the frost elven archers on the walls above. He motioned to his archers. "Give them covering fire!" he roared, and a row of archers stepped forward and fired on the keep above. Some of the frost elves above ducked as the arrows passed where they had once been, but a few unfortunate ones fell. Delavon watched one of their bodies crumble and fall in a heap at the base of the keep's wall and then turned his attention back to Derrith and the two satyrn. They had nearly reached the safety of the elven lines and were making a beeline for the elven king. The two frost elven women were close behind them. Delavon turned to one of his attendants. "Send for King Garoth," he said and started working his way back behind the lines where he could talk to them when they arrived.

King Garoth arrived just moments before Derrith and the two satyrn. Derrith approached him and bowed deeply to the elven king, and the two satyrn followed suit. The two frost elven women seemed to look confused and just hung back quietly. They were clearly out of breath and had a look about them that Delavon found disquieting as if they had survived something horrific.

"My King," said Derrith between gasps of air. "Uligart has fled the Obsidian Keep with the Gate."

"Where has the wretch-king gone?" asked Delavon. He looked at the three of them and saw the vicious scars all over the upper body of the satyrn Keeper. "And what's happened to you all?"

"My King, we are all that remain..." began Derrith, but Faljon cut him off.

"My Lord, there is no time," said the Keeper in an urgent tone. "Uligart flies north on the back of a wyvern. He has the gate and the human Keeper. He intends to open the gate, and we believe he's heading for Elfwood while we are distracted here. We need to make haste." Delavon saw the look in Faljon's eyes and thought that it looked as if the satyr might run on without waiting for a reply from him.

Derrith glanced over at Faljon, and then looked his king in the eyes. "If he opens the Gate in Elfwood and finds a way to harness its power..."

"Great Gods of old..." said Delavon. "He's managed to pull us away." Turning to Garoth, he said, "We need to head back to Elfwood, now!"

"We'll never get back there in time," stated the dwarven king. "We may as well lay a siege here; it'll be just as useful."

"I will not stand here while my Kingdom is the place from which our entire world crumbles." Delavon looked at his men ahead and prepared to call them back.

A voice came clear through the clamor of uncertainty, ringing like a clarion bell. "Kaitlynn will not fail us." It was Shanja who spoke, and everyone else turned and looked at her. There was a calm certainty to her voice, and she spoke with authority. She looked at Faljon and said, "you told us she was still armed. She will not let our two worlds fall. Not after everything she has already done. Not after everything she has already fought for. This is not her home, but if this world falls, so does her own. She will not let that happen."

"Hmph!" snorted the dwarven king. "I wouldn't trust a single human to be able to stop that mage. We're all doomed one way or another. We might as well go down fighting here and take as many of his men with us as we can!"

"She's no mere human," said Derrith. He glanced back and forth between Faljon and Shanja, and then looked his king straight in the eyes. "She is a Keeper, in far more than just title. She will do her duty." He put a hand on Faljon's shoulder, turned to him and said, "I know you wish to stand beside her, but when she stands in Elfwood, it will not be alone. If you love her, trust her." Faljon looked up at the elf, closed his eyes, and then slowly exhaled and nodded.

Garoth stood and watched the scene in front of him. After a moment of silence passed between them all, he turned to Delavon and said in a low voice, "The centaurs will do no more good here in a siege. Take them. Ride back as fast as you can. I can't promise that it won't be too late, but I understand that you can't stay here with your kingdom in danger. I will stay here and see this castle fall, if for no other reason than to honor King Halcor, so that he shall not have died in vain."

Derrith turned and looked at the dwarven king and said, "These two women were the concubines of Uligart. They've been held against their will, and they led us out through a cave about a mile back down the pass. The cave will bring you out right inside the tower of the keep itself."

"I will make great use of this information," said Garoth, "and we will bring this castle of evil down from within as well as from without."

Delavon bowed deeply to the dwarven king, and said, "You are an honorable dwarf, King Garoth. I leave my men in your charge."

"Go," said Garoth. "I've had enough goodbyes from good friends as it is." With that, he turned and headed back towards the front lines of the army that he would now command alone. He passed a centaur that had been acting as a messenger and sent him off to rally all their remaining forces with King Delavon. He watched as the centaur galloped off and then looked back at the elven king. A single tear trickled down his haggard face and softened a spot in his coarse beard. He wiped it away and then began yelling commands to his troops. By the time he looked back to where Delavon had been again, he saw the king riding off with the elven captain and the two satyrn on the backs of four of the remaining centaurs, with the rest of the horsemen galloping along after them.

81

The wyvern crashed down through the canopy of trees, flying past the houses built among their vast branches. It landed in the clearing below after dropping the painting on the ground nearby. It lay its body down close to the ground, allowing Uligart to dismount, and then the frost elven king pulled Kaitlynn down roughly. With her hands tied behind her back, she couldn't keep her balance while climbing off the beast's back, and she crashed down to the ground, landing on the same left shoulder she had hurt when she first arrived in Somalie. She was pretty sure the bruise that had just finally healed a few days ago was going to be back if she lived through this ordeal.

Uligart took the opportunity to lean the Gate against a tree before going back and grabbing Kaitlynn and pulling her up to her feet. She looked up and saw a number of elves running along the wooden walkways above. Behind her, she heard Uligart's robes shift as he turned to the wyvern and said, "Kill them. All of them." He then grabbed her and dragged her in front of the painting.

Her mother was standing there within it, looking at her. The brushstrokes almost seemed to be running down her cheeks, but Kaitlynn realized that it was the way the painting represented the fact that there were tears streaming down her face. Kaitlynn looked at her mother's emerald eyes. For the first time, she saw how old her mother had gotten. She was in her early sixties but had always looked much younger than that. But her vigil on the other side of the painting hoping to see any sign of her missing daughter had aged her significantly. Above her, she heard the screeches of the giant wyvern and the screams of the elves above.

Uligart stood behind her with his good arm wrapped in front of her. He brought his hand up in front of her, brought the cold blue flame into his hand again and let it tickle the bottom of her chin. She felt a shiver run involuntarily throughout her entire body, but she tried not to let her fear show. She watched through the painting as her mother pulled the painting off something and laid it on the ground in front of her. Kaitlynn saw her mother's tennis shoes crushing the snow in front of the painting, and then watched with awe as she saw the painting starting to grow, slowly at first, and then more rapidly as it expanded. As it enlarged itself in size, the picture within changed from a series of complex brushstrokes into the very real image of her mother looking back through the opening at her from the same spot in the wood behind her father's house where she had entered Somalie.

82

Uliah didn't have to go far before she saw the source of the screeching. The wyvern was massive, at least twice the size of the one they had fought before they'd entered the mountains. It had a helpless villager in its mouth, and it bit down cutting the elf in half. At the same time, it was thrashing its massive tail through one of the elven houses. Without hesitation, she whipped an arrow out of her quiver and let it fly at the beast. The arrow hit the beast in the chest, but it barely entered its skin. She saw a few elves with swords and shields rushing forward, but it flicked its tail and sent two of them flying before impaling a third with its poison stinger.

Uliah pulled out another arrow, and this time aimed for the beast's massive wing. She hit it as it prepared to take off again, but the small hole she put in its wing didn't seem to make any difference. The beast looked at her and began swooping right at her. She said a silent prayer to the Keeper of Souls for her unborn satyrling and prepared herself for the inevitable.

Just over her shoulder, she heard a woman's voice quietly utter some sort of incantation in elvish. She looked over her shoulder and saw Queen Reliara standing there, resplendent in her flowing jade-green silk gown, with both of her hands out, palms up and balling them into fists. Uliah looked back and saw the canopies of the very trees themselves reaching out and wrapping themselves around the wyvern. It fought to escape the grip of their branches and managed to break a few of them as it thrashed against their embrace. But the trees were large, and the forest was thick. The dense branches continued to wrap around the beast, and then Uliah saw a giant branch push itself out of the wyvern's chest with its massive heart impaled upon it. The beast gave a final screech of pain, and collapsed, its weight supported like a marionette by the branches that were wrapped around it.

Uliah looked back over her shoulder at the elven queen and saw a steely determination on her normally soft and beautiful face. She glanced over at

Uliah and said, "Protect your child. I will protect my kingdom." She then jumped over the railing of the walkway, her gown trailing in the air behind her, and dropped to the ground slowly. Uliah looked over the railing and saw that the Gate was open on the far side of the clearing, and there was a strange figure in a white robe facing into it. "Must be Uligart," she thought as she pulled another arrow and started running down the length of the walkway to get a better shot. It was then that the whole world seemed to start shaking.

83

"Let my daughter go," said Rebecca in perfect satyrn. Her voice had a slightly melodic quality as the sound of it passed through the Gate to Kaitlynn's ears, but there was a weak quality to it as well, as if her throat had a lump in it. "I opened the Gate, pass through if you must. But let my daughter go."

"Stupid woman," Uligart replied. "There's nothing your world can offer me. It's the power of the Gate itself that I want." The frost elf let the frostfire fall from his hand and stuck it through the open gate. He began chanting something that Kaitlynn couldn't understand, and the surface of the gate started to ripple like the water of a pond. It started slowly at first, but then as the ripples came faster, they started to resemble waves. It was then that the ground began to shake. Kaitlynn fought to keep her balance and looked through the painting. Through the distortion of the waves on the painting's surface she could see her mother fighting for her footing as well.

Kaitlynn looked down and saw that Jali's dagger was still in her left boot. She lifted her leg up behind her, but with her hands bound behind her, she couldn't reach its handle. She put her leg down and steadied herself against the growing tremors, and then threw herself shoulder first into Uligart, knocking him to the ground and away from the Gate.

84

Faljon rode, the sun setting in the west, among a party of twenty-two centaurs. King Delavon had told him that there were about thirty of the centaurs left, but that these were the only ones healthy enough to ride to Elfwood. Derrith and Shanja rode on the backs of two other of the horsemen, both of them off to the king's left, while he rode to the king's right.

There were just exiting the Frostspire Mountains and passing the remains of the wyvern when the ground began to shake. Some of the centaurs toppled over as the ground beneath them moved, and they went down in a tangle of horse hooves and men's arms. Faljon held on as tight as he could and hoped the centaur he was riding would be able to maintain its balance, as the shaking only seemed to be getting worse.

Shanja looked over at him. She was holding on for dear life herself, but she said to him, "Trust her."

"I do," he replied, and all of a sudden the ground stopped shaking.

Everyone looked around at each other for a second and then King Delavon turned to one of the Centaurs that was rider-less and still standing and said, "Take two others of your kind and stay with any who are wounded. We ride on." With that, their number dwindled from twenty-two to thirteen, they continued towards the Elfwood, knowing they were still at least two days ride away.

85

Rebecca steadied herself as the ground stopped shaking. She looked through the gate and saw that the waves had stopped. She couldn't see the strange frost elf in the large white robes, but she saw Kaitlynn, sprawled on the ground, her arms still tied behind her back. However, Rebecca also saw one other thing that she hadn't noticed before. There was the hilt of a dagger sticking out of her daughter's boot. With nary a second thought, Rebecca jumped through the Gate and dove for the dagger.

86

Uligart stood up and looked down at Kaitlynn as she tried to get up. "Foolish child, you are no longer useful," he said as he raised his hand up and began creating a large ball of frostfire in his hand. He reigned back as if to throw it at her when an arrow hit him in the meaty part of his leg and sent him off balance. The frostfire flew harmlessly over her head and hit the stream that ran through the clearing, instantly freezing a large patch of it. Kaitlynn looked up in the direction that the arrow had come from up on the walkway above. She saw a female satyr, with a bow in her hand and her long blonde hair tied in two pigtails that fell down across her chest.

"That was for Peton, *you wretch*!" screamed Uliah down at Uligart, as he pulled the arrow out of his leg. He looked up at her and laughed, and then raised his left hand and pointed its blackened and disfigured shape at the walkway beneath her feet. The boards turned rotten all at once, and her leg slipped through. Her bow fell harmlessly to the ground as Uliah held on to the rope railing above, trying not to fall through. She knew that even if she survived the fall, her satyrling likely would not. Uligart continued laughing, but then a stream of brilliant orange fire flew right past his head, silencing him. He turned and regarded Queen Reliara with a sneer.

"You dare bring destruction to Elfwood?" she said, her eyes cool. Her right hand had a ball of orange fire floating in it. Uligart brought his ice blue frostfire back to his own hand, and at once they struck out at each other, the fireballs colliding between them and burning each other out. They threw two more at each other, and they neutralized each other once again.

They both took a few steps towards each other, and Uligart shaped the icy blue flame in his hand into a sword. The tip and blades of it seemed to flicker, and the air around it seemed to crystallize and drop the occasional flake of snow to the ground. Reliara looked at him and shaped her own flame into a sword as well, its orange blade shimmering as the air around it seemed to move in its heat. They closed the gap with each other at a snail's pace, eyeing each other up, and then their two swords clashed with a loud hissing sound as they swung at each other.

Kaitlynn was lying on the ground watching the two of them duel, transfixed on the two blades. She almost didn't notice the dagger get pulled out of her left boot until the ropes binding her hands behind her gave way. She looked up and saw her mother staring down at her.

"Quick, run," Rebecca said. She looked at Kaitlynn with pleading eyes and put her hand on Kaitlynn's cheek. "We can close the gate behind us and forget about this place. You'll be safe."

Kaitlynn looked at her mother. She thought about Faljon, her dead friends, and then glanced back at the two dueling elves. Her eyes had gone as cold as steel. "Give me the dagger, Mom," she said. "I'm the fucking Keeper of the Gate." Her face filled with grief, Rebecca closed her eyes and nodded. The dagger slipped out of her hand and fell to the ground, and Kaitlynn swiftly grabbed it and leaped to her feet in a single motion.

Uligart and Reliara were still engaged in their duel and their magical swords clashed against each other time and time again. Each time they clashed together there was a loud hiss. They swept their blades at each other again and held them against each other, staring at each other across the crossed blades of flame and frostfire. Uligart took the opportunity to slam his boot into the Queen's knee, causing it to buckle. She went down in a heap, her leg giving out underneath her.

Uligart looked down at her and laughed. He swung down at her to finish her off, and she blocked with her flame blade again but knew that she was fighting a losing battle if her leg wouldn't hold her. She looked up and saw the evil gleam in his ice blue eyes staring right through her as he laughed at her, and then his laughter was cut off in a gurgle of blood, as an elven dagger slashed across his throat from behind him. All at once, his frostfire blade went out and his good right hand went up to his neck. He pulled it away and looked at it, and he saw his hand-painted crimson with his own blood. It squirted like a geyser from his neck and flowed down his darkening robes.

"Did you forget about me?" asked Kaitlynn, a grim smile twisting the corner of her mouth. He turned and looked behind him, and saw her standing there, the dagger in her hand, and his blood dripping from it.

He raised his hand to try and grab her, but Queen Reliara's flame blade protruded from his chest. He looked down, and his eyes glazed over as the last thing he saw was the blade burning through him, and his robes catching on fire. He fell over then and left the world of Somalie forever.

Kaitlynn looked down at Queen Reliara, who had collapsed to the ground. "Are you all right?" she asked, holding out a hand to help her up.

"My leg, I believe it's broken," the queen replied, "but I am otherwise unharmed. If not for you, Keeper, that would not be the case."

"I'll get her some help," called Uliah down from up above. She had managed to get herself clear of the rotten wood on the walkway above, and other than a nasty looking gash on her leg seemed to be all right.

"Thanks, Uliah," replied Kaitlynn. "Good to see you again," she added with a smile, looking up at the satyr. She watched as Uliah ran off with a heavy limp, looking for someone to help the Queen. She then wiped the blood off her dagger and tucked it back into her boot. She didn't look forward to having to tell Uliah about Jali, but that would have to wait until later.

"We are all in your debt, Keeper" Queen Reliara said to her, her voice strained with the effort of trying to sit up through the pain.

"I'd have been dead myself without you and Uliah showing up," replied Kaitlynn, she knelt at the Queen's side and took her hand. "Squeeze as hard as you need to, I'm right here, my Queen," she said. Reliara nodded her head and then lay back on the ground.

Rebecca slowly walked over and put her hand on her daughter's shoulder. She looked down at the smoldering body of the strange pale elf that had threatened to take her daughter away from her. His blood was still pouring out of the gaping wound where her daughter had slit his throat. Her darkest thoughts consumed her. Everything she had done to Danny, all the vows she had broken were to protect her daughter from this possible fate, and she had failed utterly and completely. Her daughter was a killer, out of necessity of course, but it still shattered her heart into a million pieces. She took a deep breath, let her tears flow freely and resisted the urge to spit on the dead elf for fear that she might accidentally put out the fire consuming him.

It wasn't long before help came.

87

Kaitlynn had sent her mother back through the Gate. She had gone reluctantly, but in the end, she had gone and told Kaitlynn that she would watch for when she was ready to return. Kaitlynn then took it upon herself to tell Uliah the unfortunate news about Jali's death. She and Uliah had held each other and cried for a long time once she was done. Kaitlynn decided to share the small house with Uliah while they waited and hoped that the others would return. She brought the Gate with her so she could watch it and keep it safe.

The Queen had given them free reign of the kingdom, and Kaitlynn took advantage of the opportunity the following day to use the hot springs and get herself cleaned up. One of the Queen's attendants had brought her some new clothes as well, a perfect gown made of luxurious green silks. Her armor, the tunic, and tights that she had been given were returned to her as well once they had been washed.

At just past midday the day after, King Delavon rode into Elfwood along with Faljon, Shanja, Derrith, and all the centaurs that had been able to make the trip. Kaitlynn ran down to the lift and waited for the party to come up. Once they did, she bowed to the King and then took Faljon in her arms and kissed him passionately. When their lips finally pulled away from each other, she saw Uliah giving Shanja a hug. They switched partners and then she went and gave Derrith a hug as well. The elf stiffened a bit at first but then put his arms gently around her as well.

Queen Reliara was waiting for them all on her throne. She did not rise when her husband entered, and he saw the wooden splint on her leg. "My Queen," said King Delavon as he bowed down before her. He took her hand and kissed it gently, and then she pulled him in close and held him tightly.

88

It was almost six days after the battle with Uligart (and about four days since King Delavon had returned with what had remained of Kaitlynn's companions) when King Garoth returned victorious with the rest of the army. They had crushed the remains of Uligart's forces by attacking through the tunnels below and laying down fire with the siege weapons from above. Leaderless, the remaining goblins and frost elves had surrendered. The goblins had gone back to their swamps beyond the mountains, and the frost elves had sworn fealty to King Delavon and Queen Reliara again.

The King and Queen had ordered a great feast to be held to commemorate their victory, and honor the fallen, particularly King Halcor of the Centaurs. His crown was placed on a silk pillow at the seat of honor in the center of one of the massive tables that had been placed in the clearing below the city in the trees. Sharing the table were King Delavon and Queen Reliara were King Garoth, Kaitlynn, Faljon, Shanja, Uliah, and Derrith.

There was music and dancing, and Kaitlynn and Faljon spent as much time as possible hand in hand as they danced or talked. The Queen was out of her splint, as her people's healers had kept working on repairing her leg, but she still moved with an unusual amount of effort. Despite this, she took her husband's hand and danced as much as she could. Uliah was the only one that Kaitlynn could see wasn't drinking, but she was still laughing and having a great time. Even Shanja, sad as she had been, seemed to enjoy herself.

After a long day of celebration, the party finally wound down. The centaurs had already ridden off. One of Halcor's attendants had taken his crown to give to the king's young colt, who would inherit his father's kingdom. King Garoth and his dwarves were preparing to march west and return to their own mountains as well. But before he could go, King

Delavon and Queen Reliara pulled him aside and spoke for some time about rebuilding the old alliances. It was decided that one of King Garoth's attendants would stay behind as an ambassador, and one of King Delavon's would march back to the dwarven lands as well. It turned out that there was also one other matter to attend to.

The two kings and the queen motioned Kaitlynn and the three remaining satyrs that she had left the Keeper's Wood with to step forward. The four of them all took a knee before the three royals.

"The four of you, for your service to Somalie, deserve some sort of reward," said King Delavon, "What can we do for all of you?"

"My Kings," said Faljon, his voice shaking slightly. "I would like to petition to be allowed to undergo the change." Uliah and Shanja gasped, and Kaitlynn turned and looked at him with a look of surprise. "I love Kaitlynn and would like to go with her to Earth if she will have me. Shanja is ready to be the Keeper of the Gate of Somalie."

"I couldn't ask you to do that," said Kaitlynn. "I know how much being the Keeper means to you. And you'd be giving up so much of your lifetime. I wouldn't want to take that away from you."

"I'm certain, and this is what I want" replied Faljon. "I can help you guard the Gate from Earth. And even if I couldn't, I would still choose you over the many extra years I would have to live without you." Kaitlynn blushed, and then nodded as the tears ran freely down her face.

"Keeper, I can't take over," said Shanja. "I have not gone through the trials."

Faljon turned and looked at Shanja with admiration and said, "What you have just gone through is far more rigorous and painful than my trials. You are far more ready than I was." Shanja looked away from him and nodded. He saw a tear start to run down her cheek, but she wiped it away before it got far. Faljon looked back at Delavon and said, "I know what I'm asking for is forbidden by the Treaty of the Sundering. But this is one of the reasons that we created the change in the first place, not what it got corrupted into."

King Delavon and Queen Reliara looked at each other. She gave him a slight nod, and then he turned and looked at King Garoth. The dwarf looked up at him and said, "Aye, I'm fine with it."

"Very well, we will allow it," stated the King of the elves. "We wish you happiness and joy, Faljon and Kaitlynn. You have done a great duty to us here in Somalie, and this entire world owes you."

"Both of our worlds owe you," added Queen Reliara, "even if those on Earth may never know of your heroism. You deserve all of the happiness that you can find with each other." She took her husband's hand in her own, and Kaitlynn took Faljon's as well.

"We shall leave for Keeper's Wood tomorrow then," said Faljon. "Any of the satyrn that joined you in battle that needs to return as well can come with us. We'll take care of everything else when we get there."

The two Kings and Queen bowed deeply to Kaitlynn and the three satyrs, and they all lowered their heads. King Delavon bade them rise, and they did so. Kaitlynn looked down at Faljon, her eyes still glistening with tears.

As everyone else slowly dispersed, she led him by the hand back to the room they had been sharing. She walked into the room and looked into the painting that was leaning against the wall. She saw her mother sitting on the couch, looking up at her. She stood and walked over to the painting on the other side and smiled at Kaitlynn. She looked down and smiled at her mother as well, and then shook her head. "I'm not ready yet Mom," she thought to herself.

Faljon walked over and looked down into the painting as well. He saw Rebecca and forced a smile at her. She was Kaitlynn's mother, even if she had abandoned her duty. He was going to have to learn how to get along with her, but he would do so for Kaitlynn's sake. He gave her a wave, and then took Kaitlynn's hand in his own again. She could make out a look of surprise on her mother's face forming in the brushstrokes. Kaitlynn turned and smiled at him, and then she reached down and turned the painting around so that it faced the wall. She figured her mother would have a pretty good idea of what was about to happen, but she didn't really need her watching it. She stood up straight, reached for the silk ties behind her neck that held her dress on. She pulled and undid them, letting her gown fall to the ground around her. She gave Faljon a sly smile and pulled him towards the nearest bed.

89

They headed out the next day. Kaitlynn and all the satyrs said their goodbyes to the residents of Elfwood and made their way back to their homes. Many of the satyrs went off in other directions, but about ten of them joined Kaitlynn and her friends as they made their way back to Keeper's Wood. Kaitlynn, Faljon, and Shanja took turns carrying the Gate as they made their way back to the satyr's home over the next few days.

When they finally saw the familiar woods in the distance, both Shanja and Uliah smiled. But Faljon looked a little sad. Kaitlynn was carrying the Gate in her hands at the time, and turned to him and said, "If you want to stay here, I understand."

He looked over at her and forced a smile. "No, I want to go with you," he said with certainty in his voice. "I will miss my home though."

"We can stay for a little bit if you want," she said to him. "I've been gone so long that I'm pretty sure that I'm going to have to find a new job when I get home at this point anyway, so I don't see much point in rushing back for anything."

He nodded at her and said, "I would like that, I think. And I would like to get used to my new body before I go to your world."

"So would I," Kaitlynn replied with a sly smile and a gleam in her eye, which made Faljon smile his normal toothy grin at her as well. "We are going to have to get you some clothes when we get to Earth though," she added. "That's disappointing." They both laughed at that, and they continued until they reached the edge of the woods.

When they arrived, they found two new guards at the entrance to the path. They greeted the satyrs warmly, though Kaitlynn wasn't sure if she'd met these two before. The bodies of Golkan and Lillia were gone, and Kaitlynn was grateful for that at least. They stopped and raided the gorkaberry bush that was nearby, and then many of the other satyrs started heading off in various other directions into the woods. Kaitlynn looked around and saw that only Shanja and Uliah remained with her and Faljon. She looked at the two women and smiled. It was good to be in their presence, and she missed the friends that she had made that hadn't survived their adventure.

She popped a couple of the gorkaberries into her mouth, and her legs started to feel sturdier, and the weariness of the trail left her. She looked up and saw that the sun's rays were getting dimmer and knew that it would be dark soon. She turned to Uliah and said, "Let us know if you need to stop."

Uliah nodded and said, "I'm ready to be home as well. Besides, the gorkaberries helped. I'll manage." She smiled at Kaitlynn and started off again.

Shanja turned to Kaitlynn and said, "I'll carry that from here. Tis my duty now, and I'll see to it that it never leaves these woods again."

Kaitlynn handed the painting over to her and took Faljon's hand. One step in front of the other, they stuck to the path until they reached the stairs in the woods that had drawn Kaitlynn into the painting in the first place. Faljon walked over to the makeshift post where the painting had hung before and pulled it out of the ground. He tossed it over his shoulder and began leading the others up the steps for the last time.

As they passed out of the fog and into the clearing above, Uliah stopped. "This is where I head off," she said. She turned and looked at Faljon and Kaitlynn and said, "Promise you'll come back and meet my satyrling. I would like that very much."

Faljon and Kaitlynn nodded and smiled. "So would we," said Kaitlynn.

"Who knows, maybe they'll bring back a satyrling of their own," chided Shanja with a smile. Faljon looked at Kaitlynn and she blushed.

"One thing at a time," she said, trying to hide her face behind her hands. Shanja and Uliah started laughing.

"You don't always get to plan these things," said Uliah with a shrug. She gave them each a hug in turn and then walked off, away from the sound of the waterfall, skirting the edge of the tall grass.

By the time the last three of them made their way down the steps on the other side it was well after dark. Faljon put the post down on the ground, and they brought the Gate into his burrow. He turned and looked at Shanja and asked her, "Will you be all right on your own?"

"I won't be on my own," she replied. "I'll see my satyrlings in the morning. I'll have to tell them, of course..." her voice trailed off as she wiped away a tear. She coughed once, and nodded before continuing, "I'll be fine."

"Once I leave, if you want to take my burrow..." Faljon offered

"Tis kind of you to offer," she replied. "We'll see how I feel after sleeping alone." She stepped forward and gave them both a hug. "I'll get a group together tomorrow and start planning the ritual. I wish you nothing but happiness together." She walked out, and Faljon and Kaitlynn stood in the door of the burrow and watched her walk away. Once she was far enough down the trail that they couldn't see her anymore, Faljon pulled the door closed with a sigh. He turned around and saw that Kaitlynn was already bedding herself down for the night. She motioned for him to join her, and they held each other until they drifted off to sleep.

90

The following day, Faljon went to work setting up the post for the Gate with a view of the stairs and the waterfall by his burrow. While he worked on that, Kaitlynn searched the surrounding woods for a number of large rocks and set six of them up in a line so that they would be visible in front of the pool in the painting. When everything was all set up, Faljon used his claws to carve the names of the six fallen satyrs in the stones in the order they had fallen: Gorkan, Lillia, Hammel, Peton, Delok, and Jali. The two of them stood next to the post and looked at the scene in front of them.

"Tis a fitting tribute," said Faljon, his voice solemn. Kaitlynn looked over at him and nodded as she wiped a tear away from her cheek. She reached out and took his hand in her own, and they stood there looking at the memorial and the beautiful scene behind it for quite some time. Eventually, Faljon went back into his burrow, brought the painting out and hung it on the post. "Tis a clearing here, so it will have to be moved in order for it to be opened," he told Kaitlynn. "This way there can be no accidents where somebody wanders through again. But if Shanja takes my burrow, there will always be a Keeper close by to let us through."

"I like it," she replied. "Besides, this scene is beautiful. I'd love to just stare at this when I get home. I think this was an amazing idea, Faljon." The satyr beamed at the compliment but kept staring at the memorial with sad eyes. "Whatcha thinking?" asked Kaitlynn, running the palms of her hand up and down his arm.

Faljon let out a heavy sigh, and said, "These deaths were my responsibility," he said. "As Keeper, it was my failure to protect the Gate that led to this."

Kaitlynn turned and looked at him. She placed her hand on his chin and turned his face to look at her. "You can't let guilt define you. If this is what you love, don't give it up because you think you failed."

Faljon looked at her with his dark emerald eyes. Kaitlynn felt a shiver go through her body as if he was staring right into her soul, as he said, "I'm not giving it up; I'm choosing you over it." Kaitlynn looked down at him and smiled, and then kissed him deeply.

91

I t was just after midday the following day when Shanja arrived with five other satyrs. She gave hugs to both Faljon and Kaitlynn and then paused as she was pulling away from Kaitlynn when she saw the graves by the bank of the pool, with the waterfall behind it. She went over and knelt in front of the stone marked with Delok's name as the tears rolled down her face. Kaitlynn walked over to her to check on her and put a hand on her shoulder. Shanja looked up at her and smiled.

"This is amazing," she said, as Faljon stepped up to join them. "You two..." her voice trailed off again, but she stood up and gave them a group hug this time, holding them even tighter than before.

Two of the other satyrs, one male, and one female came over and joined them by the graves and looked down at the marker for Delok. Kaitlynn noticed that the female one was pregnant and realized that these must be Shanja's children Junis and Hcya. When she finally composed herself, Shanja introduced them to Kaitlynn. She could see that they regarded her with a bit of distance, and she couldn't quite blame them. They had only just found out about their father, and she had been a part of the reason that he was now gone.

Before returning to the others, Shanja pulled Faljon aside and told Faljon that she would take him up on her offer to take his old burrow. "I hadn't seriously considered it until I saw the memorial by the waterfall," she said, "and how you positioned the Gate so that you can see it from Earth. I want to be here, where this is."

Faljon nodded and said, "Then tis yours," to her. "I expect we will leave by tomorrow." She nodded and then gave him a rueful smile before turning and heading back to the center of the clearing.

Shanja and the other five satyrs sat in a circle in the clearing. She left a space for Kaitlynn to join them to her right and motioned for Faljon to lie in the middle of the circle. Her two satyrlings sat to her left. With some instruction from Shanja, Kaitlynn put her hands on each side of his head, and the others all reached out and put their hands on his shoulders, hips, and ankles. Kaitlynn could see the scars on his left shoulder where the snow cat had dug its claws into him under Shanja's fingertips. She looked down at him and smiled, and he smiled his toothy grin back at her.

Shanja looked over at her and explained how the ritual worked, "Use your love and bring all of the warmth to your hands. In your mind, picture what a human man should look like. The image will burn into his mind, and we will all see it as well because we will all be connected. We will then all use the image, to craft his new body." Kaitlynn nodded her understanding.

Shanja turned her attention to Faljon and said, "This will hurt, are you sure?" He nodded emphatically, and she looked around at the rest of the group. "Let's begin," she said.

All of the satyrs closed their eyes and waited for Kaitlynn to begin the ritual. She pictured Faljon in human form in her mind. She kept the details as vague in her mind as possible, as she didn't want to feel like she was crafting him to suit her so much as letting him become the human version of who he already was. She brought the image of him into her heart, and she could feel her body growing warmer. She directed the warmth entirely into her hands and through them and into him.

Faljon gasped, and then all the other satyrs brought the warmth to their own hands. He could feel himself sweating all over, and his entire body began to glow in a bright greenish light. He closed his eyes to protect them from the glare, and that's when he felt the first changes beginning.

It felt as if all of his bones were stretching, and it was like the growing pains of his youth, only much worse. As his body grew, he could also feel the bones and muscles in his lower body changing shape. His hooves started to soften, and he could feel his tail start to shrink. It felt as if his head was being driven in with a hammer as his horns retracted into his head, and then his teeth started to round themselves out as well. He balled his hands up into fists to keep himself from screaming and noticed that his claws were not digging into the flesh of his palms. In fact, he had no claws at all.

The whole process took about ten minutes to complete, but to Kaitlynn, it felt like an eternity. She could see that his body was shining brightly even with her eyes closed. She could also feel Faljon's head changing in her hands, and could hear him grunting to hold the pain in. But she didn't want to look down and see what was happening to him.

Once it was done, and the greenish glow that had managed to get through her tightly closed eyes faded away, she heard him gasp one last time before his entire body relaxed. She kept her eyes closed, afraid to look, hoping that she hadn't disfigured him in some way.

"Kaitlynn, tis over," said Shanja, her voice barely above a whisper. "You can look."

Slowly she opened her eyes and looked down at the man now lying naked and unconscious in front of her. It was decidedly Faljon, but now human. She could see that he was breathing as if he were asleep. The thick horse-like fur, the claws, the horns; they were all gone now. She could see fresh stubble on his face, which was new. He still had all the scars he had picked up on their journey to retrieve the Gate, but some of them seemed bigger than before. She looked at him and realized it was because he was taller now by more than eight inches. He was not more muscular but was clearly well toned in general. She tried to look as discreetly as she could at his genitals and found that she was not disappointed at all. She smiled until her entire face seemed to shine, and then bent down and kissed him on the forehead.

"He'll need to rest for a little while," said Shanja as she stood and put a hand on Kaitlynn's shoulder. She paused for a moment, as if uncertain of what to say next. "Did we get everything right?" she finally asked, not knowing how else to phrase such a delicate question.

"Yes!" exclaimed Kaitlynn, a fresh batch of tears running down her cheeks. She stood up and embraced her friend and whispered, "He's perfect. It's still him, but human. I wouldn't want any more than that. I just hope he's okay with it once he wakes up."

Shanja smiled, and said in a low voice, "If you show him how much you like it, I'm sure he'll be fine with it." The two women pulled back from each other, and Shanja raised an eyebrow at Kaitlynn.

Kaitlynn looked back over at Faljon, sleeping softly in the grass. She bit her lower lip and looked back at Shanja. "I'll take it under advisement," she said with a sly grin, causing Shanja to laugh.

Shanja said her goodbyes and walked off with her two satyrlings. The others had all gone already. Kaitlynn waved and watched them go with a smile until only she and Faljon remained in the clearing. She turned around and saw him sitting up with his back to her. She walked up behind him and knelt, wrapping her arms around his upper body.

"Is this right?" he asked her, his voice covering a yawn that tried to escape.

"You're perfect," she replied and kissed him on the cheek.

He tested his new legs slowly, flexing the muscles in them. Kaitlynn watched his skin ripple with a gleam in her eyes and bit her lower lip again. She walked around in front of him and offered him her hands, and he took them. She helped him up slowly and slid an arm under his to give him a little support as he figured out how his new limbs worked. She slowly let him go and he took a few steps on his own. She saw that instead of looking down at him, she was now looking up a little bit. "I can get used to this," she thought to herself.

"How do you feel?" she asked him.

"I feel good," he replied. "Different, but good."

Kaitlynn walked over to him and put her hands on his waist. "Let me see how you feel then," she said with a sly grin, and then ran her hands slowly up and down his sides. She could feel the firmness of his muscles just beneath the skin. He put his hand behind her head and gently pulled her lips up to his. After they had been locked in an embrace for a few minutes with her hands running up and down his sides, Kaitlynn raised her arms up over her head, inviting him to take off her tunic. He accepted the invitation with a smile, pulling it up over her head slowly and then dropping it on the ground behind him. She reached behind her back and unclasped her bra, and then kicked off her boots. Faljon ran the tip of his tongue over one of her fully erect nipples while gently caressing her other breast. Kaitlynn let out an involuntary gasp and ran the fingers of both of her hands through his hair.

Kaitlynn looked over his shoulder and saw the waterfall behind him. She smiled to herself and then started kissing his neck. She could feel him getting hard between them, and while keeping one hand on the back of his head, started pulling down her tights with her other hand. He grabbed them in both of his hands and helped her pull them off, panties and all.

"Under the waterfall," she whispered, while she nibbled gently on his earlobe. She felt him nod slightly, and then he scooped her up into his arms and carried her into the water. She couldn't believe how strong he was considering everything he had just gone through during the change.

Once he entered her with the water pouring down upon their bodies, she found herself impressed with the stamina he still had as well.

She had completely forgotten about the painting hanging on the post in the clearing with a perfect view of the waterfall.

92

Kaitlynn and Faljon stood in front of the painting in the woods. They had leaned it against a tree by his stone stove, and Shanja stood behind them. She had arrived early that morning and helped them prepare to leave Somalie for Earth and had brought a few things to put in her new burrow as well.

Kaitlynn had neatly folded her new silk gown into her backpack and had tucked Faljon's sword underneath for safekeeping. She was wearing her tunic and tights, with her armor on over the top. She had her sword in her scabbard and her shield clasped to her left arm. Faljon was wearing Kaitlynn's winter coat and nothing else. Luckily it came down and covered him in the upper thigh, but she was going to need to get him some clothes as soon as possible.

Kaitlynn turned around and gave Shanja a long hug. She hated to leave her friend behind but knew that her time here was running short. Faljon waited his turn and then gave Shanja a hug as well. They turned around and saw that the painting had grown. Kaitlynn's mother stood in the clearing on the other side and regarded the two of them. Her face was stoic, and Kaitlynn couldn't tell what was going on behind her eyes, but she thought that she sensed a fire there. She had a feeling that there was going to be a confrontation, and soon. She pushed the thoughts out of her head for a moment and regarded Somalie for one last time. The beautiful trees, the sound of the waterfall of in the distance ... she would miss this place more than she had ever thought possible. There was something magical about it all that called to the deepest part of her soul.

Kaitlynn took Faljon's hand in her own and looked over at him. Their eyes met, and she said, "I love you," to him as she stepped into the painting and back to her own world. He smiled and walked through with her. They turned around and saw Shanja standing there with tears in her eyes, waving to them. They returned her wave for a minute, and then each picked up a side of the painting, lifting it off the ground. It shrunk in their hand until it was its normal size again. Kaitlynn stole a glance through it and saw Shanja's form emblazoned in the brushstrokes, her hand still raised in a sorrowful gesture of goodbye.

93

Kaitlynn turned with the painting in her hands and regarded her mother. Rebecca was staring daggers at both her and Faljon. "Took your time, didn't you?" she said more than asked to her daughter.

Faljon looked back and forth between the two women, and then said as politely as he could muster in perfect English, "It's good to see you again, Rebecca."

"Faljon," was all she said in return. He had been the Keeper of the Gate of Somalie on her one trip there, and she remembered him well. It wasn't every day you were introduced to a satyr.

Kaitlynn took a deep breath, and then said, "Let's at least get inside before we have this out, okay Mom?" She walked off towards the trail that led back to the house, making sure to hold the painting above any thorn bushes that were still blocking the path. Faljon moved gracefully through them all without managing to prick his exposed skin at all. Rebecca trailed behind, moving methodically in the distance.

Kaitlynn led them back to the house and keyed in the code to open the garage door. Faljon watched in awe as the gate opened all on its own. He saw the two cars in the garage, and he looked at them for a few minutes, not quite comprehending what he was seeing. Kaitlynn walked through the door and put the painting down on the ground so that she could hold the door. She looked back and saw Faljon standing outside the garage, just staring. It occurred to her that he was going to have quite a bit of adjusting to do in his new world.

"I may have mentioned that Earth's a little different than Somalie," she said with a smile. She waved him in, and he followed her into the house. She picked up the painting, and once inside the room, placed it back on the mantle.

Faljon looked around and smiled. "This room looks very familiar," he said.

"Might be the only thing that will look familiar where we're going," replied Kaitlynn. "My home is in a completely different part of the country. It's a city in a desert. It will be much harder for people to get through the Gate in a place like that."

"And how are you getting him there," said Rebecca as she entered the room behind them. "He can't fly without ID. Have you even thought this through?" There was a tremendous amount of frustration in her voice, and Kaitlynn could see that her mother was angry, but frankly, she didn't much care. She had plenty of pent-up frustration to get out at her mother as well.

"Faljon," she said quietly, "The last room at the end of the hall upstairs is my room. Go make yourself at home. Mom and I need to *talk*." The last few words came out slightly strained, and Faljon picked up on the change of inflection in Kaitlynn's voice.

"I am here for you," he said his voice quiet, but firm.

"I know," she replied, "But I need to do this myself." He nodded his understanding to her and headed up the stairs, taking his time to look around and figure out where he was going. "Left at the top of the stairs," she called after him. She waited until she heard the door to the room above close before she said, "You have a lot of nerve being angry at me, Mom."

"Oh really?" replied Rebecca, sounding hurt. "I watched some crazy elven wizard threaten you, and I'm just supposed to forget about it and wait for you to have another week's worth of sexual escapades? And you left the curtains open last night, FYI." She shook her head and threw herself down on the couch. "How could you make me worry like that?"

Kaitlynn felt the rage building up inside of her, but she remembered her surroundings and realized she was still dressed like an elven warrior. She pulled her sword and shield off and propped them up in the corner so that she wouldn't be tempted to use them, and then turned back to her mother.

"You had a duty, and you left," she said. "You never told me anything about who we were, or who I was. You didn't prepare me for this at all," she said while motioning to the painting on the mantle. She paused and took a deep breath. "You ran away from everything, and you hurt both me and Dad just so you could run away. Don't even start in on me about *my* choices." She balled her hands up into fists and forced herself to take a step back. "And frankly, Mom, I don't really give a shit if you saw me fucking him yesterday. I expect that you'd better get used to the idea."

Rebecca's face went bright red, and then she buried her face in her hands. Kaitlynn could hear her start to sob. Through a strained voice, her mother said, "I did everything I did to protect you." She sniffled once and then continued, "I didn't want this life for you. I wanted you to just be a normal girl who could make her own choices."

Kaitlynn felt a laugh escape her throat and then turned on her mother. "You wanted me to be able to make my own choices, so you lied and took the choices away from me? That's bullshit, Mom, and you know it. I can't believe you would try that line of shit on me." She shook her head as she paced back and forth. "You ran. Maybe it was out of fear for me, maybe it was out of fear for yourself. I don't know. But don't try to make this about anything else. You ran and left your duty with Dad. He wasn't even one of us, and he loved you. He loved me."

"And I loved him too," replied Rebecca quietly. "You may not believe it, but I did. Being the way I was to him was the only way I could keep myself from running back to him. But that would have meant having you near that damn Gate. So I had to be strong, for you. I had to protect you. You may not believe me, but everything I did was to keep you from having to go through everything that just happened to you."

"You don't even know what happened to me!" screamed Kaitlynn, bending down right into her mother's face. Now she had tears running down her cheeks as well. "I made friends and watched some of them die! I fell in love and that man chose me over his own world! And I wouldn't give any of it up because for the first time in my life I finally feel like I know who I am! Do you get that?" She stood up and brushed her hair back out of her face without thinking. "Do you get any of that at all, Mom?" she said, her voice back to its normal volume. Her mother nodded her head slowly and then reached over to the end table for a tissue. Kaitlynn realized that that box hadn't been sitting there the last time she had been in this room.

"I'm so sorry, Katie," her mother said, looking up at her through her tears. "I'm sorry for everything. I thought I was doing the right thing."

Kaitlynn looked down at her mother. She looked pathetic, and it killed her to see her like that. She reached down and unbuckled her armor and took it off. She placed it down with her sword and shield and then sat down on the couch next to her mother. She wrapped her arms around her and pulled her close. "I love you, Mom," she said after holding her for a few minutes. "I always will love you."

"I love you too, Katie," her mother replied, returning the embrace.

"Mom, it's Kaitlynn," she whispered. "You know I hate that nickname."

"Yeah, I know," Rebecca replied. "But you'll always be my little girl, no matter how much of an adult you become."

They sat there together on the couch and cried into each other's arms for about a half an hour. Finally, Kaitlynn said, "I think I'd better go rescue Faljon from my room." They both laughed at that.

"But seriously, Kaitlynn, how are you getting him home?" her mother asked. "He won't be able to fly."

Kaitlynn nodded. "Yeah, I know," she said. But we can drive Dad's old car. It's technically mine now. It'll take about five days to drive across the country, but I'm pretty sure I'm going to need a new job at this point anyway. If Jeff can find a buyer for this place soon, that should give me a bit of a cushion to find something new at least. And then I can sell Dad's car once we get home unless Faljon's a quick learner behind the wheel."

"He won't be able to get a license, or any ID at all really. His name's a bit unusual for most people too," said Rebecca. "Just give it some thought."

"Yeah, that's true," replied Kaitlynn. "Maybe he'll be okay with me just calling him 'Jon' in public. I'll talk to him about it."

And what are you going to tell your uncles and cousins about where you've been for the last few weeks?" her mother prodded. "You can't exactly tell them the truth," she added.

Kaitlynn smiled at that. "Well, I can tell them a version of the truth," she said. "I met a guy. Then I kinda ran off with him to escape my real-world problems and we fell in love."

Rebecca laughed at that. "Yeah, I guess that's pretty much the truth, isn't it."

"Yeah," replied Kaitlynn with a smile. "They don't need to know I fought a wyvern, goblins, lizardmen, a couple of large white saber-toothed tigers, and an evil elven wizard, right?"

"Wait, what?" asked Rebecca, her face stunned.

Kaitlynn laughed. "Let me go rescue Faljon from my room and then we can tell you all about it," she said. "And then we can tell everyone else I'm okay after we buy him some clothes."

94

It was nearing the end of March, and Kaitlynn had just finished packing her things into the car. The painting was wrapped in brown paper and lying on top of her suitcases in the trunk. She wasn't sure where she was going to hang it in her apartment yet, but she was looking forward to finding a good place for it. There were memories on that canvas, and she didn't want to ever forget them, or the people that she'd met in that other world.

Jeff had sold the house for almost thirteen thousand dollars over market value. They had signed the papers and turned the keys over about half an hour earlier, but the young couple that had bought the house had been really good about everyone coming around and letting them say their goodbyes before Kaitlynn and her boyfriend "Jon" drove back to Arizona.

Kaitlynn took a deep breath and looked around at all of her family. Her mother had flown back to Arizona a couple of days before, but her two aunts, two uncles, and two cousins were all there with her. Candice was there too, which Kaitlynn found to be quite nice. Apparently, Candice and her cousin Jeff had hit it off very well indeed and were working on becoming an item. She pulled her friend aside and they gave each other a hug.

"My God Kaitlynn," whispers Candice under her breath, "I told you to get laid, and you ran off and found a man."

"Apparently so did you," replied Kaitlynn. "He's my cousin, so go light on the explicit details, okay?" They both laughed at that, and Candice nodded at her. "But seriously, it's going well?"

Candice nodded again. "Yeah, he's really understanding about the job," she said. "We mostly just see each other on the weekends. But it's nice, you know."

Kaitlynn nodded. She did know indeed.

She looked around at everyone else. Faljon was wearing a nice powder blue dress shirt, a pair of jeans, sneakers, and a pair of aviator sunglasses with a nice brown leather jacket flung over his shoulder. Kaitlynn thought he looked pretty good, and like he almost belonged on this side of the Gate after all. It had taken a couple of trips to the store to find a few outfits that had worked, and that he could find comfortable. He was still getting used to the idea of clothes in general, and the lighter the fabrics the happier he was about it overall.

Kaitlynn started to go around giving everyone hugs, and Faljon started shaking everyone's hands. Candice stepped in and gave him a hug and said something to him that made him blush a little, but he gave her a nod and hugged her back. Kaitlynn put her hand up over her mouth and laughed a little as she could only guess what Candice had said, but she knew that it was probably filthy; the woman had no filter when it came to those things, but Kaitlynn was starting to find that refreshing. She would have to try and keep in touch with her in the future, and maybe they could take turns visiting each other. It would give her a chance to come home and see the town she'd grown up in, every once in a while at least.

After saying goodbye to most of the rest of her family, Kaitlynn gave Jeff a big hug. "Thank you for doing such a great job selling the house," she said. "And take care of Candice."

Jeff gave her a smile and said, "You bet I will." He gave her another hug, and then he went over and stood next to Candice and took her hand in his. She looked up at him, and Kaitlynn thought she saw something sweet in her friend's eyes as she did. That made her smile, and she looked over at Faljon.

"Time to get going, Jon," she said, and she opened the driver's side door to the car. Faljon hopped in on the other side and buckled his seatbelt on the first try for the first time. He let out a slight sigh, and Kaitlynn giggled a little bit. She turned and looked at Faljon, and he was looking back at her. "I love you," she said to him.

"I love you too," he replied with a smile. He gave her a toothy grin, but it was very different from his old one. The old pointy teeth he used to have were gone and replaced with a human set. Kaitlynn reached into the glove box and pulled out a brand-new pair of Ray Bans that she had picked up for the drive, put them on, and waved one last time to her family and her father's old house, before pulling out of the driveway for the last time.

95

The raven sat on a branch of one of the trees lining the backyard of the house and watched the strange metal carriage pull away with the two Keepers in it. It had watched the group of satyrn perform the strange magic that had transformed the one from a satyr into a human and had become incorporeal and followed them through the Gate. It had spent the last week here on Earth watching and waiting, wondering if it could get revenge for its master's death.

But the longer it had waited for its vengeance upon them, the more it began to come to a different realization. It was free now and could go wherever it wanted and eat whatever it wanted. Its old master no longer mattered to it, for it was its own master now. In this new world on this side of the Gate, there were so many new things to eat. It had already sampled some of the local wildlife and was looking forward to trying them all.

It looked down at the group of humans below. It hadn't tried human flesh yet, but it was looking forward to the opportunity. But as it looked at them all down in the driveway, it decided that there were too many of them to risk it. It was very hungry though, and it took to the air, flying off into the woods looking for something fresh to kill.

Acknowledgements

You never really understand until you write a book that it's not a truly solitary experience. It takes a village of people who are there to support you in order to ever get anywhere. Here are just a few of the amazing people that have helped me on this journey:

My aunt, who writes under N.W. Moors, has been an invaluable resource with beta reading, as well as helping me understand the ins and outs of the self-publishing world. Without her help, I would truly be lost in the woods. Look her up online, you might enjoy her novels.

My mother, Betsy Carola, has been a lifesaver by taking over my website and managing my social media presence. As a part-time author and full-time father (plus my "real" job), I already have a ton of things on my plate, and her help and encouragement have been fantastic.

My fiancé and editor, Vanessa Redmon, without whom this work would not look nearly as good and my life would be far less complete.

I'd also like to thank Fay Lane for a fantastic cover refresh for this edition of the book. Richard over at FantasyMapInk, put together an outstanding piece of cover art for the previous edition (especially after my original cover artist bailed on me). But after six years it was time for a new look and having seen Fay's work on so many other of my fellow author's works, I was extremely excited to work with her—and she did not disappoint. If you need cover art for your own work, reach out to her at https://faylane.com, you will not regret it.

But most of all, I'd like to thank you, the reader. Without you, this would just be a "hobby." And while hobbies are nice, a storyteller without an audience defeats the entire purpose of the endeavor. I hope that you've enjoyed your foray into the magical world of Somalie. We may come back someday. We'll see....

If you did enjoy this novel, please leave a review on either Amazon or Goodreads. As an independent author, reviews are our lifeblood. There's no better marketing than word of mouth, and online reviews are equivalent of twenty-first-century water-cooler talk. So, I would be eternally grateful if you would spread the good word.

Thank you once more and hopefully, we meet again, in this world or another. You never know what I've got rolling around in this strange brain of mine.

To learn more about my other books as well as get updates on my current projects, you can visit my website at www.mattcesca.com. Feel free to subscribe to my newsletter while you're there.

Out Now. Start reading today.

The Forbidden Scrolls Trilogy

By Matthew Cesca

He left her for dead.

It was supposed to be a job like any other – sneak in, grab the scroll from the vault,
and get out. It didn't matter to Juliya what the young sorcerer wanted it for, he was paying well enough. That is, until he double-crossed her.

Now Juliya has a choice: track down Frost Dirvent and the forbidden scroll of fire that she stole for him, or be turned over to the guards.

Despite her misgivings, Juliya must work with a group of adventurers to track down Frost and reclaim the scroll before he can use its powers against an unsuspecting world. But the journey to stop him will take her to the last place she ever wanted to return to: Home.

The Forbidden Scrolls

It took a few minutes for Juliya's eyes to adjust to the light, but eventually she opened them, the glare almost blinding her as she did so. Once they had cleared, she glanced around, wondering for a moment why the afterlife looked like the inside of the tower she had just been in the night before. It hit her she must actually be alive. "Thank the gods," she thought to herself. "That would have been a hell of a letdown if this was what the other side looked like."

She laughed a little bit involuntarily, and that's when the pain hit her. It was like her entire torso was on fire, causing her to let out an involuntary grunt. She looked down and saw that instead of wearing a shirt, what she assumed to have been once white bandages across much of her chest and midsection were all coated in the crimson shade of her own blood. She tried to sit up, but to move even a few inches was agonizing, and she laid herself back into the bed in a hurry. She had no idea where she was or how she got there.

"So, you're awake," said a voice from across the room. It sounded male but relatively young to her ears. Maybe not young, she thought, but perhaps inexperienced. She cautiously turned her head and looked over in the direction that the voice had come from, and she saw a familiar face: the same boyish looks and bright blonde hair that she had seen on her foray into the monastery the night before, his brown eyes glaring at her. The trickle of blood her sap had left emanating from the fresh lump on the back of his head seemed to have been cleaned up, but he looked haggard nonetheless as if he had perhaps not gotten much sleep since the night before.

"I guess so," she said flatly, trying not to betray any emotions she might have about her current situation. "How did I get here?" she asked, turning her head and looking back at the ceiling.

"Mister Titus heard you fall and went up to check on you in your room," the young guard replied. "It's a good thing too, or else you would have bled out."

So the tavern owner had heard something. She filed the information away in the back of her mind for later. She would need to question him and see if he saw where Frost and his foreign bodyguard had gone.

The young blonde guard walked over to her and placed two fingers on the inside of her wrist. "Your heart is strong now, that's a good sign. And the High Priest will want to speak to you now that you're awake." He walked back over to the door, keeping an eye on her as he went, and opened the door slightly and murmured something to someone on the other side before closing it once more. Juliya could see him out of the corner of her eye sit down in a chair by the door, but she continued to stare up at the ceiling.

A few minutes passed before there was a light rapping at the door. Juliya turned her head slightly to get a better view and saw the guard stepping aside to let another man in. He was tall, with short blonde hair, blue eyes, and sharp features. His pointed ears gave him away as elven, and his silvery-blue robes seemed to almost reflect with a soft glow of the sunlight coming into the room from the window high above them. He walked over and pulled up a chair from the corner of the room before he sat down next to the bed. He looked down at Juliya and gave her a warm smile.

"Well, you're looking better," he said to her. "Let's see how that wound is coming along." He started gently lifting the bandages near her hip and working his way slowly up her midsection while inspecting the wound. Juliya couldn't bring herself to look down and see it for herself. She remembered seeing the life pour out of her body the night before. Worse yet, she remembered feeling it. "Well, some of these have opened back up a bit," he said after examining them for a moment. "I'm guessing that you moved when you woke up?" He looked her in the eyes, and she nodded reflexively in response. "Well, let's see what we can do about that." He clasped his hands with the palms together as if in prayer, and he began to chant something under his breath.

Juliya was fairly adept at reading lips; it came with the territory of her chosen vocation. Sometimes she had to sit on the other side of a room and watch two people speaking to get information for a job. Sometimes it was recovering the information itself which was the job. But she did not recognize whatever language the elf was speaking. After he had repeated the same unfamiliar refrain a couple of times, he unclasped his hands and laid them on her midsection with the fingers splayed right above the wound. As he placed his hands on her, she could feel her body growing warmer and the pain began to subside. The whole while, the priest continued chanting peacefully under his breath. When he finally lifted his hands off of her and stopped reciting the unknown language, the warmth stayed in Juliya's body for a moment and then slowly faded. The pain from the wound had faded as well.

"Let's see how it looks now," the priest said, examining her wounds below the bandages again. "Oh yes, that will do nicely." He looked her in the eyes and said, "It looks like you won't be needing these anymore," while lightly touching one of the blood-soaked bandages. "I'll allow you to take them off in private after I leave if you would prefer. There's a spare tunic laying at the foot of the bed for you."

Juliya looked at him somewhat incredulously. "You're saying I'm healed?" she asked. He simply nodded his head. Testing herself slowly, Juliya attempted to sit up. The pain she had felt earlier had gone. She arched her back slightly in a stretch, and again, felt nothing. Her curiosity overcame her, and she looked down and ripped the bandages off of her shoulder and chest. There was a ghastly pink scar that started at her shoulder and cut across her body where the wound had once been. She poked at the part of the scar that had cut across the fleshy part of her breast but felt no pain. "I don't suppose there's anything you can do about the scar?" she asked, and the priest shook his head. He was looking at her face sympathetically, but also with a sense of professional detachment. Juliya noticed the young guard behind him seemed to have far less control over where his eyes wandered. Juliya smiled at him over the priest's shoulder and blew him a kiss, causing him to blush and look away.

"Braddock, could you give the young lady and I a moment please?" the priest said without looking over his shoulder. Juliya noticed though he had phrased the request as a question, it was clearly intended as an order.

"Ah, yes Your Grace," replied the young guard, regathering his wits about himself. "I'll be right outside." He slipped out the door and closed it gently behind him.

"I apologize for Braddock," said the priest. "He is young, and clearly needs to learn a little more decorum."

Juliya smiled despite herself. "I wasn't offended," she replied. "Frankly I'm glad that someone would still look at me like that with this scar," she added with a light laugh dancing in her voice. Besides, she had decided the young man probably deserved a good look after the knock on the head she had given him the night before. Call the debt settled, she thought as she grabbed the tunic from the foot of the bed and pulled it on over her head. It was a little bit large for her slight frame, but it would do for now until she could get some fresh clothes.

"Well," began the priest, "It's time we talk about what brought you into our care." Juliya felt a lump forming in the back of her throat and fought hard not to swallow. "You appear to have run afoul of someone particularly deadly. In fact, if not for Alabaster Titus hearing some sort of commotion in your room, it might have been too late to save you." The Priest paused again. "I'm sorry, where are my manners, I am High Priest Elithias. And you are?" He waved his left hand slightly as he asked her the question.

"Juliya," she answered. It was strange, but she suddenly felt as if she could trust this man.

"And where are you from?"

"Felbreach, originally," she replied. "I came here from Tethis though."

"And are you part of the guild?" he asked.

"Not anymore," she answered truthfully. "I worked for them in Felbreach, but once I got out of there, I decided to live for me instead of for others."

The priest nodded. His face still seemed sympathetic to her.

"Felbreach is a dark stain on the kingdom for the way they treat half-elves like yourself," he said. "The church has petitioned the king many times over the years to step in and do something with no result. I fear the war with the Destan Empire keeps much of his attention."

"The only way you get out of a place like that is by doing it yourself," replied Juliya flatly.

"Yes, indeed," replied Elithias. "You are to be commended for making a life for yourself. However," he paused, and looked at her gravely, "the thing that you stole from the vaults below this tower is an extremely dangerous artifact, and it needs to be found. I need to know where it is."

"I don't know," she replied truthfully.

Elithias's head cocked slightly to the side. "But you know who has it, yes?" She nodded. "Tell me."

"His name is Frost Dirvent," she replied.

"Dirvent?" asked the High Priest. "Are you sure?"

"Yes," replied Juliya.

"That is a very old family name," said Elithias, both his gaze and his voice seemingly far away for a moment before he seemed to come back to reality.

Juliya shrugged. She'd had no recognition of his name prior to meeting him, though she was certain she'd never forget it now. Almost as an after-thought, she added, "And he has a Destan bodyguard whose name I don't know. He was there when Frost hired me to do the job in Tethis, and then he's the one that attacked me last night after I got back to my room; the one who did this," she added, motioning loosely at the scar on her shoulder that was showing beneath the oversized tunic, her eyes narrowing in anger as she did so.

"Three days ago," replied Elithias. Juliya froze for a moment at this revelation. "You were unconscious for three days. I had to bring you back from the brink of death slowly in order for the magic to take hold and not cause more permanent damage. Healing magic of that magnitude can be a tricky proposition." He waved his left hand slightly again, and Juliya suddenly felt guarded again. It was as if her head had been released from some sort of fog. "I apologize for that, but I needed to know the truth," said Elithias.

"You used some sort of magic on me," said Juliya, her voice shaking.

"Yes," he replied. "I had little choice in the matter, and it's a good thing that I did. The situation is potentially quite dire."

"Why, what's so important about that scroll?" asked Juliya, her eyes narrowing at the priest.

Elithias paused and stood, put the chair back into the corner, and then said to her, "Because the magic described in that scroll is forbidden. The last time a scroll like it was cast some ten thousand years ago, it destroyed a vast city that stretched all the way from here to what is now known as the Storm Mountains. The crater which was caused by the destructive power of its magic has since filled in with a vast lake just to the east of here. But deep beneath the waters lay what ashes remain of the ruins of the first great human civilization here on Teren'vei."

Juliya froze somewhat. She'd heard tales of older civilizations which had populated the world long before but had assumed that those were fairytales of a sort.

"I don't need any sort of magic to know that you did not know what you were getting into," continued Elithias. "You are young, and freshly out of a rather terrible situation. I imagine you have plenty of street smarts, but little formal education. But luckily those skills can still serve us here in these circumstances."

"Serve you how?" she asked, her voice guarded.

"We will need your skills to help track down the scroll," he replied flatly.

"You seem to think I have an altruistic streak," Juliya said dryly.

"No, I make no such assumptions," responded the priest. "But you've proven that you do have a predisposition towards self-preservation by extricating yourself from Felbreach. And I believe that I can trust in your desire for revenge. Am I right?"

Juliya's eyes were cold steel. "Yes," she replied. "I'd very much like to stick my dagger in his throat. But I don't play well with others. So, if you're looking for a friend, I'm not really your girl."

"Well, if you have no interest in helping us, I suppose that I'll have to turn you over to the town's guards then," said Elithias, "Such a shame really." He turned and started to walk towards the door.

"Ok, I'll bite," Juliya said. "What do you want me to do?"

The High Priest took a deep breath, and let it exhale slowly. Without looking back over his shoulder at her, he simply said, "Everything." He lowered his head and shook it slightly before adding, "For now, get some rest," and then he slipped out the door.

The room went quiet, and Juliya was left to her own thoughts. "What the fuck happened?" she wondered to herself and thought back to the last thing she remembered; the heist, and then Frost's betrayal.

The Forbidden Scrolls

Three days ago...

Juliya hid in the dark recess behind an archway at an intersection and waited for a pair of monks to pass. With her hood pulled down low to cover part of her face, she kept her dark brown cloak clasped tightly against her body to help her merge with the shadows. The dark stone walls of the ancient monastery were mostly barren, which made it easier for her to fade into the dark corners of the hallway. The two monks continued on down the corridor oblivious to her presence within their midst. She waited a moment until they were both about thirty feet down the hall before she slowly exhaled the breath she had been holding tightly in her chest and then crossed to the passage beyond.

The job she had been hired for was a simple snatch and grab, the type she'd done a hundred times before. However, this job had paid mysteriously well, and when the coins were flowing Juliya had made a habit of not asking too many questions. This was a policy that had worked for her so far in her relatively young life.

Staying in step with the shadows, she continued to make her way through the building towards the room she was looking for. Her employer had given her a detailed map of the structure, an old abandoned watchtower on the top of a single mountain just to the north of the small town of Barhnal. The priests had converted the tower into a monastery some one-hundred and fifty years ago. She wasn't sure how her patron had gotten his hands on the map, and she hadn't asked him either. But she had studied the map and memorized its every minute detail over the last five days since taking the job. She knew every inch of the tower's layout.

The door she was looking for was just a few meters ahead of her on the ground floor. According to the map, this entrance led to the stairway into the catacombs which had stood beneath the mountain for as long as the tower had stood above it.

Eventually, Juliya came to a door with a single guard standing in front of it. She hid in the shadows near an archway and watched him for a minute. The guard was young, maybe even a little younger than herself. It was hard to tell with humans sometimes as they all seemed to age at a different pace. It was all somewhat confusing to Juliya, how the different races all aged differently, and how it affected a half-breed like herself as opposed to a purebred human. It was something she didn't quite understand.

She studied him for a bit, watching for patterns in his movements. After getting a good gauge of his patrol routine, she slipped something off of her belt without making a sound and waited until the guard looked the other way before she slithered out from her alcove and cracked him once in the back of the head. As he started to fall she grabbed him, supporting his limp body against her own, and with grace and precision, she slid him down against the wall into a seated position. He had been a fair bit heavier than she was, but Juliya had been doing this sort of thing for a long time and knew just how to support his superior weight. She glanced around quickly to make sure that she hadn't been noticed, and then put her sap back on her belt. She slipped the left sleeve of her cloak up towards her elbow and from a band around her wrist produced a set of lock picks. She knelt down by the door, examining it quickly for traps. Seeing none, she went to work on the lock, listening with her ear against the door for the tumblers to click into place. It took her only a moment or two to find the correct positioning before the lock opened. A smile creased her lips as she put her tools away and then opened the door slowly to make sure it didn't creak in the silence of the hallway. She peered inside, and once she saw no one was there, dragged the unconscious guard through the door and out of sight.

Inside the door, there was a small landing of about five feet before a flight of stairs spiraled down into the darkness below. She noticed the torch sconces along the wall going down the staircase, but she could see in the dark well enough naturally and proceeded down the steps while treading lightly and hugging the wall. She descended for what seemed like an eternity, though it was likely only twenty minutes before the stairs came to their destination deep within the mountain.

Before her at the landing at the bottom of the stairs stood another door, this one ancient in appearance compared to everything she had seen in the tower above. She examined the door for traps and almost missed the simple light blue rune just below the door's handle. It looked like it had faded through the ages. She reached into a pouch on her hip and produced about half a handful of yellowish powder. She bent down and blew the powder onto the rune on the door. As the powder covered the symbol, there was a slight green flash, and then the powder fell to the floor and the rune was gone. The magical trap destroyed; she pulled her lock picks out of her left wristband again and went to work on the door.

This lock was far older than the one in the monastery above, but also far more intricate. She could feel the time ticking away as she worked at it, knowing it would only be so long before someone noticed the missing guard above. Finally, the tumblers clicked into place, and she bypassed the lock. She opened the door deliberately and peered into the darkness within.

The room beyond had once been the dungeon of the old watchtower long before the priests had repurposed it. The cells still stood with their barred doors closed, lining both walls of the room beyond. Juliya slipped into the room and took a quick inventory of her surroundings. There were six cells on each wall to her left and right. The far wall was comprised of barren shelves covered in cobwebs that looked to be about as old as the room itself. Juliya wondered to herself what must have adorned those empty shelves once upon a time, before putting the thought out of her mind and returning to the job at hand. She started with the cells on her right first, searching for the artifact she'd been hired to find.

Each cell had been converted into a vault for some old thing or another the priests above had determined to be better hidden away than known to the citizenry of Teren'vei. Juliya had no idea what most of the items in these cells were, but she did her best to dampen her natural curiosity and focus on the task at hand.

In the first cell, she saw a greenish orb sitting on a pedestal in the center of the room. The orb was sitting in a claw-like stand made of gold. Juliya wondered how much she could fence the golden stand for but decided against it. The job she had been hired for would pay more than enough, and there was no need to risk more time and increase her chance of getting caught by the guards and monks above.

She moved on to the next cell, and in this one there was another pedestal in the center of the room. However, this time there was a black onyx skull with a ruby in each eye slot sitting atop the platform. A wave of nausea overcame Juliya when she looked at it, and she decided to continue her search as quickly as possible if only to keep herself from getting physically ill. It was in the third cell on the right where she came upon the artifact she was looking for.

Sitting on a stand on top of the pedestal in the middle of the cell was an ornate ivory scroll case embossed in intricate gold-leaf flourishes and details. Still holding her lock picks in her hand, Juliya went to work on the cell door, which she opened with relative ease.

She stepped forward, standing in front of the pedestal and examined it for a moment. It didn't take long for her to recognize the weighted pressure plate on the top of the pedestal. She smiled to herself again, and then reached under her cloak, producing a scroll case of her own. This one was plain and empty, and Juliya knew she'd have to get the exchange just right. She reached out and grasped the scroll in her right hand, feeling its weight in her hand and comparing it to the scroll in her left without lifting it. The ivory scroll was definitely heavier, which was much better than the alternative. She reached into the pouch on her hip again and took about a quarter of a handful of the yellowish powder and poured it into the plain scroll tube she had brought with her. She held it flat in her outstretched hand and swished the tube around in the air until the weight seemed evenly distributed, and then reached out and grasped the ornate tube again. The weight now felt right to her, however, she knew there was still a chance the trap could go off and she wasn't sure what the end result of that occurrence would be.

Juliya leaned in over the scroll, keeping the dummy case in her left hand as she grasped her target with her right. She would have to be unbelievably quick on the transfer to stay safe. She took a deep breath and held it for a moment, and as she exhaled in a short puff from her nose, she swapped the two scrolls in the space between heartbeats. She paused for a second waiting for the trap to go off, but the seconds passed, and nothing happened. She had done it!

She had to suppress the nearly overwhelming desire to burst into a bout of uncontrollable laughter. She placed the ornate scroll tube into a pocket on the inside of her cloak with a smirk and stepped out of the cell. Closing the door behind her, she made her way out of the vault and back up to the world above.

At the top of the stairs, she paused and saw that the young guard was still unconscious. She could see a lump forming on the back of his head and a small trickle of blood discoloring his sandy blonde hair as he slumped over. She bent down on one knee and lifted his head up momentarily to make sure he was still out, before letting his chin drop softly to his chest once again. As she stood back up, she made her way to the door and listened with her ear pressed against it for a moment to make sure that no one was coming before opening it a crack and peering out. Seeing no one, she slipped out the door and flitted back into the shadows of the corridor as she made her escape into the night.

About the Author

Originally from a small New England town shrouded in mystery, Matthew Cesca currently resides in the unforgiving deserts of Arizona. He has a teenage son and is surrounded by an assortment of cats.

Matt is a fantasy, science fiction, and horror author with multiple published works and just as many works in progress. He asks that you not get too attached to any of his characters. It rarely ends well for anyone involved.

You can also interact with him as @AuthorMattCesca on Instagram, Threads, TikTok, and YouTube.

www.ingramcontent.com/pod-product-compliance
Lightning Source LLC
Chambersburg PA
CBHW021138310726
48971CB00002B/388